TRAGIC LIES

A RIXON HIGH NOVEL

L A COTTON

Published by Delesty Books

TRAGIC LIES

Edited by Andrea M. Long
Proofreading by Sisters Get Lit.erary Author Services
Cover Designed by Lianne Cotton
Image from CJC Photography

Never be ashamed of a scar. It simply means you were stronger than whatever tried to hurt you.

~ Unknown

PROLOGUE

DARKNESS CONSUMED ME. Cold, unforgiving darkness.

It coursed through my veins, an unrelenting storm dimming every speck of light.

"Peyton. Stay with me, you have to stay with me," a voice said somewhere in the distance.

But it was cold.

So freaking cold.

My teeth chattered as I slipped deeper into the black abyss cocooning me.

I just wanted to close my eyes. To drift away... away... away.

It would be easier... the pain would stop.

Everything would just—

"Peyton. The EMTs will be here any—thank fuck, they're here." Warm hands held me, trying to tether me to the light. "They're here. Down here."

But the lull of the darkness was too strong. It cloaked me, smothering out all of my senses. Except the chill. That didn't abate. It was in my bones; icy-cold water coursing through my veins. My body trembled as I hovered on the thin ledge between consciousness and unconsciousness.

"Down here," the voice said again, a featherlight touch running across my face.

"What happened?" another voice asked.

"Peyton... sh-she fell in the river. I dragged her out, but she was under for at least half a minute."

"Okay, move over and let us do our job. Peyton, can you hear me?"

I tried to answer, only a murmur escaping my lips.

"We're going to get you warmed up and into the ambulance, okay?"

Something rustled around me, wrapping me up like a burrito, then I was lifted onto a gurney, the air whooshing around me.

"X-Xander?" Panic swarmed me as I fought against the claws of darkness, my eyes flickering open. The edges of everything were blurry but I saw his face. The deep lines of concern, the grim curve of his lips.

"I'm here." He loomed over me. "I'm right here."

"D-don't leave me."

I was scared, so freaking scared.

She was gone... my mom was gone, and I was all alone in the world. And I was supposed to want this. I was supposed to feel a deep sense of relief.

But all I felt was bleak despair.

I was alone.

And as the darkness consumed me, and I lost the fight against the bitter cold, the last face I saw was his.

CHAPTER ONE

Peyton

MY MOM WAS DEAD.

Seven days, eight hours, and twenty-five minutes, give or take.

I didn't want to count the time. It seemed so pathetic to mourn the loss of a woman who never wanted me around. A woman who loved her next high more than she ever loved me. A woman who, in the end, had given me a parting gift I would never forget.

A gift that wasn't a gift at all but more like a curse.

So yes, mourning Kate Myers was as undeserved as it was pathetic.

Yet, I couldn't stop.

Seven days, eight hours, and twenty-six—

"Peyton?" My best friend Lily touched my arm, startling me.

"Yes?" I blinked over at her.

"I asked if you wanted any more pizza?"

"No, I'm fine."

"You barely ate your slice." Concern laced her words.

"Not hungry." I didn't meet her eyes, I couldn't.

Lily was my best friend in the whole world. The girl who knew me better than anyone. She knew my flaws and insecurities, my hopes and dreams. But she didn't *know*.

How could she?

Lily had a family who supported her. She had two amazing parents who were there no matter what. I mean, they'd taken me in more than once when my mom couldn't put food on the table or keep her shady associates out of the house.

"Go on now, you little brat. Stay in your room and don't come out until I say."

"But, Mama," I sniffled, my stomach cramping with hunger. I'd only had a bruised banana for breakfast and if she made me go into my room now, who knew how long I'd have to stay there for. Sometimes, she forgot about me for hours. "I don't like it when you—"

"I said go," she snapped. "And you don't come out until I say." She shooed me away with her bony, stained fingers, ignoring the tears rolling down my cheeks. Sometimes, when she was like this, I hated her. God, I hated her so much.

I shook the thoughts away. I wasn't a small helpless kid anymore. I hadn't been for a while. Still, I would never forget my childhood.

I'd lived with the Fords over the summer and the start of senior year before Mom got clean, again. Then I went home to be with her.

What a fucking mistake that was.

A shudder ran through me as I stared out of Lily's bedroom window. She had one of those window seats overlooking her family's huge yard. There was something peaceful about sitting there, watching the trees sway gently in the frigid Pennsylvanian wind.

"I'm worried about you," she said.

"You don't need to be. I'm fine."

I internally cringed at the words.

"You know, nobody's expecting you to return to school tomorrow. It's still—"

"Lily," I snapped, finally looking over at her. "I said I'm fine."

"Sorry." She perched on the end of her bed. "I'm doing it again, aren't I?"

"You're not doing anything. I just... I'm fine. School will be good for me." I needed to keep busy, to do something —*anything*—rather than sit around all day. When I stopped and my mind was still, the images ambushed me. Blood. So much freaking blood. My mom's dull lifeless eyes as she stared up at me, her wrists shredded open.

"I'm sorry I ruined Thanksgiving weekend."

"Peyton, you didn't ruin anything. We wanted to be here for you."

Lily and her family had big plans before my mom took a razor to her wrists and I... well, I got drunk, went down to the river, and ended up in hospital. Not my finest moment. But I was okay now. It was a lapse in judgment. A split second where I just wanted it all to stop.

The pain and heartache.

The constant dejection.

The years of abuse and neglect and never feeling good enough.

All I ever wanted was a family who loved me... a *mother* who loved me.

And now she was gone.

Emotion welled in my chest, but I swallowed it down.

I'd spent my entire life locking away my feelings, I wasn't about to break the cycle now.

"Is Kaiden nervous about the quarter-finals?" I changed the subject, turning to the one subject I knew Lily wouldn't be able to resist.

Her boyfriend. Kaiden Thatcher.

"He says he isn't. But he has to be. I mean, it's a big deal, right?"

"Well, yeah. Everyone's looking to him to bring home the championship."

"God, I'm so nervous. I know how much it means to him."

"He'll be fine, babe. If anyone can do it, it's Kaiden."

He was kind of a big deal on the football field, and despite a rocky start to his senior year at Rixon High, he had led the team to an impressive season record.

"He and Dad spent the entire day yesterday strategizing. I swear they went from mortal enemies to best friends in the space of a weekend."

I smiled but it didn't reach my eyes. I was happy for Lily, she deserved nothing but good things. But feeling happy for someone and *being* happy were two different things. And my sunshine-o-meter was all out of juice.

"If you're done eating, I'll clean up." Lily climbed off the bed.

"Actually, I'll help you."

"Yeah?" Her brows pinched.

"Yeah, a change of scenery might do me good." I hadn't stepped foot out of the Ford's house since being discharged from the hospital five days ago except to attend Mom's funeral. I could barely remember the service. Thankfully, Lily's parents had organized almost everything and all I'd had to do was show up.

Standing, I ran my hand through my long blonde hair and inhaled a shuddering breath. My body ached, weary with grief, but sleep refused to come easy since that night.

Seven days, eight hours, and thirty—I checked my cell phone—thirty-five minutes, give or take.

I grabbed our glasses and followed Lily downstairs. The familiar rumble of Mr. Ford's laughter drifted down the hall and I hesitated.

"Relax," she said, noticing. "They'll be pleased to see you."

"You make it sound like I've been holed up in my room for days on end."

Lily cast me a knowing look that had a sticky trail of regret snaking through me.

"I haven't been *that* bad," I murmured as we made our way into the kitchen.

"You're entitled to space," she said. "We just want you to know that we're all here for you too."

"I know." I swallowed over the lump in my throat. "I'm lucky to have you."

Without Lily and her family, I really had no one. Another tidal wave of emotion swelled inside me. I wasn't used to being so battered by my feelings. Usually, I controlled them. Wrangled them the way a cowboy wrangled cattle. But this was different. When I'd slipped under the Susquehanna River, the icy-cold water flooding my lungs, something inside me snapped.

Something that felt irreparable.

Permanent.

"Hey, girls," Lily's mom appeared in the doorway. "It's nice to see you up and about, Peyton." She gave me a warm smile.

Mrs. Ford was the best. Kind and understanding,

compassionate and funny, she radiated love. Fierce, unwavering love. The kind of love a mother should have for her daughters, her husband, and family. She represented everything I've never had, but despite not being mine, Mrs. Ford had welcomed me into her house with open arms and accepted me flaws and all.

But her acceptance could never fully repair the damage caused by the woman I got to call mom.

"How was the pizza?"

"It was fine thanks, Mrs.—"

"Felicity. You can call me Felicity, Peyton. You're family now, sweetheart."

Her words twisted my gut. "I-I'm going to get some fresh air." I made a dash for the back door, slipping into the cool winter air. My breath drifted into the sky in a smoky tendril as I burrowed into my chunky knit sweater and sat on the swing chair. When I inhaled deeply, I could still feel it in my lungs, the icy sting of the Susquehanna River. I made myself take a breath, forcing the memories out.

I stared out at the Ford's oversized yard. The swimming pool, covered for the winter, and the seating area nestled around an impressive grill. It wasn't as fancy as some of our friends' yards, but it was still worlds away from what I'd grown up with.

I was hardly surprised when Mrs. Ford joined me on the swing. "I hope you don't mind," she said, running her hands around her mug of hot chocolate. "The weather is turning."

I managed a gentle shrug, shuffling up for her.

"Look, Peyton, I won't pretend to know what you're feeling or thinking. You have been through something no child should ever have to go through. But I want you to know that you can always come to me, with anything. You're not in this alone, sweetheart." She gently squeezed my knee. “And I know Jase is like a bumbling idiot at the moment, but it’s only because he doesn’t know what to say. He’s a man; they like to fix things. But this is one thing he can’t fix and he’s having a hard time reconciling that.”

My lip twitched. “It’s okay Mrs.—Felicity. I understand it’s weird for everyone, and I’m sorry—”

“Oh no you don’t. You’re not apologizing for anything that has happened. Apologizing suggests you’re at fault and you’re not, sweetheart, okay?”

I couldn’t meet her stare.

“Peyton, look at me.”

Slowly, I lifted my eyes to hers, swallowing over the giant lump in my throat. “What your mom did, it wasn’t your fault. I need you to know that.”

A small nod was all I could manage. She meant well, but this wasn’t something you could slap a Band-Aid and a few motivational words on.

“How are you feeling about tomorrow? You know, I can speak to Principal—”

“No.” I shook my head gently. “I want to get back to classes. The holidays are coming up. I need the distraction.”

“Well, okay, if you’re sure. But if it’s too much, you just say the word and I’ll talk to the administration. I spoke with Mya too. She’d like to see you.”

“I appreciate everything you’ve done for me; I do. But I don’t need to see the guidance counselor.”

“I think the school will insist. It’s protocol after a student…” She trailed off, and my cheeks flamed.

“I didn’t… like I told you and Jason before. It was an accident.”

“Nevertheless, it was a traumatic event.” A reassuring smile lifted the corners of her mouth. “Mya—Mrs. Bennet—is there to help you. She’ll be able to refer you for grief counselling if you want it.”

"I'm fine, really."

"Peyton, you can keep saying the words over and over, but it won't change the fact that you've been through something life changing."

Lily peeked around the door looking sheepish. "Aunt Hailee's here. And they... uh... Xander is with them."

My entire body froze at the mention of *his* name.

"He's here?" I breathed the words.

"Yeah. Do you want to go back upstairs and—"

"Lily." Her mom shook her head.

"Sorry. I didn't want you to be blindsided." She glanced at me, chewing her bottom lip.

"It's fine."

So Xander was here.

It wasn't like he'd saved my life or anything.

When I'd waded into the river that night, I hadn't ever anticipated that I would need rescuing. So when my friend's uncle had pulled me out and stayed with me until the EMTs arrived, I thought I was dreaming.

Xander Chase was an enigma. Solitary and brooding, he was a man of few words. He'd recently started helping Lily's dad out with the football team at our high school. But he wasn't like the other coaches. There was darkness in his eyes. A shadow hanging over him like thunder clouds on a stormy day.

I knew because I'd sat and watched him enough times with Lily while she ogled Kaiden from the bleachers.

"I should probably head inside and go see to our guests. If you girls need anything just holler."

"Thanks," I murmured, staring out at the yard still.

Lily took her mom's seat, lacing her arm through mine and laying her head on my shoulder. "I've been thinking, and I think you're right. Going back to school will be good for you."

"I think so." It would keep my mind off everything, hopefully.

"And after the holidays I'll be able to drive us."

My eyes snapped to hers. "You're finally going to take driver's ed?"

"Yep." A huge smile spread over her face. "I think it's time."

"Wow, Lily. That's huge." I hugged her. "I'm so proud of you."

"I couldn't have done it without you. You've always believed in me, Peyton, even when I didn't. You're one of my best friends."

"Jeez, Lil, don't get all emosh on me, you'll make me cry." And God only knew I'd done enough of that over the last week. In fact, I was pretty sure I was all cried out.

"Kaiden is going to give me a few lessons in the school parking lot when it's empty."

"You'll ace it," I said, my heart so full for her, and yet, so empty at the same time.

"You know, if you saved your wages from Cindy's you could save for a car. My parents don't want your—"

"I know you mean well, Lil. But I need to do this. I need to contribute." I wasn't her parents' responsibility, and I didn't ever want to be a burden. Helping with the groceries and the bills was the least I could do.

The rumble of voices filtered out of the kitchen window and I glanced over my shoulder, watching Lily's Aunt Hailee and Uncle Cameron laughing and joking with her parents. The second Xander appeared, my body froze, my heart racing inside my chest.

Every day since being discharged from the hospital, I'd hoped to see him. But he never stopped by and now he was standing right there, and all I could think was what did you say to the man who saved you?

Nothing.

I couldn't think of a single thing that could possibly express my gratitude.

"Peyton?" Lily asked and I finally dragged my eyes away from the patio door.

"I'm fine." The lie soured on my tongue. I wasn't fine. I was barely stitched together at the seams and knowing Xander was here only made everything ten times worse.

I needed to talk to him about that night. About what he saw… what he thought he saw.

I needed to explain.

But it wasn't like I could simply stroll up to him in front of all his family and friends.

God, this was awkward. And it was turning colder by the second. A shiver ripped through me, making my teeth chatter.

Lily frowned. "Are you cold? Maybe we should go inside."

"A little bit longer," I said, brushing her off. I couldn't go inside, not yet. Not until I'd figured out what the hell I was going to say.

Xander was there that night. He'd watched me wade into the river, half-naked and ass-over-elbow drunk.

He'd seen everything.

I could only imagine what he thought of me. But he hadn't stuck around at the hospital long enough to hear my side of the story. When I'd woken up, there'd been no sign of him. It hurt more than it should have.

Xander Chase wasn't my family. He wasn't anybody to me really, but I guess I'd always thought of myself as someone to his family, since I was best friends with Ashleigh, his niece.

Another blast of icy wind whipped around us and Lily leaped up. "I'm sorry, but I need to go inside."

"Okay." I gave her a weak smile. "I'll be in soon."

"You're sure—"

"Go. I'm fine."

God, I hated that word.

Lily hesitated, but I added, "Go. I'll be right in, promise." I just needed a chance to catch my breath.

With a small nod, Lily disappeared inside, and I burrowed myself deeper into my sweater.

I liked it out here, under the stars. It was peaceful. A place to lose yourself in nothing.

The door clicked open again and I half-smiled, ready to tell Lily that I was fine again. But it wasn't Lily at all.

Xander loomed over me as he slipped a packet of cigarettes from his jeans and put one between his lips. Mesmerized, I watched as he lit the end and inhaled a deep lungful of tobacco. It was only then I realized he wasn't looking at me. He was also staring out at nothing.

"So I was sitting here thinking about all the things I wanted to say to you," I blurted. "But now you're here and I can't think of a single thing." Nervous laughter spilled from my lips like an out-of-tune instrument. "I guess I just want to—"

"Stop."

"E-excuse me?" My mouth went dry as I fidgeted with the hem of my sweater. Xander still didn't look at me, inhaling another hit of his cigarette, holding it in for a second before exhaling a controlled tendril of smoke.

"You don't need to thank me." He flicked it to the ground and dragged his boot over it.

"But I just wanted to explain—"

"I'm not your therapist, kid." His eyes finally slid to mine, dark and tortured.

If I wasn't so lost in his hard gaze, I might have flinched

at his use of the word *kid*. But as it was, I was trapped. Suspended in his sterling gray eyes.

Before I could get out so much as another word, Xander ducked back into the house like he hadn't just rendered me speechless.

And obliterated any image I had in my head of him as my hero.

CHAPTER TWO

Xander

A MINUTE after I rejoined my brother and his friends, Peyton slipped back into the house.

"There you are, sweetie. Hot cocoa?" Fee asked her.

"No, thank you." She hovered away from us, inching toward the door. Like a deer caught in the headlights, she had big doe eyes brimming with panic.

"It's good to see you, Peyton." My brother's wife, Hailee said.

"You too, Mrs. Chase." I'm just going to—" She thumbed to the door and bolted toward it, but not before her startled gaze slid right past mine.

I was a dick before, outside. But I didn't have time for teen girl drama. From what I knew about Peyton, she'd had it rough. And until that night down by the river, she'd hidden it well.

She was one of my niece's best friends, so I'd been around enough over the last three years to notice her. Peyton liked to be in the spotlight. She liked the attention and praise. But there was something else lurking behind her bubbly blonde veneer.

"Xan?" Cam's voice pulled me from my thoughts, and I blinked over at my brother.

"Yeah?"

"I said, are you okay?"

"What? Yeah? Sure." I drained my beer, hating the way his eyes crinkled with disapproval.

"Did you talk to her?" he added.

"What is there to say?"

"Don't be a dick." He tsked. "She's been through a lot. A little sympathy would go a long way."

"Cameron," Hailee shook her head discreetly.

"She thanked me; I said no problem." My shoulders lifted in a dismissive shrug. "Life goes on, right?"

He glared at me, but it wasn't anything new. Cameron had been riding my ass my entire life. Fourteen years older than me, he'd practically raised me. Our relationship was complicated to say the least, but family was family, and he was the only brother I had.

"Got any more beers?" I asked Jase, and he flicked his head toward the refrigerator. "Help yourself. But you'd better not roll into work tomorrow hungover. The quarter-finals are right around the corner."

"Relax, boss," I sniped. "I know the rules."

Jase had given me the assistant coach gig at the high school after me and Cam got into a huge row about money. As in, I had none, and he was sick of bailing me out. But he didn't know what it was like for me. He had an amazing wife, good kids, and friends who loved him.

My brother had it all, while I'd spent the last ten years slipping deeper into his shadow.

"Glad to hear it," Jase grunted. "Everyone is expecting us to bring home that championship again."

"You put too much pressure on yourself." Fee wound her hand around his waist and leaned up to kiss his jaw.

Something inside me twisted. I'd never had that, never wanted it. But I wasn't twenty-one anymore. Getting drunk at Bell's and picking up a different girl every weekend had lost its appeal a long time ago. So while I had no plans to settle down, watching my brother and his best friends with their women and families did remind me of everything I didn't have, and probably never would.

"How are things with Kaiden?" Cam asked Jase.

"He's my star quarterback and my daughter's horndog of a boyfriend... how do you think things are?"

"You haven't killed him yet." Fee smirked. "I'd call that progress."

"He's a good kid, he is," Jase let out a heavy sigh, rubbing a hand over his jaw. "But the idea of him and Lily... See, I can't even say the words."

"I don't envy you," Cameron said. "I thank God every day that Ashleigh hasn't gotten herself a boyfriend yet."

"At least you've only got Leigh to worry about. I've got three teenage girls living under my roof."

"How's she holding up, really?" Hailee asked.

"Peyton is strong," Fee replied. "But I worry about her. The strongest glass usually shatters the most."

I glanced over at the door. Maybe I'd been too hard on her earlier. But it wasn't like I owed her anything. So I pulled her out of the river? I would have done the same for anyone else.

"She's lucky to have you," Hailee added. "I can't even imagine what it must be like to lose your mom so young." Her eyes found mine, widening with regret. "Shit, Xander, I didn't—"

"Relax, it's fine." I brushed her off. As far as I was concerned, it was ancient history.

I'd been eight when my mom lost her battle with a brain tumor. I barely remembered it. One day she was there, the next she wasn't. Yet, sometimes I remembered too vividly. Even all these years later, I could smell the cloying scent of the hospital, the monotonous beep of the machines keeping her alive. It was a mind fuck.

"I'm going for a smoke." Not sticking around to hear my brother's grunt of disapproval, I ducked outside and lit up another cigarette. I didn't even like the disgusting things, but it focused me. Kept me from turning to other vices.

I sucked on the end, inhaling so deeply that my lungs burned, then let the smoke trail out of the split in my mouth.

What I really wanted was a bottle of Jack and my couch. I rented a small place downtown, a couple of blocks over from Bell's, the local bar we liked to frequent. I liked it because it had a great view of the river, and I often ventured down there on the nights when sleep didn't find me.

That's how I'd stumbled across Peyton that night. I liked to be outside, in the dark when no one else was around. There was something settling about that time between twilight and dawn when the rest of the world slept.

Sometimes I passed the odd jogger or dog walker, but usually I had the stretch of sidewalk along the Susquehanna River to myself.

My brother's gruff laughter pierced the air, and I shook the thoughts out of my head. I wasn't trying to be a hero that night, I did what any half-decent person would have done. But I'd seen the way she looked at me earlier... with fucking stars in her eyes.

I wasn't looking to be anyone's white knight though.

Especially not hers.

THE NEXT MORNING, I rolled up to the school in my beat-up Chevy pickup. It looked like a piece of crap, but it ran like a dream thanks to the hours I spent fine tuning her. A group of girls looked over as I pulled into a parking spot, nudging each other and giggling. My arrival at Rixon High had caused quite the stir which is why I tried to keep to myself.

Grabbing my bag off the back seat, I put a Raiders ball cap on backwards and climbed out. It was cold as shit out, my lungs smarting when I inhaled a deep breath.

"Yo, Coach," a voice called, and I turned around to find Kaiden Thatcher jogging toward me.

"What's up, kid?"

"I was wondering if we can go over some plays again? I want to be ready for the next game."

"You're ready, Thatch." Slinging my bag over one shoulder, we walked toward the gym together.

"Yeah, maybe. It's just a lot... you know?"

I glanced over at him. Kaiden hadn't had it easy, transferring to Rixon High in senior year. He was at a new school, commanding a new team, but he'd done it. The kid had beaten the odds to lead the Raiders straight into the playoffs. And he'd done it while his family imploded. His dad was a real piece of shit. A drunk with an old grudge against Jase. He was back in rehab but not before he'd knocked Kaiden around. The whole thing was a shitshow.

I knew better than most that life was hard. It was messy and painful and sometimes it was too fucking much, but I couldn't ever imagine lashing out at the ones who were there for me. That shit was messed up.

"Word of advice," I said. "Enjoy it. You've worked your ass off to get here. It's senior year. You have a full-ride in the bag and your future is all mapped out. Whatever happens in the quarter-finals is just the icing on the cake."

The bitter sting of regret snaked through me. I remembered my brother saying something similar to me once, when I was just a senior in high school. Before everything turned to shit.

"Try telling that to Coach Ford and the rest of the town," he murmured.

He wasn't wrong there. Football was life in Rixon. People didn't just like it, they lived and breathed it. And the pressure was on the team to bring home the championship again.

"Yeah, I won't argue there, kid."

"*Kid*, really?" He rolled his eyes. "I'm eighteen."

"And still so much to learn." I winked, chuckling.

I follow Kaiden into the locker room, the hustle and bustle, and noise is like stepping back in time. There had been a time I'd lived for this. The weight of shoulder pads, the smell of freshly mowed grass, the glare of the Friday night lights. I'd been the guy to beat. An unstoppable force of nature. I'd poured all my anger and grief and pain into football. And for a while, it had worked.

But nothing good lasted forever.

Kaiden headed for his guys, while I made my way into the assistant coaches' office.

"What time do you call this, Chase?" Coach Huckley said.

"Looks like I'm right on time to me." My eyes went to the clock hanging above his head.

"You're two minutes late."

"Give the guy a break," Coach Macintosh interjected. "A couple of minutes isn't going to hurt. Besides, you're talking to a real-life hero, right there."

"Mac." I shook my head, hating the way he was looking at me.

"That was some heavy shit, Xander. Makes you wonder

what the hell a seventeen-year-old girl was doing down there at that time of night."

In a town like Rixon, where everyone knew everyone, news travelled fast. So it was hardly a surprise that Peyton's accident had become the hot topic on everyone's lips. One of the attending EMTs was good friends with one of the town's biggest gossips, which meant that unfortunately for me, there was no keeping my name out of the incident.

"Obviously up to no good," Huckley grumbled, skirting his eyes over the clipboard in his hand.

I glowered in his direction. It didn't sit right with me, hearing him talk about Peyton like that. It shouldn't have surprised me though.

Most of the guys on the staff team were decent. But Huckley didn't appreciate me walking into the job with little to no qualifications. And part of me got it, I did. But I needed this. More than he would ever know. So for the most part, I let his veiled jibes and disapproving glances roll off my back. I knew what people thought of me. Xander Chase, down-and-out. The guy who'd had the world at his feet and blew his shot. But they hadn't walked in my shoes. They didn't know what it was like.

They'd never fucking know.

"Guys, let's go," Jase stuck his head around the door, his eyes going to mine. "You good?"

I gave him a sharp nod, not missing the way Huckley glared at me. He didn't like that Jase had stuck his neck out on the line for me. He didn't like it at all. But Jase was as good as family, and he knew I needed a shot at something better. Something to get my life back on track.

"The boss has spoken," Coach Macintosh plucked the toothpick from his mouth and chuckled. "Better not be late."

We filed out of the office and walked through the empty

locker room. Jase was a firm but fair kind of guy. He expected his players to give their all and in return he gave his. But the next week would be on a whole other level. It was the quarter-finals, and the whole of Rixon was looking at him and the team to bring home the championship.

Which meant the heat was also on me, because like it or not I was a part of this team now.

We joined the huddle, waiting for Jase to issue instructions for our morning practice. We all knew the routine, but he liked to start every practice with a pep talk.

"Okay, bring it in," he said. "Saturday marked the first day of a new season. Playoff season. And you went out there and got the job done. But the hard work isn't over. We can't afford to get complacent because those other teams are going to come at us and come at us hard. I need you all to be on top of your game. Listen to your coaches, memorize every play in the book and then memorize them some more, and turn up to practice every day and put in the hard work. You feel me?"

"Yes, sir." The team's unified response echoed around the field.

"Good, now get out there and show me what you got. Thatcher, you're with Coach Chase, we're going to need you in peak condition, son."

"Yes, sir." Kaiden jogged over to the ball sack and plucked one out. "Ready when you are, Coach." He threw the ball at me and I caught it with ease.

"Let's put you through your paces." I smirked. Kaiden was a good kid, but he knew he was good.

After setting up the drill, we got to it, focusing on his throwing accuracy. "How's it going with Lily and her old man?" I asked as he hiked another ball toward me.

"Okay, I think. Why? Has he said something to you?"

"No, kid. But if I didn't know better, I'd say Jase actually likes you."

"Fuck you, *Coach*," he grumbled. Anyone else on the team and I might have chastised them, but Kaiden was different. He'd been dealt a shitty hand and I'd taken a shine to him since taking the coaching position a few weeks ago.

"You kiss your mother with that mouth?" Laughter rumbled in my chest, as I changed the angle on the target.

"What about you anyway? Everyone's calling you a hero."

"Yeah, well, I wish they'd stop." I swallowed over the giant fucking lump in my throat.

"Can I ask you something...?" Kaiden's look was pensive.

"Sure, kid."

"Do you think it was an accident?"

"Peyton says it was." The hand rubbing my jaw masked my expression. Or at least, I hoped it did. I didn't want to get into this with him, or anyone for that matter. Peyton was alive. She was going to be okay and get the help she needed. Accident or no accident, it was done.

But as I said the words, something deep inside me twisted. Because I wasn't sure what I'd seen that night. All I knew was I'd dragged a barely conscious girl from the icy depths of the Susquehanna River and watched as the ambulance carted her off to Rixon General. A girl who, by all accounts, had always been so vibrant and full of life.

"Yeah, but what do *you* think?" Kaiden stared at me as if I had all the answers.

But even if I did, it wasn't any of my business.

And I had no plans of getting involved.

CHAPTER THREE

Peyton

"THERE SHE IS." My friend Bryan bounced over to us, pulling me into a bear hug. "I've been worried about you, Myers," he whispered, and I gently eased back to meet his crinkled expression.

"I'm fine."

"Really?" His brow arched. "Because I—"

"Yo, dude, give the girl some room," his friend Gav nudged him back. They played on the team with Kaiden, and it's how we'd fallen into this weird friendship. Well, me and Bryan at least. "It's good to see you back, Peyton."

"Thank you." I didn't like the way they were all watching me. Sympathetic stares glittering with pity.

"Guys, stop." I yanked open my locker and stuck my head inside, grateful for the reprieve. If I would've known how weird they would all act, I probably would have had second thoughts about coming back today.

But there was no going back now.

I was Peyton Myers. I didn't cower or hide from anyone,

and I wasn't about to start now. Even if everyone was throwing discreet looks in my direction as if I was an exhibit in a zoo. I knew rumors were flying around school. I'd heard at least five of them just on the walk into the building.

Apparently, she was skinny-dipping drunk.

She was wandering drunk along the river and fell in.

I heard she got pushed.

Rixon High was a melting pot of gossip and my name was the word on everyone's lips.

Of course I'd heard *those* rumors too—the ones that talked about me trying to kill myself. But I let them roll off my back. It was an accident. A spur of the moment mistake.

That's all.

"Peyton?" Lily's voice yanked me back into the moment.

"Huh, yeah?"

"I asked if you're ready to go to class?"

"Yeah, of course." I grabbed a couple of textbooks and slammed my locker shut, the sound reverberating through me.

"See you at lunch?" Bryan asked, his eyes lingering a little too long.

Bryan Hughes was a good guy, but he was a mistake I didn't plan on making again. We hooked up a couple of times. It wasn't supposed to happen, but he'd worn me down with his charm and goofy humor. And besides, I liked sex.

Or at least, I did... *before*.

Now, I just felt numb. Like my insides had been yanked out of my body, ground through a meat processor, and then shoved back in. My heart was a shredded ball of flesh in my chest, barely beating.

Not how I ever saw my senior year going.

But I'd been thinking about things a lot over the last few

days. I turned eighteen in just a few weeks. Christmas Eve, in fact. I'd walk into the new year as an adult. An adult with no home, no family, and no real plans for the future.

My job at Cindy's Grill gave me enough money to help the Fords with their weekly groceries and a couple of smaller bills, but it wasn't enough to save for college or a security deposit on an apartment. Graduation was still another six months away. Six months in which I could be earning better money. I could pick up more hours at Cindy's or try to get a few hours at one of the various stores downtown.

But I really didn't want to drop out of high school. Getting my diploma was key to getting better employment or maybe even taking some community college courses.

I needed a plan and fast. But I was exhausted. Weary and numb. Plans could wait, at least for today.

"Yeah," I whispered, giving him a weak smile. Bryan was a good guy. Funny and loyal, he had a bright future ahead of him playing football at Michigan. He was perfect boyfriend material without a doubt.

There was just one huge problem...

Giving my heart to someone, that definitely wasn't part of any plan I had.

"PSST," Bryan whisper-hissed while Mr. Keefer scribbled some algebra on the board.

"What?" I mouthed over at him.

"Want to come over tonight and hang? My parents are out of town."

"I don't—"

"Ssh."

We both turned to find Carrie-Anne Trombley glaring

at us. Bryan flashed her a blinding smile and whispered, "Jealous, Caz?"

"Please don't call me that." She glowered, but I caught a subtle hitch in her voice.

Interesting.

Did prim and proper bookworm Carrie-Anne have a crush on Bryan? He was everything she despised. Jock. Goofball. All round cocky athlete who paid more attention on the football field than he did in the classroom.

"You love it," he chuckled.

"Something you'd like to share with the class, Mr. Hughes?" The teacher turned his attention to our corner of the room.

"No, sir. Just giving the ladies what they want."

A round of snickers broke out around us, and Carrie-Anne grumbled, dropping her head onto her arms. The girl needed to relax; she was wound tighter than a drum.

"Okay, okay, settle down." Mr. Keefer rolled his eyes. "And perhaps try the art of silent seduction from now on."

I smothered the laughter bubbling in my chest. God, it felt good to laugh. But the second I realized it, the feeling evaporated.

The back-and-forth emotions were exhausting.

As soon as Mr. Keefer was done explaining the equation, he sat down and left us to solve some problems. I went through the motions working out each answer.

"Psst, Pey, can you help me?"

"*Bryan*!" I shook my head.

"What about you, Caz?" He turned his attention to her, and I watched out of the corner of my eye as she blushed.

"No, I'm not helping you. It's bad enough we got paired together in English."

"Hey, I'm a great partner."

She snorted at that. "Whatever, Bryan. Do your own work."

"Jeez, someone needs to get laid."

Carrie-Anne gasped, kicking his chair. "Asshole."

He went to speak, but I leaned over and pinched his arm. "Bryan..." I warned.

"What?" He mouthed around a knowing smile. He knew he pushed her buttons, but did he like it?

Did he like her?

I didn't know how to feel about that.

I didn't want to be with Bryan, but we'd had sex and I liked his company. His parents owned this huge house across the river. They had an indoor pool and home theater. It was pretty amazing.

I'd grown up in a trailer until we'd finally moved to a small house downtown, the summer before I started Rixon High. We'd barely had a yard let alone a pool. We'd had a revolving door of men though.

"So, tonight... you in?" Bryan grinned, and my expression softened. He was a hard guy to say no to.

"Fine, I'll see what Lily and Ashleigh want to do."

At least if we all went to Bryan's it would keep my mind occupied. I'd wanted to go back to work, but Cindy had insisted I take the week off.

"Yes." His brows shot up with excitement. "I'll make it worth your while." He winked and I rolled my eyes again, but I couldn't deny his whole 'treat Peyton like nothing bad happened' routine was working for me. I didn't want to keep rehashing that night or talking about my mom. I wanted to put it firmly in the past where it belonged.

And figure out what the hell I was going to do with my life.

"So ARE we going to talk about the fact you and Bryan are basically FWBs, or we are still pretending that isn't a thing?" Ashleigh said as she drove us across the river.

Mrs. Ford had been reluctant to let us go, but as Lily reminded her, she and Ashleigh were eighteen now. And Bryan was Kaiden's best friend. Felicity loved Kaiden. I didn't blame her. He had pulled Lily out of her shell and given her the confidence to live her life unapologetically. We all loved him for it. Even her dad; not that he would ever admit it.

"FWBs?" Lily asked, glancing back at me.

"Friends-with-benefits."

"But you're not, right...?" She frowned. "I mean, it happened like, twice."

Ashleigh snorted, and I slammed my palm against her headrest. "You promised."

"Promised? There was a promise?" Hurt flashed over Lily's face. "But you said—"

"It's not a big deal," I said. "We hooked up a few times."

"Define few." She gave me a pointed look.

"He picked me up from Cindy's a few times and we... you know." I shrugged because it wasn't a big deal.

At least, not to me.

"Oh wow, I really don't know what to say to that. My best friend has an *FWB*, and she didn't think to mention it."

"It's not a big deal," I repeated.

"So why did you keep it a secret? Although not a secret from *everyone* apparently." Her eyes slid to Ashleigh.

"I found out. She didn't tell me."

"Can everyone just calm down a second?" I huffed. "I didn't tell anyone because I knew you'd all make a big deal about it. I don't like Bryan like that; I don't. But he's nice and he makes me feel good and he gets it."

"Gets what?" Lily's expression softened.

"That I can't be with him."

"But why? You just said it yourself. He's nice and makes you feel good."

"I just can't..."

"Oh, Pey." She reached between the seats to grab my hand. "You deserve to be happy."

Happy, yes. But most relationships didn't end happily. They ended in heartache.

It's why I kept my distance and didn't let anyone get too close. I could do sex. Sex was a transaction; a simple case of give and take. But catching feelings... that was a dangerous thing.

Ashleigh turned onto Bryan's winding driveway. His house always took my breath away. Since ninth grade, I'd grown up with Lily and Ashleigh and their beautiful homes and generous parents, worlds away from my own life. But there was something different about coming here. Bryan liked me. I knew that. Felt it every time he set his ocean eyes in my direction. It was just another thing setting us apart though. His family was rich. Really freaking rich, and my family was... gone, leaving me behind with nothing. I guess deep down, I didn't want people to think I was using Bryan. The way I knew some people thought I used the Fords.

A trail of shame snaked through me.

"What is it?" Lily asked, studying me.

"Nothing," I said, averting my eyes. "It's just been a hard few days."

It wasn't a total lie.

"I know. But we're all so proud of how you've handled everything. You're amazing, Peyton. I hope you know that."

I appreciated her kind words, but I didn't feel very amazing. I felt numb; worn down by people's pity and words of sympathy. I'd never lost anyone before, except my sperm donor, and I could barely remember him. It wasn't the same. But losing my mom, no matter how much of a waster she was, felt like losing a small piece of myself.

The car ground to a halt and we all climbed out, but my best friends didn't take the shuddering breath I did, letting my mask slide into place.

The front door opened, and Bryan grinned at the sight of us approaching. "Ladies, welcome to Chez Hughes."

Ashleigh snickered, ducking inside. Lily went next, leaving the two of us.

"Myers," he said in that thick, lilting rasp of his.

"Hughes," I quipped, the faintest smirk tugging the corner of my mouth.

But then his smile melted away, replaced with blistering concern. "Do you want to talk about it?"

"No, I really don't."

"Yeah, okay." He ran a hand over his jaw. "But I want you to know I'm sorry, babe." Bryan opened his arms. "I'm so fucking sorry."

I fell into his embrace, soaking up his comfort. His strong arms like a blanket wrapped around me. My fingers twisted in his t-shirt as I swallowed down the unrelenting rush of emotion trying to claw its way up my throat.

"Thank you," I whispered.

He gently eased me back and stared down at me. "Whatever you need, I'm here, you feel me?"

I nodded, too choked up to reply.

"Come on, I already loaded a movie and there's popcorn."

This. This was why I liked Bryan. He made everything so easy. It was impossible not to be swept up in his charm.

He tucked me into his side and guided me down the hall to our friends, but the second we found them in the home theater room, he released me. I loosened a breath and his eyes slid to mine, a smile there.

"Go," he flicked his gaze to the huge sectional, "get comfortable."

Lily and Kaiden were already curled up on the smaller couch, lost in their own little world as he whispered sweet nothings to her.

My chest cinched.

"Peyton." Gav gave me a small nod.

"Hey."

He went back to his conversation with Ashleigh. The two of them seemed to gravitate toward one another whenever the six of us hung out, but he didn't show any interest in her. I wondered if it was because he knew her interest was elsewhere.

Not that she'd ever admit it.

Folding my legs beneath me, I pulled the soft blanket off the back of the couch and over my body. Bryan pulled a small coffee table over and planted a tub of popcorn on it and my favorite soda.

"Milady." He flashed me a blinding smile.

"You're such a goofball."

"Yeah, but you love me."

Guilt ploughed through me. I liked him. I liked him a lot... but I didn't... I couldn't...

My face must have said it all, because Bryan let out a thin breath as he settled beside me, remote in hand. "It was a joke," he said. "I was joking, babe."

"I know." I didn't meet his piercing gaze.

"Are you all set for Friday?" Ashleigh asked.

"Hell, yeah." Bryan puffed out his chest. "That championship is ours. Right, Thatch?" He glanced over at Lily and Kaiden who managed to tear their lips off one another. She buried her face into his shoulder, blushing.

"Yeah," he said.

"Jeez, man, don't sound too enthusiastic."

"Bry," Gav warned with a little shake of his head.

"You have nothing to worry about," Bryan added. "We're stronger than ever and we're thirsty for it. The whole team is. Besides, the girls will be there to cheer us on, right?" He looked over at me and winked. "Our very own lucky charms."

"He's got a point," Kaiden said to Lily, brushing his nose along hers. Intimately. "With you in the crowd, wearing my number..." His eyes darkened as he leaned in whispering something to her, and only her.

"Get a room," Bryan mumbled, hitting the remote and dimming the lights. The screen lit up and the opening credits started to roll.

"Hey," he whispered, and I mouthed, "What?"

"You are coming to the game, right? I missed you last weekend."

"I guess." My shoulders lifted in a small shrug. Lily and Ashleigh's entire family would be there to support Jason and the team. I always went with them, but I'd stayed at the house for the opening game of the playoffs, too weak and upset to attend. Now I was able to go, something felt different.

And not only because I was a part of their family now.

CHAPTER FOUR

Xander

I LIVED for this time of night. The silence. The stillness. A canvas of stars twinkling against the inky night.

My mom had told me once, when I was just a young boy scared of what the future held, that whenever I was afraid, whenever things felt too much for my little mind to process, all I had to do was look to the sky and wish upon a star and she would be with me.

I didn't remember much about her, but I remembered that.

As I sat on the embankment of the river, staring up at the night's sky, I felt her.

I always did.

Maybe it was the three glasses of whiskey I had before heading down here, or maybe it was all the shit floating around in my head, but being out here, under the vastness of the stars, I felt her.

"Hi, Mom," I gritted out. Her name, a bittersweet taste on my tongue.

If anyone could see me now, they'd think I'd lost it, sitting here, talking to the silence. Staring at the sky like it held all the answers.

I couldn't explain it, had long given up trying... but the hole in my chest left by her, by my father, felt that little bit smaller when I was out here.

It was late, past midnight. I expected to see the odd jogger or dog walker. I didn't expect to see the flash of blonde out the corner of my eye.

"Xander?" Peyton croaked. Hands stuffed in her hoodie pocket, she blended with the shadows save for the golden braid hanging loosely over one shoulder.

"What the fuck are you doing out here?"

She flinched at my tone, and I let out a heavy sigh as I raked a hand down my face. "Shit, I didn't mean... it's late. Does Jase know you're out here?"

"What do you think?" Her lips thinned as her eyes darted to the ground beneath her feet.

"So, you snuck out?"

"I couldn't sleep." She peeked back at me.

"It's at least a fifteen-minute walk to their house. Anything could have happened to you."

I knew Jase, and I knew if he found out about this, he'd probably put a lock on her windows. She was his responsibility now, his ward. *Because she's still a kid*, a little voice warned me as I ran my eyes over her again.

Peyton didn't look like a kid though. All long legs and shapely curves as she stood there bathed in moonlight. She had these big blue doe eyes, full of pain. It was that haunted look on her face that hit something deep inside me.

I knew that look.

I'd lived with it every day since I was a four-year-old kid learning about things—*seeing things*—no kids that young ever should.

"I'll walk you home," I said, starting to clamber to my feet.

"Wait," she blurted out. "Just give me a few minutes. I feel like... I feel like I can't breathe in that house."

My brows knitted together as she slowly approached me, dropping her baby blues to the patch of grass beside me. A silent request.

Before I could stop myself, I nodded, and she sat down, kicking her long legs out in front of her. "I didn't know you'd be down here," she whispered.

"I come here sometimes."

"Is that how you... saw me?" The words caught in her throat.

"Yeah."

"Lucky me." Strained laughter spilled from her lips, and I peeked over at her and our eyes collided. Something passed between us, something that shot through me like electric shock.

What the fuck?

My eyes narrowed and the sound died as she swallowed hard.

"Listen, Xander, I—"

"Don't," I hissed.

I didn't want to do this.

Not now.

Not ever.

But Peyton had other ideas, as she said, "I just want to thank you." Her quiet voice shook. "Is that such a crime?"

"I know what you were doing, Peyton," I said slowly, calmly, making sure she absorbed every syllable.

"I-I don't know what you mean," the blood drained from her face. "It was an accident. I fell."

My brow lifted, heavy with accusation. "We both know you didn't fall."

I'd watched her wade into the water. Watched as she lost her footing and disappeared under and didn't so much as fight to break the surface.

"And now you're down here again... you've got to realize how that looks." My lips thinned with disapproval. "You should let me walk you home."

She inhaled a sharp breath. "You think I... it's not like that, I just... I needed some fresh air, I swear. I'm not—" Peyton's eyes fluttered close as her hand drifted to her throat. When they opened again, she looked at me with such aching I felt it right to the pit of my stomach. "Please... you can't tell anyone. They wouldn't... no one would understand. I wasn't trying to... do *it*. I just..."

"Relax," I said. "I'm not going to tell anyone." I don't know why but there was something in her expression that made me believe her.

"You're not?" Relief washed over her, and the faintest of smiles traced her lips.

"No. I've been there, kid. I wish I could tell you it gets easier. That the pain, the grief, subsides over time..." I trailed off, staring back out at the river. At nothing.

"But it doesn't?" Peyton let out a thin, pained breath.

"It dims," I added, "but it's always there."

"Do you come here a lot?" she asked.

"I like the view." Dropping back on my elbows, I stared up at the sky again.

It was a bad idea, being out here with her. But something inside me, the part blotted out with my own grief and pain, wanted to throw her a lifeline. Besides, my brother had suggested I talk to her.

Fuck only knew she looked like she could use it.

"You're right." Peyton sank back into the grass and let out a soft sigh. "It is beautiful."

Silence fell over us, neither of us rushing to fill the void. Peyton seemed lost in her own thoughts, and I was all too happy to drown in mine.

"I knew," she finally spoke, her voice like a whisper on the cool breeze. "The second I got home and called out for her; I knew something wasn't right."

Shit.

She was going there.

"Listen, I'm not sure—"

But Peyton didn't hear me. Or if she did, she didn't care as she went on. "I searched the house for her and when I saw her, lying there in a pool of blood, it was like something fractured inside of me."

"Fuck," I hissed, hardly able to imagine what that must have been like.

I'd been through a lot—seen a lot. I'd watched as my mom lost her battle to the tumor growing in her brain. But it wasn't the same.

"She was just laying there, dead. Her eyes still open, staring up at me."

I felt her shudder beside me, and the strangest sensation hit me.

I wanted to comfort her. I wanted to take away her pain.

But I didn't. Even though she was so close it would have been easy. Too close, like she assumed that night had connected us in some way.

"I always thought it would be easier," Peyton said, heaving a ragged breath. "I thought it would be better to have a life without her rather than putting up with her bullshit. I said that to Lily. I said—"

"Don't," I said gruffly. "Don't try and pin this on yourself."

"But I said it. For a second, I thought my life would be

easier if she overdosed... What kind of person does that make me?"

"We all think shit. Doesn't mean that deep down we want it to come true." I glanced over at her and her big blue eyes met mine, brimming with tears.

It twisted something inside me.

It shouldn't have, but it did. And it was there... between us. A huge ravine, her on one side and me on the other, and that night filling the void.

This was dangerous territory.

Territory, I had no right crossing.

"We should go," I said coolly, needing to put an end to this. She was hurting... hurting bad, and I wasn't the right person to comfort her.

"G-go? But I thought—"

"It's late. Too late for you to be out here alone."

"But I'm not alone." Her eyes softened.

Softened at me.

Fuck.

She had that starry-eyed look again. Dreaming of white knights and heroes come to save the day.

But I wasn't either of those things.

Especially not for her.

Suddenly feeling uncomfortable, and way out of my depth, I clambered to my feet and said, "Come on. I'll walk you home." Because Jase would kick my ass six ways to Sunday if he knew I'd ever let her walk back alone in the middle of the night.

"And if I don't want to go?" Peyton lifted her chin in defiance, fire flickering in her gaze.

"Don't make me call Jase."

Hurt flashed there. "You wouldn't."

"Try me." My hand slipped to my jean pocket where my cell was buried.

"Fine." She leaped up and stormed off, back up the embankment to the sidewalk.

Rolling my eyes, I jammed my hands into my pockets and took off after her. But Peyton stayed one step ahead of me, so I gave her space, trailing behind like a babysitter. Because I was the adult here and she was acting like a spoiled brat.

Except, she wasn't.

Something akin to guilt slithered through me. She'd wanted space. Fresh air to breathe. I got that, probably better than most people. But it didn't change the fact that she was down by the river—the same river she'd almost drowned in over a week ago—in the middle of the goddamn night.

Rixon was a small town, full of community spirit and low crime rates. But it didn't mean she was safe out here. Bad things still lurked in the shadowy corners of town. I knew; I'd wandered across them enough. Drug dealers concealed in graffiti-stained alleys, seedy bars on the edge of town, the occasional dolled-up woman down by the trailer park looking to make a quick buck or two.

Rixon was like every other town in the country. You just had to look a little harder to see past the quintessential small-town veneer to find the cracks.

Peyton didn't let up as we followed the river toward Jase's neighborhood. Anger and disappointment swirled off her like a storm.

"Wait," I called, as she took off around the side of the house.

"What?" She slowed, glancing back at me.

"Don't sneak out again," I said.

"Or what? You'll rat me out to Jason?"

I nodded sharply, and her eyes widened.

"Asshole," she breathed, but then her expression

dropped, giving way to a young girl barely holding on. "You know. I just thought..." Peyton inhaled a sharp breath, and I saw her shudder even from my position on the sidewalk. She was at war with herself. With what she wanted to say and what she knew she shouldn't.

"Forget it. It doesn't matter." Disappointment flashed in her eyes. "See you around, *Coach Chase*," she seethed before slipping into the gated yard.

She was gone.

Just like that.

I ran a hand over my jaw as I shucked further into my jacket and took off in the opposite direction toward my apartment building. I should never have let her sit down with me. I should have nipped it in the bud before it became something else. Some kind of weird hero worship.

I'd saved her. But it wasn't a debt I wanted her to repay.

In fact, I wanted everyone to forget. I wanted to go back to being regular old Xander Chase, living in the shadows.

Not that there was much chance of that now I worked with Jase and the team. No, I was in the spotlight whether I wanted it or not.

My brother's voice flitted through my mind. *It's time to do something with your life, Xander. She'd want more for you than this. They both would.* His words from our last big argument. I'd gone to him for yet another handout, after being let go by the foreman on the construction site where I'd been working. My weekly tab at Bell's burned through my severance pay and when rent day rolled around, I didn't have enough to cover it.

It had been the straw that broke the camel's back.

Cameron had stood there, disappointment gleaming in his eyes as he berated me like a child. Like I was an eighteen-year-old hothead again and he was a thirty-four-year-old man trying to do the right thing.

I loved my brother, always had, always would, but somewhere over the years, things between us had become fraught. He couldn't understand why I was so intent on wasting my life and I couldn't stand to be held to his measure.

He'd given me the money, of course he had. But it came with an ultimatum—handle my shit or consider myself cut off from big brother's bank account.

He'd threatened it before. But something about this time was different.

Feeling the bitter sting of shame snap at my heels, I pulled out my smokes and placed one between my lips, lighting it up. The tobacco filled my lungs, but I welcomed the burn. I didn't look back as I crossed the street and melted into the shadows of the sidewalk that would lead me downtown to my apartment.

Hopefully, Peyton would heed my warning and rethink any future plans to sneak out. But something told me she wouldn't. Because I'd been her once. A wounded animal trying to protect itself. It was the only reason I didn't plan on telling Jase.

At least, that's what I kept telling myself.

THE NEXT DAY AT SCHOOL, when I glanced over at Peyton across the parking lot, she didn't look twice at me.

It shouldn't have stung nearly half as much as it did.

In hindsight, maybe I'd been too hard on her. She was clearly hurting, lost and afraid. But she wasn't my problem. Jase and Fee were keeping a close eye on her, Mya too. Peyton had plenty of people around her to lift her spirits.

Including Bryan Hughes, one of Rixon Raiders' defensive tackles. He bounded over to her and slung his arm around her shoulder, drawing Peyton into his side. She beamed up at him, but it didn't reach her eyes. Did he notice? Did he see the way she recoiled slightly at his touch?

I noticed.

I shouldn't have fucking noticed.

If Bryan did, he didn't let on, as he and their small group laughed and chatted about whatever high school seniors talked about these days.

Fuck, senior year felt like a lifetime ago. For a moment, I'd had it all. The world at my feet.

Until I hadn't.

Shaking the miserable thoughts out of my head, I made my way toward the building.

"Morning, Coach," Kaiden called over and I found myself looking over at them again.

Peyton's gaze immediately darted to the ground, and I felt like a complete asshole. I didn't want to play therapist, but I didn't want her to think—

Oh, who the fuck was I kidding? That's exactly what I wanted her to think. She was a teenager. A messed up, emotionally unstable teenager. The last thing she needed was some misplaced crush on the guy who had saved her.

A guy who was just as messed up and emotionally unstable as she was.

"Shouldn't you all be heading for class?" I said as I reached them.

"Nah, we have time," Bryan grinned, tucking her further into his side.

Peyton caught my eye but quickly looked away. My brows furrowed, a strange tugging sensation spreading in my chest. It wasn't guilt. I had nothing to feel guilty about.

You were a bit of an asshole to her last night. I shut down the little voice. She was a senior. She needed to turn to her friends, kids her own age. She didn't need me offering her reassurance or some sage words of advice.

But as I walked away from them, I felt her eyes on me. I felt them burning into my back begging me for something.

Something I didn't ever want to acknowledge.

CHAPTER FIVE

Peyton

I COULDN'T BREATHE.

All day, as I went from class to class, the heavy weight on my chest grew and grew until I was suffocating under its oppressive presence.

"Peyton?" Lily whispered, and I blinked over at her. "Are you okay?"

"I'm... fine." I let out a thin breath, forcing myself to smile. "I'm fine."

She studied me, her eyes crinkling with suspicion. "You've been quiet."

"It's just hard, ya know?"

"I know." She smiled warmly, squeezing my hand. "You did good today."

I wasn't so sure about that.

I'd thought yesterday would be the hardest. But today, today was something else entirely. It wasn't the stares or even the whispers... it was the memories. The image of her laying there, wrists cut open, blood pooled around her like a dark ruby river. My head and heart couldn't reconcile that. The sheer desperation someone had to feel to *do that*. I'd never once, not in my almost eighteen years, no matter how bad life got, thought about physically hurting myself. But now I couldn't stop thinking about it.

About what it felt like as she ran the razor blade over her skin. Did she cry? Did her hands shake and body tremble as the cold steel met her soft flesh?

Bile washed in my stomach and I inhaled a shuddering breath.

"Peyton?"

I brushed Lily off as we headed toward the football field. She wanted to watch Kaiden practice. She always wanted to watch him. Not that I blamed her. Kaiden was one of the good ones. The kind of guy who would cherish her heart and keep it safe. The kind of guy I'd always imagined meeting when I was a young girl, lost and afraid of the world.

But life had hardened me, built layers of stone around my heart. I enjoyed flirting with guys, being the center of their world for a fleeting moment. I liked kissing and the feel of skin on skin. I liked the distraction.

But I didn't like feeling vulnerable.

"Oh my God," Lily nudged my arm as we sat down in the bleachers. "He's got it so bad." I followed her line of sight and found Bryan waving in our direction. "You know, he's worried about you." She laced her arm through mine.

"I know." But it didn't change anything.

"You're definitely coming to the game Friday?" She changed the subject. "If you want to stay home, I can—"

"No, Lily, no way. You need to be there for your dad, for Kaiden. I'll come."

It was in Pittsburgh, so we'd be staying overnight.

Lily burrowed into my side and let out a weary sigh. "I wish I could make it all better for you, Pey."

"It's okay... I'll be okay." The lie soured on my tongue. I wasn't sure I'd ever be okay again. I'd always thought it would be easier if my mom was dead. She never loved me, never doted on me the way Felicity doted on Lily and her sister. All she'd ever done was take and take, uncaring how her actions and barbed words affected those around her... affected me. But she took her own life knowing *I* would find her, and I couldn't move past that.

Couldn't get over the fact she despised me enough to do that.

I'd always known she hated me.

I just hadn't realized she hated me that much.

"I'll be back." Lily squeezed my arm as she dashed toward Kaiden. He dropped his bag and caught her, hoisting her to him.

A faint smile traced my lips. A few weeks ago, she would never have been so brave.

"Hey," Bryan and Gav approached me.

"How's my favorite girl?" Bryan hooked his arm around my waist and pulled me close.

Strained laughter spilled from my lips as I rolled my eyes. "I thought we agreed, less touching?"

"We did?" His brow arched knowingly, a playful smile tugging at his mouth. "Huh, I don't recall—"

I elbowed him in the ribs, and he yelped, clutching his chest. "You wound me, Myers."

"About time she put you in your place, man." Gav winked at me.

Lily and Kaiden finally joined us and the four of them launched into a conversation about the game Friday night.

Bryan kept his arm around me, and for as much as I knew it was a fine line to walk with him, I made no effort to remove it. The truth was I didn't want him, but I liked his comfort. I liked the feel of his strong arms braced around me.

A trickle of awareness ran up my spine as I glanced over at the door where Jase and Xander appeared. He barely looked twice in my direction. And it bothered me.

It shouldn't have.

He didn't owe me anything. But I guess I thought… I don't know what I thought. All I knew is, when I woke up in the hospital, cold and confused, I'd immediately looked for him.

The man who saved me.

The man whose voice had tethered me to this life.

"I'll pretend I can't see this," Jase said, throwing Lily and Kaiden a bemused look.

She burrowed into Kaiden's side, fighting a smile. "We're just hugging, Dad."

"Yeah, well, I'm no fool. I know hugging leads to kissing, and kissing leads to—"

"Oh my God, *Dad*." Her cheeks pinked, as the guys chuckled. Kaiden didn't seem embarrassed or even intimidated by Jase. He was completely at ease, holding his girl in front of her father.

Good on him.

Lily deserved to have a guy who fought for her, who stood up for her and loved her without reservation.

My chest ached as my eyes fluttered to the ground. When I lifted them again, Xander was looking at me. No, not looking at me; he was staring at me, his brows drawn tight with concern.

My breath caught, my lips parting on a soft exhale. It seemed to shake him free from his thoughts and he ran a hand down his face. "I gotta go," he said to no one in particular.

"You need a ride?" Jase asked, and Xander shook his head.

"I'm heading to Bell's."

"You sure that's a good idea on a school night?"

"As good as any." He smirked and walked off without so much as a backward glance.

"Hey, you okay?" Bryan murmured against my hair and Jase cleared his throat.

"Something you two want to tell me?" He eyed us carefully, a flicker of concern there when he looked at me.

I tried to wiggle out of Bryan's hold, but he only pulled me closer. "No, sir," he said smoothly. "We're just friends... right, babe?"

"Bryan," I hissed.

Laughter rumbled in his chest. "You don't need to worry, Coach. I know the deal. Peyton doesn't date."

Oh my God, I was going to kill him. Knee him in the balls and—

"Peyton?" Jason asked.

"We're just friends."

"Friends," he murmured, his eyes looking to the sky as if he was asking for some kind of divine intervention. When he looked at us again, he said, "I thought I'd seen it all... done it all, but here I am with three teenage girls under my roof. Remember your curfew," he added, before taking off toward his truck.

"And Kaiden?" Jason glanced back at the last second.

"Yes, Coach?"

"If I catch you sneaking out of my daughter's room one

more time, I'll string you up by your balls on the football field. Got it?"

"Got it, Coach." Kaiden swallowed hard.

Lily's eyes bugged out as she slapped a hand over her mouth.

"You okay there?" he whispered against her hair.

"He... he knows."

"He's Jason Ford. Of course he knows," Gav chuckled.

"B-but... oh my God."

"Relax," Kaiden said. "He's cool."

"Cool about us... about me... *oh God.*"

Even I smiled at Lily's freak out. "Kaiden's right, babe. Your dad is the coolest. If he cared that much, he'd put bars on your windows and a lock on your door."

"Yeah, I guess."

"So what are we doing?" Bryan changed the subject. "Or are you two... ya know." His brows waggled.

"Asshole." Kaiden punched him in the arm. "I told Aaron we'd go hang out at his house."

"Sounds good to me, let's roll."

"Peyton, you coming?" Lily asked, and I glanced between her and Bryan. It wasn't like she and Kaiden would make me feel unwelcome if I rode with them but playing third wheel wasn't exactly my idea of fun. Especially not right now.

"I'll ride with Bryan and Gav."

"You're sure?" Concern glittered in her eyes.

"Yeah. See you there."

THE BENNET TWINS lived in a house not all too dissimilar to Bryan's, minus the indoor swimming pool and home theater. It was a beautiful place overlooking the river, and

Mr. Bennet, one of Lily's dad's best friends had given his son Aaron free reign of the garden shed, letting him and his friends turn it into a hangout. There was a huge sectional facing a flatscreen, a pool table, and even a makeshift bar area. It was where we usually hung out since Lily's sister Poppy was best friends with Aaron's sister Sofia.

I liked it here, but I never truly felt one hundred percent comfortable seeing as Aaron and Sofia's mom—Mya Bennet—was the guidance counselor at Rixon High, the one person who probably knew more about me than I was ever willing to tell.

"Leigh, you're up," Aaron called, holding out the cue for her. Ashleigh regularly kicked the guys' ass at pool, and usually I enjoyed watching, enjoyed teasing them about it.

But not tonight.

Tonight, I wanted to be anywhere but here.

"You need a drink? Snacks?" Bryan asked from beside me. He'd sat there nearly all night, like a sentinel watching over me. It was as sweet as it was suffocating. But I didn't have the heart—or energy—to tell him I needed space.

"No, I'm good." I gave him a weak smile and his eyes narrowed, shimmering with concern.

"We could always get out of here?" He let the words, the insinuation, hang between us.

"I don't—"

"Shit, that was a dumb thing to say. I just want to help, in any way I can." His expression softened.

"I know. You're a good friend, Bryan."

"Friend, right." His lips thinned and a bolt of guilt went through me.

I knew he wanted more than friendship, but I couldn't give it to him.

"You should lay off the candy, Bry," Gav said, dropping down beside him. "You'll have your work cut out for you

Friday. The Panthers have one of the best offenses in the state.

"Let them bring it," he shrugged, "I'm ready."

"We're ready," Kaiden added, pulling Lily down on his lap. She nuzzled his neck, and it wasn't long before they were making out.

"Get a room," Aaron yelled.

Kaiden flipped him off over his head and snickers rang out around me.

These people were my friends. Ten of us crammed into the renovated shed. Yet, I'd never felt more alone as I did then, sitting there among their chatter and easy laughter.

It wasn't that I wanted them to be awkward around me. I didn't. I just couldn't stand the pity stares and sympathy in their eyes every time they looked at me. But the truth was, it wasn't them at all.

It was me.

Something had changed inside me that night. Intrinsically altered. And the things I used to take comfort in and enjoy no longer seemed significant.

"You want to go home?" Lily asked me while the guys talked about the upcoming game. I shook my head.

"I'm fine." Because being at the Ford's, in my spacious bedroom with its own bathroom and views of their yard, was another kind of torture.

My skin vibrated, my stomach awash with emotion. It wasn't grief, or even heartache. It was something else entirely.

Lily let out a small sigh and I pressed my lips into a thin smile. She wanted to help; they all did.

But this wasn't something anyone could fix. It was something I had to deal with alone.

Alone.

I guess that was something else I had to get used to.

Ashleigh gave us a ride back to the house. Lily and Poppy wanted to raid the refrigerator before bed, but I declined any food, grabbing a bottle of water and going straight up to my room. I felt like I couldn't breathe, a tight band squeezing my rib cage.

I closed my door and headed straight for the bathroom, gripping the counter as I stared at myself. My eyes were dull, dark circles ringing them thanks to the lack of sleep I was getting. But every time I closed my eyes, I saw her lifeless body, the blood pooled around her.

A shudder ran down my spine and I retched into the silence. Emotion balled in my throat, knotted in my stomach. I couldn't go to sleep. Not yet. I needed... I needed something—*anything*—to make it all stop.

Before I knew what I was doing, I pulled the paring knife, the one I'd swiped from the knife block downstairs, from my back pocket. I hadn't meant to take it... but it had been right there, taunting me. Calling to me. Lily and Poppy had been so distracted raiding the refrigerator that before I knew it, I'd taken it and shoved it in my pocket. My hands trembled as I pressed my thumb against the sharp blade. It stung, but there was something else too... something that unfurled shame deep inside me.

Sucking in a sharp breath, I pressed harder, wincing as a bead of blood formed there. But some of the tension inside me ebbed away.

Is this what she felt? In those minutes or hours before I found her, is this what my mom had been searching for?

My hands moved involuntarily, slipping to my jeans and pushing them off my hips. I dropped down to the bathroom floor, pressing my back to the tub as I clutched the knife in my hand.

It was a bad idea.

But it could be worse, *couldn't it*?

I could be sneaking out, getting drunk, getting into all kinds of trouble. At least I was here, safe in the Ford's house. I wouldn't go too far. Just enough to give me that burst of relief again. Just enough to chase away the oppressive weight crushing my chest.

My legs fell open, the soft skin of my thighs visible. I dragged the tip of the knife along the fleshy part of my inner thigh, angling it just enough that the blade pressed into my skin. Silent tears rolled down my cheeks as a war raged inside me. I just wanted it to stop.

I just wanted to breathe...

An anguished cry slipped from my lips as I dug the knife harder, slicing my skin open. Blood pooled there, another cry rolling off my tongue as a shudder ripped through me. It hurt, but the release... the release was like a rush of euphoria flowing through me.

My eyes shuttered as I dropped my head back and expelled a shaky breath. I felt lighter than I had in days. But the second my eyes opened, landing on the blood trickling down my thigh, the feeling became edged with shame.

What the hell was I doing?

The knife clattered to the tiles as the tears came thick and fast, a violent storm sweeping me away, tearing me in two.

On the one hand, I felt better. The endorphins chased away the constant torrent of emotions swelling inside me. And on the other hand, I felt disgusted at myself. But as the trickle of blood slowed and my breathing returned to normal, the high dissipated and the shame simmered leaving me numb once more.

CHAPTER SIX

Xander

BEING CRAMMED on a school bus full of football players wasn't exactly my idea of fun.

The ride to Pittsburgh was long, noisy, and by the time we reached the high school hosting tonight's game, I was ready to find the nearest bar and lose myself in the bottom of a glass of whiskey... or two.

But we had a game to win, and the work was only just beginning.

"Okay, listen up," Jase stood, grabbing the overhead storage rack for support. "We've got ninety minutes until kick off. I want you to remember you're not only representing the team tonight, but you're also representing the school and the whole goddamn town. Everyone's looking to you, so don't screw it up."

He was tense, the lines around his eyes deeper than usual. I got it. Coaching a winning team was no easy task, especially in a town like Rixon. But it was more than that—he was Jason Ford, one of the most successful quarterbacks in NFL history. And although his career might have been cut short due to injury, his list of accolades certainly hadn't been.

Jase had big shoes to fill, but if anyone could do it, it was him.

The bus screeched to a stop and the door cranked open. I shook my head, smothering a smile. The football team was one of the best funded programs in state, and yet the school couldn't afford an upgrade from the heap of junk we were in.

"Okay," Jase tapped the roof, "let's go play some football."

The guys jostled one another to get off the bus, the air charged with anticipation. Until arriving at Rixon High to coach the team, I'd forgotten just how electric Friday nights could be. These young men were thrust onto a pedestal and worshipped like gods. That kind of fan worship was addictive. All-consuming. It made young men think they were untouchable. Invincible. It made them think they were above reproach.

But I knew better than anyone how precarious that position was.

"You ready?" Jase asked me when everyone else was off the bus.

"As I'll ever be." I got up and grabbed my bag. Pittsburgh was an eight-hour round trip, so the school board had sanctioned an overnight stay. Which didn't only mean keeping forty-eight football players in line at the game, it meant keeping them in line once we got to the hotel.

At least my brother, Hailee, Fee, and the Bennets were also going to be here. Football wasn't only Jason's job; it was a family affair. He, Cameron, and Asher had once worn Raiders jerseys, once walked this path to the championship. Now it was their younger generation's turn. My nephew

Avery had his time before leaving for college a couple of years ago, and now it was Aaron's turn. A junior, he had football in his blood, and I had no doubts he'd go far.

"I know this is only supposed to be a temporary thing," he said, as we filed off the bus. "But you're proving more useful than I anticipated."

"Thanks, asshole," I muttered under my breath, and Jase laughed.

"You know what I mean. The guys respond to you. I think having someone a bit younger around bridges that gap."

"Try telling that to Huckley."

"He still giving you a hard time?" Jase's eyes narrowed with concern.

"Nothing I can't handle."

"Darryn is good, but he's old school and you didn't—"

"Earn my spot. Yeah, I know." I let out a thin breath.

"Look," he pinned me with a knowing look, "don't let him get under your skin. You're here because I want you here. And I've been meaning to talk to you about making it more permanent. You're an asset to the team, Xander. What do you think?"

"I appreciate the offer, Jase, I do, but..."

"But?"

"I'm not sure I'm cut out for it long term."

"Thought you'd say that." He scoffed. "And I know you probably won't believe me, but maybe this is exactly what you need. You're lost, Xan. Maybe you need something more permanent to help you find yourself again."

"Hey, Coach," someone yelled, and Jase gave me an apologetic look.

"Go," I said, flicking my head over to where the team was slowly making their way toward the football field.

He threw his bag over his shoulder and took off toward

them. I watched as they stepped aside to let him up front, to lead them. Jase might have been a hard ass at times, but the team respected him. The other coaches respected him too.

Hell, I respected him.

And I knew he was only trying to help, offering me something more permanent than one season with the team. But was I really looking to make a career out of this? It wasn't exactly what I had planned for myself.

But neither was living in a studio apartment, driving a beat-up Chevy, with less than a couple hundred bucks in my bank account.

Fuck. Maybe I needed to consider this. I could turn things around. Shed my status as the down-and-out of the family and really make something of myself.

Nah. Who was I kidding? I'd only mess it up eventually. And then Jase would regret the day he ever invited me onto the team, and Cam would only resent me more than he did already.

One season, that's all I was good for. I'd help the team reach the finals, hopefully witness them bring home the championship, put some money in the bank, and then go on my way.

After all, I'd accepted a long time ago that there was no happy ending for my story.

"Run, *RUN*!" Jase bellowed, watching as Cole Kandon, one of the team's wide receivers, took off down the field. He was Aaron's best friend and also a junior. Fast and strong, his legs ate up the yard markers. Forty... thirty... twenty...

"Go, *GO*!" Jase's fists curled ready to punch the air. The bleachers roared behind us, the visiting crowd cheering on their team.

"Yes, yes... fuck, yes," he bellowed just as Cole slammed the ball into the end zone, the announcer's declaration of '*touchdowwwwnnn*' echoing over the speakers.

The boom of the crowd slammed into me, taking my breath away so much that I sucked in a sharp breath. Everyone was already celebrating. Even with a few minutes left on the clock, the Panthers couldn't beat us now. The Rixon Raiders were headed to the semi-finals next week.

One step closer to the championship.

Kaiden jogged over to us, Aaron and Cole hot on his heels.

"Get over here, Kandon," Jase hooked his arm around Cole's neck and smashed their heads together, not caring that Cole still had his helmet on. "That's how it's done, son. You just put us in the final four. Congratulations."

"Thanks, Coach," Cole said, but I caught a hint of hesitation there.

"Okay, get back out there and finish it," Jase clapped him on the shoulder, and they jogged back onto the field, getting ready for the field goal.

A few seconds later, the ball sailed through the goalposts. Defeat was etched on the other team's coaching staff, but when the final whistle blew, they were good sports, congratulating us on a well-deserved win.

Friends and family of the team rushed on the field to celebrate, swarming the players. Lily made a beeline for Kaiden and he picked her up, twirling her around as they laughed and kissed. Jeez, he had it bad. Completely and utterly under her spell. But Lily was a good girl, and fuck knows, she'd been through enough. She deserved happiness. She deserved someone like Kaiden. I saw a lot of my brother and Hailee in them. The unwavering love and faith in one another, and although they were only young, although they had their whole lives ahead of them, something told me they'd go the distance.

My eyes flickered past Lily, landing on Peyton. She stood on the edge of the field, arms wrapped around her waist, watching as her friends celebrated with the team. A guy approached her. I didn't recognize him. He wasn't wearing the telltale Rixon blue and white, but he wasn't wearing Panthers' green and black either.

"Xander," Cameron stepped into my line of sight, demanding my attention. "Good game."

"It was all them." I flicked my eyes to the guys, a heavy weight settling on my chest as I watched them laugh and joke and soak it all up.

That could have been you. I shut the voice down, pushing the unwanted memories down.

"Don't do that," Cam said, raking a hand down his face. "Don't sell yourself short. Jase says your input has been invaluable."

"I'm not sure about that."

"He told me he asked you to stay on after the season ends." Cam eyed me carefully.

Of course he had.

"I told him I'd think about it." The lie rolled off my tongue. A flash of blonde caught my eye, and my spine went ramrod straight when I saw the guy follow Peyton along the edge of the field.

"Xander?" Irritation hung in Cam's voice.

"Yeah?"

"You're distracted."

"I'm not... I'm fine." God, I fucking hated that word.

"I think the job would be good for you. It's about time you—"

One minute there was just the two of us, the next we

were swarmed by the team as the guys jostled to high-five me.

"Enjoy it," my brother said around a small smile, backing away. That look in his eye, it made my heart clench. Longing. Regret... Disappointment.

I knew what he was thinking. I could have had this. I could have had it all. But I'd squandered my shot.

I'd messed it up.

"Okay, go easy on me," I protested, as the guys closed in around me, their excitement bleeding into the air. It was impossible not to be swept away in it, and soon I found myself chanting alongside them.

"Raiders, Raiders, Raiders."

As the high settled, the crowd began to disperse, and Jase ordered everyone into the locker rooms to get showered and changed so we could move things to the hotel.

I lingered behind though. When he noticed, he called, "Coming?"

"I'll be there in a minute."

Understanding passed between us and he nodded, taking off after his players. The high school stadium was almost empty now, save for a few stragglers.

I walked into the center of the field, crouching down and running my hand over the trampled grass, breathing in the cold air. My eyes shuttered as I let the memories out. The harsh glare of the Friday night lights. The noise, the smell, the crackle of anticipation. I'd once lived for it, but even the promise of a future in football hadn't been enough to chase away my demons, and in the end, I'd sabotaged any chance I'd had going pro.

Burying my face in my hands, I inhaled a deep breath as I rose and prepared myself to lock all that bullshit back in its box. Back where it belonged. There was no point crying over spilt milk. I wasn't a kid anymore, and it was too late for second chances.

I started to make for the tunnel leading to the locker room, but something caught my eye over by the exit.

Peyton.

Peyton and the unfamiliar guy. He was all up in her face, whispering something into her ear. It didn't look like a friendly conversation though, her arms folded over her chest, creating a barrier between them.

Why wasn't she with the others? Waiting for the team to get done?

I was about to intervene when Bryan appeared, jogging in their direction. He was still in his kit, looking murderous as he approached them.

He hadn't even acknowledged me, his sole purpose getting to her.

Had she texted him?

It made sense. They seemed close.

Why do you care? The thought rang loud in my mind. I didn't. At least, I wasn't supposed to.

But then Bryan got all up in the guy's face and Peyton lunged forward trying to separate them.

I was moving before I knew what was happening. "You don't want to do that, Hughes," I growled, startling Peyton. She shrunk into herself, refusing to meet my eyes. "What the hell is going on here?" I demanded.

"Ask Farrow," Bryan spat, eyes narrowed with contempt.

"You," I pinned the other guy with a hard stare. "What's your name?"

"Sean Farrow."

I vaguely recognized it from Jase and the other coaches. From what I'd heard, he was bad news.

"You okay?" I asked Peyton, who nodded, still refusing to meet my eyes.

"Get out of here," I said to Farrow.

He shot Bryan an irritated look and walked off, running a hand through his hair.

"Do I need to go to Jase with this?"

"What?" Her wide eyes finally landed on me. "No! He was just..."

"Harassing you," Bryan chimed. "It's okay, you can say it."

"I can handle Sean," she murmured.

"Yeah, is that why you texted me?" His brow arched and I saw the disapproval there.

Just then, Lily and Ashleigh appeared near the bleachers, and Peyton spotted them. "I should go." She took off toward them, leaving me and Bryan watching after her.

"What happened?" I gritted out.

"She texted me saying she needed me. I came."

"This Farrow kid, what do you know about him?"

"The guy's a complete douchebag. He and Peyton had a thing at the beginning of the semester, but it wasn't serious."

"Do I need to be worried?" The words spilled out before I could stop them.

Bryan's brows drew together as he let out a steady breath. He was watching her, stalking her every move as Lily and Ashleigh led her off the field.

"I can handle Farrow, Coach." His chest puffed out.

"I don't doubt it. But you can't afford a red mark against your name." I pinned Bryan with a hard look. "If he becomes a problem, I want to know, okay?"

What the fuck was I saying?

Peyton wasn't my problem.

She wasn't my anything.

He finally looked at me, confusion clouding his eyes, but after a second, he said, "Yeah, okay."

"Come on, you need to take a shower before we leave. You stink."

A faint smirk traced his lips. "The girls dig it. All that sweat and dirt, gets them going..."

His eyes betrayed him though when they flicked back over to where Peyton and her friends had disappeared.

He wasn't thinking about girls... he was thinking about *one* girl.

The same girl who had plagued my thoughts ever since I'd pulled her from that damn river.

CHAPTER SEVEN

Peyton

AFTER CHECKING in at the hotel, Lily's dad ushered all of us down to the adjoining restaurant and let us order a late-night feast. Everyone was high on the win, excited about next weekend's semi-final in Harrisburg. But my mind was still back at the stadium.

Bryan caught my eye across the table and mouthed, "You good?"

I gave him a small nod, pretending to be drawn into Ashleigh and Poppy's conversation.

I hadn't expected Sean Farrow to be here. He hated football the way bats hated sunlight.

We'd hooked up a few times at the end of the summer, but I'd cooled things off when he'd tried to push for more.

I didn't want more. I wanted fun. A distraction. Intimacy without strings. Besides, if I was ever going to go steady—and I wasn't—it wouldn't be with a guy like Sean. He liked the thrill of the chase, that's all. As soon as I'd become too hard to get, he'd moved on with another girl in our class, Layla Hannigan.

I'd learned a long time ago that the word 'no' was like a challenge to most guys.

A shudder went through me, and Lily laid her hand on my arm. "Where did you go just now?" she asked.

"Nowhere." I grabbed my soda and drained the glass dry. "Do you think we can go soon?"

"Yeah, I heard the adults say they wanted a quiet drink once we all go to our rooms." She leaned in closer. "You're okay with rooming with Leigh and the girls, right?"

"Yeah, of course." The plan was me and Ashleigh would return to our room and then sneak into Poppy and Sofia's room, so Lily could have some alone time with Kaiden.

I never imagined I'd witness her do something so daring, so of course I didn't mind. I just hoped the girls didn't want to make a big thing about our night away.

"Good, okay." She gave me a shy smile.

"Something you want to tell me, Lil?" I teased.

"I... uh, I brought something with me."

My brows knitted. "Like a dildo?"

"What?" She stuttered. "No, I didn't bring a... one of those."

I smothered the laughter crawling up my throat. "Sorry, I thought you meant—"

"Lingerie. I brought some sexy lingerie," she whispered, color blooming along her cheeks.

"How very scandalous."

"Do you think... I mean... he'll like it, right?" Her eyes slid to where Kaiden sat flanked by his teammates.

"Babe, you could wear a burlap sack and Kaiden would still think you're the most beautiful girl in the room. You have nothing to worry about."

Relief washed over her, and she let out a thin breath.

"Okay, I didn't know if it was the right time. I mean, Mom and Dad will be right down the hall, but it isn't like we get any time alone at home and—"

"Lily?"

"Yeah?"

"Breathe, babe. You have to breathe." I smiled.

Her eyes fluttered closed and then open. "I'm being ridiculous."

"You're just nervous." I squeezed her hand. "But you have nothing to worry about. Kaiden loves you."

So much that sometimes it made my chest ache to watch.

Okay, most of the time.

Not that I would ever admit that to her. Lily would only tell me how I'd find somebody one day. If only I opened myself up to guys more.

That was the whole point though; if you opened yourself up, you were vulnerable. I couldn't be vulnerable. Not again.

"Okay, can everyone settle down." Bottle of beer in hand, Mr. Ford stood and ran his eyes over the section of the restaurant we filled. "I'm only going to say this once. When you head back to your rooms, you go straight to your rooms, and I don't want to see any of you until first thing in the morning. If I hear so much as a whisper of you breaking the rules, it won't just be running suicides you'll have to worry about." His eyes fixed on the guys. "You got the job done tonight. You represented this team, and you did Rixon proud. Don't disappoint me now."

A rumble of, "Yes, Coach," went around the room.

"Okay, get out of here. Coach Macintosh and Coach Huckley will escort you up to our floor."

It was a mass exodus as the team eagerly filed out of the restaurant. Kaiden lingered. Aaron and Cole too.

"You did good tonight, Son," Aaron's dad said, fist bumping him. "Go get some sleep." His lip curved knowingly.

"Ash," Jason warned, and he threw up his hands.

"What? They know not to break the rules."

Aaron fought a grin. "Night, guys, catch you all tomorrow." His eyes found Poppy, and she ducked her head.

The two of them were so obvious, but neither of them had fessed up to being anything more than friends.

The girls got up too. Poppy hugged her mom and dad while Sofia did the same. Lily was next, her dad whispering something to her. It didn't take a lot to figure out what he'd whispered when she swatted his chest and turned firetruck red.

"Night, Peyton," Felicity said. "We'll see you tomorrow."

"Night," I said, following Lily out of the restaurant.

The guys were waiting for us and we all rode the elevator together.

"Party in my room?" Bryan said. "I managed to smuggle some vodka and snacks in."

His eyes were heavy on me, but I didn't meet his stare. He came anyway, pressing his body against the side of mine. "Hey, Myers, you okay?"

I lifted my face to his and faked a smile. "Peachy."

"Listen, about you and Sean—"

"There is no me and Sean. He obviously got bored with Layla and decided to come crawling back to me. And now he's pissed I didn't want to hang out again."

He flinched, anger simmering in his eyes. We both knew the lengths to which me and Sean had hung out.

Everyone did.

My eyes fluttered shut as I inhaled a small breath. When I opened them again, I saw the reflection of Lily and Kaiden kissing in the mirror behind me. My expression must have betrayed me because Bryan piped up, "Can you two at least wait until you're behind closed doors?"

"You're just jealous, Bry," Gav snorted.

Bryan's heavy-lidded eyes dropped to me again, but I glanced away. His lust was like a living, breathing thing, swirling in the air around us.

The second the door pinged open, I said, "I think I'm going to call it a night."

"No," Ashleigh said. "You have to come."

"You go. I just want to sleep."

"Pey," she whispered, concern glittering in her eyes, but I waved her off.

I wasn't feeling sociable, not after pasting on a smile for the game and dinner.

We filed out of the elevator, the hall a hive of activity as the rest of the team all headed toward their various rooms.

"Let's go," Coach Huckley shouted. "We've got an early start in the morning."

Me, Lily, and Ashleigh had an adjoining room with Poppy and Sofia, so it would be easy for us to sneak into their room. But then they would have to sneak down the hall to the guys' rooms.

We all said goodnight and disappeared into our rooms. Ashleigh immediately began gathering up her things.

"You don't have to leave right this second," Lily said, chewing her lip as one of her hands slipped to the braid hanging loosely over her shoulder.

"You're nervous," I said, recognizing her tell for what it was.

"My dad will—"

"Relax, your dad and the other adults will be in the bar for at least another couple of hours reminiscing about the good old days. Besides, they probably expect you to sneak Kaiden in here."

"Peyton's right," Ashleigh added. "I mean, the Bennets trusted Ezra to stay at home. They trust us enough to not come up here snooping."

"I still can't believe they left Ezra," Lily said.

Ezra was Sofia and Aaron's foster brother. Only he didn't act like it. He'd been with the Bennets for a few years now and I knew as little about him now as I did the day he'd arrived.

"Their neighbor, Mrs. Grakinsy is checking in on him." Ashleigh was a mask of indifference, but me and Lily both knew she had a soft spot for the elusive boy who lived with the Bennets.

"Ready?" she asked me. I nodded, grabbing my small bag.

"Enjoy your night." I smirked at Lily, and she ducked her head, failing to hide her bright red cheeks.

"Yeah, Lil. Don't do anything we wouldn't." Ashleigh winked, going to the interconnecting door and opening the one on our side. She knocked on the second door and it swung open.

"Party time," Poppy grinned.

"Don't let her go too crazy," Lily said. "Dad will—"

"Never find out." Poppy blew her a kiss and pulled us into the room she was sharing with Sofia. I closed the first door, hardly surprised when I heard the lock click into place. Lily knew me and Ashleigh wouldn't do something like barge into the room to catch her and Kaiden... but she probably wouldn't put it past Poppy.

Closing the second door, I leaned against it, eyeing the two Queen beds. "I'll take the fold-out bed," I said, knowing they planned to go and get drunk with the guys.

"Are you sure you don't want to come with us?" Poppy asked.

"No, I'm tired." The lie sounded convincing.

"Okay, that was Aaron," Poppy didn't lift her eyes from her cell phone. "He said the coast is clear, so if we're going to go, we should probably go now."

Sofia leaped up and grabbed her purse, following Poppy to the door.

"You sure you're okay?" Ashleigh asked, uncertainty shining in her eyes.

"Go. I'll be fine."

"Okay, but if you need me..."

"I know."

I watched them sneak out of the room in a fit of muted giggles.

And I didn't know whether to be relieved I was finally alone or bitterly disappointed.

An hour later, sleep still hadn't found me. I'd changed into my favorite pajamas and had gotten comfortable on the fold-out bed. But the murmurs from Lily's room—my room—and the thud of footsteps overhead, along with doors slamming and laughter out in the hall made it impossible to drift off.

Frustrated, I pushed off the sheet, pulled on my hoodie and shoved my feet into my sneakers. I didn't know where I was going, but I knew I couldn't stay in here for a second longer.

Grabbing the remaining key card, I opened the door and peeked out. The hall was empty, so I ducked out of the room and hurried for the stairwell, making my way up to the rooftop. I'd seen the sign for the rooftop terrace in reception during check-in. Of course, I doubted anyone would be up there this time of year.

The fire exit door loomed ahead, and I pressed down on the bar, shouldering the heavy door. The frigid air met my warm skin and I shuddered, but there was something about feeling the cold against my face that made me inhale a deep, calming breath.

The moment I stepped onto the roof terrace, I faltered though. "You," the word fell from my lips.

Xander looked up, his eyes clouding with something. He let out a slow, steady breath. "You shouldn't be out here."

"I didn't come looking for you, if that's what you think."

"Shit, Peyton," he sighed, "that's not... what are you doing up here?"

"I couldn't sleep."

He stared at me, waiting for some other explanation I didn't have. But I added, "I needed to get out of the room." *Before I did something stupid.*

Xander tracked me as I moved to the edge of the terrace. The hotel was only five stories high, but it overlooked the city, making everything below seem small and insignificant. Before he could stop me, I climbed onto the ledge and—

"What the fuck?" He rushed over to me. "Do you have a dea—" Xander stopped himself.

"Don't worry, I'm not going to jump. I just like the feeling of being..." How did I explain it?

"Reckless?"

My eyes slid to his, and I nodded gently.

"Please, get down from there," he said, softer this time.

"Will you tell Jase if I don't?"

His brow arched. "What do you think?"

"Fine." I snapped, lowering myself back down and

going over to one of the rattan couches. "What are you doing up here anyway?"

"Couldn't sleep," Xander said, joining me. His eyes dropped to my bare legs, lingering for a second. Heat flashed through me, but I silently chided myself for being so foolish.

Xander didn't see me as anything more than an over-emotional teenage girl. He'd made that obvious on more than one occasion. And part of me hated that he'd seen me that night at the river. Not because I ever expected anything to happen between us, I wasn't that deluded. But because for the first time in my life, someone had seen me. The real me. Lost and flawed and scared.

Xander had seen me at my most vulnerable and it terrified me.

But there was another part that was relieved that it was him. Because if I was right, then he carried some of the same darkness I did. I didn't have to pretend around him.

"I'm surprised you're not sneaking into the guys' room and—"

"And what?" I snapped, hurt snaking through me.

Is that what he thought of me?

That I was just some high school hussy?

"That's not what I meant, Peyton," he said as if he could hear my thoughts.

"So what did you mean?" Indignation sat heavy in my chest.

"I was young once, you know? You think I don't know what happens when the adults turn their backs?"

"Maybe... before..." I let the words linger.

Silence enveloped us. Thick, oppressive, it squeezed my lungs until I couldn't breathe. But I didn't drop my gaze, and neither did Xander. Instead, he stared at me, his eyes studying me. Searching my face for something.

When he inhaled a sharp breath, I wondered if he'd found whatever he'd been looking for. "You should go back—"

"If you're that upset by my presence, why don't *you* go back inside?" My brow rose.

"Peyton," he sighed again. "I'm the adult here."

Damn him.

Did he think I didn't know that? That every time I thought about his strong arms pulling me out of the river, or his gravelly voice coaxing me from the darkness, I wasn't hyperaware of the fact he was a man, and I was just a girl?

I knew… and I hated it.

I hated that he looked at me and saw a weak, pathetic girl.

I might have only been almost eighteen, but I'd been forced to grow up a long time ago. It didn't matter though. Because he didn't look at me and see a young woman struggling to find her place in the world…

Xander saw the girl his friend—*his boss*—took in when she had nowhere left to turn.

He saw a charity case.

Nothing more.

CHAPTER EIGHT

Xander

THE AIR CRACKLED around us as she stared at me, defiance burning in her baby blue eyes. Despite everything she'd been through, Peyton still had fight left in her; she still had the balls to stand off against me. This girl... Did she have any idea how fucking beautiful she was?

Fuck. I didn't know where that thought had come from, but it hit me square in the chest.

She was beautiful. She was the kind of girl who pulled you into her orbit. I'd seen it with her friends, with Bryan, and that asshole Sean Farrow. Peyton lit up the room wherever she went, but the sparkle in her eyes had dimmed since the *accident*. She was lost... and she looked at me like she knew I was lost too.

"So..." she said, a faint smirk tracing her mouth, as if it was a foregone conclusion I wouldn't send her back to her room.

"You're trouble." The words rolled off my tongue before I could stop them.

Something flashed in her eyes, but she shook it away, smiling at me. "That's what life's for, right? Living." The sadness in her voice was like a punch to the gut.

I pulled out another smoke and lit it up. Peyton's nose crinkled. "Do you really like those things?"

"It's a distraction," I said with a half-shrug.

"Maybe I should take up smoking then."

"Nah, it costs a small fortune and the smell never goes away."

She lifted her sneakers onto the edge of the table and folded her arms around herself, staring at the city in the distance. "I can't stop thinking about it... about her..."

The words were small; too fucking small for a strong, confident girl like Peyton.

"I close my eyes and I see it, playing on repeat in my mind. And I can't help but think it was her final 'fuck you' to the daughter she never wanted."

The crack in her voice had me wanting to comfort her, but I couldn't. And even if I could, what did a guy like me know about comforting a girl like her? I kept people at arm's length for a reason—because my heart turned to stone a long time ago. It was the only way I knew how to protect myself from the constant ache. The hole left by the two people who loved me unconditionally.

My entire childhood was shaped by the people I loved leaving me. First my mom, then Cameron, then my dad. I spent the best part of ten years attending therapy, but nobody could fix me. And fuck only knew I hadn't ever managed to fix myself.

"I'm sure your mom loved you in her own way."

Peyton let out a derisive sound. "My mom was a selfish junkie whore who cared more about her next fix than she ever did me."

I winced at the honesty—the gut-wrenching pain—in her voice.

"I'm sorry."

"Why?" She glanced up at me. "It's not your fault."

"No one should have to endure that."

"Yeah, well, the universe was all out of fucks when it dealt me my hand," she snorted.

"What about your dad?"

"You mean the useless sperm donor that up and left when I was barely out of diapers and never looked back?"

Jesus. My jaw locked up as I imagined what she'd endured, what she'd been through. I knew a little of her history from Jase and Cameron, but I didn't know the extent to which she'd suffered. I doubted anyone did. Because Peyton played her part. She put on her armor of fake smiles and sassy confidence and wielded them with perfection. The best defense was a good offense, and she'd got it down pat.

But this girl... the girl I'd pulled from the river was different.

Even I could see that.

"I'm just... ugh," she ran a hand through her hair, yanking the ends in frustration, "I'm so freaking sick of caring."

"Caring makes you human."

"Yeah, well maybe I'm sick of that too." She threw me a sardonic look.

"Give it some time. Things will—"

Peyton scoffed. "I think we both know the whole give it time thing is a crock of shit. Time might make things easier, but it never lets you forget. And even if you could forget, it would still be inside you like a slow, festering poison."

She had a point.

I'd been around enough therapists and shrinks to know

that childhood trauma shaped you and the person you became. But Peyton was still young. She had her whole life ahead of her to turn things around, to not succumb to the dark thoughts circling her mind.

"Sorry..." Her cheeks pinked. "I didn't mean to off-load like that."

"It's fine."

It wasn't, but it was too late for her to take it all back. Besides, she obviously needed someone to off-load on. I guessed the least I could do was listen.

"I'm sure you have better things to do than sit out here with me while I have an existential crisis."

"Peyton," I said, "you've been through something huge. It's going to take—"

"Don't say it. God, please, don't say it."

"Fine, I won't say it." A faint smile lifted the corner of my mouth. "But it's true. Just take each day as it comes. And you really should think about talking to someone."

"I'm talking to you."

"I mean a professional." I gave her a pointed look.

"Yeah, I know. But I don't need a shrink to tell me what I already know."

"And what's that?"

Her eyes fluttered shut as she inhaled a sharp breath. When they opened again, her expression softened. "That I'm messed up."

"Aren't we all?" My smile grew, a strange sensation tugging in my chest.

"I guess..." Peyton stared back out at the view. "Rixon feels so small compared to this." She let out a soft sigh.

"You're a senior. You have the world at your feet."

"Maybe."

I didn't like the resignation in her voice, as if she'd already accepted her fate.

"Come next fall you'll be off to college and Rixon will be an afterthought."

"College. Right." Her shoulders lifted in a small shrug.

"You do want to go to college?" I asked.

"I have to be realistic." Peyton glanced over at me. "I have no family, no money, and a part-time job at Cindy's Grill. It isn't exactly going to pay the bills."

"You can get financial aid though."

"It's an option." She shrugged.

One she didn't look convinced about.

"You didn't go to college?" she asked me.

"No, I... I dropped out of high school."

"Oh. What happened?" I let out a steady breath and Peyton flinched. "Sorry, it's none of my business."

"It's okay. I just prefer not to relive that time of my life... I was a mess."

"You could have played football at college though?"

"Where'd you hear that?" My eyes narrowed, a lick of shame racing up my spine. I suspected she already knew some of the story from Lily and Ashleigh, but still, I didn't appreciate the pity in her eyes.

"People talk, Xander."

"Yeah." I tsked, scrubbing my jaw.

In a town like Rixon, all people did was talk.

Silence echoed around us. Peyton watched me with eager eyes, but I didn't want to open that can of worms, to dredge up old memories. My life might not have been a success in comparison to Cam or Jase, but I was in a damn sight better place than I was back then. That had to count for something.

"It's getting late," I said.

"You can trust me, you know?" Her words sank into me, taking hold.

"You're just a—"

"Kid, yeah. So you like to keep reminding me." Hurt flashed over Peyton's face. "I wish I was just a normal seventeen-year-old girl. I wish I hadn't seen half the things I've seen, heard the things I've heard. God, I wished all I had to worry about was college applications, and who's dating who."

"Peyton, I—"

"I get it. You're my best friend's uncle. You coach the football team at my high school. You're... a grown man, and I'm just a girl." Her eyes glittered with pain. "I don't want anything from you, Xander. I'm not that foolish to ever think you would see me as more than what I am, but I just thought... I thought maybe you got it. That maybe you understood."

"I shouldn't even be sitting out here with you."

Bitter laughter spilled from her lips, shredding my insides. Of all the things I could have said... I chose that.

Fucking idiot.

"I guess one of us should leave then." She stood up, moving for the door. Frozen in place, I watched her while unable to think of a single thing to say.

Peyton beat me to it anyway when she said, "Goodnight, Xander. I guess I'll see you around."

By the time we piled onto the bus the next morning, I was still thinking about what Peyton said up on the roof terrace. I'd barely slept, turning her words over and over in my head. *I thought maybe you got it. That maybe you understood.*

She felt it. The strange affinity between us. I'd originally thought it was just some lingering sense of gratitude she felt toward me for saving her life. But the more time I spent with her, the more she opened up to me, I knew it was more than that.

It scared the fuck out of me.

I'd never met someone like me before. Someone plagued by dark thoughts and enough emotional trauma to sink a ship. Sure, I'd met people over the years who knew grief and loss and pain. But I'd never met someone like Peyton.

She's just a kid.

Only, she wasn't.

She was a young woman carrying the weight of the world on her shoulders.

"Remind me never to have daughters again." Jase dropped down onto the seat next to me, the team already in their seats.

"What's up?" I asked, not sure I wanted to know.

"I caught Poppy, Sofia, and Ashleigh in Bryan's room."

"Damn. I'm surprised Hughes still has his balls." I fought a smile.

"Yeah, well, I told that horny motherfucker he'd better report to the gym first thing Monday morning for his punishment."

"Where was Lil—she was with Kaiden."

"Fuck, I'm not ready for this."

"Remember what you were like at eighteen." I gave him a pointed look. I might have only been a kid back then, but I'd heard the stories. Everyone had.

"Which is exactly why I don't like it. Kaiden is a good kid. He's good for Lily. But the idea of them... nope, can't go there," he gritted out, running a hand down his face.

"She's eighteen, Jase. It was bound to happen one day."

"You sound like Fee." His brow arched. "I expect it from Peyton. I don't expect it from Lily and Poppy."

"She wasn't with them?" Fuck, the words were like cotton in my mouth.

"Nah, she'd stayed behind. She's struggling."

"Yeah," I said.

"What the hell am I supposed to do with her? It's senior year. She has some big decisions to make, and she's got nothing."

"She has you."

"But is it enough? I always knew her mom was trouble, but I never thought... fuck, Xan." He lowered his voice, but the rumble of the engine beneath us drowned out his words. "What she did... How could she do that knowing Peyton would be the one to find her?"

"Has Peyton talked to anyone about it?"

"She's talked to Mya, but she doesn't want to see a grief counselor or a therapist."

"It's a lot to confront."

"Yeah, but if she doesn't confront it... how does that end?"

"Give her some time. It's still raw."

"Maybe you should talk to her?"

"Me?" I balked.

If he knew I'd already been talking to her, the circumstances of those conversations, I was pretty sure he'd be warning me to stay the fuck away from her.

"Just thinking out loud. I'm not actually suggesting you do it. I wasn't prepared for teenage daughters, let alone one with as much baggage as Peyton."

"You're doing a good thing, Jase."

"She's lost everything. Her mom just—fuck." His voice cracked as he ran a hand over his face, blowing out a steady breath. "Sorry, man, I know this can't be easy for you either."

"What makes you say that?" I tensed.

"I just figured it would bring back some of those bad memories."

Bad memories.

I swallowed a strangled laugh. I didn't have bad memories; I had eviscerating nightmares. I don't know why my grief had embedded itself so deep, but I'd long accepted it was never going to disappear.

"It was a long time ago," was all I said, pressing my head back into the seat rest and closing my eyes.

"You know Cam's a hard ass because he loves you, right? Because he wants more for you."

"We're not doing this," I said around a deep sigh.

"I won't push, you know that. But he's your brother. You should talk to him, try to work through some of this stuff. You've only got each other."

It wasn't true though because Cameron had Hailee. He had Avery and Ashleigh. He had a family who loved him and friends who would do anything for him. And I was on the periphery, always on the outside looking in. Maybe it was in part my own fault, but it didn't change the fact Cameron had a life, a good life, and I had nothing.

There had been a time, when I was just a kid who adored his big brother, that I thought we'd never be separated, but time had only proved me wrong. And maybe it was selfish to want to be the center of his world, maybe it made me some kind of weirdo to be that dependent on him, but I couldn't change the fact that as his life moved in new directions, I'd felt left behind, and I hadn't known how to deal with losing him.

Guilt was a powerful motivator; but add shame and bitterness into the mix and it was lethal. Too overwhelming for my teen self to deal with.

I wasn't lying when I'd told Peyton last night that we were all messed up—except I wasn't talking about anyone but myself.

To my relief, Jase didn't push. He let me sit there and

stew on my thoughts, his words. But what he didn't know was, it didn't change anything. I wasn't a kid anymore. Nobody was going to swoop in and fix me. Not unless I wanted it…

And I'd stopped wanting it a long time ago.

CHAPTER NINE

Peyton

"EVERYTHING'S SO PRETTY," Lily said from beside me as we wandered down the street, taking in the storefronts decked out with holly wreaths and Christmas trinkets. The holidays were fast approaching and with them… my birthday.

Eighteen.

On Christmas Eve, I would turn eighteen.

As if she heard my thoughts, Lily asked, "What do you want to do for your birthday?"

"I haven't really thought about it." I shrugged.

Lily burrowed into my side, leaning her head on my shoulder. "We have to celebrate. I bet my parents would throw you a party—"

"No. No parties."

"I wish I knew how to make things better for you," she whispered, but she didn't look at me.

"It's not something anyone can fix, Lil."

"I know, but it's senior year and maybe I shouldn't say

this because she was your mom, but I hate that she did that to you. I hate that she—"

Slinging my arms around her, I hugged Lily tight, burying my face in her shoulder.

"What's this for?" she chuckled, wrapping her arms around me too.

"Thank you," I breathed. "Thank you for being my best friend, for not pushing and giving me space, and for just being you, Lily Ford. I love you." Lifting my face, I gave her a smile. "You're my best friend in the whole world."

"I love you too. And I know you probably don't feel much like celebrating, but it's your eighteenth birthday. We have to do something." Lily pouted.

"Fine. Something small."

"Yay." She untangled herself from me and clapped, her smile infectious.

"You still haven't told me what happened last night, with Kaiden."

Heat flooded her cheeks, and she ducked her head. "It was... intense."

"Did he like your new linge—"

"Peyton." She pressed her hand to my mouth and glanced around the sidewalk.

"Relax, no one is listening."

"Let's go to Sprinkles and I'll buy you a cupcake and tell you all about it."

"Thank God," I shot her a bemused look, "because I was beginning to think I'd have to ask Kaiden for all the gory details."

Lily rolled her eyes, grabbing my hand and pulling me toward the small coffee shop she liked. We went inside and she said, "Grab a table, I'll order."

"Lily," I sighed, "I can afford to buy my own dessert."

"I know, but I want to treat you."

"Fine. But next time, it's on me."

She stuck out her tongue, and I waved her off as I found a table near the back. It was easier to breathe around Lily. She had a calming presence on me, always had. But guilt weighed heavy on my soul because I was keeping secrets from her.

It had been two weeks since the night when everything changed. It was no time, yet, in some ways, it felt like forever.

I'd always thought being free of my mom and her addiction was what I wanted, but I had underestimated how lonely I would feel. It wasn't that I missed her. I didn't. She'd never treated me like anything more than a burden. But then, I'd always had a mother, a parent. I'd had *someone*. Even if she loved getting high far more than she'd ever loved me, I'd had a family.

"One caramel latte and a double chocolate brownie." Lily slid the tray onto the table and sat down, unravelling her chunky scarf. "Hmm, I love it here."

"You mean you love the cupcakes."

"True." Her face lit up as she reached for her red velvet cupcake.

"So... last night..." I picked up my glass and took a sip. "It was intense."

The blush returned to her cheeks. "It was like he couldn't get enough of me. I had no idea sexy lingerie could do that to a guy."

"I wouldn't know."

"What?" Lily gawked at me like I'd grown a second head. "You mean you've never..."

"Who on Earth would I ever have bought sexy lingerie for?"

"I don't know. I guess I just thought..." Guilt glittered in her eyes.

"You thought because I've fooled around a lot that I'm experienced in the art of seduction?"

"Peyton, that's not—"

"It's fine." It wasn't, but I wasn't looking for sympathy or pity. "I've never cared enough to want to dress up for a guy, Lil," I said with raw honesty.

"I bet Bryan would—"

"Bryan has nothing to do with this conversation." It came out harsher than I intended but she needed to stop pushing. There was no Bryan and me. It was never going to happen.

I couldn't force myself to want him the way I suspected he wanted me. Besides, even if I did... it would be pointless. He had an entire future ahead of him, a scholarship to Michigan. I didn't have that.

"Sorry. I didn't mean to upset you."

"It's fine." I suppressed the urge to flinch at the word. "I'm happy for you, babe. You deserve nothing but good things."

"You deserve good things too, Peyton." Lily smiled, but it didn't reach her eyes; as if she knew what I was thinking and could sense exactly where my head was at.

"I texted Cindy earlier," I said, changing the subject. "I'm going to pick up my regular shifts starting Monday."

"You don't need to do that. Not yet."

"Yeah, I do." I needed to keep busy, not to mention the fact I needed every cent I could get.

"You're not going to listen to me when I say my parents don't want your money, are you?"

"Nope." I broke a piece of brownie off and popped it in my mouth.

"Have you thought anymore about college?"

"Jesus, Lil, if I'd have known this would turn into the third degree, I would have stayed home."

Home.

The word hit me dead in the chest. Was the Ford's house really my home now? I guess it wasn't like I had anywhere else to call mine. Before when I'd stayed with them it had always felt temporary. Even though I didn't particularly relish the idea of being at home with my mom, it had still been my house, my bedroom... my space.

For as welcome as Lily's parents made me, I was all too aware of the fact I was a guest. An outsider looking in. I was grateful, so freaking grateful, but I couldn't deny being there with them was also a permanent reminder of everything I never had and would never have.

"Sorry." She gave me an apologetic smile. "I just don't like seeing you so... so sad."

"I'm not sad, babe. I'm just... honestly, I don't know what I am. But I'll be fine." There was that word again. "Once I get back to work at the diner and get the rest of this semester out of the way, I'm sure I'll feel more like my old self."

It was a lie. That girl—the girl I used to be—had died right alongside my mom. Or maybe she had drowned in the Susquehanna River. Either way, she was gone, and everything was different now.

I was different.

If anyone could understand, it was Lily. But every time I thought about opening up to her, to confessing my deepest, darkest secrets, something held me back. She'd already been through so much she didn't need me burdening her with my issues. Not when she had finally reached a good place.

No, I wouldn't do that to her.

"I can't believe it's almost the holidays." She ran her thumb around her mug of hot chocolate. Something twinkled in her eyes and I got the sense she was holding something back.

"Lily..." I waited.

"Kaiden wants us to go away over the holidays... like together."

"Wow, that's a big deal."

"I know, right? I mean, I haven't even broached it with my mom and dad yet because hello, my dad has barely accepted that I'm dating."

"Your dad loves Kaiden."

"Yeah, but will he love him whisking me away for a romantic getaway in a cabin? A freaking cabin, Peyton."

"It sounds lovely." My chest cinched.

"Maybe we could turn it into a group thing? He'd be more willing if he knew we were all going."

"I'm not sure that's what Kaiden has in mind."

"No, you're right. He said after last night, spending time together like that, he wants more." A smile lifted the corner of her mouth, making her whole face light up.

"God, the two of you are so disgusting," I teased.

"Sorry." She pouted. "I don't mean to be. But this is all so new and exciting and scary... God, it's terrifying."

"Lil, breathe," I said, inhaling a deep breath, hoping she would copy me. She did, nodding through her deep inhale and exhale. "Better?" I asked.

"Yes, thank you. I bet you think I'm such—"

"Please. You know I would never judge you... for anything. This is a good thing, babe. It's only a few months before you'll be heading to college together."

"If I get in."

"You'll get in." Lily planned to head to the University of Pittsburgh while Kaiden had committed to Penn State. It was only a couple hour's car ride, but they would make it work. I had zero doubts about it.

"So you think I should say yes... about the cabin?"

"Errr, hell yes!"

Her soft laughter filled the space between us. "I'm so glad I have you to talk to about all this stuff."

"You have Ashleigh too, and Poppy."

"Yeah, but it's not the same." Lily beamed at me. "I can't wait until you meet your guy and we can double date."

"My guy?" I balked.

"Yeah, I mean, I know you don't like Bryan like that, but it doesn't mean there isn't someone out there for you."

Xander's face filled my head. The way he'd looked at me last night on the roof terrace. There had been a moment, when our eyes collided, and the air had crackled around us. But I shook those thoughts away. Whatever understanding I thought existed between us was clearly a misjudgment on my part. He'd made that perfectly clear.

"What is it?" Lily asked. "What's wrong?"

"Nothing," I smiled my way through the lie, "nothing at all."

"OKAY, let's go over the rules," Jason said, arms folded over his chest as he surveyed the three of us.

"Seriously, Dad, it's just a small gathering." Poppy gave him her best puppy dog eyes. "You can trust us."

"It's not you I don't trust; it's the guys..." His brow quirked up.

"It's only Kaiden and his friends, and Aaron and Cole."

"Sounds like one too many guys for my liking. Maybe we should rethink this."

"We are not rethinking this." Felicity breezed into the room. She looked stunning in a knee-length, black cocktail dress. "We haven't been out in forever. We need this."

Planting her hand on her husband's cheek, she kissed him lightly. "The girls know the rules as do the guys."

"Mom's right, Dad. You deserve a night of freedom. You work so hard." Poppy snickered. "Eat, drink, be merry, and don't rush home."

"Watch it, young lady." He jabbed a finger at her. "Or else I'll call the neighbor and ask her to come over and keep an eye on you all."

She gasped. "You wouldn't."

"Is that a dare?"

"Jase," Felicity rolled her eyes, "we need to leave or we'll miss our reservation."

"Go," Lily added. "We'll be fine. You don't need to worry."

Jason grunted, letting his wife push him toward the door. "No smoking in the house," he called over his shoulder, "no alcohol, and definitely no sex."

"Oh my God," Lily breathed, her eyes wide and skin flushed. Poppy on the other hand was chuckling.

The click of the front door indicated they had left, and Poppy let out a heavy sigh. "I thought they were never going to leave."

"What time will the guys be here?" I asked them, trying to seem enthusiastic. The truth was, I wanted nothing more than to retreat to my room and stay there. But I knew if I did that, it would only result in more questions. Or Bryan doing something stupid like coming to keep me company.

So here I was, pasting on a smile and pretending everything was fine.

"Ashleigh's picking up Sofia, Aaron, and Cole now; and Kaiden and the guys are on their way."

"I can't believe Dad actually went for it," Poppy said, grabbing bowls out of the cupboard and filling them with snacks. Felicity had gone all out, buying every type of chip and dip there was. There was pizza too, and a whole heap of candy.

It was cute, if a little over the top. But it was a big deal for the Ford sisters and their overbearing father.

"I'm pretty sure he's set up some cameras so he can watch exactly what we're up to."

"God, I hope not," Poppy looked horrified. "I told Ashleigh and Sofia to bring some mixer drinks."

"Poppy! Dad will—"

"He'll never know. Besides, it's not like we're going to get wasted." She shrugged.

"Fine."

"Like you won't be distracted with Kaiden anyway." Poppy stuck out her tongue at her sister, and I smothered a laugh. She was so different to Lily; adventurous and willing to push the boundaries. Jason had his work cut out for him where Poppy was concerned. I just wasn't sure he knew it yet.

I grabbed a bowl of chips and a soda and made my way over to the sectional on the opposite side of the room, leaving Lily to reassure her sister that she could be around Kaiden without kissing his face off.

She obviously underestimated just how much PDA they engaged in, but none of us minded, not really. Lily had spent too long living in the shadows. It was nice to finally see her step out of her shell and live.

It was kind of ironic that while she'd found herself, I'd lost myself.

A few minutes later, the doorbell rang, and voices filled the hall.

"Myers, make room," Bryan appeared in the door, grinning. Rolling my eyes, I budged over and he dove for the couch. The others filtered in behind him. Usually, their laughter was infectious, but this time it did little to ease the gnawing pit in my stomach.

"Hey," Bryan nudged me, "you okay?"

He'd asked me the same thing, the morning at the hotel. I could read between the lines—he wanted to know why I didn't join their little party. But I'd told him then what I told him now.

"I'm fine."

Even though I wasn't fine.

Not even a little bit.

The second everyone left, and Lily and Poppy headed for bed, I pulled on my hoodie and sneakers, and slipped out of the house in the cover of darkness. It had been a struggle, pretending to smile and laugh and just *be* with them. I'd always hated being alone. It reminded me of being locked in my bedroom while my mom *entertained* her male friends and then got as high as a kite.

I shut the thoughts away as I made my way down to the river. The second it came into view, I saw him, lying in the same spot where I'd found him the other night. Part of me knew I should turn around and leave, but I guess I was all out of rational thoughts where Xander was concerned, because my legs carried me toward him.

"Peyton?" he gazed up at me, brows knitted with confusion. "Are you really here?"

"What?" I frowned, then it hit me. He was drunk. "I can go." Turning on my heel, I went to leave, but his voice gave me pause.

"Wait."

"Yeah?" I glanced back.

Xander pushed up on his elbows, studying me. "Why are you here?"

"The same reason you are," I whispered.

He nodded, patting the space beside him. I wanted to believe he was extending an olive branch after last night, but he was drunk. He probably didn't know what the hell he was doing.

My stomach sank, but I still sat down beside him. I couldn't help myself.

"I went to a bar tonight." He lay back down, staring up at the inky night sky. "There was this blonde woman..."

"I'm not sure—"

"I didn't do anything. But she reminded me of you. Fuck, why did she remind me of you?"

"I-I don't know," I breathed, my heart squeezing at his words.

I lay down too, looking right at him. His eyes were closed, his brows drawn tight, and jaw clenched.

"Xander?"

"Yeah?" His eyes fluttered open as he turned to look at me.

The air turned thick around us. The strange tether between us pulling taut. I wondered if he felt it. If he did, he didn't say anything. He just stared at me. *Through* me.

"What are you thinking about?" I asked.

"That night... pulling you from the river."

Oh God. I didn't want to talk about that. I couldn't. Not again.

"I saved you," he said, quietly. A strange reverence in his voice. "I couldn't save her though."

"Who?"

"My mom." His eyes shuttered again as his chest rose with a deep breath.

My heart raced as we lay there, shoulder to shoulder. I

stretched my fingers slightly, brushing Xander's hand. I didn't mean to, but once I felt him, it was almost impossible to withdraw. But I needed to before he realized. Snatching them back, I didn't expect him to snag my hand in his.

His dark-gray eyes opened again. "You're so strong," he whispered, closing his fingers around mine. "It's been years since my mom died and I'm still not over it. I don't think I'll ever be over it."

"I... It's not the same," I got the words out over the lump in my throat. "My mom didn't love me; she didn't want me around." Pain flashed through me.

Then it was like black coffee hit Xander's system, sobering him. He pulled his fingers away from mine. "You shouldn't be out here." His expression darkened.

"I know."

"You should go," he added, his eyes dipping to my mouth. Heat unfurled in my stomach, butterflies taking flight there.

"Xander, I—"

"Go," he barked, shooting upright, burying his hands in his face. "Just get out of here."

I scrambled to my feet. "You really want me to leave?"

"Yes," it came out rough, "before I do something I'll regret."

"Fine," I hissed, "but you should try to get home too, before you fall asleep out here and get mugged or something." Forcing myself away from him, I made my way back up the embankment, almost certain I heard his voice carry on the wind.

"You shouldn't care about me, Peyton. I'll only disappoint you."

CHAPTER TEN

Xander

I WOKE to a bass drum in my head. Bleary-eyed, I pushed onto an elbow and inhaled a thin breath.

Fuck.

My skull felt ready to explode, and the second my eyes landed on the empty whiskey bottle, my stomach churned. Pushing back the sheet, I staggered to my feet and ran a hand through my bed hair. I was a fucking mess. I could barely remember getting back home last night.

There had been a blonde at the bar. A tall, thin thing who had stayed by my side even after I insisted I wasn't looking for company. She'd offered to make sure I got home okay... and I told her to take a hike.

Not my best moment.

But she'd reminded me of Peyton. All starry-eyed and seductive.

What the fuck was I saying?

Peyton wasn't seductive, she was... a kid.

Except she wasn't.

And that was the problem.

I couldn't get the image of her on the roof terrace ledge out of my head. My heart had fallen out of my chest when she'd climbed up there. But it had been her parting words that really dug under my skin.

I don't want anything from you, Xander. I'm not that foolish to ever think you would see me as more than what I am, but I just thought... I thought maybe you got it. That maybe you understood.

It shouldn't have mattered—it didn't matter that she thought so little of me.

But it did.

All day, I'd replayed those words over and over in my head until I'd needed to cleanse them from my mind. And the only way I knew how to do that involved an endless supply of whiskey on the rocks.

I could barely remember leaving the bar. Had I come straight back here? No, that didn't feel right. I'd gone... fuck, I'd gone to the river and she'd been there.

Peyton had been there.

We'd talked... we'd... No, I couldn't even think about *that.*

Jesus. I shook my head as I walked into my small bathroom. I was a fucking mess, and all over a seventeen-year-old girl in high school.

What did that say about me?

About the kind of guy I was?

If Jase or Cam could see me now...

Who the fuck was I kidding? They—especially Cam—would probably expect something like this from me. After all, I was Xander Chase, the guy who repeatedly screwed up and sabotaged any shot he had at turning his life around.

It was a miracle I hadn't messed things up with the team

yet. But part of me liked working with the guys. Coach Huckley was a grumpy asshole, but everyone else was okay; and I don't know, it kind of felt like coming full circle.

I knew I'd given up my shot back in high school, but maybe by helping the team, helping Kaiden, I was paying my dues somehow.

Splashing my face with cold water, I stared at myself in the mirror. I looked as bad as I felt. My eyes were bloodshot and sunken. I knew if Cam could see me now, he'd have a thing or two to say. It was one of the reasons I'd stopped going by his house for Sunday morning breakfast.

But there was no avoiding him today.

I'd promised Jase I would show up at theirs today. No matter how much I didn't want to. Because she would be there too.

"You look like shit," Jase said as he welcomed me into his house.

"Nice to see you too," I grumbled.

"What the fuck happened to you?"

"Let me guess," Cameron appeared, leaning against the door jamb. "Heavy night at Bell's?"

"Something like that." Running a hand over my jaw, I met my brother's hard gaze, immediately wishing I hadn't.

The disapproval in his eyes was almost too much to bear. I should have been used to it by now, but it never got easier.

"Come on," Jase said, clapping me on the shoulder. "You're going to need a strong coffee to survive today."

He wasn't wrong. The house was full of people, the noise crashing against my tender skull. We passed the den, and I spotted my niece, Ashleigh, with the Ford girls as they sat with Aaron and Sofia Bennet.

"Hey, Uncle Xan," she spotted me. "What happened to you?"

"Yeah, Coach," Aaron smirked. "You're not looking so good."

"I'd still run circles around you."

Just then, the doorbell chimed. Jase paused. "That'll be Kaiden. Go find some coffee and Advil."

"Yeah," I murmured, following Cameron into the kitchen.

"Do I need to be worried?" he asked, studying my face.

"Relax, it was a blowout. I'm fine."

"How many times have I heard—"

"I said, I'm fine," I hissed, making a beeline for the coffee maker.

Fee came over and nudged my shoulder. "Hey, everything okay?"

"Like I said, I'm fine."

"Yeah, but you know what 'I'm fine' sounds like. It sounds a lot like I'm not fine." Her expression softened but I saw the concern there.

"It was a rough night."

"Want to talk about it?"

"Not particularly." My chest tightened. I'm sure she'd love to hear all about how hung up I was over her teenage daughter's best friend.

"Well, I'm glad you're here. We all are. You're a part of this family whether you want to be or not."

My lips parted but no words came out. What the fuck was there to say? I was only here because Jase—my boss—had practically demanded it.

But then Peyton appeared in the doorway like an angel sent from heaven, and I knew I was lying to myself.

I wasn't only here for Jase.

And that's precisely why I should have stayed away.

"Hey, sweetheart," Hailee said. "How are you?"

"I'm okay thanks, Mrs. Chase."

"Peyton," my sister-in-law chuckled. "How many times have I told you to call me Hailee?"

"Sorry." Her gaze slid past her right to me. She lifted her chin imperceptibly, but I caught it. I felt it like a punch to the stomach. She was pissed... and her anger was all directed at me.

I didn't blame her—I'd been an asshole on the roof terrace and again last night at the river. But this thing between her and me, it was dangerous territory. Confusing and unexpected. And I wanted to believe it was all because I'd saved her... but I wasn't so sure anymore.

She settled her eyes on Fee and said, "I just wanted to grab a drink."

"Of course." Fee shooed me along the counter to give Peyton room to open the refrigerator.

"Do you need anything else?"

"I'm good, thanks."

The air turned thick with tension. I didn't know if it was her and me, or her and everybody else. But her presence changed things.

When she disappeared out of the kitchen, everyone seemed to take a breath.

"How is she?" Hailee asked. "She seemed okay last night at the game."

"I wish I knew. She's gotten so good at putting up walls. She says she's okay, but how can she be after... God, I can't even imagine."

"She's lucky to have you and Jase," Hailee added.

"Is she?" Fee's shoulders sank. "Because some days, it

feels like we haven't got any idea of how to get through to her."

"She's been through a lot. It's going to take time."

My eyes flicked to the door, but Peyton was gone. I knew firsthand it wasn't as simple as Hailee was making it sound. I'd had people there for me, but it hadn't stopped me from spiraling out of control.

Shit, maybe I should have come clean to Jase about everything. But the last thing I wanted was to make it worse for her. For any of them.

"I need a smoke," I said, grabbing my mug of coffee and making my way to the back door. The frigid air stung as I inhaled a deep breath, but I welcomed the burn. Placing down my mug, I lit up a cigarette and sucked in a big lungful of smoke.

I was hardly surprised when Cameron followed me outside. "I don't need a babysitter," I gritted out.

"Shit, Xan, that's not... How are you?"

"Like I said, I'm fine."

"I know things have been strange between us, but you can always come to me—"

"Funny," I arched a brow at him, "because me coming to you was exactly what landed us here."

"That's not fair, and you know it. You're a grown man. You have responsibilities. You can't keep coasting through life without a plan. Mom and Dad would—"

"Don't, okay? Just don't."

I didn't need to hear what a failure I was, what our parents would think of me if they were still here. I'd heard it enough over the years.

Taking a long drag on my cigarette, I dropped the butt to the ground and dragged my boot over it.

"You should quit that shit."

"It calms me."

"I can think of a handful more productive ways to do that." Cameron smirked. "Like maybe finding yourself a woman—"

"You're giving me sex advice now?"

"That's not... fuck you." A faint smile traced his lips. "I'm glad you came. We all are." Cameron turned to leave but placed his hand on my shoulder at the last second. "No matter what happens between us, you will always be a part of this family, Xander. I hope you know that."

His words stayed with me long after he'd gone back inside. I knew he meant well; he always did. But Cameron didn't know what it was like to feel inadequate, to feel completely alone in a room full of people. Because he'd never been alone, not truly. He'd always had Jase and Asher, and then Hailee had come along and rooted herself beside him. Cameron might have lived through our mom's death and then our father's accident, but he hadn't done it alone.

So he would never understand what it was like to be in my shoes.

With three families crammed into the Ford's house, there was nowhere to hide. Fee and Jase had covered the island in tin foil to make a huge nacho table. It smelled so fucking good that not even my hangover could put me off digging in.

"I think I died and went to heaven," Aaron groaned around a mouthful of chili beef nachos.

"It's good, right?" Poppy said. "I helped Mom make it." She beamed at him.

"Come on, Peyton, get over here and eat something," Jase said, budging over to make room for her.

"Oh, I'm not hungry. But thanks, Mr. Ford."

His jaw clenched but Fee shot him a warning look with a small shake of her head. I glanced back at Peyton. She looked so small curled up on the sectional, scrolling through her phone. If she felt me watching, she didn't look up.

"Hey, Coach," Kaiden said, and me and Jase both glanced up at him. He smirked. "Coach Chase."

Jase rolled his eyes. "Don't forget who taught you everything you know, kid."

"Jealous, Coach?" The opportunity to yank his chain was too good, and I smothered a grin.

"Hey, I taught you everything I know too, Xan."

"He's got a point," Asher added.

"Maybe the two of you should go head-to-head?" Aaron suggested. "Now there's a showdown I'd pay to see."

"Nah, Coach Ford is too old to run with the big boys these days. Isn't that right, Jase?" Laughter rumbled in my chest. It felt weird to be standing here, shooting the shit with him, Kaiden, and Aaron.

But part of me liked it. It liked the feeling of being a part of something.

Fuck. When had that happened?

Cameron caught my eye, and something passed between us. His eyes held a glimmer of relief, of hope. But I didn't dwell on it. Just because I was here, laughing and joking like I was one of them, didn't change the fact I wasn't.

"What's up, Kaiden?" I asked, trying to crack the tension that had settled over us.

"Why didn't you go to college? I mean, you were good, everyone says you were. I've seen your high school records. You could have played any—"

"Kaiden." Jase shook his head, sliding his eyes, heavy with concern, to mine.

The silence was deafening as all eyes turned to me. Fuck, I felt like the walls were closing in, the air being sucked from the room.

"Sorry," Kaiden rushed out, "I shouldn't have said anything."

"It's fine," I lied. "I was young and foolish," I swallowed over the lump in my throat, "and sometimes shit happens."

I found my brother across the kitchen. He was rooted to the spot, watching me. There was so much left unsaid between us. So much I would never tell him. So much I couldn't tell him.

"I need a smoke," I said, heading for the door.

"I'll come with you," Cameron offered, but I pinned him with a hard look.

"No, stay." I scrubbed my jaw, my skin too tight for my body. "I just need some air."

Without another word, I slipped outside; but I didn't linger near the house, I took off toward the lake.

I wanted to be alone. I needed to be alone. It was hard to explain that I'd come to crave the one thing I'd always resented.

For so long, I'd felt lonely. I'd felt like it was me against the world. Back in high school, I would have given anything to have a friend, a real friend who got me. Who understood me. But it never happened. I'd had friends, sure. I was always surrounded by people who wanted Xander the star football player. Girls who wanted a piece of me and guys who wanted to party with me. But no one ever wanted to *know* me. And maybe that was my fault. Maybe I was too intense, too guarded, too unattainable.

Dragging a hand down my face, I let out a steady breath. I wasn't looking for a trip down memory lane. All I wanted was to finish up the season with the team and worry about the rest later.

The trees created a natural arch down to the lake. It was secluded down here, quiet and out of sight from the house. It was the perfect place to get lost.

But the second I stepped out of the thicket, I realized I wasn't alone.

CHAPTER ELEVEN

Peyton

I FELT Xander before I saw him.

But I knew he wasn't here for me. Why would he be?

"Sorry," I said, lifting my eyes to his, "I'll just go." Averting my gaze, I went to slip around him, but he snagged my wrist, sending tiny shocks rippling through me.

"Stay."

Our eyes collided, and the air was sucked clean from my lungs.

"You were right," he said, so quietly I barely heard him. "I get it."

His words shouldn't have affected me as much as they did, but the relief was instant. Like a heavy weight lifted off my shoulders.

"Is that why you're hiding out here?" My eyes narrowed.

Xander expelled a heavy sigh, running a hand over his jaw. It was dusted with stubble, but it suited him. I'd never kissed a guy with facial hair before, and I couldn't help but wonder what it would feel like.

"It's hard pretending all the time." His eyes dipped to my mouth and back up, and I wanted so badly to know what he was thinking. "What's your excuse?" The corner of his mouth tipped up.

"I just needed some air."

"I didn't even see you slip outside."

"I used the front door and went around the back gate."

"Stealthy."

"Less questions." I shrugged. "You want to sit?" My hand dropped to the space beside me on the bench. It was an old rickety thing but sturdy enough.

"I need a smoke." Xander was already digging out his packet.

"I don't mind."

His brows knitted as he studied me. "You sure?"

"Yeah, my mom smoked." I didn't tack on that it was rarely straight tobacco.

"My mom always hated it." Xander sat down and I couldn't help but notice how he perched right on the end of the bench, keeping a respectable distance between us, unlike last night. "Or at least, that's what Cameron used to tell me. He told me this story once, about how Dad came home one night stinking of cigars and she made him sleep in the basement for two nights straight until he managed to completely wash the smell off him."

I watched as he placed the smoke between his lips and ignited the end. I didn't particularly like the smell, but I didn't hate it either, and there was no denying there was something sexy about the way he caressed it with his mouth.

"Peyton?" Xander's voice pulled me from my thoughts, and my cheeks burned.

"I… uh, I've never tried it. I've gotten high a couple of times, but I didn't like it."

"Don't ever let Jase hear you say that. If he thought you were corrupting Poppy and Lily—"

"Have you met Lily? She would never do that. I'm not so sure about Poppy though." I chuckled.

"Yeah, she has that glint in her eye. Something tells me Jase will have his hands full with her over the next couple of years."

"She's too busy crushing on Aaron to get into too much trouble yet."

"You noticed that, huh?"

"She thinks she's discreet, but she isn't fooling anyone. Everyone except Aaron can see the way she looks at him."

"He'll figure it out."

"Wow…" I fought a smile.

"What?" Xander took one more hit of his smoke and then stubbed it out on the bench before flicking it into the thicket.

"We managed an entire conversation without things getting weird. I think that's a first for us."

"Peyton, I—"

"No, don't say it. Whatever it is, just don't. Let me have this, *please*."

He regarded me for a second and then released a resigned sigh. "I can do that."

Xander leaned back against the bench and stared out at the lake. The water glistened in the fading winter sun. It was freezing out here, but I liked the bite of the icy wind. It kept me alert, chasing away some of the nightmares circling my mind.

"Can I ask you something?" I said.

His sterling gray eyes flicked to mine. "Depends on what you want to know."

"Why didn't you go to college?"

"Going straight for the jugular, huh?" His face was a mask of indifference even if his words were strained.

"You don't have to answer." He hadn't answered Kaiden earlier, so it made sense he probably wouldn't want to tell me. "I heard what Kaiden said. You were good. Better than good."

"Have you ever wanted something so much that you can't think of anything else? It consumes your thoughts. Becomes everything to you. Because you think—no, you know—that if you can just make it happen it will fix everything?"

Xander inhaled a ragged breath. "The thing is though once you get there, once you're at the top and the thing you wanted so badly is within your grasp, there's this moment of sheer panic. What if you don't live up to everyone's expectations? What if it doesn't fix you? What if it's not really what you want?

"Football was my way out. It was my golden ticket out of Rixon, away from all the bad memories. It was a chance for me to escape. And it was right there... so close I could almost taste it." He dragged a hand down his face, pain rolling off him. I fought the urge to reach for him, to offer him comfort. Because I knew he wouldn't accept or appreciate it.

"I got drunk two nights before the final game. Totaled my car on the way home and ended up in the hospital with a broken collarbone. It could have been worse. The doctors said had I been going any faster, I probably wouldn't have made it."

"Oh my God," I breathed, the weight of his confession like a stone on my chest.

"I spent the weekend in the hospital while the Raiders

played without me. They lost the game, and I lost my friends, my team... my future. Gone, just like that."

"I'm sorry," I said, because what else was there to say?

Pain bled from Xander making the air heavy around us.

"I turned down my offers to college after that. Cameron was furious. He didn't speak to me for almost a month."

"He wanted more for you?"

"Yeah, but that's the thing... I realized lying in that hospital bed that I never wanted it for myself. All the years spent practicing and pushing, it wasn't for me... it was for him. It was for my coaches and the school and the team. I never wanted it, other than for a ticket out of Rixon. Maybe I should have... Maybe I... shit, I don't know."

"Do you ever regret it?"

His eyes slid to mine. "I regret a lot of things, yeah. But deep down, I don't think college would have made me happy. I was chasing a dream that was never mine to begin with."

"I'm not sure I want to go to college," I blurted out.

"I'm not sure I'm the right person to give you advice there." He gave me a pointed look, but there was a hint of a smile on his lips.

I liked it when he smiled. It was rare, something to be coveted. For as foolish as it was, I liked that he gave *me* his smile. I knew it meant nothing, but it still made me feel special.

"What does Jase and Fee think?"

"I haven't talked to them about it yet. It feels weird, ya know? They took me in, and they've been so great... but I don't want to be a burden."

"Peyton, they don't think that. Not for a second."

"Yeah, maybe. But it feels like I need to make a plan and find a way forward. I'm almost eighteen, and I have nothing..."

"Jase is one of the best guys I know. He'll do right by you."

"I know. But he shouldn't have to." My chest tightened. "I'm not his responsibility."

"Just don't make any rash decisions without talking to them," Xander said.

"I won't."

"Are you getting cold?" he added when a shiver went through me.

"Not really. I've grown accustomed to it. I spend a lot of time out here."

A shadow passed over his face. "I know you've been through a lot, but it's your senior year. You don't get a second shot at that. Trust me, I know."

"Please," I gawked at him, "don't act like I can just forget everything that's happened. My life has never been a walk in the park. I didn't grow up with a family who loved me. I've always been fiercely independent. I've always..." I sucked in a shuddering breath. "I've always had to rise above my shitty circumstances. And I did it because I knew I deserved more. Something deep inside me refused to accept that was my lot. But finding her like that... it changed me, Xander. It changed me and now I don't know how to find myself again."

Tears burned the backs of my eyes and I swallowed roughly. I hadn't wanted to break down in front of him, but I was so tired of holding everything in.

"Peyton, I—"

"It's fine." I held out a hand, unable to look at him as I desperately tried to dry the silent tears rolling down my cheeks. "I just need a minute."

But the words only made me cry harder.

"Ssh, come here." Xander wrapped an arm around my shoulder and pulled me into his body. Without thinking, I twisted my hands into his hoodie, soaking up the comfort he was offering me.

"Don't cry," he said, his voice cracked. "Please, don't cry."

"I just... why? Why would she do that?" It was the question that haunted me.

Had she really hated me that much?

"I know it's hard to believe, but her pain and desperation, her decision to... end things," he choked out the words, "probably had very little to do with how she felt about you."

I lifted my face to his, inhaling another shuddering breath. "Is that your attempt at making me feel better? Because you might need to work on your delivery." The faintest of smiles traced my lips.

Xander smiled back, and the sight of him made my heart flutter. "There she is."

I didn't dare ask who he was referring to. I didn't want to break the spell we were both under.

I nuzzled his neck again, inhaling his scent. He smelled so good. So manly and clean. Before I could stop myself, my lips skimmed his throat. His entire body shuddered, an involuntary moan rumbling in his chest. I smiled, feeling a bolt of confidence go through me as I brushed my lips against his neck again.

Xander stiffened. "Peyton..."

"Sorry," I whispered, my cheeks burning, unsure of what to say or do now.

I shouldn't have done that.

God, I shouldn't have—

"Hey," he said quietly, coaxing me out from his chest. "It's okay."

It was?

Heat blossomed inside of my chest, but a sudden burst

of emotion had a fresh wave of tears sliding down my cheeks. "Sorry, I'm a mess."

"It's okay," he said again, brushing the hair from my face. I nodded, inhaling a deep, calming breath. "Better?" Xander held me still, his eyes still fixed on mine.

"A little, thanks."

He gave me a small nod before putting an appropriate amount of distance between us.

I hated it.

Hated how cold I suddenly felt. In his arms, I'd felt warm and safe and cherished.

I'd kissed him. I hadn't meant to, but the urge to taste his skin had been so overwhelming I couldn't fight it.

"Sorry, that was... fuck." His lips thinned as he buried his face in his hands.

"It's okay," I whispered.

"No, Peyton, it isn't. There are a hundred reasons why it's not okay."

"It was just a hug, Xander." I mustered the best fake smile I could, despite the fact we both knew he wasn't talking about the hug. "You don't need to get all bent out of shape about it."

He didn't look convinced, but he hadn't pushed me away and scolded me though. That had to mean something, didn't it?

"Let me guess, you're going to go back to avoiding me now?" I peeked over at him, but he was staring out at the lake.

Xander didn't answer me, and deep down, I didn't expect him to. The moment we'd just shared was already a whisper of a memory.

So much so I wondered if maybe I'd dreamed it.

He stood swiftly, a blast of cold air wafting over me. "I should get back inside."

"I guess I'll stay out here."

He finally gave me his eyes again, and what I saw made a shiver run through me.

"You're strong, Peyton," he said, thickly. "Don't ever forget that."

And then he was gone.

"Peyton, let's go," Lily yelled.

"I'm coming." I smeared on some lip gloss and blotted my lips. Checking my reflection one last time, I smiled to myself.

So maybe I'd gone a little overboard, but there was nothing wrong with making an effort.

Oh, who the hell was I kidding?

I couldn't stop thinking about yesterday. The way Xander had held me, opened up to me. The fact he hadn't pushed me away when I'd kissed him. Not really. He was a little wary, yes, but he hadn't seemed too pissed about it.

Something had changed between us.

I knew better than to get swept away in fantastical dreams where he might have felt the same tug I felt whenever I was around him. But I didn't want him to see me as just a schoolgirl with a misplaced crush.

We'd shared something, something real. A single moment where we'd both let down our walls. That had never happened to me before. But Xander knew about pain, he knew about loss, and what it was like to be on the outside looking in.

"Peyton!"

Grabbing my bag, I hurried out of my bedroom and jogged downstairs.

"What the hell took you so—" She gawked at me. "What are you wearing?"

"What do you mean?"

"You look... pretty, but isn't it a little much for school?"

"It's only jeans and a sweater, Lil." I shrugged.

She gave me a strange look. "And your hair and makeup?"

"What, a girl can't take pride in herself now?"

She might not have appreciated the effort I'd made, but hopefully Xander would.

I FOUND myself looking for him. I knew it was unlikely I would see Xander around school since he mostly spent all his time in the locker room or out on the football field, but it didn't stop me from hoping to get a glimpse of him.

"Are we watching Kaiden after school?" I asked Lily.

She looked up from her study notes and frowned. "What's gotten into you?"

"Nothing." I shrugged, tapping the pen against my lips. "It's just a question."

"Are you sure? You seem... I don't know, different."

"Because I put some makeup on?"

"Not just that..." She rolled her eyes. "I don't know, it's like you're—"

"Jeez, Lil, is it a crime to be happy?"

Because I was. Okay, so maybe happy didn't quite describe what I felt, but I'd woken up feeling lighter than I had in days, and I knew it was all thanks to a broody, dark-eyed guy I couldn't stop thinking about.

"Why do I get the feeling you're up to something?"

"Paranoid much?" My lips curved. "I thought you'd be pleased I'm feeling more like my old self."

"Of course I am, but it's okay to not be okay too, you know."

The concern in her gaze threatened to punch a hole straight through my resolve but I refused to let it.

I felt good.

I finally felt like things might be okay.

And maybe I shouldn't have pinned that all on Xander's pep talk yesterday but he'd been the catalyst at least.

Still, I silently chastised myself for searching the library for him. I wasn't going to see him here.

"I'd planned to go," Lily added. "But you don't have to come with me. I understand if—"

"I want to." My eyes flicked to the wall clock. "In fact, time's up." Butterflies swarmed my stomach at the thought of seeing him.

We quickly packed away our things and headed out, only to be intercepted by Kaiden.

"This is a surprise," Lily said, falling into his arms. She leaned up, kissing him.

"I didn't realize you were with Peyton." His eyes landed on me, and he gave me a thin smile.

"Sorry, am I interrupting something?"

"Of course you're not." Lily smiled, but Kaiden seemed conflicted.

"I... uh, actually, I was hoping to borrow you for ten minutes before practice."

"What—"

"Go, it's fine," I said, pulling on my wooly hat. It was cold today. Much colder than it had been on the weekend. I felt like a marshmallow buried under my thick coat.

"Are you sure?" Apology glittered in her eyes.

"Yeah, I'll meet you at the bleachers."

"Okay." She grabbed Kaiden's hand and smothered a nervous smile. They were so sickeningly in love. It was impossible to not feel a stab of jealousy as he led her away.

I took a slow walk toward the football field. They didn't get many spectators when it was this cold, but Lily hadn't missed a single practice since she and Kaiden got together. I'd almost reached the turn for the bleachers when I felt someone coming up behind me. My skin tingled with awareness and I knew I'd find Xander when I turned around.

Sure enough, my gaze landed on him as I stopped and turned. "Well, hello." I smiled, unable to fight it even if I tried. "You're late. Don't let Coach Ford know you're slacking on the job." Soft laughter spilled from my lips, but Xander wasn't laughing. In fact, he didn't look pleased to see me at all.

My heart sank.

"Xan—"

"Don't," he hissed. "You can't call me that here." His hard gaze darted around us.

"Relax, no one else is here." Maybe I shouldn't have found it so endearing that he was worried about being caught talking to me, but my foolish heart had already latched onto it. "I'm glad we bumped into each other," I said, finding my confidence. "I wanted to thank you for yesterday."

I searched his eyes for a hint of emotion, but there was nothing. Xander wore a mask of indifference—annoyance even—that chilled me to the core despite the already freezing temperature.

"I need to go." He dragged a hand through his hair and went to step around me.

"Wait," I grabbed his wrist. Irritation flashed in his eyes, the muscle in his jaw flexing as he dropped his darkened gaze to where my slim fingers circled his arm.

Immediately releasing him, I stepped back with a shaky breath. This wasn't the guy who had opened up to me yesterday. It wasn't the guy who had pulled me out of the river and saved my life.

Clearly, I'd misread the entire situation. *Because you're a foolish girl with no experience with guys like Xander.*

"I-I'm sorry." Spinning on my heel, I took off down the path back to the main building. Xander didn't call after me; at least I didn't think he did. It was hard to hear over the roaring of blood in my ears, the tears burning my eyes, the barbed coil of shame squeezing the air from my lungs.

Fumbling with my bag, I managed to retrieve my cell phone and quickly text Lily that I wouldn't be joining her after all. I'd built this moment up in my head all day, losing myself in the fantasy that somehow when I finally saw Xander he would be happy to see me. That I'd see even a flicker of recognition of what we had shared yesterday.

But there'd been nothing happy about the way he'd looked at me.

It hit me then, that yesterday hadn't been a 'moment.' We hadn't been equals sharing our stories. Xander had pitied me. He'd taken pity on me falling apart, and he'd done what any normal person would have. He'd offered me comfort. Not because he was compelled to do so, or because he *wanted* to... but because that's what you did when somebody was hurting. You comforted them. But I'd twisted it. I'd latched onto how good, how *right* it felt to be wrapped in his arms and I'd let myself believe it meant more.

And when he hadn't reprimanded me for kissing him, I'd stupidly, foolishly, let myself believe that Xander cared for me.

CHAPTER TWELVE

Xander

I WATCHED Peyton hurry away from me, cussing under my breath when she finally disappeared out of view.

Fuck.

I hadn't planned to hurt her like that, not again. But I'd seen the way her eyes lit up when she turned and saw me standing there. The flicker of hope pass over her face. I'd seen the extra layer of makeup and formfitting outfit underneath her coat, and I couldn't let her run with it. I couldn't let her think that yesterday was anything more than me offering her a small act of comfort.

Even if my eyes had lingered on her curves for a second longer than they should have.

I hadn't meant to reach for her yesterday, to pull her into my arms and try to absorb her pain as my own. I hadn't meant to brush over the kiss like it wasn't important. Like she hadn't crossed a huge fucking line. But she drew me in. I was man enough to admit that. Peyton intrigued me, and not only because she was beautiful and wiser than her years. It was the shadows in her eyes, the darkness she tried so hard to bury.

The truth was her fucking soul called to me. And yesterday, I'd slipped. I'd allowed myself to get close. But it was wrong on so many levels. I hadn't been there, down by the lake, comforting her the way Jase or Cam or even Asher might. As an adult, as a father figure. I'd been comforting her as a friend... something more than a friend. Someone I felt drawn to. And when she'd pulled away from me and looked up at me with tears in her eyes, something inside me had cracked wide open.

She disarmed me. Because she made me care.

A seventeen-year-old girl did what no other woman ever had.

It was fucked up. That the first person I truly felt anything for—was completely and utterly forbidden.

"Whoa, what happened to you?" Jase asked me the second I reached the locker room.

"Car trouble." It wasn't a complete lie, "sorry."

"Anything I can help with?"

"Nah, I can handle a flat tire." I threw him a smirk and he rolled his eyes.

"I'll see you out on the field."

With a stiff nod, I moved past him and headed for the assistant coaches' office, dumping my bag. Thankfully, Coach Huckley was nowhere to be seen. I wasn't in the mood to deal with his passive aggressive bullshit after the hour I'd just had trying to bring my piece of shit truck back to life.

I hung my jacket on the rack and ran a hand down my face. I needed to get it together. It was better that Peyton hated me than believed there could ever be anything between us.

When I headed out, a few stragglers were still in the locker room. "Coach expects you on the field pronto," I grumbled, pausing when I heard Peyton's name.

"Come on, Hughes, spill the beans. You and Peyton... what's going on there?"

Bryan chuckled. "Already told you, man, I don't kiss and tell."

"We all know you ran to her rescue when Farrow cornered her at the game. You're her hero." The guy—a kid named Sam—chuckled. "The question is though, did she get on her knees and thank you?"

My spine stiffened, but I wasn't sure if it was the way Sam was talking about her or if it was the idea of her with Bryan... or both.

Backing up a couple of steps, I poked my head around the locker cages and said, "Field, now."

"Shit, sorry, Coach."

I stormed away but not before I heard Bryan say, "Don't fucking talk about her like that, okay?"

I didn't stick around to hear the rest. Bryan was protective of her, and part of me was relieved she had someone in her corner. But it didn't stop the acidic taste of jealousy on my tongue.

The second I burst through the doors and into the cold air, I inhaled a deep breath trying to erase the image of her from my mind. But my eyes immediately went to the bleachers.

And even though I knew I wouldn't find her there, I still looked for her.

Peyton didn't seek me out again. She didn't come with Lily to watch the team practice, and on the odd occasion I actually ventured into the school cafeteria to grab some lunch, I never saw her.

I told myself it was for the best, that this was how it had to be. But I couldn't shake the feeling that I'd screwed up somehow. We had a big game coming up though, so I didn't have time to be distracted.

Let alone by a girl so out of reach, so forbidden, that even letting myself think about her made me feel skeezy.

The semi-final against Limmington High was Saturday in Harrisburg. It was only a short bus ride away and since we'd drawn the midday game, I had no doubt there would be big celebrations or commiserations Saturday night. It was all the guys had talked about in the locker room before and after practice.

By the time Friday morning rolled around, everyone was feeling the pressure, myself included. I climbed out of my car and surveyed the school parking lot, immediately scolding myself for looking for her. As if the universe heard my plea, I found her across the lot. But she wasn't alone. That asshole Sean Farrow was crowding her against the wall, his hand pressed against the wall beside Peyton's head as he leaned in and whispered something to her.

Before I knew what I was doing, I stalked toward them, anger rippling through me.

"Morning, Coach," a voice called, and I glanced over to find Bryan heading in my direction. "What's u—motherfucker," he hissed under his breath. "Gotta go, see you at practice." He took off, jogging toward them and it was enough to snap me out of the trance I'd found myself in.

What the fuck was I thinking? Approaching them —*approaching her*—like that?

I guess I could've pulled the staff card, but still, it was

risky. Farrow wasn't doing anything that Peyton didn't look like she wasn't enjoying. In fact, the second Bryan reached them, she looked pissed, as if he was ruining their moment.

A strange tightness squeezed my ribs, but I shook it off as I cut across the lawn, in the direction of the gym. Still, despite telling myself I didn't care, I couldn't help but glance over at them again. Peyton was all up in Bryan's personal space, her finger wagging at his face while he backed away with his hands up. Farrow looked amused, standing there with a cocky smirk as he watched Peyton hand Bryan his balls.

I was too old for this shit. Too old to be worried about whatever teen drama they were tangled up in. But fuck, if I didn't want to go over there and wipe the smirk right off the little shit's face. Bryan shook his head and walked away, his dejection obvious even from all the way over here.

"Everything okay?" I asked casually as he reached me.

"Fucking girls," he muttered, not bothering to slow down.

I lingered, watching as Farrow tried to talk to Peyton again. She brushed him off though, shoving past him and heading for the school building. I should have moved. I should have followed Bryan, because right at the last second, before she slipped inside, Peyton glanced up, finding me across the lawn. Even from the distance between us, I saw her breath catch, her eyes widen. But then her gaze narrowed, animosity rolling off her. She looked fucking adorable, all angry and worked up.

It was a bold move, one I'd no doubt regret later, but I didn't break our stare off. Or maybe she'd just ensnared me that damn good, I couldn't tear my eyes away.

Peyton shook her head, breaking the connection, and ducked inside, not giving me a backward glance.

I was still thinking about her cold stare when I entered the locker room.

"Nice of you to join us, Chase," Coach Huckley said as he passed me.

"I'm five minutes early," I gritted out.

"And yet, some of us were here thirty minutes ago. We've got a big game coming up Saturday—"

"Seriously, *Coach*," I spat the words, "you want to go there?"

Glancing around, I was relieved to find most of the guys minding their business. Huckley pulled last week's roster off the notice board and tacked the new one up. As expected, there were no big changes.

"I'm just telling it like it is." He looked me up and down, as if I was nothing more than dirt on the bottom of his sneaker.

"Chase, get in here," Jase's voice rang out.

"The boss calls," Huckley held my stare.

"Yeah, I'm going." I almost shouldered past him but managed to check myself.

He wasn't worth it. I knew that.

I'd known people like him my whole life. People who liked to remind me I was nothing more than Cameron Chase's down-and-out brother.

"Come in, take a seat," Jase said, barely looking up from the notes in front of him.

"What's up?" I asked, whipping off my Raiders ball cap and running a hand through my damp hair. I may have hit the whiskey a little too hard last night, but I was here on time.

"Here." He grabbed a manila folder and threw it across the desk.

"What is this?" I picked it up and flicked it open.

"It's the job application for the permanent position."

"Shit, Jase, I didn't—"

"You're good with the guys, you're focused, you show up and put in the work. Give me one good reason why you can't say yes to this?"

My eyes scanned the form. He was offering me a lifeline; offering me the chance to finally make something of my life.

It was a no-brainer.

"You don't need to decide right now..."

Fuck.

"Look, Jase. I'm grateful, man. I'm so fucking grateful. But I didn't earn this." *I don't deserve it.*

He had no idea that I'd been... well, whatever the hell I'd been doing with Peyton. We hadn't crossed any real lines, except the kiss—which I had no intention of letting happen again. But the fact I felt as guilty as fuck told me all I needed to know.

I was a lying piece of shit, and I didn't deserve his support.

"I'll be the judge of that," he said. "How about this? I refuse to accept no as an answer unless you give me a valid reason why not."

"Come on, Jase, that's... I'll just not turn up." I gave him a pointed look. It wasn't like he could coerce me into taking the position.

"You won't do that. You're many things, Xander, but you're not a complete asshole." Jase smirked.

"Why is this so important to you?" I asked. He'd never been so invested in my life before. Sure, Jase often played peacekeeper between me and Cameron, but he'd never gone to such lengths.

"It's time, Xan," he said.

I released a thin breath. I didn't want to do this now, here of all places. I didn't really want to do it ever.

"Did Cameron put you up to this?"

"No. *No*!" He shook his head and held up his hands. "That's not what this is. I knew you needed a break, and I gave you one, and you've surprised me at every turn. I know you probably never imagined coming back to football, but you're an asset to the team."

His words should have made me feel good, and maybe a small part of me did. But the rest of me was steeped in guilt and regret. I'd been so close to making all Cam's dreams come true and I'd blown it. I'd sabotaged my future.

I had to live with that every second of every day. I'd let my brother down—the one person who had done everything in his power to raise me right and give me everything despite the fact our parents were gone. I'd let them down.

I'd let myself down.

"Xan?" Jase's gruff voice pulled me from my thoughts. "If you ever need to talk..."

"Yeah, I know." I ran a hand down my face. I didn't need to talk.

I didn't.

"Okay, get out of here. Take that, read it, mull it over... but for the love of God, don't make a hasty decision." His eyes drilled into me, so hard I was worried he would crack my mask of indifference and see inside my dirty black soul. I'd gotten good over the years at deflecting, of playing the misunderstood guy with a chip on his shoulder.

"Okay." I closed the manila folder and got to my feet, offering him a small nod of appreciation. "I'll see you out on the field."

"Damn straight you will, we've got a championship to win."

The corner of my mouth tipped. Even now, even after his successful, albeit short career in the NFL, football was everything to Jase. I wondered what he saw when he looked at me. I wondered what he thought all those years ago when I gave up *my* shot.

As if he heard my thoughts, as I reached the door, Jase said, "Maybe it's time to lay the past to rest, Xan. Maybe it's time to move on."

If only it were that easy.

CHAPTER THIRTEEN

Peyton

"ARE you sure you don't want to come?" Lily asked me for the tenth time this morning, and it was barely eight-thirty.

"I already told Cindy I'd pick up an extra shift at the diner."

"But it's game day..." She pouted. "It's kind of a big deal."

"I know. But Kaiden and your dad will have enough fans cheering them on. I doubt they'll miss little old me."

"I'll miss you."

"You'll be fine." I offered her a weak smile, quietly adding, "I need the money, Lil."

It wasn't a lie; I did need the money. But it wasn't the only reason I didn't want to go to the game with them. Maybe it made me a coward, hiding from Xander, but I wasn't ready to see him again, not after Monday.

I'd managed to avoid him all week. It wasn't hard. He barely came into the main school building, and during lunch, I busied myself with assignments in the library. But while avoiding him was as easy as breathing, fighting the urge to search him out wasn't.

No matter how much it had hurt when he shunned me.

"You sure I can't convince you to come?" Lily pouted.

I shook my head, hoping she would drop it before I did something stupid like admit the truth.

"Fine. But you're wrong you know? We all want you there. You're a part of this family now. You're one of us."

Lily staggered back as I threw my arms around her and buried my face in the crook of her neck. "You're my best friend, babe. The best."

Soft laughter tickled my hair. "I love you too," Lily said thickly, pushing me back to arm's length. "I should probably go finish getting ready. I promised Kaiden I'd go over there and give him a good luck... kiss." Heat exploded in her cheeks.

"A good luck kiss, huh? And where exactly do you kiss?"

"*Peyton*!" she breathed.

"Go," I said, saving her anymore embarrassment. She was so cute. But as I watched her go, the ache in my chest grew heavier. Lily was flourishing, flying high and free on the wings of love and acceptance. While I withered in the shadows.

I finished up my breakfast, watching the Ford family as they breezed in and out of the kitchen, a hive of activity. And when they finally left, I released a steady breath. Lily's words still ringing loudly in my head.

You're a part of this family now. You're one of us.

I wanted to believe her, I did.

But when you'd spent your entire life not belonging, it was hard to accept anything else.

For a Saturday shift, Cindy's Grill was quieter than usual. No surprise given the town's beloved Raiders were over in Harrisburg playing in the semi-finals. It was all people talked about. So much so that when a man had asked Cindy to turn up the radio so they could hear the commentary, she'd indulged them.

"Table fifteen, order up," Calvin, the grill cook, called through the hatch as he slid the plates over to me.

"Thanks, Cal." Grabbing two napkins, I picked up the plates and made my way over to table fifteen. "Okay, I've got the burger with dirty fries and the ribs with fries."

"Smells good," the man said, grinning at his wife. I'd spied their rings when I took their order.

"If you need anything else, don't hesitate to—"

The diner erupted in cheers as 'touchdooooown' rang out through the radio speaker.

"You go to Rixon High, right?" The woman eyed my name tag, and I nodded. "I'm surprised you're not at the game."

"I'm sorry, do I know you?"

"My daughter is a senior, Carrie-Anne Trombley." She smiled warmly. "She mentioned she had a friend that worked here."

Me and Carrie-Anne Trombley, friends? I didn't have the heart to burst her mom's bubble.

"Uh, yeah," I said, trying not to frown. "We have a few classes together. She's not with—"

"Oh, she's at the game."

"She is?" I hadn't taken her for a football fan. In fact, she seemed to hate the football team with a passion. Especially Bryan.

But then, I had seen the way she looked at him sometimes.

"She didn't tell you?" The woman seemed genuinely

surprised. Weird. "Her cousin Jude is a huge fan just like our Carrie. He attends Temple University now, but came back to take her to the game."

"I'm sorry," I said, glancing over to the service counter. "I need to—"

"Oh, of course."

"Enjoy your food." Hurrying over to the counter, I pretended to busy myself.

"What was all that about?" Cindy asked quietly over my shoulder.

"Her daughter is in my class," I said. "She thinks we're friends."

"And you're not?"

"We've barely ever spoken."

"Maybe her daughter wants to be your friend?" Cindy gave me one of her trademark smirks.

"Yeah, maybe." There was still something about it that rang weird to me, but it wasn't like I'd ever tried to get to know Carrie-Anne. It was easy to judge without knowing the facts.

The doorbell jangled as a group of guys walked in. My eyes immediately went to the guy upfront. Sean.

Crap.

I'd managed to avoid him all week too, after he'd cornered me earlier in the week to apologize for what happened at the game. Sean wasn't a bad guy; he just didn't like being rejected. Male pride was a strange thing. But I didn't have the energy to get pissy about it, so we'd talked, and I'd accepted his apology. But I'd turned down his offer to take me out and make it up to me.

His eyes lit up when he found me across the diner.

"Uh oh, girl," Cindy snickered, "I know that look."

"He's... a friend."

"Aren't they always." She patted my shoulder as she

disappeared to take care of one of her tables, leaving me to deal with Sean and his rabble of friends.

I grabbed four menus and made my way over to them. "Welcome to Cindy's. Are you dining with us today?"

"Yeah, Sean's real hungry. Isn't that right, Farrow?"

"Don't be an asshole, Richie," Sean shot me an apologetic look. "We're eating." His eyes dipped down my body and back up, a small grin curving his lips. Damn, his smile, it got me every time.

It's how I'd ended up tangled up with him in the first place.

"Right this way." I forced myself to take a deep breath as I led Sean and his friends over to a booth by the window. Waiting until they were all seated, I passed around the menus. "Can I get you some drinks?"

"We'll take four Cokes," Sean said, not giving his friend time to answer first.

"Sure thing. I'll be back to take your order soon."

As I walked away, I heard Richie say, "Fuck, Farrow, you're punching way above your weight."

"Quit it, asshole, Peyton is good people."

Good people.

But not good enough. The thought came out of nowhere. But I wasn't thinking about Sean, I was thinking about the dark-eyed guy who refused to see me.

I rang their drinks order through and busied myself with making them. But a trickle of awareness ran through me.

"Sorry," Sean's voice gave me pause, and I turned slowly to find him leaning against the counter. Cindy caught my eye over his shoulder and raised a brow.

"I didn't know you'd be here today." He gave me another one of those dimpled smiles.

"It's fine," I said.

"I didn't want you to hold it against me."

"Why would I do that?"

"Richie is—"

"I can handle Richie, Sean."

"How come you're not at the game...? I figured you'd be there supporting Hughes." Something like jealousy flashed in his eyes.

"Nothing is going on between me and Bryan, not that it's any of your business."

He stood up, holding his hands up. "Relax, I didn't mean it..." I gave him a pointed look and he chuckled. "Yeah, okay. I did."

"I'm working, Sean. I should—"

"Come out with me later?"

"Sean..."

"Just... think about it. We're heading to that bar, The Tap. They have live music tonight and Richie knows the owner, so we won't be carded." His mouth quirked again. "Go on. You know you want to. Unless you were planning to party with the team."

I wasn't.

I'd volunteered to pull a double shift to keep myself occupied... and to avoid Bryan and the team when they got back from Harrisburg.

"I'll think about it," I blurted, grabbing my order pad and moving around the counter.

"What time do you get off?" Sean asked me, a sparkle in his eye.

"Eight."

"I'll be waiting," he said, giving me another lingering look that once upon a time would have made my toes curl. I wasn't that girl now though.

"Friends..." I gave him a pointed look. "Nothing more."

"Scouts honor." Sean held up two fingers before slipping back to his booth. I didn't miss him high-fiving Jake.

Another roar filled the diner, people whooping and hollering. The Raiders had done it—they'd beat Limmington and secured their place in the finals next weekend. I could imagine how wild the party tonight at Bryan's house would be, but I had no desire to go. To be around all those people, pretending everything was fine.

That I was fine.

The skin on my inner thigh burned. I hadn't taken the knife to my thigh again, but I'd thought about it. I'd thought about carving the dark thoughts right out of me.

But I wasn't that girl, I wasn't.

I wasn't her.

Tears burned the backs of my eyes, but I swallowed them down as I approached a table to take their order. I would throw myself into work. I would go to the bar with Sean and drink and laugh and pretend.

Anything to not think about my mom. About what she'd done.

About what *I'd* done.

Anything to not think about him.

Cindy let me clock off fifteen minutes early to freshen up for the date I'd told her numerous times wasn't actually a date. I used the small bathroom to change into my plain black cropped t-shirt and unravel my hair from the messy ponytail. A couple of spritzes of perfume and some lip gloss and it was as good as it was going to get without going back to the Ford's house.

"Seriously, girl, if you look that good after ten minutes, I can only imagine how you'd look after an hour." Cindy grinned at me as she wiped down the counter.

"It's the best I could do." I shrugged, sweeping my blonde waves over one shoulder.

"He'll love it. Now go, and don't do anything I wouldn't." Cindy winked before practically shooing me out of the diner.

Sean was waiting outside, propped against his truck. He let out a low whistle, his eyes full of heat and hunger. "You look—"

"Friends, remember." I levelled him with a hard look.

"Yeah, yeah. I know the rules. Let's get out of here." He yanked open the door and I slid inside.

The last time I'd been in Sean's car, things had ended a little differently.

Maybe this was a bad idea.

But I wasn't ready to go home, and I definitely didn't want to go to the party at Bryan's, despite the messages I'd had from him and Lily begging me to go.

"You okay over there?" Sean asked as he drove the short distance across town to The Tap.

"I'm fine." I offered him a weak smile. "Who'll be there tonight?"

"Richie, and a couple of the other guys. I think Jayden is bringing his girlfriend. It'll be fun."

Fun. It felt like a lifetime ago since I'd had fun. Now when I looked back and imagined myself partying and flirting and hooking up with guys, a shudder went through me. That girl had died the night I'd fallen into the river. And maybe it was for the best because although she was always up for a good time, it was all a lie.

A sham.

Sean pulled off the main street and into a small parking

lot next to an old brick building. I'd never been here before, but I knew of it.

"Ready?" he asked, and I nodded, sliding out of the car before he could get around and open the door for me.

A knowing smirk lifted the corner of his lips when I met him at the hood of the car. "You're really set on this friends thing, huh?"

"Yup." I ran a hand down my hair and flashed him a smile. "Lead the way, *friend*."

Sean motioned toward the door, a neon sign hanging above it, flickering 'live music.' I could already hear the heavy beat pulsing inside. But even over the noise, I swear I heard Sean say, "We'll see."

"Come on, babe, you're drunk," Sean said. "I should get you home."

Home.

Didn't he know I didn't have a home anymore... not that my house had ever really been a home.

"I'm fine... fine. See." I swatted Sean's chest, stumbling forward. He caught me with an exasperated sigh. "We're leaving. So are you coming or—"

Something caught my eye across the bar. No, not something.

Someone.

"I want to stay, just for a little while."

"Yeah, whatever." Sean rolled his eyes, looking past me and smiling.

"Who are you—" I glanced back. "Oh."

He was blatantly checking out his friend's girlfriend's friend. I couldn't remember her name. Hadn't paid much attention when he'd made the introductions.

"I'm gonna head out. You'll be okay getting home, yeah?"

"I... Sean, wait..." But he was already gone, grabbing the girl's hand and leading her to the exit.

Asshole.

I drained the remainder of my drink and slammed it on a nearby table before searching out the only other familiar face in the bar.

"Coach Chase," I grinned, "I didn't expect to find you here." I stumbled toward the table he was perched on, falling straight into a pretty brunette. "Oops, sorry."

"A friend of yours?" she asked Xander, arching one of her perfectly plucked brows. The liquor in my veins settled a little as I took her in. She was pretty, beautiful even, and she was standing close to Xander. Too close.

Oh my God.

Was he here with her?

On a date?

My stomach roiled as I tried to right myself, but the room spun, and my arm shot out to grab...

Xander's arm.

"Shit," he grumbled. He looked good, too good, standing there in his jeans and a dark shirt, the sleeves pushed up to his elbows in that sexy way guys did. His hair was an imperfectly styled mess, strands falling into his eyes a little, disguising their dark depths.

"Sorry, Tash, but I should probably deal with this," he said, curving his arm around my waist. It felt nice to be so close to him again.

It felt right.

"Do you need me to come. I can—"

"No, stay. I'll tell Harry to put your drinks on my tab. Stay, enjoy the music." He started leading me away.

"Is that your girlfriend?" My head lolled against his arm. "She's pretty, really pretty."

"You're drunk."

"So drunk." I hiccoughed, smothering a giggle with my hand. "Sean and his friend Rich—"

"That little shit brought you here and got you drunk?"

"Little shit?" I peeked up but Xander wasn't looking at me. He was too focused on leading me out of the crowded bar.

"She okay?" One of the security men asked as we reached the entrance.

"Don't worry, Shane, she's a friend. I'll make sure she gets home okay."

"I bet you will."

Xander tensed beside me, and I was sure I heard a muted cuss slip from his lips, but everything was spinning so fast I couldn't be sure of anything.

"Jase is going to lose his shit when he—"

"No." I gripped Xander's arm tight. "You can't tell him. Please, you can't... I just need to sober up and then I'll be okay." I pulled on his arm and his hard gaze found me. "Please, Xander."

He loosened a breath. "Come on, I have my truck around back."

Keeping his arm tight around my waist, Xander led me around the back of the bar to the small parking lot. He opened the door and bundled me inside. My eyes felt heavy, much like my limbs.

"Thank you," I whispered as he leaned over me to get the buckle. He looked up, his eyes darting to my mouth. Heat flashed through me, tightening my stomach. Sometimes, like right now, and when we'd been down at the lake, I swear he looked at me like he wanted to kiss me.

And I wanted him to. God, did I ever.

The air was nonexistent as Xander stared at me, but I could feel the warmth of his breath tickle my face. He inhaled sharply, shaking his head, as if to break the tension between us. Pulling away, he slammed the door shut and went around to the driver's side, folding his body inside.

"An hour," he grunted. "You have an hour to sober up and then I'm taking you home."

"Well in that case, I need food," I grumbled. "Lots and lots of food."

Xander took me to a drive-thru and ordered me a supersized portion of fries and a Coke. The sugar would stop me crashing, he said, and the carbs would soak up the liquor.

By the time he pulled into the shadowy parking lot, I'd already devoured half of my fries.

"What?" I said, licking the salt off my fingers. He just shook his head. "Want some?"

"No, I'm fine."

"So who was that woman back there? Tash." I peeked over at him. I already felt better, the world no longer spinning. But I had the makings of a gruesome hangover brewing.

"A friend."

Okay. So he didn't want to talk about her. It wasn't my business who Xander spent his time with. But it didn't stop it eating away at me. She was so pretty and put together and mature, exactly the kind of woman guys like Xander dated. The kind of woman they settled down with.

Suddenly, I didn't feel very hungry. Closing the lid on my fries, I dumped the container in the brown paper bag.

"You okay?" he asked.

"Yeah, I feel better, thank you."

"Ready to tell me what happened tonight?"

I avoided his heavy stare. "I already told you, I was with Sean and his friends."

"And they plied you with alcohol, got you wasted, and then, what? Abandoned you?"

"It wasn't like that." Shame washed over me as I remembered Sean's advances when we'd first gotten to the bar. A hand on my knee. An arm around my shoulder. He'd broken his promise and I hadn't taken too kindly to being ambushed. When his friend, his girlfriend, and her friend showed up, he'd backed away from me.

Now I knew why.

Xander snorted, the derisive sound making me flinch.

"I'm a big girl," I sniped, finally meeting his stare. "I can take care of myself."

"You were in a bar, alone and drunk... not exactly what I call taking care of yourself."

Glancing away, I pressed my forehead against the cool glass, my eyes shuttering at his words. There was so much anger in his voice. But what I couldn't figure out was his motivation.

"I should take you home," he said, and I wondered if he noticed I flinched at that word.

Home.

I still didn't know how to truly feel about that.

Twisting around to him, I laid my head against the seat and said, "Just a little while longer, please."

"Peyton..." He let out a heavy sigh.

"Please."

"Ten minutes." His lips thinned with disapproval, a contrast to the small smile gracing my lips.

"Thank you."

CHAPTER FOURTEEN

Xander

THE AIR in the truck was too thick, but I only had myself to blame. I shouldn't have intervened. Or at least, I should have taken her straight to Jase's and let him deal with her. But I couldn't do it.

I couldn't do the right thing where Peyton was concerned.

She was under my skin, and the second she had stumbled over to me at the bar, I'd lost all sense of reason.

Fuck only knew what Tash and Shane thought of it all, but I'd deal with them later. Right now, I couldn't think about anything besides the girl half-asleep in the seat next to me. Her eyes were heavy, her long blonde hair spilling over her shoulders like a golden waterfall.

She was too damn beautiful for her own good.

"You didn't come to the game?" I asked.

"I had to work..." She peeked up at me, surprise swirling in her eyes.

"And here was me thinking you might be avoiding me."

"You can't say things like that to me..." Her breath caught, and she was right.

Damn, she was right.

I wasn't supposed to be encouraging this... whatever *this* was. But I'd looked for her today and noticed her absence almost immediately. Jase had confirmed she was working a double shift at Cindy's Grill, but I suspected that wasn't the only reason she stayed away.

And I couldn't blame her.

God, I was a fucking mess. And all over a girl I could never have.

Because this—her and me—it wasn't an option.

Ever.

And yet... it didn't stop me from imagining things.

"Who's Tash?" Peyton whispered, stroking her fingers up and down my worn leather seat.

"A friend."

"A friend you like to fuck?"

"Peyton." I swallowed roughly. That word on her lips... it was sinful. Heat splashed inside me.

Get a fucking grip. I clenched my fist against my thigh. I needed to take her home, right now. Before I did something reckless, something I couldn't ever take back.

Something that would doom us both.

"I was jealous, seeing you with her," she said brazenly.

I wanted to believe it was the liquor in her veins talking, but when I dropped my gaze to hers, I saw the honesty glittering there.

Peyton meant every single word.

"We're not... together."

Why the fuck had I said that?

Maybe I should have told her we were and put an end to this thing brewing between us.

"You're seventeen," I said, feeling sick to my stomach.

"I'm eighteen soon."

"You're just a kid."

Her breath hitched. "Is that really what you see when you look at me? A kid?" Peyton sat up, fixing her eyes right on me. "Because other men don't look at me like I'm a kid. They look at me with lust in their eyes. *You* look at me with—"

"Stop, just stop." I sighed deeply. "This... us, it can't ever happen. You're in high school, Peyton. And I'm... I'm no good for a girl like you."

Not to mention the fact I worked there.

Hurt etched into her expression but she didn't look away. "Being with you... it makes everything quiet, Xander."

Fuck.

Fuck!

"Sometimes it feels like I can't breathe." Her voice was quiet. Too fucking quiet. "Everyone around me is getting on with their lives and I'm... I'm stuck. I dream about that night constantly. I dream about slipping under the water and feeling it fill my lungs. The cold water turning my blood to ice.

"I dream about you pulling me out. You think my friends want to hear that? That they want to know that I can't get the image of my mom out of my head... the blood. So much blood."

Silent tears guttered down her cheeks, shattering some piece deep inside me. Before I could stop myself, I pulled Peyton into my arms, sliding one hand into her thick waves and cupping the back of her head as I tucked her against my body.

"Ssh, I got you, I got you," I whispered, gently rocking us as she sobbed quietly.

I knew what it felt like to be alone, to carry such a burden. My mother hadn't neglected me, not at all. She'd loved me fiercely and fought to stay with me. But when she had finally lost her fight with the tumor, something inside me had broken, and never quite fixed itself.

I could barely remember her, just a glimmer of her soft voice and warm smile. The lingering memory of her singing to me and holding me. Twenty years later, I couldn't remember much at all about her, but I could remember every minute without her.

Peyton's slim fingers twisted into my sweater and I inhaled a sharp breath as she pressed herself closer.

The right thing, the wise thing, would have been to gently slide her off my lap and take her home. But as I held her, I realized we were past that. Past the point of pretending something wasn't happening between us.

Even if I couldn't act on it, even if I wouldn't act on it, I could do this. I could hold and comfort her.

I could let her know she wasn't alone.

But then I felt her shift. Her cheeks brushed mine, her warm lips skating across my face as she inhaled a shuddering breath. Then she was kissing me. Barely a whisper of a touch, yet I felt it all the way to the pit of my stomach.

"Xander," she whispered, turning her head slightly and sliding her mouth against mine again. Harder. More determined.

My entire body shuddered as I smothered the involuntary moan rumbling in my chest. "Peyton, no..."

"Please, Xander. Give me this." Her palms flattened against my chest, sliding up to my shoulders as she kissed the corner of my mouth, flicking her tongue over the seam of my lips.

Jesus. It felt good.

Too fucking good.

It felt like temptation and salvation, and sweet, sweet torture.

"Stop," it was a ragged breath, "you have to stop." I released a long breath, forcing my body to calm the fuck down. She was so close, too fucking close. And I wanted to kiss her. I wanted to fist my hands in her hair and crash my lips down on hers and kiss her until I didn't know where I ended and she began.

But she was drunk, and I was...

I was screwed.

So fucking screwed.

"Y-you don't want me?" Peyton lifted her tearstained face to mine, the raw vulnerability in her voice like a punch to the gut.

"We can't," I said again. Only this time, I wasn't sure who I was trying to convince more. Peyton or myself.

"I see." Her entire body tensed as she started backing away, scrambling to her own seat. "I think you should take me back." She tucked her hair behind her ear, refusing to meet my gaze.

"Yeah." I exhaled another steady breath, firing up the truck. It rumbled to life, drowning out the violent thud of my heart against my chest.

We'd crossed a line.

I'd crossed a line.

And I wasn't sure where we went from here.

THE RIDE to Jason's was almost unbearable. Peyton didn't speak, let alone look at me. I'd done some fucked up things in my life but tonight topped them all.

When I finally pulled up just down the road from the Ford's, it was a little after eleven. I didn't know where Jase and Fee thought she was, but Peyton didn't seem worried as she grabbed the handle and went to shoulder the door.

"Thanks," she murmured, "for… everything."

The words lashed my insides.

"I can come to the door and explain—"

"It's fine. I texted Fee earlier."

She had?

Dread snaked through me, but Peyton let out a bitter laugh. "Don't worry," she sniped. "I didn't tell her who I was with."

"That's not—"

"It doesn't matter. I should go." Her eyes barely met mine.

I had to fight the urge to pull her back inside the car and drive away so we could finish what we started, but if I went there…

I doubted getting charged with a corruption of minors' sentence would be the worst thing that would happen to me.

"Fuck," I rapped my knuckles against the steering wheel, watching as Peyton slipped quietly into the Ford's house.

I was a mess.

This whole fucking thing was a mess.

Once Peyton was safe inside, I floored the gas and sped off toward my side of town. But the ride did little to ease the memory of her lips on my skin. She may as well have branded me.

The second I got back to my apartment, I checked the mirror in the bathroom just to be sure she hadn't, because fuck, I could still feel her soft lips right there, pressed against my skin. I was rock hard just thinking about it, and before I knew it, I'd stripped out of my clothes and stumbled into a cold shower. But I didn't find any solace there. Peyton was like a ghost I couldn't exorcise, a beautiful nightmare I couldn't escape.

There was something very fucking wrong with me because the desire coursing through me didn't tamper down under the cold spray. Giving in to the temptation, I gripped myself roughly and thrust into my hand, groaning into the waterfall.

My thoughts hit me like a runaway train, slamming into me with such force, such clarity. I couldn't do anything but picture her on her knees, those pretty pink lips wrapped around my dick.

"Fuck," I grunted, jacking myself harder, lost to the imaginary feel of my fingers in her hair, her tongue and teeth driving me to the point of ecstasy. I'd guide her right, show her how I liked it. And when she'd made me come, moaning her name, I'd lay her out on my bed and show her just how much I appreciated her.

How much I wanted her.

"Fuck. Fuuuuck!" I came hard, jerking into the shower spray. My chest heaved as I tried to catch my breath, tried to process what the hell had just happened.

I'd imagined Peyton before... but never like this. And God, now I'd pictured her like that, I wasn't sure I would ever be able to look at her the same way again.

She was just a teenage girl.

Except she wasn't.

And the more I tried to fight it, the more I seemed to screw up.

SUNDAY, Cameron summoned me to his house for dinner. Technically, the invite came via Hailee, but only because she liked to play peacekeeper between us.

"Uncle Xan," Ashleigh said as she opened the door. "You came."

"Let me guess. Your dad wasn't expect—"

"Xander." Cameron appeared in the hall and gave me a sharp nod.

"I brought a bottle of wine." I offered it to him, and he took it. "How was the party last night?" My attention turned to my niece who looked a little worse for wear.

"Ugh, don't ask," she grumbled.

"I think you should tell Uncle Xander all about how you came home drunk and puked in your trash can."

I let out a low whistle. "No wonder you look so pale."

"I'm never drinking again." Ashleigh balked.

"That's what we all say, kid, until the next time someone offers you a drink."

"Good thing you're grounded for a month then, isn't it?" Cameron flashed her a smug grin.

"Mom," she yelled. "He's doing it again."

"Doing what?" I mouthed at my brother.

"Apparently, now Leigh's eighteen, I can no longer treat her like a child. But what she seems to forget is that it works both ways. If she makes childish decisions, she'll—"

"Okay, Dad. I get it." She threw up her hands. "I screwed up. At least I came home and didn't stay out and let some guy corrupt me and—"

"Whoa," Cam said, frowning. "Let's not have this conversation before we eat."

"Whatever you say, Dad." She sauntered off down the hall.

"Sometimes she makes Avery look like a dream."

"I guess guys are different," I said as if I knew anything about parenting.

"Yeah, with him all I had to worry about was him knocking up some poor unsuspecting girl." He ran a hand over his jaw, looking to where Ashleigh had disappeared into the kitchen. "Girls are... they're a different thing altogether."

"Don't be too hard on her. She's a good kid."

"Yeah, it could be worse. She could be like Peyton."

"What that's supposed to mean?"

Shit.

It came out far too sharp.

Cameron's brow knitted together. "Come on, Xan. I know you don't know much about her, but before everything, it was pretty obvious she was... a free spirit."

"Jase seems to think it's hardly any surprise given everything she's been through."

"Yeah, she's had it tough." A flicker of regret shone in Cameron's gaze. "That was a shitty thing for me to say. Peyton is a good kid even if she's a little misguided. Leigh loves her. Lily too. And I can't imagine what it must have been like, finding her mom the way she did..."

"They're in high school. They're supposed to screw up and experiment and make mistakes."

Fuck knows I had.

From the way Cameron was staring at me, I knew he remembered what I was like at that age all too well.

"I don't envy Jase," Cam admitted, "that's for sure."

"Look at us, having a normal conversation."

"Stranger things have happened." He regarded me. "Did you make a decision about Jase's offer yet?"

"No, and I'd appreciate it if you didn't start. I have some things to figure out first."

"What things?"

"I'm not doing this—"

"There you two are." Hailee slipped out of the patio doors and came around to Cameron. Leaning down, she grazed his cheek with her lips. "Dinner won't be long.

Xander." She smiled at me. "I'm glad you came. We both are."

I gave her a small nod.

"We're just discussing the job at the high school," Cameron said.

I wanted to bang his head against the wall. He couldn't just leave it alone like I'd asked.

"And?" Hailee looked at me expectantly.

"I'm still deciding."

"Well, I'm sure you'll make the right decision for you."

"There's only one decision to make here, surely you know that?" Cameron studied me.

"I didn't ever see it being a permanent thing."

"That's bullshit, Xander, and you know it."

"Cam!" Hailee warned, squeezing her husband's shoulders. "Xander is a grown adult. He can make his own decision."

"I just don't understand what there is to decide." Cam slumped back in the chair, letting out an exasperated breath. "It'd give you stability. A real shot at getting out of that shithole apartment. You'd get a full package: health insurance, a dental plan... all that stuff."

"If I'd have known coming would have turned into a third degree I would have gone to Bell's."

"I asked him to play nice," Hailee added, before disappearing back inside.

"I just don't understand what you're so scared of?" There was no malice in his voice this time, only genuine curiosity. But it was easy for Cam. Always had been. He'd been old enough when Mom had died to get on with life, same with Dad.

I knew he hadn't had it easy taking care of me, but he'd had Hailee by his side, not to mention Jase and Asher.

I stared at him, at the brother who'd raised me. The guy

who'd always been there. And I'd never felt more distance between us.

"You don't get it," I whispered.

"Try me. For fuck's sake, talk to me, Xander. I don't see what the problem is." His eyes narrowed and he ran a hand over his jaw. "Jase did you a solid by offering you the job with the team."

"I know that."

"So what is there to decide? You'll never get another shot like this. It's the right call and you know it."

"It's not that simple."

"You're worried about letting him down? About falling back into old habits—"

"Don't," I gritted out.

"Don't what? Try to talk to you?" His lips pursed. "Try to understand what the hell you could possibly have to think about? It's a good job. It's the right—"

"I'm not a kid anymore, Cam. You don't need to pull the father figure routine with me."

He stiffened. "What the hell does that mean?" It came out cold.

"Nothing," I huffed, glancing away. "It means nothing."

"You know, Mom and Dad would want more for you. They'd want nothing more than to see you succeed... succeed at something."

He might as well have punched me in the stomach. I stared at him, slack-jawed and speechless. The blood drained from his face. "Shit, Xander, I didn't—"

"Whatever." I went to get up, but Hailee called, "Cam, a little help please."

Her voice was like a bucket of cold water over the tension brewing between us. My brother let out a small sigh of frustration while I pulled out my smokes.

"You need to quit that shit," he gritted out as he stood.

"I'll get right on it, *Dad*."

I regretted the word the second it tumbled from my lips. It was a low blow, I knew that. But I wasn't a kid anymore and I was so fucking sick of him always thinking he knew what was best for me. It was tough shit if he didn't like the decisions I made.

He gave me a lingering look before going back into the house. I could finally breathe again. Dropping my head back against the wall, I inhaled a breath. It was so damn cold it made my lungs smart, but I welcomed the burn.

It was always the same between us. Cameron held my mistakes against me, and I resented him for it. But along the way, it had gotten messy, miscommunications getting tangled up until there was no unravelling the past. And the kicker was, I knew... I knew I'd screwed things up back in high school. That one split decision had set me on a dark path. I couldn't handle the disappointment, the gut-wrenching guilt, the way Cameron looked at me after the accident. But instead of getting through it, together, we'd only drifted further and further apart.

A minute later, Ashleigh slipped outside and joined me. "I thought I'd find you out here," she said.

"What's up, kid?"

"Sometimes I wonder if you say that to piss me off or to remember that you're the adult now." She snickered, poking her tongue out at me.

"Trust me, I don't need a reminder," I said, leaning down to put out my smoke.

"I wish you'd quit that. It's such a disgusting habit." Her nose screwed up.

"Could be worse." I shrugged.

"It's just so... unattractive."

I glanced over at her and arched a brow. "Thanks." It came out sarcastic.

"You know, if you quit you might have a better chance at getting a girlfriend."

I almost choked on my own breath. "A girlfriend? Where the hell did that come from?"

"I heard Mom and Dad talking... I guess they think it's time you settled down or something."

Peyton's face popped into my head.

I was officially going to hell.

"Uncle Xan?" Ashleigh whispered, and I wondered what she saw to make her sound so concerned.

"I'm not sure this is a conversation you and me should be having."

"I'm eighteen now. I know all about the birds and bees." She rolled her eyes.

"I really don't know what to say to that."

Ashleigh chuckled. "Maybe Mom could set you up with one of her artist friends from the group?"

"Been there, done that. It ended badly." The woman had been nice enough, but I wasn't exactly the kind of guy with much to offer someone. We'd gone on two dates before she realized I had no real plans for the future.

Most women my age were looking for Mr. Right, not Mr. Right Now, and when they realized I had no plans to settle down, they never called again. Tash was the exception.

She was like me—damaged—and for a while, it had been good between us. Unconventional, but good.

Now she was one of the few people I called a friend. She'd already blown up my phone this morning about last night. But I wasn't ready to deal with her meddlesome ways. She knew me. She knew I didn't play the hero.

She also had no idea that the girl she'd briefly met last night was the same girl I'd pulled out of the river.

"Uncle Xan, can I ask you a question?" Ashleigh's voice pulled me from my thoughts.

"Sure, Leigh Leigh." I smirked at the nickname I'd called her when she was a child.

"How do you tell if someone likes you or not?"

"I... I'm not sure I'm the right person to answer that."

"Because you've never been in a relationship?" She gave me a mocking smile. "Come on, you must have liked someone, you're almost thirty."

Yeah, I'd liked someone. One of her best friends.

"You got yourself a crush, Leigh?" I teased, trying to deflect the spotlight burning down on me.

"I... no, it isn't like that. We're friends... at least," she dropped her gaze, "I think we are. He's confusing."

My eyes narrowed. "He a good guy?"

She pressed her lips together and met my gaze. "He's kind of a lone wolf."

"Anyone I know?" My brow arched.

"Like I'm going to tell you. Forget it." She leaped up, "forget I said anything."

"My advice," I offered before she could escape, "make him work for it. You're a good kid, Leigh. You deserve to be treated right."

Her eyes widened as if she was seeing me in a whole new light, and then she disappeared inside.

Leaving me alone.

Just the way I liked it.

CHAPTER FIFTEEN

Peyton

"WHAT HAPPENED TO YOU LAST NIGHT?" Lily asked me as we studied in her bedroom.

"I told you, I hung out with Sean."

"At the bar." She gave me a pointed look.

"Yeah... there was a band."

"Are we going to talk about the fact that you went to a bar with Sean Farrow instead of coming to a party with your best friends?"

I let out a deep sigh. "There's nothing to say. I didn't feel like being around loads of people, and Sean—"

"You went to a bar, Peyton. Full of people. So don't give me that." She closed her notebook. "Talk to me."

"I just couldn't do it. It's hard to explain."

"Try... for me, please."

Sitting up, I closed my legs and tried to figure out where to start. "Honestly, I didn't plan to go anywhere. But Sean turned up at the diner, and when he asked me to go with him, I said yes."

"Do you like him?"

"Sean? God no." That ship had long sailed. Not that there had ever been anything between us. It was a fling, nothing more.

"So why did you go with him?" Confusion clouded Lily's eyes.

"Do I need a reason?" It came out more defensively than I intended. Lily wasn't the enemy here. She was my friend. My best friend. But she wouldn't understand.

"Is it because of Bryan? Because you know, he gets it. He knows you don't like him like that."

"It's not about Bryan, Lil."

"So what is it?"

"I just..." I inhaled a deep breath. "Sometimes, when I'm with you all, it's hard."

Her expression fell. "Peyton."

"It's not anything anyone has done or said, it's just me... I'm not... I'm not the same."

She reached over and grabbed my hand. "It's going to take time."

"Please don't think it's you, it's not. I just... I can't do the getting excited about college and the future, not yet."

"God, I wish you'd have told me. I can see how hard it must have been."

"It's fine, really. I don't expect people to put their lives on hold because something bad happened to me. But I also can't pretend that everything is okay all of the time either."

Silence fell over us. I didn't want to make Lily feel bad, but the truth was, it wasn't about her. It was about me. It was my burden to carry, my pain to endure.

My journey to live.

And I didn't have all the answers right now as to how she could help me.

"Did you and Sean... you know...?" A faint smile traced her lips.

"No, we didn't have sex. That's not what last night was about, Lil."

"Oh, okay."

"I just needed to get out of my head." I'd needed to think about anything besides Xander, but that had backfired when I'd spotted him across the bar.

God, I still couldn't believe I'd done that. Accosted him while he was with his friend, and then kissed him like that while we sat in his truck.

I was an idiot, and a glutton for punishment apparently. But sitting there, wrapped in his arms, I'd felt it, the tether between us.

It was there, no matter how much he fought it.

I didn't want to ever be that girl though, tricking guys into being with me. How pathetic he must have thought I was, throwing myself at him like that.

"Peyton?" Lily's voice snapped me out of my trance.

"Yeah?" I forced a weak smile.

"Are you sure there's nothing else?"

She knew.

Of course Lily knew I was keeping something from her. But she probably thought it had to do with my situation, and not her uncle's brother.

No wonder Xander had no hesitations in stopping me. There was so much at stake, too much. Lily and Ashleigh would never look at me the same if they knew the truth. If they knew how I felt about Xander, if they knew what I wanted from him.

Shame burned through me.

I hadn't meant for it to happen. To develop these feelings for him. But I had and now I didn't know how to make them go away.

Because I didn't look at Xander and see a silly high school crush. I saw a guy who had spent most of his life shielding himself from those around him. I saw a guy who built walls around his heart and vowed to never let anyone inside. I saw a guy with pain in his eyes. A guy with darkness in his heart.

I saw a kindred spirit.

I saw myself.

And in the few moments we'd talked, and opened up to each other, I saw past all that. Whether he knew it or not, Xander had let me in and now I wanted more.

I wanted to know the guy he never let the world see.

I wanted it so badly it hurt.

Tears welled in my eyes and Lily reached for me, pulling me into her arms. "Oh, babe, don't cry. I'm here. I'm right here, Peyton. It's going to be okay. I promise, everything will be okay." She hugged me and I held on tight.

Because in that moment silence was a better answer than all the things I wanted to say and never could.

"Peyton, wait up." Sean jogged over to me, his dirty-blond hair falling in and out of his eyes with every step.

"I really need to get to class," I said, hoping to avoid a scene.

He'd texted me yesterday apologizing for abandoning me at the bar. It wasn't like I could tell him I got a ride home with Xander, so I'd made up some story about getting a ride with a friend's family member, knowing it was unlikely he would ever put two and two together.

"Just a minute, yeah?" He gently grabbed my wrist, my eyes immediately going to the spot where his fingers held me.

"Sean..."

"Come on. I said I was sorry."

"It doesn't matter. It was a mistake, Sean," I said, yanking my arm away. "I should never have gone with you."

"Why do you have to be such a fucking bitch all the time?"

I jerked back as if he'd slapped me in the face, my cheeks burning. It didn't help that a group of juniors walked by at that exact moment, snickering at us. At me.

"What did you just call me?" I seethed.

"You heard me. You're a fucking cocktease, Peyton. Acting too good for me."

"I... that's not what I was doing."

"Oh, come on, babe." He sneered. "You were practically begging me to fuck you over the summer and now you're acting like—"

"How dare you?" My voice quivered as tears stung my eyes. "We were never dating. I didn't owe you anything then, and I sure as hell don't owe you anything now. You asked me out. I told you I'd come as your friend... I didn't promise you anything. Besides you weren't that bothered, you left with another freaking girl."

"Yeah, only because you—"

"Oh my God, get over yourself. How many times do I have to say it? I'm not interested."

"That's bullshit and you know it." He went to reach for me again, but I batted his hand away.

"Don't touch me. Don't you dare touch me."

He snorted, stepping into my personal space. "Such a high opinion of yourself, when you're nothing more than trailer trash with a tight pussy."

His words slammed into me with such venom I couldn't believe I was looking at the same guy as the one who had begged me to go out with him Saturday.

"You're a fucking mess," he spat the words.

"Back the fuck up, Farrow." Relief sank into me at the sound of Bryan's voice, quickly chased away by fear as he stepped between us and right up to Sean.

"I always knew you were a piece of shit."

"Go fuck yourself, Hughes."

"Say that again, asshole." Bryan etched closer, shoving his face into Sean's.

"Bryan!" I shrieked, grabbing his arm. "Don't."

"I heard what he said," he seethed. "You think I'm going to let him talk to you like that?"

"You two deserve each other," Sean taunted. "You're so fucking desperate to play hero and she's the damaged princess. Good luck trying to piece her back together."

Before I could stop him, Bryan launched himself at Sean and the two of them crashed into the wall, throwing fists and elbows.

A scream tore from my throat as someone yelled, "Fight!"

Kids scrambled to our quiet corner of the quad, forming a semi-circle around us as Bryan and Sean beat the crap out of each other. Ashleigh rushed to my side, lacing her arm through mine. "Oh my God, what happened?"

"I... I don't—"

"Okay, okay, break it up," Jason waded into the fray. "Break it the hell up. Now." He hauled Bryan off Sean and shoved him to the side. "Stand down, Hughes. Stand the hell down."

Blood gushed from Sean's nose. "You fucking asshole," he snarled.

"Walk it off, Farrow. Straight to the nurse's room." He swung around and pinned Bryan with a murderous look. "I'll deal with you later. Get the hell out of here. All of you."

Ashleigh started to lead me away, but Lily's dad wasn't done. "Peyton, a word please."

Oh God.

My heart leaped into my throat.

"Want me to stay?" Ashleigh whispered, but I shook my head.

"It's fine, go. I'll catch up with you later."

I didn't meet Jason's piercing stare as we waited for the crowd to disperse.

"Let's walk," he said.

I fell into step beside him as we walked away from the school building and around the side toward the gym.

"Want to tell me what that was all about?"

"How do you know it had anything to do with me?" I peeked up at him.

"Peyton, I may be what you kids consider old, but I'm no fool. There are only two reasons guys fight like that. Because they're ass over elbow drunk, or over a woman. And since it's no secret Bryan has a soft spot for you..."

"Fine, you got me." I inhaled a ragged breath. "But I didn't know that was going to happen."

"I'm not blaming you, Peyton." Jason held open the door to the locker room and ushered me inside.

It was strange being in here when it was empty. Not that I made a habit of sneaking into the boys locker room. I didn't. But me, Ashleigh, and Poppy had snuck in once or twice to prank Aaron.

"Sit," he said, motioning to the chair opposite his desk. "Now, why don't you tell me what really happened?"

"Bryan was just defending me."

Anger flickered in his eyes, but not the wild kind that had been simmering in Sean's gaze earlier. No, this was the calm, controlled type of anger that came with years of learning to harness your emotion.

"Did Sean...do something to hurt you?"

"He... he said some things. Things I'd rather not repeat."

"Peyton, I can't help you if you don't tell me what happened."

"I went out with him Saturday, as friends," I quickly added. "He misread the situation."

"You said you were hanging out with friends Saturday."

"I was... or at least, I thought I was." My eyes darted to my hands.

"I see." His words were tight. "And where were you hanging out?"

"It wasn't like... that." I lifted my gaze to his. He was Lily's dad, the man who had taken me in when I had nowhere else to go. I owed him. I owed him more than I could ever repay. But still, it felt weird talking to him about this stuff. And it had nothing to do with the fact I was still keeping some things to myself.

"Hey, Jase—sorry, I didn't realize you were busy."

My heart fluttered at Xander's voice. I felt him behind me, felt the tension rippling off him.

"What is it?"

"It can wait," he said. "Is everything okay?" His eyes burned holes into the back of my head, but I didn't glance back because I knew if I did, I'd give myself away.

"Nothing I can't handle," Jase said. "We'll be done soon and then we can go over those game tapes."

"Sounds good." Xander tapped the door. "I'll be in the assistant coaches' office."

Jason gave him a small nod, waiting for him to leave. "Sorry about that."

"It's okay," I said, trying to get a hold of my emotions.

My skin felt too tight, my chest constricted. Could Lily's dad see the change in me? Hear the rapid beat of my heart in my chest? Could he see the stain in my cheeks, no matter how hard I tried to silently will myself not to blush?

"I know it hasn't been easy for you, Peyton, and I know I'm not very good at this kind of thing, but it's important to me that you know I'm here, okay?"

"Thank you." I swallowed over the giant lump in my throat. "I'll be forever grateful to you and Felicity."

"We know it's going to take time for you to heal, but we're here for you. Every step of the way."

Tears pricked the corners of my eyes. "I should probably get to class."

"Of course." He smiled. "And you come straight to me if Sean Farrow causes you any more issues. I'll be having a firm word with him and Bryan. I suspect Principal Kiln will also want to talk to them, but I'll do my best to keep your name out of it."

"Thank you." I stood, smoothing my hair from my face. "I'll see you later."

"You will. And Peyton?" he said as I reached the door. I glanced back. "You're too good for a guy like Sean Farrow."

I walked out of there with shame on my heels.

If only he knew.

I DIDN'T GO BACK to class, not after everything. Instead, I slipped around the side of the gym and hid in the shadows. The building kissed the tree line bordering this side of the school. Kids came around here all the time at recess to smoke, but it was empty right now.

Pressing my head against the brick, I inhaled a breath, shuddering at the icy-cold air flooding my lungs.

Everything was such a mess.

I shouldn't have gone with Sean Saturday night.

Although I knew I didn't deserve his cruel words, I also knew that I was partly to blame for giving him false hope. I'd told him I wasn't interested, but it hadn't stopped me from drinking with him, dancing and laughing. But I'd just wanted to feel something other than the gnawing numbness I felt every second of every minute.

Sometimes it wasn't numbness at all. Sometimes it was pain so deep, so vast, that it felt like the only way to get rid of it would be to slice open my chest and bleed out.

I'd gone with Sean to feel something else, to lose myself in the noisy crowd and cheap liquor. I'd gone because the thought of going back to the Ford's alone was so terrifying, partying with Sean had seemed like a better option. Even when deep down, I knew it was a terrible idea. I'd created this mess... and now I had to deal with the consequences.

"Peyton?" My head whipped up to find Xander standing there.

"What do you want?" It came out sharp.

"What happened?"

"Why do you care?"

His stare was aching. "Come on. That's not... Shit, do you know what I even risk being out here?"

"So why are you here?" I glared at him, my body trembling with rage and frustration.

"I wanted to make sure you were okay. I heard there was a fight..."

"I'm fine. You should go."

"Yeah." But Xander made no move to leave. We stared at one another, locked in some silent battle of the wills.

"I can't do this," I said, shoving past him. Tears threatened to burst free as I grappled with my emotion. But I completely froze when a hand brushed mine.

Xander's hand.

My breath caught as I dropped my gaze to where his

hand lay against mine. But I was too confused, too weary, to try to decipher what it meant. His mixed signals were giving me whiplash.

So without another word, I walked away from him...

And I didn't look back.

CHAPTER SIXTEEN

Xander

LETTING her walk away from me was one of the hardest things I'd ever done. Something was wrong. And not just with us. But with her.

I'd heard there was a fight and the second Bryan Hughes and Sean Farrow's names were mentioned, my mind instantly went to Peyton.

Had that little shit done something to her? Said something?

Peyton was already so fragile. Strong yes, but her strength was cracked. Fractured. And I hadn't helped matters. But I had responsibilities. I worked here, and she... she was a student here. Did she understand the kind of shitshow that would rain down on us if the truth came out?

I'd always been a morally gray character, but I drew the line at the corruption of a minor. Even if her soul called to mine like a moth to a flame.

Fuck.

Everything was so fucked.

I pounded my fist on the wall, wincing with the bolt of pain that ricocheted up my arm.

"Chase?" A familiar voice said. "What the hell are you doing out here?" Coach Huckley appeared, eyeing me with disdain.

"Just needed a smoke," I lied.

"You need to quit that shit, and no smoking on school property. You should know better than that," he sneered.

"It's been a rough morning. Give a guy a break, yeah?" My brows quirked up, but his grimace didn't budge.

"You're lucky I caught you out here and not a group of kids. It sets no example for—"

"I get it," I snapped, growing tired of his bullshit lectures. "We should probably head back inside." Barging past him, I went to turn the corner, but his voice stopped me at the last second.

"I know he's offered you a permanent position, Chase."

"That's between me and Ja—Coach Ford." I glanced back.

"That's the thing though, a decision like that affects all of us."

My brows pinched. "If there's something you want to say, Huckley, then spit it out."

His tawny eyes narrowed, full of contempt and judgment. "You don't deserve to be here. Good men were overlooked for you."

"Say what you really mean," I grumbled. "Look, Darryn, you don't like me, fine. But I'm here to do a job and while I am, I'm going to do it. If you have a problem with that, take it up with the boss."

I didn't look back as I went around and slipped inside the gym.

"Problem?" Jase said the second I reached his office.

"Just Huckley doing his civic duty to remind me I don't belong here."

"I know the guy can be a little... difficult—"

"Difficult? He's just waiting for me to drop the ball so he can pounce."

"He's harmless." Jase let out a small sigh.

"We'll see."

Five minutes earlier, and he would have caught me and Peyton. That would have been all the ammunition he needed.

"You wanted to see me earlier?"

"I was hoping to get Wednesday afternoon off," I said.

"It's the final week of practice, Xan. We have a lot—"

"It's the anniversary of his death."

"Shit." Jase sank back in his seat. "Of course it is. Sorry, I didn't—"

"Relax, there's no reason you'd remember. But I usually visit him and Mom and—"

"Of course, take some personal hours. We'll be able to hold the fort without you. Just make sure you're back on Thursday with a clear head." He gave me a knowing look.

"I will. We have a championship to win."

"Damn right, we do."

A faint smile traced my mouth. "I'm going to get a start on those game tapes," I said.

"Good. I want you to make sure Kaiden is ready for Bridderton. They have a big defense."

"He'll be ready."

"Okay, get out of here and I'll check in on you later."

"You got it, Coach."

Memories assaulted me. Ten years ago, I'd stood in this very office on the cusp of my senior year championship game. Coach Hasson had looked to me to lead the team all the way... All I had to do was want it.

"Xander?" Jase's voice pulled me from my reverie. "You okay over there?"

"Yeah, Coach, I'm okay."

What choice did I have?

It wasn't like I could go back in time and change a damn thing.

WHOEVER DECIDED to push the football championships to the last weekend before schools got out for the holidays had severely underestimated how amped the student body would be.

Everyone was talking about the upcoming game *and* their plans for the holidays. It was chaos in the halls.

"Xander, wait up," Mya Bennet cornered me as I made a rare trip to the school cafeteria. But after hours of studying game tapes and drinking nothing but strong coffee, I needed sustenance.

"What's up?" I said, taking her lead to step aside for the steady stream of kids.

"Have you spoken to Peyton lately?"

Everything inside me froze. "I saw her at Jase's a couple of times. Why?"

"I'm worried," she said. "She's refusing grief counselling. And I heard there was a fight this morning, but when I asked her about it, she brushed me off saying it was just a misunderstanding."

"I get you're worried, but what does it have to do with me?"

"You saved her, Xander. And I know you're not entirely comfortable with the idea that Peyton sees you as... her savior. But I just thought maybe she might have tried to talk to you. You're right though, I'm probably overstepping. It's a delicate situation with you working here and knowing her outside of the school too."

"Look, Mya, I'm not really sure what you want me to say." I dragged a hand down my face. "I did what anyone else would have done."

"I know. Sorry. I'm just finding her a tough nut to crack. She's been through so much. I don't want her to jeopardize her senior year."

"Have you tried asking her what she wants?"

Mya's brows knitted together. "What do you mean?"

"Like you said, she's had her whole world tipped on its side. And everyone's so eager to fix things for her, but has anyone stepped back and bothered to ask what she wants?"

Surprise shone in Mya's eyes. "You know, you ever want to quit football, I could use an extra pair of hands in the guidance counsellor's office."

"You're joking, right?" I didn't know the first thing about giving advice and guidance.

"I'm serious, Xander. After everything you've been through, I think the kids could really benefit from having someone who understands what it's like."

"What it's like?" I asked, choosing to focus on that rather than the fact it sounded like she was offering me a job.

"Yeah," her expression softened, "being an outsider, trying to find your place in the world." I didn't like the way she looked at me, through me, as if she saw straight past my defenses.

"I'm not that guy, Mya."

"Don't sell yourself short. I really think—"

"Mrs. Bennet, can I have a minute please?" A student chose the perfect moment to interrupt.

"Sure, Terri, what's up?"

"Can we... uh... go inside?" The girl motioned to Mya's office.

"Sure. Go right in and I'll be there. Sorry," Mya said to me. "Looks like duty calls."

"It's fine. I need to get back anyway."

"What I said... It's just another option, no pressure." She gave me a warm smile before disappearing back into her office. I didn't speak to Mya a lot, sometimes in passing and at the occasional gathering I attended with my brother and Jase, but that had to be one of the strangest conversations I've ever had.

I wasn't guidance counselor material. I barely had my own life on track. Not to mention the fact I was thinking highly inappropriate things about one of her students.

Shaking the thoughts from my head, I continued on to the cafeteria, only to walk straight into Kaiden, Bryan, and Gav.

"So the rumors are true then?" I said to Bryan, noting the bruise along his jaw.

"Why don't you ask that fucker Farrow," he grumbled.

"I thought I warned you not to do anything stupid." My brow arched.

"Yeah, well, you didn't hear what he was saying to Peyton."

My spine went rigid. "So you were fighting over a girl."

"Not just any girl, Coach, and you know it." His eyes met mine, and for a second, I wondered if Bryan knew more than he let on. But there was no way... I was just being paranoid, it was just because he was aware I knew her outside of school.

"You're lucky Coach Ford isn't making you sit out Saturday's game," I said, knowing full well that Jase would fight tooth and nail to keep his best defensive tackle in the starting lineup.

"He started it," Bryan protested.

"Yeah, but you should have known better," Gav gave him a pointed look. "Farrow is a real piece of work, but he isn't worth getting benched for."

Bryan ran a hand through his hair, glancing up at me, and I knew exactly what he was thinking. Sean Farrow wasn't worth it, but Peyton was.

I knew because I was thinking exactly the same thing.

She'd been with Farrow Saturday night; she'd been drunk with him.

Anger flashed through me. Bryan wasn't the only person standing here that wanted to go teach Farrow a lesson. But I was the adult here, I was supposed to be the voice of reason.

Fuck.

When had life gotten so complicated?

When you pulled her near-lifeless body from the river.

A shudder ripped through me as I gave the guys a small nod and excused myself. If I stood around to listen to any more talk of Sean Farrow and Peyton, there was every chance I would do something stupid.

And I'd done enough of that already.

I DIDN'T SEE Peyton over the next couple of days, and despite looking for her around school, I knew it was for the best. It was bad enough that we'd be spending the holidays together. It was Jason and Felicity's turn to host, so there was no escaping. Even if I only turned up for the food, he expected me to be there.

It was Wednesday afternoon, and I was ready to head out.

"You good?" Jase asked me before I reached the door.

"I'm okay."

"Good. Go do what you gotta do then come back tomorrow with a clear head, okay?"

I managed a small nod. Today was never easy, but it felt different this year. Or maybe I was different.

Slinging my bag over my shoulder, I yanked open the door and slipped out of the locker room. No doubt Huckley would have something to say about me taking the afternoon off so close to the finals, but the team was ready. Kaiden was ready. There wasn't anything more we could do except put all the practice and hard work into play on Saturday and hope it was enough.

I'd almost reached the parking lot when I noticed a flash of blonde out the corner of my eye. Turning, I watched Peyton as she hurried out of the side entrance of the school grounds.

Where the fuck was she going? There was still three hours until the final bell.

Hopping in my truck, I backed out of my parking spot and headed for the gates, taking a right, in the same direction Peyton would be headed. My mind was reeling with reasons she would be leaving school in the middle of the day. Had something happened with Farrow? Had he said something to her again? Had he... hurt her?"

Fuck. My hands tightened around the wheel as I surveyed the sidewalk for any sign of her.

"Bingo," I breathed, spotting her up ahead. It was a dreary day, with dark, angry clouds swarming overhead. It looked like it might storm. Even so, it wouldn't stop me doing what I needed to do, not today.

Peyton on the other hand...

I eased my foot off the gas and wound down the passenger side window. "Hey."

"Xander? Oh my God." She clutched her throat. "You almost gave me a heart attack."

"What are you doing?" I asked, keeping one eye on the road. "Are you stalking me?"

Laughter rumbled in my chest. "Seriously?"

"Ugh, whatever. Just... go." She adjusted the knitted hat, burrowing deeper into her coat just as a loud crack of thunder rumbled overhead. "Crap." Peyton almost jumped out of her skin.

"Want a ride? It's looking nasty out here."

"No, I'm fine. I need the fresh air."

"Get in the truck, Peyton."

"You can't tell me what to do. Besides, someone might see." One of her brows lifted.

"I don't see any other cars, do you?"

Another crack of thunder reverberated in the sky, fat drops of rain falling.

"Shit," she muttered, glancing at me and back to the sidewalk.

"Last chance," I said.

"Fine... *fine*!" Peyton stormed over to the truck and yanked open the door, climbing inside.

"If I keep rescuing you like this, you're going to get used to it."

Her eyes slid to mine, narrowed with suspicion. "Did you just make a joke?"

"I wouldn't call it a joke per se."

She rolled her eyes. "You know what I mean. You seem... different."

"Don't read too much into it," I grumbled, taking the turn for Rixon cemetery.

"Uh, the Ford's live in the other direction."

"I know."

"Okay then. Guess we can add kidnapping to your list of flaws." Peyton let out a resigned sigh, and I peeked over at her. She'd been crying if her swollen eyes were anything to go on. But she still took my breath away. She was so fucking beautiful.

"I have a list?" The playful edge to my voice surprised me. But she looked so sad, so broken... in that moment, I would do anything to make her smile.

"It doesn't matter," she said quietly.

Too fucking quietly, as if she had no fight left inside her, and I refused to believe that for a second.

"Go on, try me..."

"Well, you're arrogant, for starters." She finally looked at me. "And brooding and you're grumpy, so freaking grumpy."

"Say how you really feel." I smirked, glancing at her.

"You say one thing but do another, and you give me all these mixed signals. It's confusing." Her voice turned small again. "You're confusing."

"I'm sorry." It wasn't enough but it was all I had right now.

The air in the truck turned thick again, the silence almost too much to bear. But I didn't know what to say to fix things, and she wasn't wrong. I was all those things and more. Peyton saw me. She saw me in ways nobody ever had, and it scared the shit out of me.

"Where are we going anyway?"

"You'll see," I said, taking the turn for the cemetery. It was on the edge of town, bordering the dense woods leading down to the lake. I came here twice a year no matter what. Always had, always would.

But I'd never brought anyone here before.

"The cemetery... you brought me to the cemetery. Well, this isn't creepy at all." Peyton wiped her hand through the condensation on the window. The rain was pelting down, bouncing off the hood of my truck.

I pulled into the small dirt parking lot. There was a pavilion, so I grabbed my rain jacket from the back and climbed out, shielding myself with it while I ran around to open Peyton's door.

"Have you lost your mind? It's torrential—"

"Scared of a little rain?" My lips pressed together as I fought a smile.

Her eyes narrowed. "Who are you and what have you done to the Xander Chase I know and—" She stopped herself, swallowing whatever she'd been about to say.

"Come on," I reached for her hand, disarmed by the skitter of electricity that flowed between us. If Peyton felt it, she didn't say anything as I held the jacket over her head, closed the door, and ushered her into the pavilion.

"It's really coming down," she said, dropping down on the stone bench lining the wall. A wisp of cold air drifted into the air and I watched, transfixed on her soft pink lips.

"Xander?"

I blinked. "Huh?"

"Is something wrong?" The faintest of smiles traced her mouth.

That mouth.

God, the things I imagined doing with that mouth.

"I like your hat." I said, sitting down beside her. Close enough to touch her but still far enough to resist.

"My hat." Peyton absently reached for it. "It's just a hat."

"But it looks good on you."

"Are you… flirting with me?"

"Do you always say whatever's on your mind? Even if it can land you in trouble?"

Her smile grew. "Especially if it can land me in trouble."

Jesus. This girl.

"Tell me what happened today at school," I changed the subject.

Her walls immediately slammed up and she dropped her gaze to her hands, wringing them together.

"Was it Farrow again? Because if it was—"

"You'll what?" There was no accusation in her voice, only mild curiosity. We were treading dangerous waters, quickly drifting to where the pull was too strong, and if we weren't careful, soon we'd be drowning with no escape.

I needed to stop. The teasing and flirting. The playful words to get her to smile.

"Sean is an asshole," she whispered, slowly meeting my eyes again. "He said some really shitty things about me the other day. I thought it was the last of it when Bryan introduced him to his fist, but apparently, he doesn't know when to quit."

"What happened... with him, I mean?"

"You really want to know?"

"I wouldn't have asked if I didn't."

Peyton regarded me for a second, and I didn't blame her hesitation. I had been giving her mixed signals. But what she didn't realize was every time our paths crossed, it was getting harder to do the right thing. To walk away.

"You've got that look again," she said, so quietly I barely heard her.

"What look?"

A beat passed.

The air crackled.

And she said six little words that sent my world spinning.

"Like you want to kiss me."

CHAPTER SEVENTEEN

Peyton

XANDER DIDN'T BLINK. He didn't do anything. Just stared at me as if he was seeing me for the first time, and I wanted to believe it meant something. I wanted so badly to believe that this was it, the moment we ignored all the rules and gave into this thing building between us.

But he didn't lean in.

Again, he didn't kiss me.

He didn't do anything.

Dejection sank into me. Cold, cruel dejection. God, how many times was I going to do this? Wait for him to make a move? To prove me right and confirm what I felt every time we were together.

"Why did you bring me here, Xander?" I managed to force all of the hurt out of my voice. I didn't even sound angry, just resigned.

"My parents are buried here. I come here every year to see them. Twice, actually. Once on the anniversary of my mom's death and once—"

"On the anniversary of your dad's death."

He nodded. "He died seventeen years ago today in a collision. Three-and-a-half years after I lost my mom. I was eleven."

"I'm sorry."

"Me too."

Without thinking, I reached for his hand. It didn't matter that I still felt the tang of rejection on my tongue. Xander had comforted me when I'd needed it most. I could do the same for him.

As our fingers twined together, I don't know who was more surprised. Me or him. But it felt so natural to be close to him, so right. Like a part of me knew he was mine, regardless of what society said.

Love wasn't always an easy road; it was often hard and messy and chaotic. Not that I loved Xander. But I knew I was falling for him. I'd collected the scraps of attention and comfort and soft moments and now I wanted more.

I wanted everything.

"It's my birthday soon," I blurted, wishing the rain would drown my words out.

It didn't.

Xander tensed beside me, reading the hidden meaning in my words. There were only twelve days until I turned eighteen. Twelve days until my age would no longer be an issue.

"The rain is letting up," he said, untangling his hand from mine, the moment gone so quickly part of me wondered if I'd imagined it.

If it didn't hurt so much, I would have been impressed with how effortlessly he burned hot and cold with me.

"I'm going to go..." He got up and motioned to the nearest row of headstones.

"I'll wait here," I said, suddenly feeling out of my depth.

He'd brought me here, to the place he visited his parents. It was too intimate to not mean something. Wasn't it?

I wished I knew.

I wished I had experience with guys like Xander. Older guys with life experience and stories to tell. I'd lived a lot for my almost eighteen years, but I still felt so clueless around him. I was ruled by my emotions and it showed.

But I'd vowed a long time ago, to never be anything less than myself.

The rain had created a mist over the cemetery, and I watched as Xander moved down a row to two headstones side by side. I knew he and Ashleigh's dad had lost their parents when Xander was a young boy, but I couldn't imagine what it must have been like for him to watch his mom suffer only to lose his dad in a tragic accident three years later. He'd been eleven and had his entire world ripped apart. My heart ached for him: for the boy he was then and the man he was now. It was obvious Xander carried a lot of unresolved grief and pain over what happened.

Cameron and Hailee had raised him. What a huge responsibility for them when they were so young themselves. But there was also something so beautiful about two brothers who stuck together when their worlds imploded. From the little snippets I knew about their relationship now though, it wasn't all sunshine and rainbows. I'd been to enough Ford and Chase family gatherings to know Xander didn't always show, and when he did, he often kept to himself.

The vibration of my cell phone pulled me from my thoughts, and I dug it out of my pocket.

. . .

Lily: You skipped class?

Peyton: I just needed some air. I'm okay. I'll be home later.

Lily: Where are you? I'm worried…

Thick, sludgy guilt slithered through me.

Peyton: I'm okay, I promise. A couple of Sean's groupies cornered me in the girls bathroom.

He'd spread a bunch of lies about me. I guess rejection was an excuse to be a cruel asshole because the things he'd told them…

Inhaling a ragged breath, I wiped my eyes and texted Lily back before she could reply.

Peyton: I'll be fine. I just couldn't stay there for another second. Please, don't worry about me.

Lily: Not possible. You're my best friend. It's what we do.

I texted her back a heart emoji and silenced my phone, shoving it back in my pocket. The truth was, when I'd fled from school, I hadn't been thinking about anything other than getting out of the bathroom. The walls had begun closing in around me while Layla and her friends taunted me about Sean.

Before I knew it, I'd burst out of the main entrance to school and spilled into the cold winter air... and I'd kept walking. I'd just kept going until I was out of the gates.

Cocktease.

Trailer trash.

Whore.

Their words had washed over me like an unrelenting storm. I knew my classmates thought I was a notorious flirt. Before... everything, it had been true to an extent.

I'd enjoyed the attention. It filled that gaping hole inside of me. The part of me that craved to feel normal. To *be* a normal teenage girl. But I wasn't reckless with my body. I didn't sleep with guy after guy. That wasn't who I was.

I'd watched my mom's revolving door of guys. Men who would use her and hurt her and make her cry out in pain. I had no desire to become that... none. But flirting, kissing, getting hot and heavy with a guy made me feel good. I never promised more than I could give, and I was always, always safe.

"Peyton?"

Xander stood before me, his eyes crinkled with concern. I hadn't even heard him approach, too lost in my thoughts.

"You're crying."

"I'm not—" I touched my frozen fingers to my cheeks. "I didn't realize. Did everything go... okay?" I asked.

"Yeah." He joined me on the bench again. "It never gets any easier, even after all this time."

"You miss them."

"Every second of every day," he admitted. "I never got over it, losing her. It changed me. Therapists tried to label it, to help my dad and brother understand it, to help me understand it. But I always knew what the problem was... something inside me broke the day I had to say goodbye to her. Maybe it was my heart or my sense of reason or some part of my brain. I don't know... but I wasn't the same after that."

"Xander..." My breath caught, his pain like a living thing in the air around us. I wanted to reach for him, to comfort him, but I was so scared of being rejected again.

I couldn't stop myself though. Because he was hurting, and I needed to show him he wasn't alone.

Lacing my arm through his, I tangled our hands together. Xander dropped his gaze to where our fingers twined, and I held my breath, waiting for him to pull away.

He didn't.

"It doesn't have to mean anything," I whispered, laying my head on his shoulder as we stared out at the cemetery.

"It does," he replied after a beat. "It means... a lot."

My heart stuttered, and I was desperate to know what he was thinking. But now wasn't the time to push for answers.

"I found it impossible to make friends," he said quietly. "I had attachment issues, trust issues, anxiety, depression. You name it, I had it. By the time high school rolled around, I'd gotten really good at pretending. I was good at football, really good, and it became a way for me to communicate. People didn't want to know how I was. They wanted to know about my stats and my performance on the field. It was easier to play along than have them look too closely."

"I get that. You hid behind it."

"I did. But by senior year the pressure was unbearable. I felt like I couldn't breathe... Slowly, game by game, practice by practice, I cracked. And because I'd gotten so good at pretending, nobody noticed... until it was too late."

Xander drew in a sharp breath as if saying the words physically hurt him. Or maybe it was the truth behind them. Or the vulnerability of telling me.

Whatever it was, I knew then, that I was right. Xander and I were the same. Our stories weren't identical, but who we were, who we'd become was.

"Does Cameron know?"

"He knows... bits. But he never understood why I threw it all away."

"Maybe one day you should tell him." I peeked up at Xander, surprised to find him watching.

"God, you're beautiful."

"I..." Heat flooded my cheeks as I tried to dip my eyes and give myself a second to catch my breath. But Xander's finger slid under my jaw, forcing me to look at him. "You're brave and beautiful and you deserve so much more than..."

"Than?"

Him.

He was going to say him.

But he let out a steady breath and said, "The hand you've been dealt."

My heart cinched. He was determined to keep things between us innocent when I wanted nothing more than to climb into his lap, take his rugged face into my hands, and kiss him until we were breathing for each other.

"Thank you," I said, forcing down the urge to kiss him, "for telling me."

"I don't know why but it comes easy with you." His fingers moved to my cheek, pushing a loose curl back inside my hat. A shiver ran through me at the intimate touch, the suggestion in his words.

But I knew what he meant. For the first time, I found myself wanting to open up too.

His eyes dropped to my mouth again, and I could practically imagine his lips ghosting over mine.

"Xander..."

"Fuck," he breathed, the air crackling between us. "I know better. I should know better..."

He wasn't talking to me; he was at war with himself.

"It's okay," I whispered.

"No, it isn't." He pulled me into his arms, burying my face in his chest. My hands slid over his shoulders as he dropped his chin to my head, holding me. "Nothing about this is okay."

Xander was holding me like he never wanted to let go. And despite how much I wanted him to kiss me, this was somehow so much more.

"Come to the game Saturday."

"I have to work," I said, my words muffled by all the layers between us.

"Change your shift. You should be there... I want you there."

"You do?" I pulled away, peeking up at him.

His eyes glittered with possessiveness. "I didn't like looking for you in the crowd last weekend, knowing you weren't there."

"Oh." My stomach coiled tightly at his gruff words.

He closed the distance between us, leaning in to brush his nose along mine. It was a whisper of the kiss I wanted so badly my body ached for it. But still, he didn't give it to me, his mouth hovering just out of reach.

Butterflies fluttered wildly in my stomach. "What are we doing, Xander?"

"Nothing... we're doing nothing." His words were tight, tense. Almost as tense as his body beneath my touch.

"Okay," I said softly.

If it made him feel better to pretend we were doing nothing, to pretend this meant nothing, I could play along.

So long as he didn't shut me out again.

"Are you hungry?" he asked me, and it was such a one-eighty on the intense moment we'd just shared, laughter bubbled out of me. "What?" He smiled.

"Yes, I could eat." Anticipation trickled through me. He wasn't going to take me back to the Ford's like this was a mistake. He was going to feed me.

"Come on. I'm freezing my ass off." Xander stood, taking my hand and gently yanking me to my feet. I expected him to pull away, but he surprised me again, by keeping a hold of me all the way to his truck.

"Careful," I said as he held the door open and waited for me to slip inside. "A girl could get used to this." A smile played on my lips.

Xander shook his head, giving me a disapproving look, but I saw the twinkle in his eye.

He liked this: the banter, the tension, and intensity. Even if he didn't entirely accept it.

I liked it too.

I liked it a lot.

"This isn't the drive thru," I said minutes later when we pulled up outside a building on a quiet block downtown.

"This is my place."

His place?

"Oh."

"We don't have to... I just thought that we could eat in comfort."

"Comfort, sure." I shot him an amused smile.

Xander's brows crossed. "Let's get one thing straight, Peyton. This isn't some attempt to get you—"

"I know, I'm messing with you. It's just food."

"Right."

"In your apartment."

He cussed under his breath. "This was a bad idea. I'll take you—"

"Wait." I snagged his arm. "I'm just joking. I do that sometimes... when I'm nervous."

Understanding filtered into his eyes as he leaned in. "Do I make you nervous, Peyton?"

This was dangerous territory.

So freaking dangerous.

Like a forbidden dance of push and pull, but it was impossible not to be swept away in the moment.

"You said something about feeding me?" My brow arched, trying to lighten the moment. Because when he looked at me like that, all sultry and serious, my heart beat so hard in my chest, I couldn't breathe.

A smile tugged at the corner of his mouth and he laughed. Xander laughed and it was a sound I wanted to bottle and keep with me always.

Jesus. Less than a couple of hours with him, and I wanted to bottle his laugh and memorize his smile.

"So demanding," he muttered, before climbing out of his truck, and coming around to open my door.

I could get used to this.

To Xander doting on me, opening doors, and insisting on feeding me. But I knew real life didn't work like that. Whatever this was, I would enjoy every second.

And only hope I survived the fallout.

CHAPTER EIGHTEEN

Xander

PEYTON LOOKED at home curled up on my small couch, tucking into her lo mein. I'd thought it would be awkward, bringing her here, letting her see where I lived. In fact, the second I opened the door and let her inside, I thought it was a huge fucking mistake. But in true Peyton fashion, she'd taken one look around my small apartment, declared her love for it, kicked off her shoes and gotten comfy on my couch.

I stood in my small kitchenette watching her. I'd never met anyone like her. Before the accident, I would have said she was just like every other seventeen-year-old kid, but Peyton had layers. Layers she didn't show the world. And I knew if I peeled them back, one by one, I'd find a girl beyond her years, but with a vulnerability she didn't often let people see.

She'd had it tough; I'd gleaned that much from Jase and Ashleigh. Peyton had filled in some of the gaps, but I still didn't know her whole story. And for the first time in my life, I wanted to.

I wanted to know her.

I knew I wasn't supposed to. It was wrong, on so many levels. But I couldn't seem to stop myself. Peyton pulled me in, she made me smile. She made me laugh, and that hadn't happened in a really long time.

"I know you're watching me." She glanced over at me and smiled. "Come, eat. I'll never manage all of this."

I'd ordered from my favorite takeout and watched Peyton eat her body weight in lo mein and sesame chicken.

"It's good, huh?" I said, joining her on the couch.

"So good." She licked her lips and I imagined kissing her, again.

I couldn't think about anything else, and she knew it. It lingered in the air around us. Taunting me. Tempting me. But if we crossed that line there would be no going back, and it wasn't only my life I stood to ruin.

"Open," she ordered, shuffling closer to me. With impressive skill, Peyton scooped up a piece of chicken with her chopsticks and lifted it to my mouth.

Her eyes lit up, watching as I savored the aromatic flavors. "I don't think anyone's ever fed me sesame chicken before," I said.

"Well, I guess there's a first time for everything." Her cheeks pinked as she helped herself to some more noodles. "So a little birdie told me you're coming to the Ford's house for Christmas dinner?"

"I said I'd drop by."

"Don't sound too excited."

"I'm not a fan of the holidays." I shrugged.

Peyton put the nearly empty container on the table and tucked her legs back under her body. "Why does that not surprise me."

"When I was younger my brother and Hailee always tried to make a big deal, but I preferred when it was just the three of us."

"What was it like growing up with them?"

"I idolized Cameron back then. All I ever wanted was to live with him and Hailee. I remember him being away at college and I hated it. I was in second grade and it just felt... wrong being apart from him. It wasn't a good time for me."

"And now?"

"Now what?"

She rolled her eyes. "You know what I mean."

"We grew up." I let out a long breath. "I grew up, and I don't know... things changed."

"I always liked the holidays. It was the one time of year my mom usually managed to pull herself together." Her hands twisted in her lap and I could sense her discomfort.

"You don't have to tell me..."

"No, I want to. It's just... it's not easy remembering how bad things were."

"It was always just you and your mom?"

Peyton nodded. "I don't ever remember my dad being around. She told me he lived across the river in Halston. He never bothered to show up and I never bothered to look him up. We lived out on the trailer park until I was eleven, then we moved to the other side of town. I was so excited to finally live in a real house. But I quickly realized we'd only traded one nightmare for another.

"My mom had a love/hate relationship with crack."

Fuck. What she'd endured... I knew it had been bad, but I didn't know how bad.

"She turned tricks to feed her habit, so I was used to a stream of men coming and going. I got really good at hiding or staying away. We had this neighbor, Mrs. Harrison. She'd let me stay over sometimes if my mom was messed up. She used to bake me cookies and let me watch cartoons to my heart's content."

"Peyton..." My voice cracked.

No child should ever have to endure that.

But Peyton hadn't only endured it, she'd come out the other side stronger. Brave and beautiful and confident.

"When I met Lily, I was so excited to have a friend, a real honest-to-God friend. She didn't look at me and see the girl with the junkie mom and thrift store clothes. She saw me. I'll never forget that."

"She's a good kid."

Peyton winced and I immediately regretted saying it. But it came naturally to refer to them as kids. Because that's what they were—my friends' kids. High schoolers. Teenagers.

Kids.

Jesus, what the fuck was I doing?

"Oh no, I know that look." Peyton's hand drifted to her throat. "You're about to tell me this was a mistake and that you should take me back to the Ford's."

"You mistake me for a good guy," I said quietly.

"You saved me."

"I also broke about a hundred moral boundaries with you."

"I know one moral boundary you didn't break with me." A faint smirk played on Peyton's lips.

"Would it scare you if I said I wanted that? That I wanted you?"

Dangerous territory... I was letting conversation slip into dangerous territory again.

"Why would it scare me?"

"Because I'm not some cocky little shit who doesn't know his way around a woman's body."

Her breath caught, her eyes big and bright and

brimming with curiosity. "Don't say things like that to me unless you mean them," her eyelashes fluttered, "it isn't fair."

"Nothing about this is fair," I whispered, my arm sliding along the back of the couch to gently tug the ends of her hair. She'd pulled off her hat earlier and woven her golden waves into a braid over one shoulder.

I wasn't sure if she was even aware of it, but Peyton leaned into my touch, a soft whimper spilling from her lips.

Jesus. It was a serious test of restraint to not go to her, to pull her into my arms and kiss her the way I'd wanted to ever since that day down by the lake at Jase's house.

I wasn't even sure how we'd gotten here, to a place where I was seriously considering breaking every rule I had for her.

I'd never had anything that was just mine. Usually, I sabotage everything good in my life because I didn't know how to do... *this*. I didn't know how to let someone in.

But Peyton was different. She knew what it was like to grow up feeling alone in the world, to feel abandoned. Peyton knew... when so many didn't.

Our stories weren't the same, but our souls, our souls were.

"What are you thinking?" I asked her, my fingers still toying with the ends of her hair.

"You were right." She let out a heavy sigh, staring at a spot on the wall. "That night you found me, I think there was a part of me that just wanted it all to stop. I think there was part of me that wanted it..." Slowly, her eyes lifted to mine, filled with so much anguish the air *whooshed* from my lungs.

A part of me had known the truth but hearing her admit it was gutting.

"Do you still feel like that?"

"No... I mean, I'm not suicidal, Xander. That's not what this is. But in that moment, I just wanted... I wanted to un-exist."

"Come here." I tugged her braid gently and she shuffled closer, burying herself into my side. I slipped my arm around her shoulder and held her tightly. "If you ever feel like that—"

"I don't. Not like that night. But sometimes things build up inside me and it feels like I might explode." She pressed a hand to my chest and peeked up at me. "I cut myself."

"What?" It came out harsh, her confession shredding something deep inside me.

She flinched. "It was only once..." Panic etched into her expression. "I-I needed to know what it felt like. What she felt... I needed to understand."

"Peyton, that's..." I didn't know what the hell it was. But it didn't sound good.

"I haven't done it again. I felt... God, I felt so ashamed afterward. But there was something else. This... this great sense of relief. Like all the pent-up frustration and emotion had a way out." Tears collected in the corner of her eyes. "I can understand how people chase that feeling again and again."

"I'm glad you told me." Without thinking, I curved my arm around her neck and pulled her closer, dropping a kiss on her head. "But I think you need to talk to someone, a professional..."

"Yeah, I think you're right."

"Yeah?" I jerked back.

"Yeah. I wasn't ready before... but I think I'm ready now."

I leaned down, touching my head to hers. "You've got so much to live for, Peyton."

"Yeah?" She curled her hand into my sweater,

anchoring us together. Her vanilla lip balm taunted me as the air turned thick around us.

"Peyton," I whispered, "this is a bad idea."

"A terrible idea." Her mouth curved as she moved closer, ghosting her mouth over the corner of mine.

"If I kiss you—"

"You don't have to kiss me," she said, sliding her hand to my jaw and pressing a finger against my lips. My body was a tightly coiled spring, rigid beside her. If she kissed me...

Fuck.

My control was slipping. Her scent, her silky blonde hair brushing my cheek, her fingers twisted into my sweater... I was barely holding on. Yet, I couldn't move. I couldn't do the right thing. Ensnared by her words, her touch.

"Peyton..." It came out ragged as I tried to drag air into my lungs. My tongue darted out to wet my lips, catching the tip of her finger. She smothered a moan, her eyes growing hooded as her gaze darted from my mouth to my eyes and back again.

Fuck. Fuck. Fuck.

Heat curled down my spine, a direct line to my dick which strained behind my jeans, desperate to feel her.

I was in so much fucking trouble.

"I just want to try something," she said, her eyes alight with mischief.

Gingerly, she rose up on her knees and straddled my lap, wrapping her arms around my neck. I didn't move. I didn't dare breathe. Watching as she settled on me and leaned back in to touch her head to mine. Her fingers toyed with the ends of my hair, the way I had done earlier with her braid.

"Is that a gun in your pocket or are you just happy to see me?"

Laughter rumbled in my chest as I choked out, "I can't believe you just said that." My arm curled around her waist, pulling her closer. Peyton's lips parted on a gasp.

"That's... better." She smothered a giggle.

"Stop," I chuckled again, dipping my head, I pressed a kiss to her collarbone. "You don't need to be nervous with me."

"You have met you, right?"

Lifting my face, I grinned. "I am pretty awesome."

"And vain apparently." She rolled her eyes. "But seriously, is this okay? Because I kind of got the impression you didn't want to—"

"Stop." My finger on her lips cut her off. "If I didn't want this to happen, it wouldn't be happening." Like I had any control over myself around her.

It should never have gotten this far... yet here we were, on the precipice of something.

Something I didn't want to overanalyze.

"You still haven't kissed me," she teased, brushing her nose along my cheek, chasing it with her lips.

"Maybe I'm waiting for the right time," I said.

"You mean until I'm eighteen?"

"Peyton, a few days isn't going to change how I feel about you." I gave her a pointed look, but she was staring at me with eyes brimming with confusion.

"How you feel about me?"

"You think I make a habit of bringing women back here for takeout in the middle of the afternoon?"

"You mean, you don't?" She gave me a shy smile.

"I think you know the answer to that."

"Maybe." Peyton pressed her lips together. "I didn't expect... this. I used to watch you at practice, you know. I used to joke with Lily about you... but I didn't think... I never thought that I'd be here now."

"That night changed things." I realized that now.

I'd never looked twice at Peyton before that night. And I'd tried really fucking hard to forget all about her. But I knew enough about trauma to know it bonded some people. I'd been there that night. I'd watched her wade into the river. I would never forget that.

"What?" Peyton searched my eyes. When I didn't reply, she added, "You just went rigid. What are you thinking?"

"About that night—"

"Please, can we not...? I already told you I'll talk to someone."

"I will never forget that night, Peyton." I brushed the stray hairs from her face.

I didn't know if it was the realization that if I hadn't stumbled across her that night things could have ended very differently; the overwhelming connection I felt as she gazed at me when I dragged her from the water; or the knowledge that life was too precious, too short and expendable. But I knew if I didn't kiss her right here, right in this very moment, I would regret it.

The second our lips touched, all the doubts melted away. We weren't two people separated by age and society's rules, we were two people bound by grief and trauma and a connection that couldn't be denied.

Peyton whimpered as I slid my hand into her hair and deepened the kiss, curling my tongue around hers. "Xander," she breathed, rolling her hips against me.

Fuck, she felt good.

Too good.

It would be so easy to lose myself in her.

She rolled her hips again, and a groan crawled up my throat. "Peyton, stop." My hands left her hair, stilling on her hips. "We have to stop."

But I was still kissing her, still tracing my lips over her

jaw and down the slope of her neck as she rocked against me, clutching my sweater as if she didn't want to let go.

"Peyton," I choked out. "We have to slow this down..." *We have to stop.*

Rigid, she eased back to look at me. Her skin was flushed, her eyes glittering with hunger. Fuck me, she looked beautiful.

A small, uncertain smile played on her lips. "I like kissing you," she said.

I like it too. The words teetered on the tip of my tongue, but I swallowed them down. "We have time," I said, inhaling a ragged breath.

She stared at me, the desire in her eyes dimming a little. "Do we? Because I feel like this is a dream... and when I wake up, you'll go back to avoiding me."

My jaw clenched as I tried to get a hold on the need coursing through my veins. "It won't be like that. Not this time. I promise."

I needed to figure out how to navigate this while causing the least amount of damage. Because this—her and me—it was happening. But I knew it wouldn't be easy.

I ran my thumb over her jaw and her eyes fluttered. "Don't break my heart, Xander," she whispered, her eyes fixed right on me. "I'm not sure I'll survive it."

CHAPTER NINETEEN

Peyton

XANDER DIDN'T GIVE me a ride back to the Ford's. I wanted to walk. I needed space to think, to process everything that had happened.

He didn't like the idea of me walking across town, but I'd insisted. Besides, it wasn't like he could deliver me to their doorstep without an explanation. One I knew neither of us had right now.

There had been no more kissing or touching or holding one another, and for as disappointed as I was, I couldn't deny part of me was relieved. Because kissing Xander... it had been completely overwhelming. Even as the cold air brushed my face, I could still feel the warmth of his mouth against mine, taste him on my tongue.

I burrowed into my coat, trying to protect myself as much as I could from the bitter wind. Lily had called twice since her text. She was worried and I knew she had questions. Questions I didn't want to answer.

Questions I couldn't answer.

Because this thing between Xander and I, it had to remain a secret. The second it became public, it would implode. And I refused to let that happen, not when it was so new and fragile.

He'd kissed me.

Xander Chase had kissed me with such intensity I was pretty sure he'd ruined me for all other kisses.

I touched a finger to my lips, smiling like a fool as I crossed the street into the Ford's neighborhood. We hadn't talked about what the kiss meant or what it didn't mean but I knew something had changed between us.

But my bubble burst the second I stepped foot in the Ford's house though.

"Peyton, in the kitchen, please." Felicity called.

The hairs along the back of my neck stood to attention as I slipped off my fur-lined boots and went into the kitchen. Lily and Poppy were seated at the breakfast counter, both wearing grim expressions.

"Is everything okay?" My skin vibrated. Did she know where I'd been? Had they somehow found out about Xander?

Panic welled inside me.

"Why don't you take a seat, sweetheart."

Sweetheart was good. It was a pet name. She wouldn't be calling me sweetheart if she was about to reprimand me.

"Okay, guys, you're starting to scare me." Strangled laughter bubbled up my throat.

"Principal Kiln called. You skipped class this afternoon?"

"Yeah, but I can explain..." I started. "I had a moment and needed to get out of there."

"You didn't think to go to Mya's office or ask to see the school nurse?"

"I wasn't exactly thinking straight."

"Principal Kiln is concerned," her eyes crinkled with concern. "He said there was a fight..."

"It was nothing." I cast Lily a 'help me' look, but she only mouthed, "I'm sorry."

"I know things have been hard, Peyton, but we can't help you if you don't talk to us. If you're finding school difficult—"

"I'm not."

"So what happened? Walking out in the middle of the day isn't like you, Peyton, and we can't just let it slide because—"

"I'm sorry, okay. Some girls were saying some things and I let it get to me. I didn't want to make a big deal about it, but I couldn't be there. So I left. I told Lily I was okay."

"Girls?" Lily finally spoke up. "What girls?" There was a protective edge to her words, and pride blossomed inside me.

There had been a time our roles were reversed; when I'd defended Lily from the mean girls and vipers of Rixon High. She'd come such a long way.

But still, I said, "It doesn't matter." Because I didn't need her or anyone else fighting my battles.

Besides, it wasn't even really about them... it was how the small things added up. It was how the halls at school felt too small suddenly. How I'd be sitting there in class and then the image of my mom's bloody, lifeless body would fill my head.

For the first time in a long time, I wasn't in control of my emotions. *That* was the issue.

Lily and her mom watched me quietly, studying me like I was a puzzle they needed to solve.

Inhaling a deep breath, I finally lifted my gaze to

Felicity and said, "I think I'm ready to talk to someone… about everything."

A slow smile tugged at her mouth as relief washed over her. "I think that would be a really good thing, sweetheart."

FRIDAY MORNING AT SCHOOL, I felt… different. There had been a time school had been my savior, a chance to escape my shitty life and be a regular teenage girl. But after everything, I realized I wasn't a regular teenage girl.

I never had been.

Most girls my age were worrying about college applications and making plans for graduation and the summer beyond that. I was worrying about how I was going to afford to survive.

The Ford's had been great, but I couldn't stay with them forever. And come summer, Lily would be going off to college. No, staying with them long-term wasn't an option. Which meant I needed money.

I needed a plan.

And the more I thought about it, the more I realized sticking around to graduate high school next May was only going to delay the inevitable.

But I needed to know if the alternative was even viable. Which is why I headed straight for Mrs. Bennet's office.

"Come in," she called as I rapped my knuckles on the door.

"Hey, I was wondering if we can talk."

Smiling warmly, she beckoned me inside. "Peyton, how are you?"

"I'm okay."

"I'm glad you decided to stop by. I've been worried about you."

"Actually, I didn't come to talk about... what happened."

"You didn't?" She sat back in her chair, waiting.

"I... what would it take for me to graduate early?"

"Graduate early? Where is this coming from, Peyton?"

"I have nothing, Mrs. B. No home, no family... no money."

"Sweetheart, that isn't true." The sympathy in her eyes was almost too much to bear. "You have your friends, and Jason and Felicity. You have a home with them."

"And I'm grateful. I'm so grateful for everything they have done for me. But it's not a long-term solution."

"What about college? You can apply for financial aid—"

"With all due respect, Mrs. B, we both know college is out of the question given my current situation."

"I disagree. If you want something badly enough nothing is out of reach, Peyton."

My mind flickered to Xander, and I wondered if she would say the same thing if she knew how much I wanted him.

"I can't think about college right now," I said. "Not while I have bigger things to deal with." Like my immediate future.

"Have you talked to Jason and Felicity about this?"

"Not yet. I wanted to make sure I knew my options first. I'm eighteen next week. I need to be able to stand on my own two feet. I need to know that if my circumstances change again, I can support myself."

Her eyes widened with understanding. "You're worried you might end up alone again?"

"I have to be realistic. Lily's family did an amazing thing taking me in, but I'm not their responsibility. And this is just something I need to do. If I graduate early, I can get a full-time job. I can save some money."

Mrs. Bennet ran a hand over her tight spiral curls. Even

in her mid-forties, Sofia's mom was stunning. It was hardly a surprise some of the guys at school had a crush on her.

"You're serious about this?"

"I am."

"I'll make some inquiries. It's not something the school board typically approves, but you make a compelling case."

"Really?" Disbelief coated my words. "You're not going to try to talk me out of it?"

"You're a good student, Peyton, with a good GPA. Of course you'd need to have the right number of credits, but we can figure that out."

"Thank you, thank you." I couldn't believe how easy it had been to convince her.

"Believe it or not, I am on your side." She gave me another warm smile. "And I understand your situation more than you think. I admire your resolve and strength. You're a bright girl with a bright future ahead of you. Don't ever forget that."

A tidal wave of emotion rose up inside me and I bit back the tears. I'd never grown up with that kind of praise and reassurance. My mom had never showered me with love or positive affirmations or pride. I was only ever a burden... a nuisance.

"Thank you," the words came out thick, "that means a lot."

"All I ask is that you remember it's okay to ask for help, and it's okay to accept help. Once we know if graduating early is a viable option, talk to Jason and Felicity. This isn't a decision you should make alone."

"I will, I promise." I got up to leave, but she wasn't done.

"Felicity called me last night. She said you're ready to talk to someone."

I wasn't surprised. They were best friends. It was a

strange dynamic. Lily and Poppy's dad was the football coach, and Sofia and Aaron's mom was the school guidance counselor. They were all friends long before they started working at Rixon High.

"I am. She already contacted a therapist."

"Good. I think you'll find it helpful to have a safe space to talk about everything that's happened. But know my door is always open too."

"Thank you, Mrs. B."

She gave me a small nod. "Now get to class before your teacher complains I'm making their student tardy."

I'd entered her office full of trepidation. But I walked out feeling something I hadn't felt in a long time.

Hope.

"Peyton, wait up."

I glanced over my shoulder to find Carrie-Anne Trombley hurrying after me. "Uh, hey," I said. "Do you need something?"

"Actually, I've been trying to talk to you all week."

"You have?"

"Yeah, but I didn't know... it doesn't matter. Can we talk for a minute?"

I was on my way to the library. Lily, Poppy, and Sofia had taken their lunch to the football field to watch the guys' final practice before their big game tomorrow. But I'd made up some excuse about having a paper to finish.

"Uh, sure. Okay." I motioned to a quiet alcove and she followed me in.

"I know you saw my parents last weekend at Cindy's, and I just wanted to explain..." She flushed. "Wow, okay, this is so awkward. I... I don't exactly have many friends, but you probably know that already. My mom worries, but whatever. It's not like I care." There was something in her eyes that told me she probably did care.

"Anyway, I mentioned that I sit next to you and Bryan in a couple of classes, and she kind of latched onto it, and she seemed so relieved that I'd made some new friends that I kind of let her believe it."

"That's... I don't know what to say to that." It was kind of sad and more than a little bit weird.

But strangely, I got it too.

"You like him."

"What?" Her cheeks burned.

"Bryan, you like him."

"I-I don't... he's a dumb jock."

My brow quirked up. "So you didn't go to the game last Saturday to watch him?"

"No," she whisper-shrieked. "I went with my cousin because he's a huge football fan."

"Funny story, your mom told me you're the huge fan."

"Dammit," she muttered under her breath.

"Relax," I smirked, "I'm not going to tell him."

"He doesn't even know I exist." Sadness crept into her expression. "Not when he only sees you..." Carrie-Anne trailed off and a pang of guilt flashed through me.

"It's not like that between us. We're friends."

"But he wants more."

"Guys are funny things. They usually want what they can't have. But Bryan thinks you hate him. Piece of advice. Maybe if he knew you were into him, he'd feel differently."

"No. No way." She shook her head, panic glittering in her eyes.

"Fine. Are you going to the game tomorrow?" An idea struck me.

"I don't have a ticket."

"I can probably get you one, if you want to come?"

"I... I don't have anyone to go with."

"You can come with me and my friends. There'll be a party afterwards." One I hadn't decided if I would go to, but I couldn't avoid my friends forever. And maybe Carrie-Anne would be a good buffer.

"Why would you do that for me?"

"Because I know what it's like to feel like you don't fit in. And because Bryan is a good guy."

He deserved to find his happy ending.

"Okay. I'll come."

"Awesome. Give me your number and I'll text you all the details when I've spoken to my friends."

Carrie-Anne and I exchanged numbers and stepped out of the alcove... just as Layla and her friends were walking down the hall.

"Oh look, it's trailer trash Barbie and the school nerd."

"Go fu—"

"What is wrong with you?" Carrie-Anne stepped forward, and I realized she was shielding me from them. My mouth dropped open, hardly able to believe that quiet, book smart Carrie-Anne was defending me. "Her mom just died. Show some goddamn respect."

A ripple went through the air and even Layla looked shocked at Carrie-Anne's words.

"Carrie-Anne, it's okay," I said, grabbing her arm.

"No, it's not." She stared Layla down. "Being a bitch doesn't excuse being an insensitive asshole."

A couple of her friends snickered, and Layla whirled on them. "Let's go," she hissed, shooting me and Carrie-Anne one of her best sneers.

"God, I hate her," Carrie-Anne said the second they were gone. "What?" she said, finally meeting my gaze.

"You surprised me is all."

"In... a good way?" A faint smirk graced her lips, and it occurred to me that perhaps there was more to Carrie-Anne than she let people see.

"What?" she asked, as I studied her.

"Nothing." I smiled. "Nothing at all."

"Carrie-Anne? You invited *Carrie-Anne Trombley* to the game?" Bryan stared at me like I'd grown a second head.

"Yeah, is that a problem?"

"No, but... Carrie-Anne? She's kind of a know-it-all." His face screwed up.

"Have you ever tried to get to know her?" I arched a brow.

"You have met her, right? She's pretty vocal about her disdain for the football team." He took a long pull on his beer.

We were at the Bennet's house, all crammed in Aaron's shed. Lily had begged me to go with them and I hadn't been able to deny her puppy dog eyes. I knew she felt bad for the ambush yesterday. But I wasn't angry.

"She stood her ground against Layla."

"What do you mean she stood her— Layla is who's been giving you a hard time?" Understanding flashed in Lily's eyes.

"I can handle Layla."

"Hey," Ashleigh slipped into the shed and made a beeline for one of the beanbags.

"So?" Aaron asked.

"He doesn't want to come." Disappointment shone in her eyes.

"Told ya. I've asked E like five times and he was pretty clear he wouldn't be there tomorrow."

"I just thought... it doesn't matter."

"He's coming Christmas day though, right?" Poppy asked.

"Yeah," Aaron let out a steady breath, "Dad said he has to be there. Gave him the whole, 'you are part of this family' speech."

"Aaron," Sofia warned.

"What? I'm just telling it like it is."

"Yeah, but you know it isn't easy for him."

"He doesn't even try, Sis. It's like he's... ah, I don't know."

I could count on one hand how many times I'd spoken to the twins' foster brother Ezra in the last three years, but I got it. More than ever, I knew what it was like to feel displaced. It wasn't about people's generosity; it was about self-worth and knowing your place in the world.

So yeah, I got why Ezra might have been having a hard time living with the Bennets. Sometimes you had to accept yourself and lay your past to rest before you could accept that family wasn't always what you were born into, that sometimes it was what you made for yourself.

"I can't believe this time tomorrow we'll know if we're the champions or not," Bryan kicked out his legs and folded his arms behind his head.

"Make yourself comfortable, why don't you," Aaron mumbled.

"Don't mind if I do," Bryan quipped.

"You'll do it," Lily said. Curled in Kaiden's lap, she kissed the underside of his jaw. "You've worked too hard not to win."

"If only it was that easy, Lil." Aaron chuckled.

"Well, I believe you can do it."

"Fuck yeah." Bryan drained his beer and slammed it down on the table beside him. "I've dreamed about this since I was a kid."

"Yeah, and fuck knows you were never going to win it as an Eagle." Aaron smirked.

"Low blow, man." It was Kaiden's turn to chuckle. "You're not wrong though. Coming to Rixon High wasn't all bad."

"Yeah," Bryan snorted. "You got the girl and the football team."

"Asshole," Kaiden leaned over and smacked him upside the head.

But Bryan had a point. When he, Kaiden, and Gav had transferred to Rixon High after their school burned down, nobody could have predicted Kaiden would become the Raiders star player.

"Fucker, that hurt. Peyton, babe, care to kiss it better?"

My brows pinched as I gawked up at Bryan. "Relax, Myers, I'm joking." His smile said one thing, but the intensity in his eyes said something else entirely.

Thankfully, Kaiden and Aaron started discussing strategy for the game tomorrow and Bryan moved along the couch to join them.

Ashleigh slipped into his space and looked at me. "What's going on with you?"

"Me? Nothing, why?"

"I don't know. You seem… I mean, I get it. But you went really tense just now…" She lowered her voice. "When Bryan said that. Did something else happen with you two?"

"No, I just…" I couldn't tell her the truth, that I was thinking of Xander, of what he might say if he saw Bryan flirting with me.

"And this Carrie-Anne thing… that's what exactly?"

"I don't know," I said. "I felt bad... she had no one to go to the game with. And she stood up for me with Layla."

Ashleigh's brows knitted together. "If Layla is giving you a hard time, you should have told me. I'll deal with Layla Hannigan."

"She's just jealous because Sean dumped her and came after me again."

"I still can't believe he and Bryan—"

"Did somebody say my name?" Out of nowhere, Bryan slung his arm around Ashleigh's shoulder and grinned at us.

"Is it possible to love yourself any less?" she grumbled.

"You're talking to high school football royalty, baby." He flashed her a toothy grin.

"God, make it stop." She swatted him away, shirking out of his hold. "I need a drink."

"Your loss," he called after her.

"You're such a goofball," I said.

"But you dig it, right?"

"I..."

"Ouch. She hesitated." He fell back against the couch, clutching his heart and pretending to be wounded.

"I told you already, you're punching above your weight with Peyton, bro," Aaron winked at me. "You should lower your expectations to somebody else. Someone like... Carrie-Anne, for example."

Bryan shot up, frowning. "Seriously? That is never going to happen. Not in a million years. She's... annoying."

"Have you met you?" Kaiden chuckled.

"I think there's more to her than meets the eye," I added, and everyone looked at me.

"Oh shit," Bryan gawked at me, "tell me you didn't invite her tomorrow in some lame attempt to set me up with—"

"What? No!" I lied. "As if I'd ever do that."

"Good," his eyes darkened, narrowing right on me, "because I'm not interested in her."

He didn't finish his sentence out loud, but I saw the words written on his face.

I'm interested in you.

CHAPTER TWENTY

Xander

"KAIDEN?" I said, noticing he hadn't followed the rest of the team out onto the field. "What's the matter?"

"I'm not sure I can do it."

My brows knitted as I sat down beside him. "Do what?"

"Go out there... lead them." His eyes flicked to mine, nervous energy rippling off him as his leg bounced up and down.

"I feel like I'm going to puke, Coach."

"Nah," I clapped him on the back, "you've got this, Thatch."

"But what if... what if we lose? What if I screw it up?"

"Not possible." I shook my head. "No one has worked harder than you this season, Kaiden. You're a great player and an even better leader."

He exhaled a long steady breath, rubbing a hand down his face. "I want to win. I want it so fucking much. But I feel like I'm losing it."

"Hey, hey," I gripped his shoulder, "you've got this.

You're ready for this. Do you really think Jase would have entrusted the team to you if you weren't?" I smirked, and Kaiden returned it with a weak smile.

"Listen. Whatever happens out there tonight, whether we win or lose, as long as you know you gave it your all, that's all you can do. Either way, you got us here. And you deserve to be here, you hear me?"

"Y-yeah." The color slowly returned to his cheeks. "I can't believe I'm freaking out like this."

"It happens to the best of us, kid. You think Jase hasn't puked in a trash can before a big game?" I stood, offering him my hand. "Now come on, you're no good to the team sitting in here."

He took my hand and let me pull him up. "Better?" I asked, and he nodded.

"Thanks, Coach, for everything."

"It's all part of the job." I winked, hooking my arm around his shoulder and leading him out of the locker room into the tunnel. "Hear that? That's all for you, Kaiden. Soak it up."

His eyes were wide with awe as we stepped out onto the field. Jase caught my eye, frowning as he mouthed, "Problem?"

"It's all good," I mouthed back, shaking my head slightly. "Ready?"

"I think so, Coach. Thanks."

"Good, now get out there and show everyone why we're the best; why you're the best, kid."

He jogged off toward the team, then slowed down and turned around to face me. "Hey, Coach?"

"Yeah?" I called.

"I couldn't have done it without you." He grinned before joining the rest of the team, like he hadn't just punched me in the damn chest.

THE ATMOSPHERE WAS ELECTRIC, the fourteen-thousand strong crowd like a constant boom of thunder as the team went head-to-head with Bridderton.

"They've got this," Jase murmured from beside me, one hand squeezing my shoulder and the other gripping his playbook like it held the secrets of the universe.

"Run, RUN," he yelled, jogging along the sideline as Cole took off, sprinting with the ball.

"Go, GO," the words seemed to echo from all directions as the sea of red and white jerseys closed in on him.

Forty... thirty... twenty...

"Run. *RUN*!" Jase was coiled as tight as a spring watching his player duck and dodge their defensive line.

"He's got it... he's—"

"Touchdoooown!" The announcer's voice was drowned out by our spectators as they celebrated the third touchdown of the game.

"Yes. YES!" Jase thrust his clenched fist in the air, shooting me a shit-eating grin. "We've got this, we've got it."

He wasn't wrong. The team was dominating the game, executing play after play. Kaiden and his offensive line were an unstoppable force against Bridderton's defense. By the time the fourth quarter rolled around, the championship was so close we could taste it.

"You good?" I asked Kaiden, and he nodded. His face was flushed, his body vibrating with adrenaline. It was hard not to be unaffected. The roar of the crowd, the buzz in the air, the lingering scent of sweat and wet grass.

"You've got this, it's yours," I said, clasping him on the shoulder. "All you've got to do is reach out and take it."

He nodded again, inhaling a bottle of water like it was air.

"Okay, gather round," Jase yelled, beckoning his team in for one last pep talk. "At the beginning of the season, the championship was ours to lose. Ours to defend. And by God, did we defend it. You've put in the work, showed up, and given your all... and we're this close." He pinched his fingers together. "This fucking close. People say it's not winning that matters; but standing here, so close I can almost taste it, I say to hell with that. I don't know about you, but I don't want to go home a loser today. What do you say?"

"We want to win, Coach," Kaiden said, the voice of his team.

"Damn right, we do. We go out there and keep pushing. Keep applying the pressure. And we show everyone in this stadium today why the Rixon Raiders are the best. Why we're the ones to beat." He ran his eyes over every single player, pride radiating in his eyes. "Raiders on three."

Hands piled in as the huddle tightened, shoulder to shoulder, teammate to teammate.

"One... two... three."

The crowd seemed to echo the word with us.

"Raiders!"

"Jase, we need to talk," I said over the noise.

"Later," he grinned, holding his hand around my neck and touching his head to mine. "We did it, we fucking did it, Xan. You and me, there's no stopping us."

Guilt coiled through me. Fuck. I need to talk to him. I needed to tell him I couldn't accept the permanent position. But he was so happy, everyone was so fucking happy.

Some of the guys appeared. Crowding us, bouncing up and down, chanting, '*Raiders, Raiders, Raiders*.'

"We did it, Coach," Kaiden grinned. "We fucking did it."

"Damn right, we did, son. You deserve this, kid. You deserve it so much." The two of them hugged while Lily, and Kaiden's mom watched from the sidelines. The second the whistle had blown, our supporters, friends and family had spilled onto the field to celebrate with us. It was chaos. News crews waited in the wings to interview key players. They'd want to talk to Kaiden no doubt. He'd commanded the field with maturity and precision. Playing far beyond his eighteen years. Bridderton's defense couldn't stop him. He'd thrown pass after pass, letting the ball fly down the field and find his players. He'd even pulled a couple of touchdowns out of the bag. Kaiden had it. He had what it took to go all the way.

"Congratulations," a voice said over my shoulder and I turned to find my brother.

"Thanks," I said. "But it was all of them." Flicking my head over to the team, I smiled.

They deserved it, and I couldn't deny part of me was sorry that I was probably going to have to walk away.

Maybe I could have made it work here, under Jase's direction. Part of me wanted it, but I couldn't do it. I couldn't lie to him anymore than I had already. It was already gnawing away at me. Even if this thing with Peyton didn't go anywhere, I had to walk away from the team. It was the right thing to do—the only thing.

My head was a fucking mess. It wasn't like I could come clean to Jase or my brother—definitely not my brother. Not yet, while I didn't really understand whatever it was growing between us. But if it got out... She'd already survived too much; she wouldn't survive the shitshow that would come with that.

I searched for her in the crowd. She wasn't standing

with Lily, Felicity, and Kaiden's mom; or Mya and Sofia as they hugged Aaron, beaming with pride. She wasn't with Hailee and Ashleigh either who lingered behind Cameron, probably giving the two of us some privacy.

"I'm proud of you, Xander."

My brother might as well have reached into my chest and ripped out my heart.

He was... *proud.*

Fuck, I couldn't remember the last time he'd said those words to me. The broken lost kid in me stood a little taller. But I wasn't a teenager anymore and this moment wasn't going to fix years of tension between us. There was too much unresolved shit, things we'd both said out of frustration, too many things we'd never had the balls to say.

"I should probably go congratulate them," I said, my skin too tight, the air in my lungs too thin.

I needed her.

I needed Peyton.

But when I stalked away from my family and found her, she wasn't alone.

Hughes was spinning her around, the two of them laughing and hugging. Golden blonde hair fell down her back like a river, her eyes wide with pride. Bryan dropped her to her feet and gazed down at her with that look. The way a guy looked at a girl when he wanted more than just their smiles and laughter.

Don't do it. Fuck. He leaned in, sliding his arm around her waist and pulling her closer. Panic etched into Peyton's expression as she stared up at him like a deer caught in headlights. And I stood there... watching them, unable to do anything as another guy—a fucking teenager—kissed my girl.

Yet, she wasn't, was she?

We hadn't made any promises to each other.

Peyton pushed him away, staring up at Hughes with confusion. She said something to him and then backed away, spinning on her heel and taking off into the crowd. He let out a deep breath, running a hand down his face and muttering a string of cusses. His head whipped up, finding me across the field. I dropped my gaze, stalking off in the direction of Peyton. It was a bad idea, going after her. But all rational thought had gone out of my head the second I saw Bryan put his fucking mouth on her.

The constant barrage of congratulations and handshakes made getting through the crowd like wading through mud. But eventually, I reached the opposite side of the field and scanned the bleachers for any sign of Peyton.

But there was nothing.

Fuck.

Where was she?

"Coach," Bryan jogged over to me. "What's up?"

"Nothing," I said, forcing myself to remember he was just a kid. A kid who had far more right to kiss Peyton than I ever did. "Congratulations, Hughes. You deserve it." Squeezing his arm, I gave him a nod. "Don't you have family to celebrate with?"

"My parents couldn't make it." Disappointment etched into his expression. "They... they're out of town."

"I'm sorry to hear that. But you know what they say, when your parents are away—"

"It's time to play." Laughter crinkled his eyes. "You're not like the other coaches." Something passed over his face, but I excused myself, ready to get the hell out of here.

"You'll be at the party tonight?" he called after me.

"Yeah," I glanced back.

He gave me a curt nod and I couldn't place the strange expression on his face.

THE SECOND we entered Bell's, the noise hit us like a tsunami.

"Holy shit," Kaiden breathed from beside Jase.

"Soak it up, ladies," Jase said, beaming with pride as he stepped aside to let the entire team enter ahead of us. He took the time to shake each player's hand and congratulate them individually. A true leader and respected coach.

Part of me envied him, his relationship with the guys, the way they looked up to him.

"Xander," he said, motioning for me to go inside. "We couldn't have done it without you." Understanding passed between us. He'd seen just how nervous Kaiden was, and I suspected he knew what had happened.

I slid my hand against his and gave him a thin smile. "I don't know about that, Coach."

"It's true. You gave him the strength he needed to get the job done tonight."

"Thank you." I gave him an appreciative nod. "But I still need to talk to you."

"Talking can wait." He grinned, as if he knew exactly what I wanted to say. "It's time to celebrate."

I slipped inside and surveyed the bar. The place was crammed full, a sea of Raiders blue and white. Music blasted out of the speakers, people laughing and drinking and celebrating their beloved team's victory.

"Coach, get over here," Kaiden beckoned me over.

"What's up?" I said.

"I just wanted to say thank you, for everything."

"Like I said before, it was all you, Kaiden."

"Yeah, well, we still wanted to show our gratitude." Bryan and Gav burst through the crowd with a yard of ale.

"What the—"

"It's on us," Kaiden grinned.

"Guys, I'm not sure—"

"*Chase, Chase, Chase,*" they all started chanting.

"Is this okay?" I mouthed to Jase who had joined us, along with my brother and Asher.

"It's one night," Jase shrugged, wearing a smug grin, "and technically school's out for the holidays. Besides, last time I checked, you're old enough to—"

"Fine. But just one."

The guys erupted as I positioned myself with the yard glass. "Three, two, one... Drink!" they yelled and I tipped it back, gulping down the beer as quickly as I could.

Done, I wiped my mouth with the back of my hand and rolled my eyes. "You'd better be lining up Coach Ford, Huckley, and Macintosh for their turn?" I said.

"Already on it, Coach." Gav and Bryan disappeared into the crowd again.

"Was that really necessary?" I asked Jase, breaking away from the guys to stand with the adults.

"Let them have their fun. They deserve it."

A flash of blonde caught my eye and I looked past my brother and his friends to find Peyton across the bar. In the middle of her friends, she smiled and chatted, but I saw the shadow over her face.

I always saw it.

As if she felt me watching, her eyes lifted to mine, and for that single beat I was ensnared in eyes so blue, the noise, the crowd, and the music all melted away until there was only her and me.

Two lost souls twined with grief and pain.

Her breath hitched but then her lips curved into a full luscious smile.

Fuck.

She was beautiful. Like a beacon of golden light in the

dimly lit bar. I wanted to go to her. It pulsed through me, a steady heartbeat I couldn't ignore.

"Xander?" someone said.

"I... I need to go smoke," I replied to no one in particular, making my way toward the back of the bar. I didn't expect her to follow, but my heart stuttered in my chest when I felt her behind me.

People came and went from the hall leading to the bathrooms, and at the end, a fire exit led to the dark alley. The alley I had every intention of going to smoke in.

I slowed right by the door to the women's bathroom, making a show of retrieving my packet of smokes. My other hand dangled at my side and I felt Peyton brush her fingers against it as she whispered, "it didn't mean anything."

Relief slammed into me.

I hadn't realized how much I'd needed her to say the words until that moment.

I didn't dare look at her. If I did, I knew I wouldn't be able to resist pulling her into the alley with me. Pushing her up against the wall and kissing her the way I'd imagined ever since watching Bryan put his mouth on her.

Peyton lingered, her hand still brushing up against mine.

One of us needed to move. The second voices reached the hall, I broke away, striding for the fire exit. I burst through the door and slipped into the shadows, lighting up my smoke.

What the fuck was I doing?

Everyone we knew was here tonight. Every single person. I needed to keep my distance.

I needed to—

The door swung open again and she stood there, wide-eyed and breathless.

"You can't be out here," I said, dropping my smoke to the ground as I stalked toward her.

Peyton met me halfway, gazing up at me with so much intensity, it was like she'd reached into my chest and fisted my heart.

"I had to see you," she breathed.

"If anyone saw you come out here."

"They didn't." Peyton slid her hands up my chest. "I waited until the hall was empty."

Smart girl.

But it didn't change the fact that anyone could stumble across us out here.

"I didn't kiss him back."

"I know." I dropped my head to hers and breathed her in. "But for a second, I thought maybe you and Hughes—"

"I don't feel that way about him." Her eyes softened.

"I came after you. Back at the stadium, I came after you... You've got me all tied up in knots, Peyton."

"I can't stop thinking about you either... about kissing you again." Her cheeks flushed as she stared up at me through thick lashes.

"Shit," I rasped, my thin rope of resolve fraying. "Come here." Grabbing her hand, I pulled Peyton further into the shadows, pressing her against the wall. Her soft laughter washed over me, her smile snapping the remainder of my control.

Caging her in with my hand against the brick, I slid my fingers along her neck and kissed her. The tiny moan that escaped her lips was like a siren's call and I erased the distance between us, fitting the hard line of my body against her soft curves.

Why did this feel so right?

Why did *she* feel so right?

The questions flew out of my head when Peyton dipped her hands under my sweater and ran them up my chest.

Jesus. Her touch was like kryptonite, threatening to bring me to my knees.

"Peyton," I murmured, licking her mouth, curling my tongue around hers and kissing her deeper.

"More," she purred, pulling me closer. Close enough that she felt my dick straining behind my jeans.

Her eyes went wide as she broke the kiss.

"What is it?" I asked, trailing my mouth down the slope of her neck and nipping her collarbone.

"I want you," she whispered, hesitation coating her words.

"Peyton..."

Days.

She was eighteen in a matter of days.

I brushed the hair from her face and tucked it behind her ear. "Soon," I said.

"You mean after my birthday." Her gaze darted to the ground.

"Hey," I slid my finger under her jaw and tipped her face back to mine. "It doesn't matter, not to me. But it'll matter to everyone else. If anyone finds out..." I didn't finish that sentence because the reality of our situation wasn't something I wanted to think about.

"I hate this. I practically raised myself. My mom killed herself and left me with nothing. And in a week, the state will deem me an adult, but I can't choose who I want to be with?"

"It's not that simple," I exhaled a steady breath.

"I know," Peyton gave a resigned sigh, "but it doesn't make it any easier to accept."

Curving my hand around the back of her neck, I kissed her forehead. "We'll figure it out."

"Promise me, we—"

"Peyton?"

She went rigid in my arms and my eyes shuttered at the sound of Bryan's voice.

"What's going on?" He stepped closer and I released Peyton, turning slightly to meet his confused gaze. "Coach?" His expression darkened.

"Oh my God, Bryan," Peyton stepped forward, but I kept a hold of her hand. Bryan noticed, his sharp glare homing in on our fingers threaded together.

"No." He shook his head, backing away. "No way! She's... and you're..."

"Bryan, please." Her voice cracked as she pulled away from me and went to him. "I can explain."

"You're fucking her?" Anger flared in his eyes, and I stepped forward.

"Watch your tone," I snapped.

"Please, stop, Bryan." Peyton put herself right in front of me. "Please. I can explain... just let me explain, okay?"

His eyes cut to me again.

"Go back inside, Xander," she whispered.

"What?" I gaped at her.

"Please, just go." Peyton glanced at me, pleading in her eyes.

"I'm not leaving you out here."

"Fine, then we'll go. Come on," she started leading Bryan back to the door as if she needed to protect him... from me.

Peyton managed to shove Bryan inside, looking back at me for a second before she followed him in.

And I remained rooted to the spot, wondering what the fuck had just happened.

CHAPTER TWENTY-ONE

Peyton

"WHAT THE HELL WAS THAT?" Bryan seethed the second the door clicked shut behind us.

"You can't tell anyone," I rushed out, "you have to promise not to—"

"He's like thirty or something," Bryan pinched the bridge of his nose. "Are you... together? Is that why you acted weird earlier when I..." Hurt flashed in his eyes and I hated myself.

"I never meant to hurt you."

He scoffed at that. "But Chase, really? He's a teacher—"

"He's not, not really."

"Like that matters. You're a senior, Peyton. You're not even eighteen. What are you thinking?" Desperation coated every word. "What the hell are you—"

"It wasn't supposed to happen, I swear." Tears pricked my eyes, my heart crashing wildly in my chest. "But after the accident... we..."

"You let him take advantage of you."

"What? No. *No*! It isn't like that. He gets me. He knows what it's like. I didn't ever think he'd feel the same… I swear, I didn't—"

"Stop, just stop." Bryan stepped back, putting some distance between us. If anyone wandered into the hall, hopefully they would just think we were having a lovers spat. Because the last thing we needed was an audience for this conversation.

My eyes flicked to the door. Xander hadn't tried to come back inside, not that I blamed him.

"Don't tell me you're actually thinking of going back out there to him?"

"He would never hurt me."

"Wake up, Peyton, he's fucking a seventeen-year-old. He's sick in the—"

The *crack* of my palm across Bryan's face filled the hall. He stared at me with disbelief, and I snatched my hand back, hardly able to believe what I'd done. "I'm sorry. I shouldn't have done that. But we haven't… he hasn't touched me."

"So, what was that just now because from where I was standing it didn't look innocent."

Guilt sat heavy in my chest. "We've kissed, nothing more."

"Shit, Peyton. This is crazy. You have to know that, right? He's—"

"I care about him, Bryan. I care about him a lot." I pushed the hair from my face as I stared up at him. My friend. One of the few people that I'd let into my life this year. "I know it's a mess and I know you don't understand my reasons, I don't expect you to. But I'm asking you, as my friend, not to say anything. Please?"

"I don't like it. I don't like it at all." Indecision flickered in his eyes.

"I know. But I can't help how I feel."

"You swear he hasn't made you do anything you didn't want to?"

"Bryan," I let out a small snort. "You know me. Do you really think I'm the kind of girl who can be persuaded to do anything she didn't want?"

"Shit, Peyton." He ran a hand over his jaw. "I don't know what I'm supposed to do here."

"Be a friend, Bry," I whispered, stepping closer to him and wrapping my arms around his waist. "That's all I've ever asked."

"A friend. Right." Dejection rippled off him, but he didn't argue with me, pulling me into his chest and holding me tightly.

"I'm sorry I dragged you into this."

"I'm sorry I wasn't the guy you needed me to be."

"Bryan." I looked up at him and gave him a weak smile, my heart aching. "It was never about you."

"I really thought I could win you over. I thought if I put in the groundwork and stayed the distance..."

"I'm sorry. But you'll make some girl really happy one day."

"Peyton?" A meek voice said, and I looked down the hall to find Carrie-Anne standing there, glancing between Bryan and me.

Crap. The universe was really out to mess with me tonight.

"Oh, hey, Carrie-Anne. We were just... I got a little upset." I untangled myself from Bryan's hold and put some distance between us. "But I'm okay now."

"Oh, I... I think I'm going to head home."

"No, don't do that," I blurted. "Bryan was just about to go get another drink. Why don't you take Carrie-Anne with you?"

"The fuck?" He glared at me with clenched teeth. I nudged his arm and whispered, "Please."

His eyes fixed on mine and he gave a small shake of his head in disbelief. I knew what he was saying. That I was demanding too much. But he'd do it, because it was me asking. "You thirsty, Trombley?"

Her eyes lit up but if Bryan noticed, he didn't react. "I guess I could stay for one more drink."

"You should," I said, shooting her a warm smile. I wanted to suggest Bryan could show her the Raiders cabinet full of newspaper clippings and paraphernalia, but I didn't want to push my luck.

He reached Carrie-Anne and glanced back at me, mouthing, "You owe me."

I nodded, and I knew he didn't only mean for playing babysitter to Carrie-Anne.

"Thank you," I mouthed back.

They disappeared back into the bar, but I remained, needing to catch my breath for a second.

I waited to make sure the coast was clear, and then slipped back outside to explain everything to Xander.

But as I scanned the shadows, I realized he was gone.

Xander didn't return to the party. I spent the next hour on tenterhooks, keeping one eye on Bryan while I searched the bar for any signs of him.

"Who do you keep looking for?" Ashleigh asked me as we stood with Lily, Kaiden, Poppy, Sofia, and her brother.

"No one," I said dismissively.

"Is it Bryan and Carrie-Anne? Because I thought you were trying to set them up."

"I was... do they seem to be hitting it off?"

"You have seen them, right? It's got disaster written all over it."

I glanced over at the two of them. Bryan was talking to Gav while Carrie-Anne lingered at his side looking every bit as uncomfortable as he did.

"Ugh, I should probably go over there," I said.

"Uh, yeah you should." Ashleigh gave me a small nudge and I approached them.

"Hey, are you enjoying the party?"

Carrie-Anne's eyes darted around me. "I'm not sure I fit in here."

"Sure you do. You know you didn't have to stay over here with Bryan and Gav, you could have joined us."

"I didn't... I mean... I wasn't..."

God, she was so nervous.

"I get it. It's a lot."

"Yeah." She nodded, tucking a strand of her mousey-brown hair behind her ear.

"Come on," I said, motioning toward my friends. "Come talk to us."

Bryan looked up then, frowning. "What's going on?" he asked.

"Well, since you're both doing a stellar job of ignoring Carrie-Anne, I'm rescuing her." Lacing my arm through hers, I pulled her away, but Bryan wasn't done.

"We need to talk," he said, and I flinched, inhaling a sharp breath.

Carrie-Anne noticed, her brows furrowing.

"Not here," I replied thinly.

Bryan reached for me, grabbing my arm. "Peyton, we need to—"

"I said *not here*." I shrugged him off and guided Carrie-Anne away, but she stopped me before we reached my friends.

"What's wrong?" I asked.

"What's going on with you and Bryan?"

"What do you mean?"

"Oh, come on, Peyton. I'm not stupid. He's into you. Everyone can see that."

"Carrie-Anne, that's not—"

"It's okay, I get it. You don't like him like that so you thought you'd try and push him toward... someone else."

"I just thought... I'm sorry."

She shrugged. "It is what it is. Deep down, I knew a guy like Bryan would never be into a girl like me."

"It was a dick move," I said. "But I've watched the two of you in class. There's something there."

"Yeah, it's called he thinks I'm a pretentious nerd and I think he's a conceited jock."

"Why did you agree to come then?"

"Because for one night, I wanted to know what it was like to be seen."

"Carrie-Anne... people see you."

She gave me a weak smile. "We've been in the same class since ninth grade and this semester is the first time you've ever talked to me."

"I'm sorry." Shame burned through me.

"It's never really bothered me before."

"What changed?"

"It's senior year. I don't want to graduate with all these regrets." Her gaze flickered to Bryan.

"You should tell him."

"E-excuse me?"

"What have you got to lose?" I smiled.

"Uh... everything."

Soft laughter bubbled in my chest. "Don't be ridiculous. The worst that can happen is he can say he's not interested. But you'll never know if you don't tell him how you feel."

"I wouldn't even know what to say... besides, I'm not you."

"Bryan knows I don't like him like that. We're friends, *just* friends."

"I don't know... you saw what just happened. He practically ignored me the whole time."

"He's a guy. They're kind of dumb when it comes to girls." I smiled. "Just think about it. You might be pleasantly surprised."

Bryan flirted with Carrie-Anne; I'd seen it. There could be something there, and he deserved to be happy. They both did. The fact they were polar opposites wasn't a bad thing.

"I'll think about it," she said. "But can I ask you something?"

"Sure."

"If you think Bryan's such a good guy, why have you written him off so easily?"

I looked at Carrie-Anne and inhaled a sharp breath. "Because when it's not there, it's not there."

And when it was, it was.

Bryan was a good guy. One of the best guys I knew. But he wasn't the guy I wanted.

He wasn't Xander.

FOUR DAYS LATER, I hadn't seen or heard from Xander. I knew he couldn't exactly turn up at the Ford's house asking to see me, but I thought... I didn't know what I thought.

I just needed to know we were okay, that Bryan discovering our secret didn't change anything.

It was hardly surprising that when Felicity yelled I had a visitor my mind instantly went to Xander. Deep down, I knew it wasn't him, but it didn't stop my heart from fluttering as I leaped off the bed and fluffed my hair, imagining what it would be like to discover him at the door waiting for me.

He'd come inside and tuck me into his side and declare to everyone that we had something to tell them. Naturally, they would be surprised at first, but once they saw how serious we were about each other, they would understand. Then we could be together without fear of recrimination or judgment from the people closest to us.

"Peyton?" Felicity said, and the image shattered, sending a shiver through me.

It would never be like that because life wasn't a fairy tale. It was hard and messy, and it hurt, and I knew everyone would freak when the truth came out.

But all I'd ever experienced was a life of neglect and disappointment. Was it so wrong to want something for myself? Was it so wrong to want Xander, the one person who got me better than anyone else?

"Hey," Bryan stood at the door, hands in his pockets, bundled in his jacket and scarf. "I was hoping we could talk."

"I... uh, sure."

"Wanna get something to eat?"

"I'm working at five, so we could eat at Cindy's before my shift?" That sounded a damn sight better than having this conversation in the house where too many people could overhear.

"Let me just grab my purse and jacket," I said. "You can wait inside."

"Come in, Bryan." Felicity beamed, shooting me a knowing glance. From the faint smirk on her lips, I knew I was never going to hear the end of this.

I rushed upstairs and grabbed my things, praying that

she wouldn't pry too much. I trusted Bryan, but what if he'd decided that the right thing was to tell someone about what he saw?

"Okay, I'm all set."

"Have fun you two."

There was far too much suggestion in Felicity's voice.

"Cindy said she might need me to stay until lock up, but I'll text, okay?"

"If you need a ride home, call Jason."

"I'll be fine,"—they already did enough for me—"but thanks." I ushered Bryan out of the door and followed him to his car.

"Peyton, I—"

"Not yet," I said, slipping past him and climbing inside.

I knew this was coming, and yet, my heart still drummed at the prospect of talking about it.

Bryan knew.

He could wield that knowledge against me. Against Xander. If he was anyone else, someone with less morals or pure intentions he could use it as leverage.

But of all the people who could have found us the other night; in a way, I was glad it was him.

"Go on then, whatever you want to say, spit it out," I said, the second the car rumbled to life.

"Shit, Peyton... I don't even know where to start."

"If you came to try and talk some sense into me, you wasted a journey. I know the risks, Bryan, it doesn't change anything."

"He's ten years older than you, have some sense—"

"Age is just a number."

"So you're telling me you wouldn't freak out if Lily or Ashleigh or Poppy came to you and told you they were dating a guy ten years older?" His eyes slid to mine and I pursed my lips.

Of course I'd freak out.

But I also liked to think I would give them a chance to explain before jumping to conclusions.

"This is an unusual circumstance," I huffed.

"Because you almost..."

"Died. I almost died." I flinched, shame nipping at my heels. "You can say it."

"You're fixated on him. You've got some kind of hero worship—"

"He saved me. He pulled me out of the river and saved me, Bryan. Of course there's a connection there. But it isn't just about that. Look," I let out a deep sigh, "I don't know how to explain it."

"Try, Peyton. Try for me. Because I spent most of yesterday trying to weigh up if I was doing the right thing not telling anyone."

"Bryan, you promised." Panic welled inside me.

"I know, and I don't want to break your trust." His expression softened. "But this isn't right, Peyton."

Bryan found a parking space on the road near the diner and cut the engine, running his hands around the steering wheel. "Where do you honestly see this going? You're a senior with your whole life ahead of you, and Xander is... you've heard the stories. He's unpredictable and isn't exactly looking to settle down. You can't trust him, Pey."

I jerked back as if he'd slapped me. "That's not fair. You don't know what he's been through..."

"And you do?" He chuckled bitterly. "Wake up, Peyton. He's grooming you. He's—"

"Stop, just stop. It isn't like that. I..."

"What? You what?" His eyes drilled holes into the top of my head, but I couldn't meet his eyes.

"I don't have to pretend with him. I don't have to plaster on a smile. I don't have to keep trying to be somebody I'm not. There's a reason I keep people at arm's length, Bryan. I'm broken." *Irrevocably, irrefutably broken.*

"Peyton, that's not—"

"Stop trying to tell me how I feel." The words came out in a rush of frustrated breath. "I have spent years perfecting my armor, but for the first time in my life I feel like I can finally let my walls down."

Because Xander knew. He knew what it was like to stand on the outside always looking in.

I'd been the pretty one, the popular one who liked to flirt with the guys and enjoy herself. But that girl was a fake. She was a ruse, hiding a life's worth of pain and fear of never being good enough.

The girl Bryan had fallen for didn't exist. He'd fallen for the ideal. The girl I pretended to be to hide the cracks, to mask the life that had chewed me up and spit me out.

He released another heavy breath, his eyes flicking to mine. "You're sure he didn't—"

"Bryan, I swear to you. I want this..." My eyes dipped and lifted back to his slowly. "I want him. He's not pressuring me. If anything, I'm the one pushing for this more. He's a good guy."

"Fuck." He shook his head as if at war with himself. "Okay."

"So you won't tell anyone?" I held my breath awaiting his answer.

"No, I won't tell anyone. I don't like it, but I think I get it... you can't help who you fall for."

"Thank you." The air was thick around us, filled with regret and guilt.

"I just wish it could have been me," he said quietly.

"I know. I'm sorry."

Bryan shrugged, offering me a half-smile that didn't

reach his eyes. "You deserve to be happy, Peyton. But it isn't going to be easy with him. You know that, right?"

"I know." But was anything worth having easy?

"So what happens now?" Bryan searched my face, but I didn't have all the answers, not when there was so much still to figure out.

"Actually," I said, an idea forming in my head. "Can you do me a favor?"

"Why do I not like the sound of that?"

"Please… for me?"

It wasn't fair to use his feelings for me against him, but I didn't have anyone else to trust with this.

"Fine." He shook his head. "Just tell me what you need."

CHAPTER TWENTY-TWO

Xander

THE KNOCK at the door was unexpected. No one visited me at my apartment except delivery people bringing me pizza or Chinese takeout, and I'd cooked my own meal this evening.

"Just a minute," I called, running the towel through my hair again. My shorts hung low on my hips as I padded to the door and opened it. "Yeah—Peyton?"

My heart almost exploded out of my chest. "What are you doing here?"

"Can I come in?"

"I… uh, yeah… come on." I stepped aside and let her pass, sticking my head outside to make sure no one had seen her. My eyes landed on the familiar car backing out of the parking lot.

"Hughes brought you here?"

"He gave me a ride home from work. I asked him to make a detour."

Jealousy burned through me, laced with something else. Something I didn't want to think about.

"What are you doing here?"

Peyton winced at the sharpness in my voice, but she wasn't looking at me. Her eyes were fixed firmly on my chest, her cheeks burning bright red. But it was nothing compared to the fire I felt searing into my skin as she drank in her fill of my body.

"I'll grab a shirt," I murmured, making a beeline for my bedroom.

What the hell was she doing here?

I hadn't stuck around at the party after Bryan discovered us outside in the alley. It was cowardly, running away like that, leaving her to deal with the fallout. But I knew if I stuck around, I'd end up doing or saying something I regretted.

So I left.

Being caught was a sobering reminder that this—us—was a mistake. If Bryan told Jase... I didn't even want to imagine what would happen.

But the fact Peyton was the first one to show up here suggested Hughes had kept our secret. For now.

"Can I get you a drink?" I said, stepping back into the living room. Peyton looked all kinds of awkward standing there.

"I didn't come because I needed a drink, Xander. We need to talk," she said, lifting her chin slightly, determination glittering in her baby blues.

"Yeah, I guess we do." I motioned to my couch, and she sat at one end while I took the other.

"Bryan isn't going to tell anyone."

"That's... good." I ran a hand through my hair. "That's good."

"Yeah." She gave me an uncertain smile. "And now it

means we'll have someone to cover for us."

"What do you mean?" I frowned. Because surely she didn't mean...

"He gets it," she said. "He'll cover for us. I can say I'm hanging out with him, and we can... spend time together."

"Back the fuck up, you asked him to do that?"

"Yeah, I mean... I thought... You're angry." Disappointment washed over her as she pressed her lips together.

"I... shit, Peyton. I don't know what to say. Bryan finding out wasn't a blessing, it was a reminder that this can't work." It could never work, and I was a fucking idiot for thinking it could. "If he tells Jase or—"

"He isn't going to. We talked. He understands."

I scoffed at that. "And why do you think he agreed?"

"What?"

"Why do you think he offered to keep our secret?"

"Because he's my friend."

"Are you really that gullible? He's just waiting for you to realize that this isn't what you want..." Confusion clouded Peyton's eyes and I added, "He's biding his time to swoop in and comfort you when it all goes to shit."

Because it would, I realized that now.

I had nothing to offer Peyton. She was a senior with her whole life ahead of her. She needed encouragement to chase her dreams, not a reason to be shackled to Rixon.

That's what I would become.

A burden.

An obligation.

She would use me as a reason not to go after the things she wanted. I didn't ever want to become that to her, not after all the shit with my brother.

"What are you saying?" It came out tight.

"We were lucky it was Bryan who found us." I glanced

away from her, unable to stand the hurt in her eyes. "We can walk away now and—"

She bolted off the couch, staring at me with utter disbelief. "Walk away? You want to... end things?"

"Peyton, be reasonable. Bryan saw us." I'd seen the look in his eyes, the absolute disgust. It would be ten times worse when Jase and my brother found out. We would become a local scandal; *Peyton* would become a local scandal. I couldn't do that to her, no matter how much I wanted her. She deserved more. She deserved to walk around town with her head held high. She deserved to be taken on dates without fear of being sneered at, pointed at, and laughed at. She deserved a relationship she wouldn't have to defend at every turn.

Peyton wanted this now, but would she still want it when she was the main source of town gossip?

I'd spent ten years living life as the local pariah. I didn't want that for her.

And deep down, she didn't want that for herself.

She couldn't.

"I can't believe you're breaking up with me," she stared at me with utter disbelief.

"We weren't even together. You can't—"

"Don't, just don't." Her body trembled as she held up her hand. "You're a coward, Xander Chase. And part of me knew... deep down, part of me knew you might run when things got hard. Because that's what you do, right?" She swallowed back the tears collecting in the corner of her eyes. "You sabotage any shot you have at happiness because you're scared... you're scared of never being good enough, of being abandoned again."

Anger lashed at my insides. "You don't have any idea what you're—"

"Please! Spare me the sob story," she heaved a ragged

breath, "I spent years, *years* begging for scraps of attention from my mom, doing anything I could to make her notice me, to care. I watched her do despicable things for her next hit, listened to her..."

A shudder ripped through her. "I spent years thinking I wasn't good enough." Her eyes narrowed, the sparkle dimming until she stared at me with cool indifference. "I let you in. I let you in because I thought we were the same. I thought we could face our fears.... together." She cut me with a scathing look. "I guess I was wrong."

"It's for the best," I choked out, even though every word felt wrong.

I'd been so certain Bryan finding us was a sign, a sign to put an end to this fantasy.

"Well then." Peyton dried her eyes. "I'll see myself out." She stormed toward the door while I just stood there.

This was the right thing, the only decision.

So why did it feel like my chest was cracking in two?

Because you care. You care, you fucking idiot.

I did care—I cared enough to let her go.

Peyton would move on. She would heal and find a guy her own age with similar hopes and dreams, and she would be happy.

She reached the door, hesitating. Waiting for something.

"Peyton," I said, and she glanced back, heartache etched into every line of her face. The knot in my stomach tightened. "I'm sorry."

"Yeah, me too." She slipped into the night, the door swinging shut behind her. The echo reverberated through me, like a gunshot to the chest.

It was for the best.

It was.

So why did it feel like I'd just made the biggest mistake of my life?

"You look like you could use this." Tash slid a glass toward me.

"Thanks," I snatched it up and downed it in one.

"It must be bad," she said, leaning back against the bar. "Harry, another round."

"Coming right up, Tash."

"I didn't expect to see you here this late on a Wednesday night."

"Didn't expect to be here." I nursed my empty glass. Already five drinks in, I felt the warm trickle of whiskey in my veins, but it offered me no comfort tonight.

"Want to talk about it?"

"Not really."

"Since you've been avoiding me, I'm thinking it has to do with the drunk blonde the other weekend."

My jaw clenched, Peyton's face flooding my mind. She'd looked so hurt, so fucking disappointed when I'd told her that it was for the best.

It was a mess.

I was a mess.

"You know, she looked young, Xander. Too young for—"

"Leave it, Tash."

"Come on," she nudged my shoulder, "talk to me. We used to talk about stuff, didn't we?"

I didn't like the suggestion in her voice.

"We can talk. But she's off-limits."

"Aha, so this mood *is* because of the blonde."

My eyes snapped to hers. "I said—"

"Yeah, yeah. I heard you. But I've never seen you like this, Xander. Not over a piece of ass."

Because I'd never cared enough before.

Lips pursed, I met her narrowed gaze, and her expression went slack. "Oh my God, you like her." She let out a low whistle. "Xander Chase has a heart after all."

"Jealousy doesn't look good on you, Tash," I smiled, immediately regretting it. She wasn't the enemy, but I was miserable and drunk, and fuck, I'd messed up earlier.

But when Bryan had stumbled upon me and Peyton in that alley Saturday night, my natural reaction was to go on the defensive. It was my default setting. The way I'd protected myself over the years.

Now it wasn't only my feelings I had to protect, it was Peyton's, and I didn't know what the fuck to do with that. All I knew was she deserved more—she deserved a life I could never give her.

"Ha, you wish." She clapped me on the back. "Been there, got the t-shirt, and I'm not looking for a repeat."

"Good to know." I snorted, unconvinced by her bravado.

Tash was like me. Broken. Bruised by her past trauma. She'd never asked for more, but sometimes I caught her looking at me, wondering. I never brought it up though because I wasn't interested.

"Seriously though, this isn't like you. Do I need to be worried?"

I knew what she was asking. She'd seen me at my worst more than once.

"No, I'm fine," I said.

"Well, okay then," she snatched up her drink and pushed mine toward me. "Drink up and then I'll let you kick my ass at pool."

A faint smile traced my lips. In all the years I'd known

her, Tash had never come close to beating me. But it didn't stop her from being a good sport and playing me.

"You're on," I said, downing my drink. "Harry, a bottle of water, please."

"Water, I'm impressed." Tash teased. "Who knows, maybe there's hope for you yet."

"You rack up the balls, I'm going for a smoke."

"Ugh, I spoke too soon," she grumbled.

"Sorry to disappoint."

The words rang through me. That's all I'd ever been. To Cameron, to my team and Coach, to myself... I was almost thirty years old and what did I have to show for it?

Being with Peyton made me want to do better... to be better. But I'd already pushed her away.

She was right. I'd done what I always did when someone started to get too close, or things started to get too hard.

I ran.

Back then, I'd been too young, too self-destructive to see it. But for the first time in my life, I knew I'd fucked up.

The question was, what was I going to do about it?

"XANDER?" Peyton gawked at me as I entered Cindy's the next afternoon. The whole place had been decked in Christmas tinsel and trinkets. Even Peyton was wearing a small Santa hat attached to a hairpin.

"I mean Welcome to Cindy's." She cleared her throat. "Can I get you a table?"

"Yeah, that would be good."

Grabbing a menu, she motioned for me to follow her. "Is this one okay?"

"It's fine, thanks." I slid into the booth and accepted the

menu from her, our fingers brushing. Peyton sucked in a sharp breath and quickly snatched her hand away.

"Drink? I mean, what can I get you to drink?" A pink blush tinted her cheeks.

"Can we talk? What time do you get off?"

After playing pool with Tash last night, she'd given me a piece of unsolicited advice. She'd grabbed my face in her hands and told me to fix whatever was broken.

It sounded so simple.

I knew it wasn't.

But I also knew that I didn't want to go through life like this. Alone. Bitter and brooding.

What Peyton and I shared was rare. It was ours. And I didn't want to give it up. But I was so fucking scared of the fallout. Not for me. I didn't give a shit about me. But for Peyton.

"I'm working a double. I don't get off 'til late." She shut down that line of conversation, barely looking at me. "Can I take your drink order?"

"I'll take a thick chocolate shake please."

"One thick chocolate shake coming right up." She went to walk away, but my hand shot out, snagging her wrist. "Please," I pleaded.

Peyton's eyes dropped to where I was holding her, cold and detached. The message was clear, and I released her arm.

She was pissed. It was nothing more than I deserved, but I needed her to give me a chance to fix things. To explain.

Before I could get another word out though, she headed for the service counter. My leg bounced beneath the table as I tracked her around the diner. But she didn't look at me. Not until she came back with my drink.

"Are you ready to order?"

"Peyton, come on. I know I—"

"Stop, just stop," she seethed under her breath. "This is my job, Xander. The place where I work. You can't just come in here and do this. It's not fair."

Guilt snaked down my spine. "You're right, I'm sorry. I'll take the Cindy's special with fries, please." I handed her my menu, unable to resist brushing my fingers over hers again.

Peyton's eyes fluttered closed as she sucked in a sharp breath.

"I just want to talk..."

She cut me with a scathing look. "I think you said enough last night."

Peyton avoided me after that, letting the other server bring my food. I tried to get her attention... and failed miserably.

Maybe this was a bad idea.

But I had no other way of seeing her and I didn't want the first time we saw each other to be Christmas Day at Jase's.

After barely touching my food, I settled my check and left. She didn't want to talk to me, fine. But I refused to give up that easily.

So I sat in my truck and waited.

Two hours later, I watched as Peyton slipped out of the diner and glanced up and down the street. I held my breath, half-wondering if she was waiting for someone to pick her up. But no one came. Without thinking, I turned off the engine that had been keeping me warm and climbed out of my truck.

"Peyton," I called, aware of the risk, but it was late, the streets quiet.

She turned slowly, her eyes narrowing with disbelief. "Stalking isn't a good look on you," she snapped.

I held up my hands. "I just want to talk. Please?"

Just like before, a crack of thunder rumbled overhead as the sky lit up with forks of lightning.

"Unbelievable," she muttered.

"It's your call." I inched back, tapping the side of my truck.

"Fine... fine. But you can take me straight back to the Ford's."

Even now, Peyton hesitated to call it home. And I hated that, hated that she felt unable to let herself put down roots there.

But I got it.

I fought a smirk at the way she stomped toward my truck and yanked open the door, slipping inside. I could deal with her attitude if it meant having a chance to at least talk to her.

But I couldn't deal with the thought that I'd lost her, not when I'd only just found her.

CHAPTER TWENTY-THREE

Peyton

RAIN PELTED off Xander's truck like the steady beat of a drum. It was hypnotic. At least, it would have been if I wasn't strung so tightly. I shouldn't have agreed to let him give me a ride. But yet again, a storm had nudged us together.

Maybe it was an omen.

Maybe our relationship—or lack thereof—was a storm. Something we had to weather to find a rainbow on the other side.

It was a nice thought, but it was nothing more than that. Xander had made his feelings about us—about me—perfectly clear last night.

"If you don't want to give me a ride," I said, "I can call Bryan."

It was the wrong thing to say. Xander's hand squeezed the steering wheel so tightly his knuckles turned white as he sucked in a harsh breath.

"You're jealous... of Bryan."

Unbelievable.

"Is this the part where you tell me you don't want me, but you don't want anyone else to have me either? Because if it is, you can save your—"

His hard gaze slid to mine, rendering me speechless. "You know it isn't like that."

"Actually, I don't. Or can't you remember the part where you broke it off? And then reminded me that you weren't ending anything because we were nothing in the first place?" The words poured out in a rush of anger and frustration.

"I fucked up, okay? I panicked..."

"It doesn't matter." I dropped my eyes to my hands.

"It matters. Why do you think I waited tonight?"

I didn't look at him. I couldn't. I wasn't only angry at him; I was disappointed in a way I hadn't expected.

Xander was the person who got it. He was the person I'd confessed some of my deepest, darkest secrets to, and then he'd cast me aside like I was nothing.

He'd compounded every self-doubt and worry I'd ever had.

He'd made me feel worthless.

"Peyton, please—"

"Just take me to the Ford's house, Xander. It's late, and I'm tired." And I really didn't want to do this.

I propped my head against the cool pane of glass. Xander let out a resigned sigh and finally gunned the engine, backing out of the parking lot. I could hardly make out the diner through the sheet of rain, but Xander navigated the streets of Rixon with ease.

Only, he didn't take me back to the Ford's. He took the road out of town, down to the lake.

"Xander..." It was my turn to sigh.

"I made a mistake, Peyton. I got scared." The truck

rolled down the dirt road and came to a stop. Applying the handbrake, Xander turned to me, and I couldn't fight it. I couldn't resist the tether pulling taut between us.

Our eyes collided and my heart fluttered at the intensity in his eyes, the utter regret and desperation.

Stupid foolish fickle heart.

"I didn't tell you this yet, but I'm going to decline Jase's offer to go permanent."

"Wh-what?"

"This—us—is going to upset a lot of people, Peyton. I work at your high school. That's not okay. I'm pretty sure it's beyond not okay. I could be in a lot of trouble, and I can't keep lying, not to Jase."

"Xander, I would never—"

"It doesn't matter. If Principal Kiln chose to make an example out of us, it wouldn't end well for me. Not to mention what it would do to your reputation."

"I don't have a reputation in Rixon." Not a good one anyway.

"You really want to be that girl?" His expression softened but I saw the frustration in his eyes. "The girl who is dating a twenty-eight-year-old guy with no prospects?"

"I don't care about any of that. Besides, you forget that I'm living with my friend's family because I have nowhere else to go."

A shadow passed over his face. "Bryan saw us, and I panicked, and I realized I needed to do the right thing by you and walk away."

"That's bullshit and you know it. I'm old enough to make my own decisions."

"I realize that now."

He did?

I startled. "I'm still angry with you."

"I know you are."

A beat passed while I tried to process what he was saying.

"So you don't want to... stop this?"

Hope bloomed inside me. But hope was a dangerous thing. Too many times, I'd given my mom another chance... and another, and every time, she disappointed me. She hurt me over and over until my hope became a sharp jagged thing I resented.

"No." A faint smile traced his lips. "I knew the second I let you walk out I'd fucked up."

"I know it won't be easy, but nothing in my life has ever been easy, Xander."

"Yeah, I get that." He reached for my hand, tangling our fingers together. "Is this okay?"

I nodded, relishing the feel of his thumb moving back and forth over my skin.

"I'm going to talk to Jase as soon as possible. The sooner he knows I'm not taking the job, the sooner we can figure out how to tell everyone."

"Okay," I whispered. It was what I wanted—to be acknowledged and not secreted away—but I also wanted to enjoy him without the scrutiny and judgment of our friends and family.

"After the holidays," I blurted. "Can we wait until after the holidays? I didn't tell you yet, because I'm not sure if I can, but I asked Mya about graduating early."

"You what?" He went rigid.

"Don't worry, it's not something I'm doing because of... us. I'd already decided I want this. I need my independence, Xander. I need to stand on my own two feet. If the school board says yes, I could graduate as early as the end of January."

Indecision flickered in Xander's gaze, but then he nodded. "Come here." He gently pulled me over the center console and onto his lap. My thighs cradled his legs as I straddled him.

Xander slipped his arms around my waist and held me. "Three days," he leaned in, whispering the words against the corner of my mouth.

"Does it really matter?"

His lips trailed over my jaw and down the column of my neck. Pleasure trickled through me as I arched into him.

"Consider it foreplay," the words formed against the hollow of my neck. "So fucking beautiful."

Xander's fingers drifted over the curve of my breasts, expertly dragging his thumb over my nipples. A moan caught in my throat as I gently rocked my hips, seeking out more friction.

I could feel him, thick and hard, pressed up against my stomach as I moved above him, imagining a much different scenario. One involving less clothes and more skin.

He framed my face with his hands, eyes searching mine, deep and intense. "What?" I whispered, my heart stuttering in my chest so much it felt hard to breathe.

"You slay me, Peyton."

And then he kissed me.

His hand curved around the back of my neck, gripping me possessively as Xander licked and teased the seam of my mouth, coaxing me to let him in. My hands fisted his hoodie as I fell willingly into him, the feel of his lips, the heat of his body beneath me.

"Xander," I breathed, kissing him harder, deeper. Our tongues slid together, slow and searching. Xander's fingers twined in my hair and he yanked gently, giving him better access to trail hot open-mouthed kisses over my jaw and down my throat.

"I must taste lovely," I chuckled, all too aware that I'd just worked a six-hour shift at Cindy's Grill.

Xander met my gaze, pure need glittering there. "You think I care?" He rolled his hips, showing me exactly how much he didn't care.

A bolt of lust shot through me.

"More," I panted.

But I saw the torment in his eyes. Xander wouldn't cross that line. Not here, not yet. But God, I needed him to touch me. I needed something to tamp down the flames threatening to burn me inside out.

Feeling a lick of confidence, I shifted above him slightly and then lowered myself down. Right over him. His throaty growl made my skin vibrate, sending delicious shivers shooting through me.

"Fuck, Peyton." His hands slid to my ass again, pulling my body closer, rocking me against his hard length. "This is dangerous..."

"We're not doing anything." I leaned in, smirking against his mouth as I kissed him. "Not really."

He chuckled darkly, kissing me back with as much desperation as I felt.

This wasn't wrong.

It wasn't.

How could it be wrong when it felt so right?

I hooked my arm around his neck, letting my tongue tangle with his as I rolled my hips, pretending that we weren't separated by layers of clothes. Pretending that he was inside me, loving me.

I tensed.

"What's wrong?" Xander's brows drew together as he searched my face.

"Nothing." I smiled, pushing the overwhelming thoughts out of my head. I dipped my hand under his hoodie, finding the hard plane of his stomach.

"Fuck," Xander choked out. My hand slipped lower,

grazing the slight dusting of hair disappearing into his jeans. But his hand snagged mine, his eyes conveying everything he wouldn't say.

Not here.

Not like this.

Not yet.

"I want to feel you," I whispered, slowly rocking against him.

His eyes shuttered as he hissed out a breath. When they opened again, they were so dark I couldn't see the rings of his irises. Xander buried his hand in my hair, dragging me closer until we were nose to nose.

"When I get inside you for the first time it won't be in my truck."

"It won't?" My voice quivered.

"I want to take my time. To acquaint my hands with your skin, my lips with every curve and dip of your body." He kissed the corner of my mouth, teasing me, making my stomach clench. "I'll lay you out and bury my face in your pussy and lick you until you're begging me to fuck you."

My breath hitched, waves of pleasure building inside me as I rocked above him with reckless abandon.

"Would you like that, Peyton?" he crooned. "Would you like me to fuck you?"

"Yes... yes." I was close. The feel of Xander's dick pressed up against me combined with his dirty words detonated inside me.

"Imagine I'm inside you, imagine me filling you... stretching you..." His mouth moved to my ear, teeth grazing the sensitive skin there. My fingers clutched his hoodie tighter as my body began to tremble.

"Look at me," Xander's hand slipped around the back of my neck again, threading into my hair, anchoring me in place as he stared into my eyes. "I want to see you fall apart." He thrust up and it was enough to make me shatter.

The wave crashed over me and I cried out, my chest heaving as pleasure radiated deep inside me.

Dragging his thumb over my bottom lip, Xander inhaled a ragged breath. "Beautiful," he whispered, burying me against his chest.

I didn't know how long we stayed like that, but when he finally nudged me away, my heart had calmed, and the lust had cooled between us.

"I should probably—" I went to clamber off his lap, but his hand shot out, clamping around my waist.

"What—"

Xander's mouth crashed down on mine, kissing me with so much intensity I felt winded.

When he pulled away, I was flushed all over and breathless again.

"Come on," he said with a knowing smirk. "I'll take you back."

Ellis: What are you doing for your birthday?

I rolled onto my back, unable to stop grinning at Xander's message. After he'd given me a ride back to the house last night, he'd asked for my cell phone and saved his number under Ellis.

When I'd asked him why Ellis, he informed me it was his middle name.

. . .

Me: Lily and Ashleigh are insisting we go for lunch at Sprinkles and then I have a shift at the diner.

Much to Lily's disappointment. But I'd told her—and the rest of her family—that I didn't want any fuss. It was almost Christmas. People had enough to worry about in the way of buying gifts and celebrations, to be worrying about my birthday as well.

Besides, I wasn't sure I could handle being the center of attention for the day.

Ellis: Do you think you can escape for a couple of hours after work?

I bit my lip.

Me: Why, what did you have in mind?

Ellis: It's a surprise. What time do you get off?

Me: Seven.

Cindy always closed early on Christmas Eve to give her staff time with their families.

. . .

Ellis: I'll pick you up.

Me: I'll meet you. Your place?

My cell started vibrating and I hit answer.

"I don't like the idea of you walking across town by yourself." Xander practically growled the words. I had to smother a chuckle at his overprotectiveness.

I'd been taking care of myself for years.

"You live a couple blocks over from the diner." My eyes flicked to the door. Poppy was over at Sofia's, and Lily and Kaiden were hanging out downstairs while her mom and dad did some last-minute shopping.

"I still don't like it."

"Well, I'm not some damsel in distress you need to save... again," I added. "I can walk a couple of blocks, Xander. I'll be fine.

Besides, I didn't want to see him again with diner-scented hair and a layer of grease clinging to my skin.

"Fine. But I want you to call me the second you leave."

"Yes, *Dad*." Laughter swelled inside of me.

"Hey, I might be older than you, but I'm not that old."

This was nice, talking to him, laughing with him like we were just a regular couple. Not that we were... I mean, we hadn't discussed it.

"Peyton?" Concern laced his voice.

"I... what are we, Xander?"

The beat of silence taunted me. And then he said four little words that made my heart flutter.

"Mine. You're mine, Peyton."

"Okay."

"Okay? Is that all you have to say?" he teased.

"I didn't... we didn't talk about it. I didn't want to assume—"

"Hey, this—you and me—it's new and complicated, but I'm not looking to share you with anyone." I heard his unspoken words.

Especially Bryan.

"I don't want to share you with anyone either."

"Good. So, I'll see you on Sunday?"

"Yeah. I'll—"

"Peyton," Lily called from downstairs.

"Shit," I clambered off my bed going to the door. "Lily is coming, I have to go."

I half-expected him to freak, but he didn't. Instead, his gruff laughter filled the line. "Go, I'll see you soon."

"Bye." I hung up and flung my cell down on the desk.

"Peyton?" Lily knocked on my door.

"Hey." I opened it. "What's up?"

"We're going to meet Bryan and Gav down at Riverside. They have that cute little Christmas market. Do you want to come?"

"I'm all set for a Christmas movie marathon." I motioned to my pajamas and fluffy socks. I was going to ask her to hang out with me until Kaiden showed up.

But I didn't begrudge them. She was happy. Happier than I'd ever seen her.

"Are you sure? I feel bad leaving you alone."

"Go, eat all the holiday treats for me." I smiled.

"Ooh, I'll bring some sugar cookies back with me for you."

"Perfect."

She went to leave, but paused at the last second and said, "Is everything okay with you and Bryan?"

"Why wouldn't it be?"

"Kaiden said he seemed a little off..."

"Beats me." I shrugged, the lie coiling around my heart like barbed wire. I hated lying to her. But I wasn't ready to tell her.

The truth was, I wasn't ready to tell anyone.

Because I knew when I did, everything would change.

CHAPTER TWENTY-FOUR

Xander

I SPOTTED MY BROTHER, Jase, and Asher at their usual table at Bell's. A blast of icy-cold wind followed me over the threshold as I fought to close the door behind me.

"Xander," Kel greeted me with a curt nod. "Usual?"

"Yeah, put it on my brother's tab."

He chuckled, giving me a swift nod as I made my way over to them.

"You're late," Cameron grumbled.

"Have you seen it out there?" I unzipped my jacket and slid into the booth beside Asher.

"Yeah, it's blowing up a storm."

"How does it feel finally winning the championship then, Xan?" Asher asked, and a ripple went through the air.

"Seriously?" Cameron balked.

"Relax," Ash waved him off. "It's just a question. High school was a long time ago, right, Xander?" He looked at me and I nodded.

"Although not as long for me as it was for you." I smirked.

"If that's your way of telling me I'm old, get in line. I have enough of that from Aaron and Sofia. Apparently, I'm too uncool to hang with them anymore."

"Imagine if your old man had tried to hang out with you back when we were seniors," Jase said.

Asher shuddered. "Point taken. But I'm way cooler than he ever was."

"How's it going with Ezra?" Cam asked.

He let out a low whistle, tension radiating from him. "It's not getting any easier. You know, I thought we were over this shit, but since his birth mom got in touch, he's confused."

"You still want to go through with the adoption though?"

"Of course we do, he's our son."

"Give him time," Cam said. "He isn't eighteen until the spring."

"I had no idea you were thinking of adopting him," I said.

"Shit, me and my big mouth." Jase ducked his head and took a long pull on his beer.

"It's fine," Asher replied. "You're as good as family." He smiled at me.

I appreciated the sentiment even if it didn't feel that way anymore.

There had been a time, back when they were younger, when I'd looked to Jase and Ash as uncles. They guided me right alongside Cameron. But it was different now. They had their own families, their own kids.

They had their own issues.

"I don't know about you," my brother said to no one in particular, "but I'm ready for a few days off work."

"Things at the center that bad?"

"No, things are great." Cameron managed a fitness center, providing personal training, sports therapy, and coaching. His business had really gone from strength to strength over the last few years, and there had been a time when he wanted me to join him.

But we could barely stand to be in the same room together sometimes, let alone work together. He'd long given up asking me to join the family business.

"I'm just looking forward to some quality time with Hailee."

"Ahhh, work getting in the way of—"

"Ash, for the love of God, that's my sister you're talking about," Jase mumbled.

"And he's been married to her for almost twenty years. They have two kids. You do know how babies are made, right?" Asher's brows waggled.

"Asshole." Jase flicked his beer mat at him.

"It's just hard. Between Hailee's installation at the gallery and my clients, it's not easy to find time to just... be."

"I hear you on that," Jase said. "But now football season is over things should calm down." His gaze lingered on me and I braced myself for the question I'd promised Peyton I wouldn't answer, not yet.

"Where did the years go?" Asher provided the perfect distraction. "One second you're eighteen and think you know everything. The next minute you're raising seventeen-year-olds who definitely don't know everything. Nobody prepared me for this."

"Suck it up, buttercup," Cam chuckled. "They fly the nest, and it still gets no easier. Hailee frets more over Avery now then she ever did when he lived at home."

"Be thankful you don't have kids yet, Xan."

Our booth went silent, and Jase glared at Ash, who

looked at me with sympathy, and maybe even a little pity. Cameron was watching me too, but I didn't acknowledge him.

"Relax", I said, laughing off the sudden awkwardness that had descended over us. "I don't want kids."

"Yet." Asher frowned. "You don't want kids yet."

"Try ever," I mumbled.

"Come on, Xander, you can't know that. One day you'll meet the right woman, she'll knock you on your ass and you'll see a life for yourself that you never dared to imagine." Asher clapped me on the shoulder. "Trust us on that."

"Nah, it's not the life for me." I could barely look after myself, let alone a kid. Yet, my mind went to Peyton. Did she want that? The big wedding, the white picket fence... a family.

Fuck. Hot all of a sudden, I shucked out of my jacket.

"You okay over there?" Jase studied me.

"Yeah, I'm warmed up now."

He gave me a strange look but said no more about it. I didn't want to talk about this. Not now. Not ever. But as the conversation turned to safer topics like the holidays and the NFL season, I couldn't get my mind off Peyton. Of all the things we hadn't talked about—all the things we needed to talk about.

I wanted her.

I wanted her in a way I'd never wanted anyone else.

But I hadn't given much thought to the future. So I'd refuse Jason's job offer and Peyton would graduate early. But then what? I was broke and she had nothing. Those weren't the kind of things you were supposed to worry about in the beginning of a new relationship.

Unease coursed through me as I picked the label off my beer bottle. I knew what the right course of action was. I tried—and failed—to make it happen. But Peyton was the first thing in my life I wanted for me. Not for my brother, or my parents, or the people around me.

For me.

And I was too fucking selfish to give that up.

To give her up.

But I'd never been one to live for the future either… so, where did that leave us?

The next day, after working off a hangover thanks to Asher insisting we stay for another drink and then another, I begrudgingly braved downtown to get some last-minute gifts. It wasn't like I could turn up at Jase's empty-handed. But by the time I got back to my apartment with a trunk full of gift cards for the kids, bottles of wine and chocolates for the women, and an assortment of useless crap for my brother, Jase, and Asher, I needed a drink. I was just grateful most stores offered a gift wrap service because I drew the line at that.

I heaved the bags up to my apartment and freshened up to head back out to The Tap, but the vibration of my cell stopped me in my tracks. I smiled at Peyton's pseudonym.

Blondie: Surprise.

A rustle outside my apartment caught my attention and my heart slammed against my chest. My legs ate up the distance to the door, and I yanked it open.

"Hi." Peyton stood there looking like sin and temptation wrapped up in a blonde and blue-eyed package.

"I know we agreed to see each other tomorrow, but everyone's out again. I was sitting in that house all alone, and—"

I grabbed her hand and pulled her inside and pushed her up against the door. "You're here," I breathed, running my nose along her jaw, ghosting my mouth over her soft pink lips.

"I'm here." She grinned. "Is it okay? I mean, I didn't know—"

"It's more than okay."

The fact she'd had the balls to come here unannounced after the last time... well, it was more than I deserved.

"Were you going out?" Peyton's brow knitted as she took in my jeans and sweater. "You look..." She swallowed.

"I was heading to The Tap."

"Oh." Disappointment flickered in her gaze. "I didn't—"

"Relax," I whispered the word against the corner of her mouth. "I'd much rather be here with you."

Her hands curled into my sweater and she inhaled a shaky breath. "Yeah?"

"Yeah. Are you hungry?"

Shit. Wrong question. Her pupils dilated, heat spilling up her neck and into her cheeks.

"For food." I nipped her jaw, unable to resist the urge to kiss her. Our mouths fitted like two pieces of a puzzle, the slide of our tongues sending a bolt of lust straight through me.

Fuck, this girl.

This beautiful brave girl.

"Xander," she purred, clutching my sweater between trembling fingers. "I want—"

"Ssh," I whispered, kissing away her pleas. She was right. It didn't matter if I had her now; or tomorrow, once she turned eighteen. But it assuaged some of the deep-seated guilt I felt at even being here, kissing a girl ten years my junior.

I knew her age didn't change the young woman inside though. It didn't undermine what she'd been through, what she'd survived. It didn't change the fact that she had experienced more than most adults.

But it would matter to everyone else. It would affect the way people saw us.

Saw her.

My hands slid into Peyton's hair, and I reveled in how soft it felt against my fingers. I had imagined it splayed out on my pillow more than once. God, I wanted her. But I had to be the adult here.

I *was* the adult.

Forcing myself to break the kiss, I took her hand and smiled. "Come on. Let me dazzle you with my cooking skills."

"I thought you didn't cook?" Her brow rose with amusement.

"Ah, you got me there. But I just stocked the refrigerator. I'm sure there's something I can rustle up."

"Do you have eggs?" she asked, and I nodded. "Okay, you grab the pan and some oil. I'll need a bowl and fork too."

"Peyton, you don't have to—"

"I want to. It won't be anything impressive, but it'll taste good."

"You taste good." I leaned in, stealing a kiss. When I pulled away, she let out a contented sigh.

"I could get used to that." I grinned and she added, "now stop distracting me."

"Yes, chef." With a smile, I collected all the things Peyton asked for and hopped up onto a stool, watching as she cracked the eggs into a bowl and started beating them.

"This was my go-to meal back in middle school. Quick, easy, and delicious. I used to experiment, adding whatever we had left in the refrigerator. But my favorite is and always will be ham, onion, cheese, and tomato. Chop these please."

Peyton pushed the ingredients toward me, and I made quick work of chopping everything into small chunks before grating the cheese.

"Perfect." She added everything to the bowl and mixed it all together, before heating a drizzle of oil in the pan. "You can make it into an omelet, but I was never very good at that, so I just scramble it. Tastes just as good."

I tried to keep the frown off my face at the thought of her having to learn how to feed herself at such a young age. But when she glanced up, I realized I'd failed.

"Don't look at me like that. Some kids have to go through worse than I did."

My teeth ground together. "I hate that she didn't care enough."

Peyton gave a small half-shrug. "Do I wish things were different? Sure, I do. But I survived, Xander. I didn't let it break me."

No, she hadn't. But something had broken in her when her mom killed herself. She'd told me as much.

She turned her back to me, focusing on the scrambled eggs. I slipped off the stool and went to her, sliding my hands around her waist and dropping my chin to her shoulder. "You're so fucking strong, Peyton. I hope you know that."

A shiver ran through her and her breath hitched.

"This is nice," she whispered. "It feels like something a normal couple would do."

I read between the lines. A normal couple—we weren't one of those, but it was nice to pretend. I could imagine her, standing here in the morning in nothing but my shirt, swaying her hips to the radio while she made us breakfast.

Jesus. The thought was so clear, so real, it knocked the air from my lungs.

"Xander?" Peyton looked up at me.

"I'm fine." I forced a smile, dropping a kiss to her nose. "Your eggs are burning," I said, releasing her to put some space between us. "I'll get some plates."

I needed to catch my breath and calm myself the fuck down.

Peyton represented everything I'd ever avoided.

Commitment.

Opening my heart—my life—up to another person.

A future.

But watching her do something so simple as cooking us scrambled eggs, I realized I wanted it... with her. Screw society, screw the rules, and the consequences. Maybe I was supposed to save her that night, maybe it was fate's way of giving me everything I never knew I needed.

"Almost done." She glanced over at me and smiled. It lit up my entire dull apartment, a beacon of light in the dark. "What?" Her soft laughter drifted over to me, and I realized I was just standing there, watching her. In *awe* of her.

Without another thought, I closed the space between us. I hooked my arm around her waist, pulling her into my chest. "The eggs," she protested.

"The eggs can wait," my voice was low and rough. I reached around her and turned off the stovetop.

"Xander, I thought you were—"

I slid my thumb over her lips, silencing her. My mouth followed, licking and teasing. Peyton melted into me, folding her arms around my shoulders and kissing me back. Sliding my hands around her thighs, I picked her up, and she wrapped her legs around me.

"If you want to stop," I wound one hand into her hair, gently pulling. "Now is a good time to tell me."

"I want you," she said. "I think I've wanted you since that night you pulled me from the river."

Inhaling a shaky breath, I carried her into my bedroom, kicking the door shut behind me. Peyton ran her mouth over my jaw, trailing her warm tongue down my throat, grazing her teeth over my stubbled skin.

"I love this," she purred, scraping her fingernails along my jaw. "I love how it feels."

Fuck. I was so hard that I wasn't sure I was going to be able to last, and I wanted to take my time with her. To map her body and learn every dip and curve, every sensitive part of her. I wanted to discover where to touch and lick and kiss to make her blush, to make her scream my name.

I didn't make it to the bed, pushing her up against the wall, caging her in with my body. She stared at me with big open eyes, fire simmering in the middle of two blue pools of ice. Raw, aching, unwavering. No words passed between us as I ran a hand from her throat, down her body, squeezing her tits hard enough to make her gasp. My hand slipped lower, down the flat of her stomach, only stopping when I reached the waistband of her leggings.

She nodded, silently giving me permission, and I dipped my hand inside, finding her wet and wanting.

"God," it was a throaty purr as I slid two fingers into her. Peyton moaned, arching into my hand, demanding more. "Xander..." Her hand went to my jeans, trying to palm me through the denim. But I nudged her away. Needing to keep a leash on my control.

"Ssh," I crooned, licking my tongue up her throat and jaw, kissing her deeply. "I've got you."

She began riding my hand, rolling her hips in time with my thrusts. Shallow at first and then deeper, stretching her.

I added my thumb, circling her clit in perfect synchrony. I hadn't even gotten her naked and I was rock hard, desperate to feel her tight around me.

"I'm gonna... God..."

I swallowed her moans, plunging my tongue deep into her mouth, dragging every inch of pleasure from her that I could. Her body trembled around me as my name fell from her lips like a prayer.

Xander... Xander... Xander...

It was the best fucking thing I'd ever heard. I didn't give her time to come down, spinning us around and walking her to the bed. Peyton landed with a soft thud, staring up at me through lust-heavy eyes. Weak against her spell, I pulled off my t-shirt and unbuttoned my jeans, letting them fall to the floor.

"You sure?" My voice was thick.

Peyton nodded, and I dropped a knee to the bed, so I could lean over and pull off her leggings and panties. A shiver rolled through her.

"Sit up," I said, and I helped remove her t-shirt and bra.

She looked like an angel, laid out before me, a halo of golden hair fanned on my pillows.

"You're so fucking beautiful," I said. But then something drew my eye. A small scar on her inner thigh. My finger grazed the healing skin.

"Xander..." Panic rose in her voice.

"It's okay." I smoothed my thumb over the imperfection, swallowing the giant fucking lump in my throat. "We all have scars, Peyton."

CHAPTER TWENTY-FIVE

Peyton

RELIEF SANK into me and I exhaled a shaky breath. I'd forgotten all about the scar, too lost in the feel of Xander touching me, the way he kissed me like he couldn't get enough.

The air crackled around us, the tether between us snapping taut as Xander crawled over me, his eyes flicking to the clock on the nightstand. I glanced at it, noticing the time. Almost ten.

"We can always wait two hours," I teased, knowing he'd wanted to wait until my birthday.

He gazed down at me, hunger simmering in his eyes. "I've waited long enough," he growled, fitting his body over mine. Hard planes to soft curves. A shiver ran through me as my hands ran up and over his shoulders, marveling at his corded muscle. His body was a work of art I wanted to admire and study. But when his lips found the hollow of my throat and trailed downward to dip between my breasts, all thoughts flew out of my head.

"Xander," I breathed, delving my fingers into his hair and arching my body into his mouth, needing more.

His tongue swept over the curve of my chest, licking and sucking, grazing his teeth over my nipple. A moan caught in my throat, heat coiling deep in my stomach. I hitched my legs around his waist, trying to rub against him, desperate for the friction. But Xander kept just out of reach, taking his weight on his arms.

I needed him now though before he realized this was a terrible idea and built the walls around his heart again.

"Xander." I tugged the ends of his hair, forcing him to look at me. "I want to feel you inside me."

His eyes darkened as he forced out a steady breath. "If we do this..."

"I know." I swallowed.

He was stalling. I'd known it the second he pressed me up against the wall and refused to let me touch him. It was his last attempt at maintaining some shred of control. Because if we crossed this line, we both knew there would be no going back.

But what he didn't know was, I didn't care about any of that.

I only cared about this, us. Together.

"I'm on birth control," I blurted, wincing at my sudden outburst.

"Shit, Peyton." He ran a hand over his jaw as he smothered a groan, one caught somewhere between frustration and need.

My cheeks burned as I said, "I don't want anything between us." Not now. Not ever.

He grasped himself and shifted forward, running his dick through my wetness. I failed to keep the moan in my throat. It felt so good, and he wasn't even inside me yet.

"I want to take this slow... but you're so wet and I've

dreamed about this." He kissed me softly, moving his lips to my ear. "I've imagined fucking you bare. God, Peyton, I need inside of you." He pressed the tip just inside and stilled, staring down at me. "No going back."

"No going back," I whispered, and Xander filled me in one smooth stroke.

Shocks of pleasure rippled through me as he circled his hips a couple of times before dragging his dick out and rocking back into me. "Fuck," he hissed, burying his face in the crook of my neck, kissing and sucking the skin there.

My body slowly adjusted to the feel of him, and I began to match his thrusts until we moved as one. Xander urged my legs around his waist so he could go harder... deeper... pushing me toward some place I wasn't sure I'd ever been.

I'd had sex before. I'd learned what I liked and didn't like, but this was... this was different. Xander knew things. He knew how to angle his hips to make my breaths come in short, sharp bursts. He knew how to ride my body in a way that made me beg for more.

He knew how to touch me, to kiss, and caress me in a way that made my head spin.

"God, it feels... *God*!" I pressed my lips together, trying to stop the needy moans from spilling out. But it was too much, too intense.

He was everywhere. Our skin slick with sweat, our kisses hungry and desperate. Xander fucked my mouth with his tongue matching the sure steady strokes as he moved inside me.

"You feel so good," he breathed against my lips. "So fucking good." His hands slid under my ass, tilting my body toward him as he went faster, hitting me at just the right angle.

"Xander... God," my legs began to tremble, an intense wave of pleasure rising inside me.

His thumb found my clit and sent me flying over the edge.

"I can feel you coming, choking my dick... Peyton... *fuck*!" He breathed the words against my neck before fixing his mouth onto mine and kissing me deeply. "I'm close... fuuuuck..." Body tense, a low groan rumbled in his chest as he jerked inside me.

For a second, there was silence. Nothing but our racing hearts and ragged breaths. Xander leaned down, brushing his nose over mine, and I let out a sigh of contentment as he captured my mouth in a soft kiss.

"That was..."

"Yeah." His eyes shuttered before settling on mine once more. "Are you okay?"

I nodded.

I waited for it to become awkward, for him to retreat into that place inside himself. But the night was full of surprises.

"Wait here," Xander pecked the end of my nose before clambering off the bed. I watched as he stalked, butt naked, into his adjoining bathroom. He returned with a washcloth. "Here."

"Thanks." My cheeks burned as I cleaned myself up.

He disposed of the washcloth and slipped back into bed with me, pulling me into his side as he lay on his back. "I tried so fucking hard to tell myself that this was wrong." His voice was thick. "But that didn't feel wrong, Peyton, not a single thing about it."

My fingers drew lazy circles on his chest. "Sometimes you don't choose it, it chooses you," I said quietly.

"What was that?" Xander asked.

"Remember I told you about my neighbor, Mrs. Harrison? Well sometimes when I'd get upset about...

everything, she'd take my face in her bony hands and tell me that."

But I'd never really understood what she'd meant until recently.

I didn't choose to grow up with a loveless mother, just like I didn't choose to find her dead on the bathroom floor. Just like I didn't choose to fall for the man who'd saved me that night.

I didn't know if I believed in life's grand design, but everything that had ever happened to me had led me here, to this moment. And I couldn't find it in myself to hope for anything different.

"I wish I didn't have to leave," I whispered, snuggling closer. My fingers traced the script tattoo over his pectoral. I'd noticed it before, but I'd never asked what it meant.

"What does it mean?"

"I was young and foolish and I'm pretty sure I was drunk."

"But what does it mean?"

"After my dad died, I did a lot of soul searching. I was young and I guess some part of me wanted answers. I had both my parents taken from me... it messed with my head." His fingers glided up and down my spine, sending shivers through me. "My therapist at the time talked a lot about acknowledging my grief, giving myself time and space to process my thoughts around losing them. I thought she was talking shit to be honest. But Hailee gave me this book on mindfulness and the same phrase kept coming up in it. Be here now. I don't know, it stuck."

I ran my fingers over the fading ink. "Do you think it helped?"

"I think I've spent the last ten years doing the exact opposite of what it means."

Pushing up on my elbow, I looked at him. "How do you mean?"

"Peyton," he let out a heavy sigh. "I'm almost thirty and what have I got to show for my life?"

I didn't know what to say to that. He had his job at Rixon High, but he was going to give that up… for me.

My stomach sank. "Can I ask you something?" He nodded, and I forced out the words. "If you and I weren't… you know, would you have accepted the job?"

"You can't ask me that. You and me did happen and I don't regret it, not for a second."

"But—"

"No buts." He leaned in and brushed his lips over mine. "You make me want more, Peyton. I've never had that before. There'll be other jobs. Other opportunities."

Everything had been perfect, but now it felt like there was a dark shadow hanging over us.

Guilt swarmed the happiness I felt, threatening to blot it all out. "I bet you regret ever walking along the river that night."

"Don't. Don't do that." He gripped my chin, his dark eyes piercing me. "Don't put words into my mouth. You want the truth?" I nodded. "The only regret I have is that things aren't going to be easy for you… because of me. Because of this."

I curled a hand around Xander's neck and touched my head to his. "No regrets, deal?"

"Deal." He exhaled a long, steady breath as if he'd needed to hear me say that. "Get dressed, I want to feed you before I take you back." Xander kissed me swiftly before sitting up.

"Actually, Bryan is picking me up."

He went rigid, glancing over his shoulder. "He's what?"

I sat up, curling my body around his and pressing my

lips to the side of his neck. "Everyone thinks I'm with Bryan. They expect him to bring me back. He's just a friend... a friend we need right now." I kissed him again.

"Fine," he said, and I could sense his disapproval. But if we wanted to see each other over the holidays we were going to need an excuse, one that people wouldn't look too closely at.

Xander pulled on his clothes and collected mine up and placed them on the end of the bed. "I'll give you some privacy." Heat blazed in his eyes as the sheet drifted off my body. "I should..." He swallowed.

"Yeah, you probably should." Desire pulsed through me, and I knew if he didn't leave me to get dressed, we'd never make it out of his bedroom.

Xander gave me a knowing smirk before leaving me alone. I held the sheet to my body, hardly able to believe I was here. It had been everything I'd imagined and more, erasing every doubt I had that this was wrong.

Nothing so wrong could ever feel this right.

Forcing my racing heart to calm, I quickly dressed and tamed my hair into a loose braid. I found Xander at the stove, reheating the scrambled eggs. "Maybe we should throw that out?" I peered around him to look at the half-cooked mulch. "I can make my other specialty instead."

Xander's brow rose playfully, and I swatted his chest. "I'll have you know the perfect grilled cheese sandwich requires a lot of practice."

"I love this." He wrapped his arms around my waist, cocooning me in the strong curve of his body.

"Me too," I said over the emotion welling in my chest.

Xander nuzzled my neck, peppering my skin with tiny kisses.

"I need cheese and bread," I said, wriggling out of his hold. "You sit there and keep your hands to yourself."

"Yes, chef." He winked.

I couldn't think with him so close, and I definitely couldn't make grilled cheese. He was a tempting distraction.

And buried so far under my skin I wasn't sure he'd ever leave.

"I HAVE TO GO," I said, trying to detach myself from Xander's mouth. "He's been waiting ten minutes already."

"Let him wait five more," Xander murmured against my lips, flicking his tongue expertly along mine.

"Xander..." I breathed, pushing his chest gently. "It's late. I need to—"

"Yeah." He broke away, heaving a harsh breath. "I know."

"I'll see you tomorrow though."

"Damn right you will, birthday girl." He trailed a finger along my jaw and pressed a final kiss to my lips. "Tell Hughes to drive carefully, you're precious cargo."

I rolled my eyes at that despite how much it made me swoon. I loved this side of Xander. Protective. Possessive. All growly and broody.

It was hard to believe he could ever want a damaged girl like me. But I felt it every time he looked at me, every time he touched me.

We lingered, fingers brushing, eyes locked unwilling to break away. "I need to go..." I said. Yet still, I didn't move.

It felt like if I walked out now, the bubble we'd formed around us would burst.

"Tomorrow," he said in a low, gravelly voice.

My cell vibrated, splitting the tension. I didn't need to look at my cell to know it would be Bryan.

"Night," I said.

Xander gave me a small nod, his heavy gaze following me as I slipped out of his apartment.

I forced myself to move down the steps and across the parking lot to Bryan's car. Judgmental eyes met mine as I slid inside.

"Don't," I said.

"What? I wasn't going to say anything." A smile played on his lips, but it didn't reach his eyes. "I thought I was going to have to come up there and drag you out."

"We were—"

"Yeah, I really don't need to know what you were doing." His jaw clenched as he forced himself to take a breath.

"Thank you. I owe you."

"Yeah, well, maybe you could not keep me waiting so long next time, and please promise not to push Carrie-Anne on me again. She's... hard work."

Guilt hit me that I'd kept him waiting outside for so long when he was doing so much for me. It hit harder when I thought of his true feelings for me. God, it would be so much easier if he fell for Carrie-Anne.

"Bryan," I sighed, "you don't even know her."

"And I don't want to. If I can't have... well, best not to go down that road. Consider this your early birthday present."

"I am sorry, you know. I never meant to hurt you or let you think that there could be more between us."

"You didn't." His hands squeezed the steering wheel a little tighter. "I just hoped... it doesn't matter. You're with Coach Chase now. Fuck, it's never going to get easier saying that."

"It's just for the holidays, then we'll figure out how to tell everyone."

"You know shit's going to hit the fan, right? I mean, I get you can't help liking him or whatever," he cast me a sideways glance, "but a lot of people are going to be upset."

"I know." It was a small price to pay. Besides, it wasn't like we were wrecking a marriage or destroying a family. Xander had no one—besides his brother and his family—and neither did I. We were two lost souls who had found some measure of peace together.

Surely the people who cared about us would see that. Once they got over the years between us, they would see how we felt about each other.

We rode the rest of the way with Bryan making small talk about his friends and the team. I didn't expect him to understand my relationship with Xander. He was his coach, his mentor. Xander was in a position of authority, entrusted with the welfare of his players, and the other students he came into contact with.

I wasn't stupid. I knew some people would look at us and assume we'd had an illicit student-teacher relationship, but it wasn't like that.

Finally, we reached the Ford's house. Bryan applied the handbrake and turned to me. "What will you tell them?" His eyes went to the house.

"They think you wanted to take me out for a pre-birthday movie."

"What movie did we see?"

"I don't know. I didn't think that far ahead."

"The Wreckage. It's an end of the world movie, something I'd watch."

"Thanks."

"Yeah." His eyes darted away from me.

"Bryan, I—"

"Let's not do this, yeah? I said I'll keep your secret and I will."

"You're a good friend, Bryan." Shouldering the door, I went to climb out, but he stopped me.

"Peyton?"

"Yeah?"

"Happy birthday. I hope you get everything you wish for." He leaned over and opened the glove compartment and handed me a small gift box. "You might as well have this."

Barbed coils of guilt squeezed my heart as I saw the gift.

"I bought it before, well, you know..."

"Thank you." I got out of the car and closed the door, inhaling a sharp breath.

I was a horrible person. The worst. Bryan didn't deserve this. But I also couldn't pretend there was something more there when there wasn't.

Bryan might have only seen me.

But I only saw Xander.

CHAPTER TWENTY-SIX

Xander

I LAY awake half the night, still able to smell Peyton on my pillows, my sheets. Her vanilla perfume was woven into the room, heating my blood.

She'd been perfect in every possible way. But I hadn't expected to feel so stripped bare afterward.

Ever since Mom got sick, when I was just a kid afraid of losing her, people had looked at me with sympathy and pity. Once she'd died, people lost their ability to see me. They only saw my grief and pain and anger at the world. My dad and Cameron tried to shield me from that, to protect me. But it only got worse after Dad died. I was so angry and confused, people's sympathy became tinged with fear. They didn't know how to reach me, what to say to me, and I grew to resent it. Even with Cameron and Hailee. It was like my instinctive defenses worked against me, repelling people rather than attracting them. But I didn't know how to make it stop.

I didn't know how to let them in.

After the shitshow in senior year, everything changed again. People no longer saw a boy damaged by the loss of his parents. They saw a teen who threw it all away, a boy who tarnished his family's name.

I was no longer a victim; I was the villain.

But staring down at Peyton as I'd loved her body, there had been no traces of pity or sympathy or fear or disappointment... I'd only saw understanding swirled with desire. She wanted me. Despite everything, this brave, beautiful girl wanted me.

I didn't deserve it—I didn't deserve her. But it was such a moment of clarity, that it shook the foundations of my soul.

And maybe she was right when she said that you didn't always choose it, that sometimes, it chose you.

I had never expected to become the hero of someone's story... I hadn't wanted it. But when she looked at me, I didn't feel like that lost boy or the cold-hearted man I'd become. I felt alive. For the first time in years, I felt like I could breathe.

I felt like maybe, just maybe, there was something better out there for me.

It was a crazy fucking notion given all the obstacles that stood between us, but I'd never been one to follow the rules, or to conform to society's rules or the small-minded expectations of Rixon's residents. And if losing my parents at a young age had taught me anything, it was that life was too short.

Peyton was my shot at something good, something besides the loveless, bleak life I'd made for myself.

With the sunrise finally peeking in through the crack in the curtains, I leaned over and snatched up my cell.

. . .

Me: Happy birthday. Enjoy your day.

I didn't expect Peyton to be awake yet, but her reply came instantly.

Blondie: It would be better if I was waking up next to you.

She added a wink emoji and I fought a grin. Jesus. She was turning me into a sap. But it was impossible to resist playing with her.

Me: Hmm, I like the sound of that. I can think of a few ways I could wish you a happy birthday…

Blondie: I'm listening…

She was game. And from the state of my morning wood, I was more than willing to oblige her.

Me: I'd pull you into my arms, your back to my chest and slide my hand up your stomach, gently squeezing your tits while my mouth trailed up the side of your neck.

. . .

My blood turned to fire as I fought the urge to palm myself.

Blondie: It feels so good, Xander… I can feel you pressed up against my ass, hard and ready…

Fuck. I fisted myself and hit dial on her number. Her voice, thick with sleep, filled the line.

"Good morning," she said.

"God, I wish you were here right now." My voice was ragged, and I heard her breath catch.

"Are you…?"

"Yeah, is that okay?" Pumping myself harder, I imagined her in bed, naked and ready for me.

"Oh my God," she breathed.

"Are you wet, Peyton? Touch yourself, slide two fingers into your pussy and tell me how wet you are."

She let out a muffled moan. "I'm soaked."

"Fuck, yeah. Finger yourself and imagine it's me. Imagine I'm there, pressed up against you as I glide my fingers in and out, circling my thumb over your clit."

"Xander," she choked out. "God, it feels…"

"Don't stop. I'm close…" My fist tightened around my dick, imagining it was Peyton's warm wet heat.

The little moans and sighs she made were enough to tip me over the edge. An intense tingle shot down my spine and I spurted into my hand, groaning loudly.

Peyton's soft laughter filled the line followed by her ragged breaths. "Oh God… Xander."

"Come for me, imagine it's my fingers you're riding."

Her orgasm hit and she moaned quietly, the sound muffled as if she was pressing her hand to her mouth.

Silence filled the line as we both lay there, in our separate beds, panting and hearts racing.

"That was a surprise," Peyton finally said.

"A good one I hope?" Fuck, I hadn't had phone sex in forever. But I could wake up every morning and do this and die a happy man.

"Very good." I heard the smirk in her voice. "But I still wish you were here... I need you, Xander."

"Tonight." The word almost got stuck in my throat.

"I'm already counting the hours. Crap, I can hear people out in the hall. I should probably go."

"Okay. I'll see you later. Happy birthday, Peyton."

The line went dead, and I dropped my cell onto the bed, shaking my head gently. I was in trouble.

So much fucking trouble.

To KILL SOME TIME—AND avoid moping around my apartment waiting for Peyton to get here—I decided to head to the gym downtown. For almost two hours, I pushed my body to its limits, burning off all the excess energy she triggered inside me.

After a quick shower, I pulled on my hoodie and grabbed my bag and left the gym, walking straight into Bryan.

"Oh, it's you." His lips thinned.

"Bryan," I said, because what the fuck else was there to say?

Disappointment and betrayal radiated from him. I knew he liked Peyton. I wasn't an idiot. I knew it was the only reason he'd kept our secret.

"Okay, this has been swell and all but I'm just going to go." He moved around me, but I snagged his arm at the last second. His eyes snapped to mine, swirling with anger.

"We should probably talk."

"I have nothing to say to you."

"Please," I said. Peyton cared about Bryan, called him her friend. And he was a good kid. I'd seen it more than once when he swooped in to rescue her from the likes of Sean Farrow.

"Fine. I'm meeting the guys at Bell's, but I have time."

"Want to get a coffee?" I flicked my head to a street vendor.

"Sure." Bryan stalked off in that direction, not bothering to wait for me.

He had every right to be pissed at me, but it didn't stop the sting.

When I reached him, he'd already ordered for himself. I placed my order and we collected them and headed to an empty bench at the edge of the park.

"Just tell me one thing," Bryan said, after an awkward beat of silence. "Do you genuinely care about her or is this just some... game to make you feel good about yourself?"

"It's not a game, Bryan."

"So you really care about her?"

"I do."

There was no use denying what I already knew.

"I didn't expect this to happen," I added. "But sometimes you can't stop these things."

"She's just been through so much... and you're... fuck, I don't know how to understand this."

"I fought it, you know?" I confessed. Maybe it was because I needed to talk to someone about it, or maybe it was because of all the people in Rixon, Bryan knew Peyton. He knew how easy it was to be bewitched by her.

"You think I don't know it's wrong, that everyone will look at me and think I'm some kind of...." I couldn't say it.

"Yeah," he agreed, only making the knot in my stomach tighter.

"Peyton isn't like other girls her age, Bryan."

"Is that how you've justified it to yourself?" He let out a bitter laugh. "Because that's some bullshit right there."

"That came out wrong. I just mean... everything she's been through; I understand what it's like to carry so much pain."

Bryan sipped his coffee as he stared out at the park. Fairy lights had been strung up in the dense trees, their trunks wrapped in huge silver bows. All we needed was some snow and it would be the perfect winter wonderland right in the heart of Rixon.

"She said something similar," he said quietly, as if it hurt him to say the words. "Just promise me one thing," Bryan finally looked at me again. "Don't hurt her."

I'd never imagined a scenario where I'd be taking advice from an eighteen-year-old kid, but here I was.

"I'll try not to."

Hurting Peyton was the last thing I wanted. If anything, I wanted to do the exact opposite. I wanted to make her laugh and smile and feel good about herself. I wanted to show her that life wasn't always a battle, that even in the darkness there were flickers of light.

"I guess that's all there is left to say then." He stood up abruptly, looming down at me. Suddenly, I didn't feel much like his elder. Under his narrowed gaze, I felt small.

"I promised Peyton I won't say anything to anyone, but once the holidays are over, if you don't come clean, I will."

I gave him a silent nod. It was a threat, one I had no doubt he would follow through on if I didn't do what he considered to be the right thing.

"If you care about her as much as you say you do, then there should be no problem telling everyone," he said, before disposing of his coffee cup in the trash can and walking away from me.

I let out a strained breath. It had gone better than I expected. It wasn't like I needed his approval or understanding, but he was Peyton's friend, and I didn't want to alienate her any more than necessary from the people she cared about.

Running a hand down my face, I drained my coffee before throwing it away. Slinging my bag over my shoulder, I made the short walk back to my truck, when an idea struck me.

It was Peyton's birthday, her eighteenth birthday and I'd gotten her nothing.

It had seemed too soon in our relationship to commit to buying her something. But Bryan's parting words played on my mind.

I scanned the row of stores. What the hell did you buy an eighteen-year-old girl for her birthday? Usually, I bought my niece a gift card for her favorite store or tucked fifty dollars into her card. But Peyton wasn't my niece, she was my girl.

I'd never done this before though, bought a girl gifts in an attempt to show my affection. Part of me almost wished Bryan hadn't left so quickly, I bet he would know what to get her.

Irritation zipped up my spine. I could do this. It didn't have to be anything elaborate or expensive, just a small token to show her that I was serious about this. About us.

Not that any token would ever do justice to how deeply she'd buried herself under my skin.

"Think," I muttered to myself, "think, idiot."

How hard could it be to pick something out for the girl who had barreled into my life and refused to leave?

The girl I'd hopelessly fallen for.

CHAPTER TWENTY-SEVEN

Peyton

"YOU GUYS," I said as I finally entered the kitchen. I'd avoided coming downstairs for as long as possible. Especially after my surprise morning wakeup call from Xander.

I was still blushing, and it wasn't from the birthday banners and balloons decorating the kitchen.

"Happy birthday, bestie," Lily sang as she came around the island and hugged me. "I thought I was going to have to come up there and drag you out of bed," she whispered.

"I just needed some time." The lie was ash on my tongue.

"Happy birthday, Peyton," Felicity gave me a warm smile.

"Gifts, let's do gifts." Poppy clapped her hands.

"First let's wait for—"

"I'm here," Jason's voice rang out and seconds later he appeared holding a cake box. "Happy birthday," he said. "I hope you're hungry because this thing could feed five thousand."

"Dad!" Lily scolded, flipping the lid on the box. "Gaaah, it's so good."

"What is—oh my God," I breathed. "You didn't."

"Oh, I did. I so did." Her lip quirked.

"My wallet says otherwise," Lily's dad grumbled as he made a beeline for the coffee maker.

"This is amazing, thank you so much." I stared at the giant personalized funfetti cake, completely overwhelmed. I'd never had a birthday cake before, not of my own anyway. And now I had one big enough to feed every single person I knew.

"I was going to make pancakes for breakfast," Felicity said, peering over Poppy's shoulder. "But Jase is right, we might need to start now if we want to make a dent in it."

"Cake for breakfast?" Lily beamed, and I nodded.

"Cake for breakfast."

We gorged ourselves on cake while I opened my small pile of presents. They were mostly gifts I could make use of—and didn't have a lot of spare cash to buy for myself—makeup, some new boots that were warm and sturdy enough for the winter, a hat and scarf. Lily had bought me a gorgeous sweater that was silky soft and a shade darker than my eyes. It would look perfect.

"Thank you so much. I didn't expect all this."

"Nonsense," Felicity said. "Everyone deserves to be spoiled on their birthday." She glanced at her husband, and he sat a little straighter.

"Actually," he cleared his throat, "there's one more thing." He produced a small envelope from behind his back and handed it to me.

"What is this?"

"Open it and see."

They had already given me too much, but the expectancy on their faces had me tearing into the envelope. I pulled out the note. Not a note, a check.

"No," I blurted, unfolding it and scanning the amount. "This is too much," I said, my eyes burning with tears. "This is way too much."

Felicity wrapped her arm around her husband and smiled at me. "We thought you could put it toward a car or a college fund. We know it isn't much—"

"Not much? Mrs. Ford, this is more than I can accept." Twenty-five hundred dollars was more than I could ever dream of. Sure, to them, it was a mere drop in the ocean, but to me, it was everything.

And it was too much.

"I can't accept this." I swallowed down the tears threatening to fall.

"It's yours, Peyton. We want you to have it. And please for the love of God, stop calling us Mr. and Mrs. Ford. You're family now."

I gawked at them, knowing I'd lost the battle. If I didn't cash the check, they would probably resort to more definitive options.

"Thank you." My voice shook. "This is... thank you."

"We know you haven't made a decision about college and we understand, but we wanted you to know you have a small pot of savings behind you. We also talked, and we'd like you to save what you give us for groceries alongside it."

"I... I need to pay my way." It was something I needed to do.

"We know, but it's too much. Instead, we thought you could buy the family takeout every now and again or treat us to a meal out."

"I..."

"Say yes," Lily urged.

My brows pinched. Was she behind this? I hadn't confided in her about most things, but she knew I needed to contribute.

Four pairs of eyes watched me, waiting. Their expectation was almost too much to bear.

"Yes, fine. Fine... Thank you."

"Excellent." Felicity beamed.

Twenty-five hundred dollars. That would be a security deposit for an apartment. Not that I could afford the actual rent payments. But maybe I could if Cindy gave me full-time hours at the diner.

"What are your plans for the rest of the day?" she added.

"I have a shift later."

"But first she promised to get lunch with us at Sprinkles," Lily said.

"You couldn't get the day off?" Jason asked.

"No." Not that I'd asked.

"I can't believe it's Christmas Eve already," Poppy turned the conversation to safer shores. "I still have a ton of gifts to wrap."

"Why does that not surprise me?" Lily replied with a soft chuckle.

"I hope you're ready for the chaos tomorrow, Peyton. There's never a dull moment when the Fords, Chases, and Bennets get together."

"We're not that bad, Mom." Lily gave her a wistful smile.

"Kaiden and his mom won't know what's hit them." Poppy added with a smirk.

It should have been a happy time, a time for joy and laughter, but I only found myself reminded of everything I didn't have... that and the fact I would have to sit with Xander all day and pretend he was nothing to me.

My stomach churned.

"I think I'm going to take a shower," I said, sliding off my stool.

"Good plan. Then we can start your birthday celebrations." Lily gave me a smile.

"Yeah, sure."

As I walked away, I felt them watching me. Felt their pity and concern. It brushed up against me like ice-cold fingers. But I wouldn't let it in.

I couldn't.

Not unless I wanted to fall apart.

"I THINK WE'RE DONE HERE," Cindy said. "Here, this is for you" She handed me a thick envelope.

"What is this?"

"Your holiday bonus. It isn't much, but—"

"It's great, thank you. Actually, I wanted to ask you something."

"Sure." She turned off the lights and walked with me to the door. There wasn't a muscle in my body that didn't ache from the busy shift we'd just worked, but it had been the perfect distraction.

"If there's a chance for me to pick up more shifts, would that be a possibility?"

Her brows knitted. "But what about school?"

"I might be able to graduate early, and I could really use the extra money."

"We can always make use of a good pair of hands, Peyton, but I don't understand... why would you want to..." Realization dawned on her face. "Oh, I see. You know I'll always find you some extra shifts, if that's what you want."

"Thank you and thank you so much for the bonus."

"Get out of here and enjoy the rest of your birthday." She waved me off. "And Merry Christmas, honey."

"Merry Christmas, Cindy."

I slipped into the inky night, pulling my coat around me. Bryan's car waited down the street and I hurried to meet him. "Hey," I said, climbing inside.

"Hey." It came out stiff. "Happy birthday."

"Thanks, and thanks for doing this. I really appreciate it. And my gift, Bryan, it was beautiful."

I'd been overcome with guilt when I opened the silver star bracelet. Lily, Poppy, and their mom had all swooned over it when I'd shown them, rolling their eyes when I reminded them we were just friends.

"No problem." He headed for Xander's building, while I pulled out my small cosmetic bag and started touching up my makeup. I'd already changed out of my work uniform and spritzed my hair and body with perfume. It wasn't ideal, but it would have to do. I didn't want to waste a second of our limited time together.

"You know, I ran into him this morning."

"You did?" My head whipped over to his, and he nodded.

"We talked."

My spine stiffened. "What did he say?"

"He echoed what you said the other night. God, I want to fucking hate him for..." Bryan stopped himself, sucking in a sharp breath. "He made a good case. I told him I'll keep your secret until the end of the holidays."

"Thank you."

He gave me a sharp nod, and guilt snaked through me.

"Oh hey," I rummaged in my purse. "I got you something." Placing the small gift down on the dashboard, I smiled over at him. "It isn't much, but Merry Christmas, Bryan."

"Shit, Peyton, you didn't need to do that."

"Yeah, I did. You've been a good friend to me, and despite what you might think, I do care about you."

"At least I'll have one present under the tree." It was a joke. He was joking, and yet, there was something about the way the laughter didn't quite reach his eyes that made my heart cinch.

"Your mom and dad are back for the holidays, right?"

"Yeah, they got back a couple of days ago. I'm looking forward to some quality family time." The sarcasm in his words made me flinch. "Don't worry about me," he added. "It's nothing I haven't endured before."

We pulled up outside of Xander's building. "I'll be back before eleven."

"Thank you," I said.

With trembling fingers, I opened the door and climbed out.

"Hey, Peyton?"

"Yeah?" I glanced back.

"I'm glad you're happy."

I shut the door and stood there, watching as Bryan drove off.

It weighed heavy on my heart that I'd hurt him, but I'd always been honest. Even when we'd been sleeping together, I had been upfront about it being just sex. Still, Bryan was the last person I ever wanted to hurt.

Sadness washed over me, but then Xander's door opened, and I felt him watching me. As I slowly turned and met his intense gaze, everything else melted away.

"Hi," I climbed the stairs to his apartment.

"Happy birthday." A faint smile traced his lips as his

eyes roamed over my body, leaving a trail of heat in their wake. "Come on."

Xander grabbed my hand and all but pulled me inside.

My eyes grew wide, landing on his small breakfast counter. "Xander!"

"It isn't much, but I thought—"

"I love it, thank you." I broke away from him and hurried over to the small birthday display. There was a balloon, a small vase of flowers, a mini cake, and a gift bag and card.

Emotion swelled inside me as I ran my hands over the petals, leaning in to smell them. "They're beautiful."

He came up behind me, slipping his arms around my waist and tugging me against his solid chest. His lips brushed the curve of my shoulder, kissing me lightly. "Happy birthday."

"Thank you." I nestled into him, wrapping my arms over his.

A sense of peace drifted over me. I'd never wanted this. Never imagined I'd be able to open up to anyone and show them the deepest, darkest parts of myself. But here I was, completely smitten with this complex, layered, and utterly gorgeous guy.

"I realized you wouldn't be able to take the flowers home after I bought them, but I figured you can leave them here... For when you come over."

"I'd like that." Tilting my head, I grazed my lips over his. Xander deepened the kiss, sweeping his tongue into my mouth, claiming me. "Hmm," I sighed, completely overwhelmed by the taste of him, the feeling of being cocooned in his strong arms.

"Can I open it?" I pulled back to look at him.

"Go ahead."

My skin hummed with excitement. I hadn't expected

him to get me a gift. This thing between us was still so new and fragile. I was just happy to be here.

With trembling fingers, I reached for the gift bag and pried it open. "What is...?" Laughter spilled from my lips as I pulled out the soft toy. It was a birthday bear wearing a party hat and holding a slice of cake.

"I love it, thank you." I turned and threw my arms around him.

"It's just a silly bear." Xander tried to play it down but what he didn't realize was, it was the first stuffed toy anyone had ever given me.

"Well, I love him."

"There's a box of chocolates in there too." He motioned to the bag. "I know it's not much—"

"Stop." My expression softened. "I love that you did this for me." Hugging him again, I buried my face in his shoulder, breathing him in.

"It's been a long time since I spent Christmas Eve with anyone," he whispered.

I lifted my face to look at him, and Xander caught me by surprise, stealing a kiss.

"It's just another day," I said, refusing to let the years' worth of memories creep in and ruin this moment.

"It shouldn't be though." His eyes flickered with something I couldn't place. "My mom and dad always made a big deal of it when we were kids. We had this tradition on Christmas Eve. She'd make our favorite breakfasts and then we'd visit the Christmas market in Halston. After that we'd spend the afternoon watching Christmas movies. She always let us open one gift before we went to bed."

Sadness washed over him, so strong I could feel it.

"Xander," I breathed, smoothing my hand against his cheek.

He blinked, pulling himself out of the memory. "It was a long time ago."

"Maybe we should start our own tradition..." I peeked up at him, hoping I hadn't said the wrong thing.

We didn't know where this was going, but I wanted to believe it wasn't something fleeting but the start of something real.

"I like the sound of that." Humor twinkled in his eyes.

"Hey," I jabbed his stomach with my elbow. "I'm being serious. We could watch a Christmas movie, order pizza, and snuggle under a blanket."

"A blanket, huh... and will you be naked under this blanket?"

I shot him a bemused look, stepping out of his hold. "You order pizza, I'll choose the movie. Do you have popcorn?"

"Uh, no. It's not usually a priority on my limited grocery list."

"Fine. We can share my cake." I grinned. "Oh, and maybe order some ice cream with the pizza."

"We're really doing this?" His brow rose, hesitation clouding his eyes.

"Oh yeah," I leaned in, brushing my lips over his, "and you're going to love every single minute."

CHAPTER TWENTY-EIGHT

Xander

WATCHING a movie with Peyton sprawled all over me was virtually impossible. Her fingers had slipped under my t-shirt a while ago, tracing lazy circles over my stomach. She didn't let them drop lower, but it didn't stop me from imagining it.

In fact, it was all I could think about.

Her laughter filled my apartment, so free and content, as she lost it again at some scene about an overgrown elf. It was a movie I remembered from my childhood, one of Cameron's favorites, but I was far more interested in her. The way her eyes widened at the funny scenes and her breath caught at the sad moments. Peyton's face was a kaleidoscope of emotion and I loved that she felt so comfortable with me.

Empty pizza boxes and ice cream tubs littered my table. After we'd finished eating, I'd sunk back against my well-worn couch and Peyton had crawled into the space between my arms, pulling a blanket over us.

"Are you enjoying it?" She glanced up at me.

"Yeah, it's great."

Her eyes rolled. "You could at least pretend you're watching it."

"I'm too busy watching you."

Peyton sucked in a harsh breath, her pupils dilating with lust.

"You should probably watch your movie," I teased. "You wouldn't want to miss it."

She poked her tongue out at me and I dove for her, sucking it into my mouth.

"Xander," she shrieked, her fingers scraping my chest as I lay her back on the couch and crawled over her.

"Movie time is over," I rasped.

"But it's almost—" The words got stuck in her throat as I ran my tongue up her neck and nipped her ear.

"You were saying?"

"Fine... *fine*. But you'd better make it worth my while, I love this movie."

Laughter rumbled in my chest as I dragged my tongue back down the slope of her neck. Peyton tipped her head back, giving me better access, and I pressed a kiss to the hollow of her throat as she wound her hands around my neck.

Rocking back on my haunches, I pulled off my t-shirt, feeling like a fucking king as her hungry gaze drank me in. "These need to go." My hands went to her pants and I shuffled back, pulling them down right along with her panties.

"Xander," she protested, but I only smirked.

"You wanted to make our own tradition, right?"

Eyes sparkling, she nodded.

"So consider this your Christmas Eve gift." Sliding my

arms under her thighs, I spread her open and buried my face in her pussy.

"Oh my God," Peyton cried, fisting my hair as I dragged my tongue up the center of her. She tasted so fucking good, I dove back in for more, licking and teasing. Adding two fingers, I swirled them deep inside her and then over her clit. Her body bowed into me, her little moans of pleasure like music to my ears.

She yanked my hair slightly, and our eyes collided over the length of her body. "More," she demanded, "I need more."

"Greedy girl." I smirked, flicking my tongue over her clit and then grazing my teeth there.

"Xander..." Her voice was caught between a moan and a plea.

Spearing my tongue inside her, I fought the urge to climb her body and fuck her into my couch. I wanted to take my time, to savor her. Our time together was finite, and I wanted to spend every single second worshipping her.

But God, I wanted to sink deep inside her too.

"God... *God...*" She panted, her grip on my hair borderline painful. It was worth it though, to see her come undone on my tongue. Her orgasm tore through her and she cried my name over and over.

Raising myself back over her body, I snapped my belt, and with Peyton's help, pushed my jeans off my hips, just enough to free my dick.

"I need you," she breathed, hooking her arms over my shoulder.

Sliding one hand under her ass, I lifted her slightly and pressed inside her, slowly. "Fuck," I choked out.

"Move... I need you to move." Peyton wriggled beneath me, but I held still, looking down at her, memorizing every single second of this.

"Can you feel me?" I said the words against her lips. "Feel what you do to me." Kissing her, I tangled my tongue with hers. Slow, leisurely licks as I pumped my hips at the same lazy pace.

"Xander," she huffed, growing impatient. But I didn't want to rush this.

"Just feel it." I pushed one of her legs back, letting me go deeper. We both groaned, pleasure sparking off around my body. She felt too fucking good. Like she was made for me, and me alone.

Impatient, she rocked her hips, pulling me into her body. It was enough to snap my last shred of control and I slammed into her, riding her hard and fast. Peyton clung to me, her soft moans the beat to our rhythm. Sweat beaded down my spine as our kisses grew hungrier, clumsier... dirtier.

This girl...

This fucking girl.

She matched me thrust for thrust, letting me take what I wanted. Giving me what I needed. And when I came to the sound of her second orgasm tearing through her, she reached inside my chest and fisted my heart, claiming it as her own.

The thought hit me so intensely, I shuddered.

I'd known Peyton had power over me.

I hadn't known she would completely obliterate my walls and steal my soul.

"You okay over there?" Peyton asked from the couch.

After we'd cleaned up and gotten dressed, I'd made the excuse of taking the pizza boxes to the trash while Peyton watched the end of her movie.

"Yeah." I forced a smile, but Peyton caught it.

"What's the matter?" She got up and padded over to me.

"Nothing, I'm—"

"Please don't insult me. I know that look. I wear it often enough." Her lips curved, but the smile melted away when I didn't reply. "Xander?"

"I just keep thinking that you deserve—"

"Not this again." She huffed. "What happened to no regrets, huh?"

I scrubbed my face. "Truth?"

"Always."

"I've never felt like this."

"And you think I have?" Her expression softened. "When I'm with you, it's like... it's like for the first time, in a really long time, I can breathe."

I wanted to tell her I felt the same, that she settled something deep inside me. She did. But more and more, I felt like I couldn't breathe around her. Because part of me was waiting for the other shoe to drop. For her to realize that she wanted more than this. More than me.

It was confusing as fuck.

"I want this, Xander." She gazed up at me with fierce determination. "I don't know how else to make you see that."

"Come here." I pulled her into my chest and dropped my chin to her head, holding her.

I had no idea what the future held, how I was going to survive tomorrow or whatever came after that. But I vowed to myself to do everything in my power not to screw this up.

"Can I give you your gift now?"

"You got me something?"

"Yeah." Her smile hit me dead in the chest.

"But I didn't—"

"You've given me more than enough." She went over to her purse and pulled something out. "It's only small." Holding out a small box, she added, "Merry Christmas, Xander."

I accepted the gift and carefully opened it, floored at the glossy black keyring inside.

"I saw it this morning in a store on my way to work. I thought it would be—"

"It's perfect." I ran my fingers over the engraving, feeling emotion clog my throat.

Sometimes you don't choose it, it chooses you.

"Every time you look at it, I want you know that I choose you." My eyes slowly lifted to hers. "I choose you, Xander."

If I thought she owned a piece of my soul already, this sealed my fate.

Peyton Myers was mine.

But more than that, I was hers.

THE NEXT MORNING was the same as the last five years. I woke up alone. No presents under the tree—I didn't have one—and no one to wish me Merry Christmas.

Except when I snatched my phone off the nightstand and rubbed the sleep out of my eyes, I had a message from Peyton that made me smile for the first time in a long time.

BLONDIE: Merry Christmas, Xander. I know we can't be ourselves today, but I'll be wishing we could be.

. . .

She'd sent an image too. A photo of her in a floppy Christmas hat and not much else if the expanse of her bare shoulders and collarbone was anything to go on.

Me: Merry Christmas. I think the rest of the image is missing...

Blondie: Flirt.

Me: With you, always.

My imagination had run away with me, picturing her in nothing but that silly little hat and maybe a giant bow for me to unwrap.

Blondie: Lily's mom wasn't kidding when she said Christmas is chaos. Poppy was up hours ago and your brother and Hailee just got here. What time are you coming over?

Me: Later. I try to avoid the gift exchange.

I checked my other messages, and sure enough, I had a message from my brother encouraging me to come to the Ford's sooner rather than later. There was one from Hailee too. But they knew I wouldn't concede.

I never did.

. . .

Blondie: Party pooper. I'll see you later xo

Blondie: p.s. I'll wear something special...

Fuck. She was going to kill me before the day was over.

Me: Behave!

Peyton replied with a collection of winking and laughing emojis, and I couldn't help but laugh. Even under all the pain and trauma, she found the strength to smile. I was in complete awe of her.

Dragging myself out of bed, I made quick work of getting a shower and dressing. I had numerous other messages from Jase, Asher, Avery, and Ashleigh. There was even one from Tash. After texting everyone back, and wolfing down some breakfast, I reluctantly grabbed the bag of gifts stowed by the door and made my way to the Ford's house.

It had already descended into chaos by the time I arrived.

"Uncle Xander," Ashleigh opened the door, lit up like a Christmas tree in a garish flashing holiday jumper. "Merry Christmas." She beamed.

"Merry Christmas, Leigh." I thrust the bag at her. "I come bearing gifts."

"Excellent. You may enter then."

Rolling my eyes, I stepped inside the house, silently ordering my heart to calm the fuck down.

"There he is," Jase appeared. His holiday jumper wasn't as awful as Ashleigh's, but it was still... interesting.

"Nice sweater," I teased.

"Yeah, well, it seems you didn't get the memo about the dress code." He motioned to my plaid shirt.

"I must have missed that one." My lip twisted with a knowing smirk, and he muttered something under his breath before approaching me.

"Merry Christmas, Xander. We're glad you're here." Jase pulled me in for a guy hug.

"Thanks, you too."

"Beers are in the refrigerator. Help yourself."

I gave him an appreciative nod and took off toward the kitchen, spying my brother and Hailee amidst a sea of shredded gift wrap.

He caught my eye. "Xander, get in here and open your—"

"I'll be right in," I said and kept walking. Despite the time, I needed a drink first. Something to take the edge off the restless energy zipping through me.

The Ford's kitchen had been transformed into something out of the holiday spread in *Ideal Home* magazine. Two tables had been pushed together, enough to seat all fifteen of us. Adorned with holiday centerpieces and coordinating dinnerware. I almost balked at the scene. My nephew Avery was a lucky sonofabitch, choosing to spend the holidays with his fiancée's family rather than join the festivities with us.

Laughter flitted down the hall, as the kids teased each other about their gifts. I made a beeline for the refrigerator, helping myself to a bottle of beer. Someone approached, and I closed the door, leaning back against the counter, expecting to find my brother or Jase.

I didn't expect to see Peyton enter the kitchen, dressed in a knee-length black sweater dress that hugged every inch of her curves. My mouth dried instantly as I stood there, gawking at her. I realized then it was peppered with tiny silver-thread snowflakes. Her own interpretation of the dress code apparently.

"Merry Christmas, Xander." A knowing smile played on her lips as she walked right up to me and moved around me to get to the cabinet above my head. The second her body brushed up against mine, a groan rumbled deep in my chest.

Fuck. Me.

She hadn't been lying earlier, when she said she would wear something special. I wanted to drag her away from prying eyes and ears and strip her out of the ridiculously tight dress and—

"Whatever you're thinking," she whispered. "Stop. Or you'll get us both into trouble." Soft laughter coated her words, wrapping around my heart, and my dick, like a fist.

"You look... fuck, Peyton. How the hell am I supposed to survive dinner with you looking like that?"

"Merry Christmas." Her eyes glittered with amusement and unrestrained lust.

I couldn't move, entranced by her smile, the scent of that vanilla fucking lip gloss and perfume she loved to wear. But I wasn't the only one frozen in place. Peyton stared at me with so much intensity, it sucked the air clean from my lungs.

No one had ever looked at me with such lust and longing.

"Peyton, I—"

"What's taking so long?" Cameron's voice boomed, too

fucking close. We jerked apart right as he entered the kitchen.

"Just getting a beer," I said, hoping he didn't notice the roughness to my voice.

Peyton grabbed a bowl and started pouring in the bag of chips she'd gotten out of the cabinet. "Snacks." She whirled around and flashed my brother a warm smile, ducking around him to disappear into the hall.

His brows knitted. "Everything okay?"

"Yeah, why wouldn't it be?"

"Look, Xander, I know things haven't been—"

"Let's not do this." I stepped forward. "Not today. It's Christmas. Merry Christmas, Brother."

"Merry Christmas. I'm glad you're here." He squeezed my shoulder, and for a second, I was just an eleven-year-old with no one but my big brother to protect me.

But we're older now. Separated by years of disappointment and shame and harsh words. And I didn't doubt for a second that if he knew what he'd really walked in on...

He would never forgive me.

CHAPTER TWENTY-NINE

Peyton

"YOU DIDN'T NEED to do this." I said to Aaron as I stared at the gift card in my hands. I hadn't expected gifts from everyone, but sure enough, when we'd all gathered in the Ford's big living room, there was a small pile with my name on them. Gifts from everyone except for Ezra. But no one minded he hadn't bought anyone anything. His presence—although coerced—was enough.

"It's nothing." He grinned.

"It's perfect." The ball of emotion lodged in my throat swelled. I realized now, sitting here, that the Ford's weren't the only ones who had accepted me into their family.

It was overwhelming.

And only made worse by knowing Xander was sitting right opposite me. We hadn't talked again, and I'd avoided making eye contact. But I felt him watching me. My dress had had the desired effect earlier, but we'd had a close call with Cameron. We needed to be more careful.

"Here, why don't you open one, Ezra?" Ashleigh said, nudging a small box toward him. I gave her an imperceptible nod, grateful for her attempt at deflecting the spotlight from me.

"Thanks," he said quietly, plucking up the gift. He unwrapped it with slow, steady fingers. It didn't surprise me given Ezra's nature. A strange expression washed over him as he lifted the lid and peered inside the box. "I—"

Apprehension glittered in Ashleigh's eyes as Ezra struggled to get out his words. I realized then, it was her gift to him. She looked so hopeful... but the light in her eyes extinguished as he set the box down and said to no one in particular, "Thanks."

Lily frowned, glancing at me as if to say. *What the hell was that?*

I don't know, I silently replied by shrugging.

"I'm going to get another drink," Ashleigh said, excusing herself. Lily went after her.

"Okay then," Felicity said. "Why don't we finish opening presents and then the party can really get started." Her laughter was strained, but it broke the tension.

Poppy and Sofia handed out the remaining gifts, and by the end, everyone, including Kaiden and his mom, had a small pile of gifts at their feet.

"This is... thank you," Kaiden's mom said, fighting the tears clinging to her lashes. "You didn't have to do all of this."

"It's Christmas," Jason grinned. "Of course we did. Now I don't know about anyone else, but I'm ready to eat."

"Eat?" His wife balked. "You ate all those pancakes at breakfast."

He patted his stomach. "And now I'm ready for brunch."

Everyone snickered. Even Ezra managed a smile, his eyes still glued to the door Ashleigh had disappeared through a minute ago. I'd never gotten to the bottom of their friendship... if you could call it that. But she was the only person who still tried to encourage him into our group.

Pockets of conversation broke out around me—the adults; Poppy, Sofia, and Aaron; Kaiden, his mom, and Xander.

"Hey," I whispered, shuffling closer to Ezra. "You okay?"

"Yeah," he said, his eyes flicking to the door. He looked like a cornered animal, ready to make a dash for it at any second.

"Wanna get some air?"

The reflection of the twinkle lights danced in his dark-brown irises. "Yeah, okay."

We got up and slipped away without question, everyone too invested in their conversations. I started to head for the kitchen, to where I assumed Lily and Ashleigh were, but Ezra turned for the front door.

"You're leaving?" I asked.

"I don't see any fresh air in here, do you?"

Well then.

I grabbed my coat off the rack, shoved my feet into my pumps, and followed him outside.

Ezra didn't stop until he reached the small wall separating the Ford's driveway and the trees bordering their property. He dropped down, letting out a thin breath.

"Not a fan of the holidays?" I asked.

"Are you?"

"Touché. What did Ashleigh get you?"

"You knew... it was from her?"

"Lucky guess." I shrugged. "What was it?"

"It doesn't matter."

Something told me it did, but I didn't push. "She likes you, you know?"

"She shouldn't." His throat bobbed as he glanced at the thick blanket of white-gray clouds overhead. This was the most I'd ever talked to him. Fake-Peyton and Ezra were worlds apart. But now... now I felt a strange desire to uncover his secrets and let him know that he wasn't alone.

"They say you tried to kill yourself that night, in the river."

I flinched at the blunt edge to his words, but surprisingly, I found no judgment there. "They say a lot of things."

"Is it... true?" His eyes locked on mine, searching for answers.

"I was in a bad place then."

"But you're not now?"

"It's getting easier." With the help of my friends, Jason and Felicity... Xander, it was slowly, day by day, getting easier.

"You're not... I mean, you don't want to—"

"Kill myself?" He let out a strained laugh. "Nah, but I like the quiet."

What a strange thing to say. But Ezra didn't expand, and I didn't have the courage to ask. Instead, I said, "You should give us a chance one day. You never know, you might actually like hanging out with us. And it would mean a lot to Aaron and Sofia... to Leigh, if you came around once in a while."

His eyes shuttered as if he couldn't quite grasp my words, the invitation there. "Yeah," he loosened a breath. "Maybe."

I nodded. "I'm going to see if they need any help with anything. Merry Christmas, Ezra."

Ezra watched me walk away. I'd almost reached the door when he called after me, "Merry Christmas, Peyton."

I'd never had Christmas dinner with so many people. The noise was deafening as everyone passed around the various side dishes. It all smelled so good. I piled my plate with mashed potatoes, green bean casserole, cauliflower with cheese sauce, and buttered peas.

"This all looks so good," I said, smiling.

Lily's mom beamed across the table at me. "I had a lot of help." Her eyes went to Hailee and Mya.

"I never had..." I stopped myself, realizing everyone was looking at me. "The ham smells amazing."

Conversation resumed, but Xander's eyes remained on my face. He was seated opposite, a couple of seats down next to Kaiden. I risked meeting his stare while everyone was busy filling their plates. He smiled. A real honest-to-God smile, so full of heat and promise it sent a shiver racing down my spine.

It was both a blessing and a curse having him here. His presence settled me, gave me the strength to smile and engage with my friends and their families. But it was also torture not being able to go to him. I tried not to imagine what it might be like if they knew.

"Peyton is right, Mrs. Ford," Kaiden said. "This is great. Thank you so much for inviting me and my mom."

"You're always welcome, son," Jason gave him a nod. "Although I think I'm drawing the line at one boyfriend." His eyes went to Poppy, and she stuck her tongue out at him.

"We'll need a bigger table next year," Asher chuckled.

"Who knows, maybe you'll bring a lady friend around next year, Xan?"

My heart stuttered as blood roared in my ears.

"I wouldn't count on it." The words rolled off Xander's tongue with smooth conviction.

I knew he was only deflecting the question, but God, it hurt—to hear him so flippantly dismiss Asher's suggestion.

"You're not hungry?" Poppy nudged me, noticing my untouched food. It all smelled so good, but now I had a pit in my stomach.

"I... I have a bit of a stomachache," I whispered. It wasn't a complete lie.

Would they ever accept us?

Would we ever be welcomed into their families?

I glanced up, my eyes colliding with Xander's again, and he frowned as if he felt the change in me. My lips curved into a small smile, but I knew it didn't reach my eyes, the reality of our situation pressing down on me.

Surely, he had to know hearing those words would hurt?

"Excuse me," I announced, standing, the crushing weight of everything too much to bear. "I need to use the bathroom."

"Better hurry, Peyton," Aaron called after me. "Before Dad eats all the ham."

Laughter filled the air as I slipped out of the room and hurried down the hall.

Frustration vibrated through me. I'd known today would be hard, but I hadn't anticipated to feel so... so out of my depth. I cared about Xander; I cared about him a lot. I wanted nothing more than to give us a real shot. But being here, surrounded by my friends and their parents, to hear him talk like that, it seemed impossible to have faith that things would work themselves out.

Inside the bathroom, I locked the door and pressed my

head against the wood, inhaling a ragged breath. I wanted someone to talk to about everything so badly. To reassure me that everything was going to be okay. That Xander and I could survive this. I needed him. I needed him in a way that terrified me. He was my buoy, keeping me afloat in a sea of darkness.

The vibration of my cell phone pulled me from my thoughts, and I retrieved it from the pocket in my dress.

Ellis: Are you okay?

Such a loaded question. I quickly typed a reply.

Me: I don't know… this is harder than I thought it would be.

Ellis: I didn't mean what I said. You know that, right?

Me: Yeah.

Ellis: We'll talk about this later.

Pocketing my cell, I rinsed my hands and stared at myself in the mirror. I'd been so excited to see Xander today, to dress sexy for him and enjoy the heated glances across the room. I hadn't anticipated how insecure it would make me feel. Instead, I felt like his dirty little secret.

The thought punched me in the chest.

When I rejoined the table, Lily shot me a questioning glance. "Okay?" she mouthed, and I nodded, slipping into my seat. Xander's stare was heavy, but I didn't meet his eyes. I couldn't.

Reluctantly, I picked at the heaps of food on my plate, trying to stave off any further concern from Poppy or anyone else. When I was done, I pushed it forward slightly, pretending to listen to the many conversations going on around the table. Kaiden commanded most of Xander's attention, discussing the football game airing later.

"Okay, okay, pipe down," Jason stood, clinking a fork against his bottle of beer. "I'm pretty sure it's tradition to say a few words before the food, but I've never been one to do things by the book. I just wanted to take this opportunity to say that I feel blessed to spend today with my family. Because that's what you all represent. I have known Cameron and Asher for the best part of thirty-five years and thank my lucky stars every day for their friendship. And now, our kids are growing up, ready to fly the nest and I realized that this is the last year we might all be together."

The women around the table were misty-eyed as my friends looked a little embarrassed at his heartfelt words.

"And I know Asher was joking earlier about needing a bigger table next year, but I want you all to know that our table will always be big enough for you and your future... partners." He swallowed over that last word.

"Okay, Dad. I think we got the message." Poppy chuckled.

"I think it's very sweet, babe." Felicity pulled her husband down into his seat and leaned in to kiss him.

"Just remember," he pinned his daughters with a hard

look, "I can handle boyfriends. I cannot handle being made a grandparent anytime soon. That goes for you too, Kaid—"

"Oh my God, *Dad*!" Lily breathed, her cheeks flushing deeply.

"Okay," Felicity leaped up, "who's ready for dessert?"

"I'll give you a hand with the dishes." Hailee got up to help.

"We're going to watch the pre-game show," Cameron said. "Shout-out when it's ready."

The men, including Xander, got up and filed out of the kitchen.

"I'm going to help them," Mrs. Thatcher said, patting Kaiden's arm.

"And then there was seven." Aaron grinned, but it fell when Ezra stood.

"I'm going to get some air."

We watched him stalk out of the back door. Ashleigh's shoulders slumped, hurt etched into her expression.

"At least he stayed for the whole meal," Sofia offered.

"Big whoop." Aaron grumbled.

"Aaron..."

"Yeah, whatever. I'm going to watch the game. Kaiden?"

He looked to Lily, and she smiled. "Go. I'm going to stay with the girls."

The second they were gone, Lily turned to Ashleigh. "Are you okay?"

"I'm fine."

But I knew that tone, and I knew that look. She wasn't fine. Not even a little bit.

"I don't know why you keep trying," Sofia said, quietly. "E is—"

"I know, but everyone deserves to have somebody in their corner." The defensive edge in Ashleigh's voice didn't surprise me. She was fiercely protective of the people she cared about. We all were, in our own way. It was one of the things I'd envied most about them when I'd first met Lily. The bonds they shared mirrored the ones their parents shared, and now I was one of them.

At least, until the truth came out.

Then who knew what would happen?

CHAPTER THIRTY

Xander

I WAS in some kind of hell.

Peyton was pissed at me, and I didn't blame her. But when Asher had teased me about bringing a *lady friend* around next year, the words had spilled out without thought. It wasn't until I saw the hurt flash across her face that I knew I'd fucked up.

But it wasn't like I could admit the truth.

Not yet.

"Is it wrong we've abandoned the kids?" Hailee asked. She was tucked into my brother's side, looking a little glassy-eyed from one too many glasses of wine.

"Nah, let them have their fun," Jase replied.

"I'm so proud of you, babe." Fee kissed his jaw. "You handled everything very well."

"Yeah, well, she's going away to college next year," he grumbled, "I guess two nights in a cabin with her horndog of a boyfriend isn't going to kill me."

"I still can't believe you agreed to that shit." Asher guffawed.

"Fuck you, man. Soon enough Sofia will be asking to shack up with her boyfriend on a romantic getaway."

"I can handle it. I'm cool like that." He winked.

"Did Peyton seem okay to you?"

My spine stiffened as I avoided making eye contact with Fee.

"She seemed quiet."

"I think it's to be expected," Mya said. "Holidays are always going to be hard for her, a reminder of everything that's happened."

"I guess. I just worry we're not doing enough."

"You are. More than enough." Mya smiled. "It's a fine line between giving her space and gently encouraging her to face everything that's happened. It's a good sign she's willing to engage with counselling."

"I need a smoke," I announced, getting up with a slight sway. I'd buried my frustrations with one too many whiskeys.

"You need to quit that shit," Cam called after me, but I waved him off, needing air.

After forcing us to eat the copious amounts of dessert, the adults, plus Aaron and Kaiden watched the game while the girls retreated to the den. Ezra had taken off earlier, after getting permission from Asher to leave. He'd managed to stay for dinner, and Asher and Mya had agreed that was better than nothing.

I could hear their laughter, the giggles and girlish shrieks. Aaron and Kaiden had joined them not long ago, and who knew what they were up to. But I didn't dare go find out. Because I didn't want to see the hurt in Peyton's eyes again.

I was a fucking coward. Bold enough to love her in the shadows but too scared to love her in public.

Not that I loved her. I didn't. Wasn't sure I would ever be capable of that. But I cared for her, more than I ever thought possible.

The cold hit me and I burrowed into my jacket as I took off down to the lake for some peace. But I found none. Pulling out a smoke, I was about to light it when the rustle of leaves caught my attention.

"I thought I'd find you out here," Peyton said. She'd wrapped a big chunky knit cardigan over her dress and pulled on her knitted hat.

"You shouldn't—"

"Relax, no one saw me. The adults are all drinking and talking, and the others are playing silly games." She kicked the frozen ground with her boot, refusing to look at me.

"Peyton..."

"The words just poured out," she whispered. "Like you didn't even have to think about them."

Through gritted teeth, I tipped my head to the sky and inhaled a deep breath. "I thought we agreed to give ourselves the holidays."

"We did." Slowly, she lifted her eyes to mine. So full of sadness and defeat. "You didn't even hesitate. I guess it just caught me off guard."

"Come here." I pulled her into my arms and gazed down at her. "What I said doesn't mean anything."

"It hurt."

"I know." Fuck, I knew, and it gutted me. "But now is not the right time."

"I don't want to hurt anyone, Xander. I don't want them to hate us. To hate you." Her eyes shuttered as she inhaled a shaky breath. When she looked up at me again, I felt winded. "But I can't stop this... I can't stop feeling this way."

"I know." Gathering her closer, I pressed a kiss to her head. "I can't either."

Peyton slid her hands inside my jacket, curling them into my shirt. "I need you."

Those three little words undid me.

Brushing my fingers along her jaw, I gently gripped her chin and tilted her face to mine. "I need you too." *More than you'll ever know.* I leaned down, kissing her. Once, twice, until our tongues tangled together in a rush of complete surrender to the connection burning between us.

"Xander." My name on her lips was a whispered prayer.

"Merry Christmas, Peyton," I breathed the words, kissing her harder, deeper. She clung to me, unwilling to let go. But we couldn't do this, not now. Not here.

"Peyton, we have to stop..."

"No, I need—"

"I know, but we can't, not here." The words tasted bitter on my tongue. I didn't want to stop. I wanted to push her against the nearest tree and spend my sweet time acquainting myself with every dip and curve of her body.

Desire danced in her eyes, but it winked out the second I pulled away from her. "I'll see you inside," she said coolly, her walls slamming back up.

Peyton whirled around and took off toward the house as I exhaled a steady breath, running a brisk hand over my face. It was the right choice, the *only* choice.

But it didn't make it any easier to watch her walk away from me.

THE NEXT MORNING, I sat eating breakfast, staring at my cell phone, willing it to vibrate. My last text to Peyton taunted me, had done ever since I'd gotten home last night after finally leaving Jase's house. He'd offered me the guest room. But I couldn't be there, under the same roof as Peyton. Not after our brief kiss down by the lake.

Me: Let me make it up to you.

I didn't know how I planned on doing that. Not when our options were limited to hanging out at my apartment, or in my truck somewhere under the cover of darkness or off the beaten track.

But I had to see her. Needed it in a way I couldn't quite comprehend.

I hated that I'd hurt her, again.

She didn't reply though. It was almost eleven and my cell phone had lit up precisely once, with a message from Cam. He wanted to build bridges. I'd sensed it last month at the team's quarter-final game. But I knew the second he found out the truth, our shaky truce would come crashing down.

So I'd kept him at arm's length.

I dumped my plate and mug in the sink and headed for a shower, but the vibration of my cell gave me pause. Relief flooded me at the sight of Peyton's nickname.

Blondie: How?

My mouth curved.

. . .

Me: I'll figure something out. Can you sneak away tonight for a few hours?

Blondie: I have work until six, but I can see if Bryan will cover for us after?

I didn't like relying on him for this, but there wasn't much choice if I wanted to see her. And I did.

I needed to see her, to put a smile back on her face. Fuck, I needed it.

Me: Do it. And listen, I'm sorry, about yesterday…

Blondie: It wasn't your fault. I just freaked out. Lily and Poppy want to hang this morning before she heads off to the cabin with Kaiden, so I'll see you later xo

Me: See you later… and Peyton, I'm sorry.

Jealousy swam in my veins, followed by a blast of shame. I was a grown fucking man, jealous of an eighteen-year-old kid taking his girl away for a couple of days. But Peyton deserved all that. She deserved to be showered with affection.

I dumped my cell on the sideboard, stripped off and

walked butt naked into the shower. But I couldn't stop thinking about it.

Peyton deserved to be treated right, and I was going to figure out a way to do just that.

My nerves were shot by the time Peyton knocked on the door hours later.

"Hey," she said around a faint smile.

"Hey." I stepped back to let her inside. Her vanilla perfume hit me as I closed the door and pulled her into my arms.

My hands slid into her hair, tilting her face to mine. "I'm sorry."

"It's okay."

"No, it's not. I didn't think... I didn't—"

"Ssh." Peyton pressed her finger to my lips. "I don't want to spend what time we have together fighting. Besides, you were going to make it up to me..." Her brow arched.

Laughter rumbled in my chest. "I was, wasn't I?"

Brushing my lips over hers, I kissed her. My tongue licked the seam of Peyton's mouth, coaxing her to open for me. She did, our tongues tangling in a slow dance of submission. Her hands curled into my sweater, anchoring us together.

"Xander," she whispered, breaking away and heaving a breath.

"I'm taking you out." I kissed her forehead.

"Wh-what? But I didn't think—"

"Relax. We're not going out in Rixon. I thought we'd go on a little road trip."

"You did, huh?"

"I want to date you, Peyton. I want to take you out and show you off to the world."

The idea had come to me earlier. Of course, we couldn't be seen out in Rixon, but there were a couple of towns close enough to drive to where nobody would know us.

"I wish you'd have told me. I would have worn something a little more—"

"You look perfect." I kissed the end of her nose. "So, Peyton Myers, will you go out with me?"

Her smile was blinding, hitting me dead in the chest. "Yes," she threw her arms around me, "I'll go out with you."

"Come on then. We need to be there for eight."

"You made a reservation?" Her eyes twinkled with excitement.

"Kind of. You'll see. Do you have gloves?"

"No, I didn't—"

"I have a spare pair." I'd picked up some earlier from the store down the block. They were only cheap, but they would do the trick.

"A date," Peyton sighed. "A real date... I'm nervous."

"Why?"

"Because you're... you, and I'm—"

"Perfect." *And I'm so fucking gone for you.*

I kissed her, taking the hat from her hand and pulling it over her blonde waves. "You're going to need this."

Peyton eyed me carefully, the air crackling around us. "What are you up to, Xander?"

Disguising the wild thud of my heart, the way my palms turned clammy, with bravado, I smirked and said, "You'll see."

"This is... I don't even know what to say." Peyton snuggled into my side as we got comfortable on our loveseat, pulling the blanket up around us.

Another twenty-nine loveseats littered the flat rooftop of The Heights at Halston, each bedecked with a heat lamp, cushions, blankets, and a dark canopy providing the perfect amount of privacy.

"How did you even find out about this place?" She peeked up at me, blonde locks spilling out of her hat. It was cold out, bitter. But it only added to the ambience of the rooftop movie night. They were screening a holiday classic, and although it wasn't my movie of choice, I suspected Peyton would love it.

"Can I get you both a drink?" A server arrived at our loveseat.

"Hot chocolate for me please." Peyton glanced up from the menu card. "Xander?"

"Make it two. And we'll take a bucket of popcorn."

"Coming right up."

"This is so cool. I've never been to anything like this before." Peyton's excitement was infectious, and I relaxed against the soft cushions with a smile.

When I'd stumbled across the listing for the rooftop movie night, it had seemed like the perfect solution to our predicament. It was romantic but afforded us a measure of privacy most other date night activities wouldn't.

Besides, it meant I could get up close and personal with her, so it was a win-win.

Peyton leaned up and scraped her fingers over my jaw, kissing me there. "Thank you."

"I'm sorry it's not a romantic dinner at some swanky restaurant."

"Ssh. I don't need any of that." Her lips ghosted over mine, and my eyes scanned the rooftop. Our loveseat was tucked away in the back, enveloped in shadows except for the faint flicker of the tiki torch marking the front of each loveseat. We were as good as alone.

I curled my hand around Peyton's neck and held her as I deepened the kiss, plunging my tongue into her mouth.

"I know nobody can see us," she whispered against my lips, "but it feels... illicit."

"We can always stop." My brow rose.

Her eyes glittered in the dark. "No, I like it." Peyton dove back in, the sounds of our kisses drowned out by the opening credits of the movie.

Approaching footsteps made me pull back, touching my head to hers. "You make me so fucking hot," I whispered.

"The feeling is entirely mutual." A wide grin spread across Peyton's face, her cheeks tinting under the candlelight.

"Two hot chocolates and a bucket of popcorn." The server placed our order on the small table at the side of the loveseat. "Enjoy the movie," she offered before melting back into the shadows.

Peyton grabbed a handful of popcorn and lifted her hand to my mouth. "Open up." She chuckled, feeding me the salty-sweet snack.

"Your turn." I snatched up a couple of kernels. She clasped my wrist, letting me feed her. When I went to pull away, Peyton sucked my finger into her mouth, swirling her tongue over it.

Desire pulsed through me, my dick jumping to attention as I swallowed a groan. She smirked up at me, amusement dancing in her baby blues.

"Keep doing that," I growled, "and you won't get to see much of the movie."

"Maybe I don't want to watch the movie." Her eyes glittered with hunger.

Fuck.

I'd thought we could come here and play at being a normal couple, but now all I could think about was dragging her back to my car, laying her out on the back seat, and finding ways to make her scream.

"Behave," I chided, nipping the end of her finger. Her soft laughter filled our little section of the rooftop, but it was barely a whisper against the noise of the movie playing on the huge screen.

I'd never been one for romantic gestures—I'd never had a reason for it. But this, right here, was something I could get used to.

And I was slowly coming to realize Peyton was everything I wanted and never knew I needed.

CHAPTER THIRTY-ONE

Peyton

I'D NEVER FELT as content as I did snuggled into Xander's side in the comfort of our own private loveseat, watching the movie on the rooftop of the hotel.

It was perfect.

His fingers toyed with the ends of my hair, my own tracing nonsensical patterns on his stomach. The seat reclined enough that we were practically laying down, our legs kicked up in front of us.

"Can we stay here forever?" I whispered against his stubbled jaw. Xander turned slightly, capturing my mouth in a tender kiss.

Everything melted away as his tongue slipped past my lips and curled around my own. It was easy to pretend we were the only two people up here, under a blanket of twinkling stars.

I leaned up, pressing my palm flat against his abs as I kissed him harder. No one had ever gone to this kind of trouble for me. He knew I loved cheesy holiday movies, so it had made my heart skip a beat when I realized what we were doing for our date.

God, I still couldn't believe I was on a real honest-to-God date with Xander Chase, the man who had saved me in more ways than one. And soon, when he told Jason he wouldn't be returning to his coaching job, and I graduated early, we wouldn't have to worry anymore about hiding our relationship.

"Fuck, Peyton," Xander rasped, his voice cracked with lust. "You taste so good. I don't think I'll ever get enough of kissing you."

His words made my chest swell as I nuzzled his neck, letting my hand slip lower. It was dark, the shadows cloaking us along with the blanket.

"Peyton," he warned as my fingers fumbled with his jean button.

"I want to feel you," I breathed the words against the corner of his mouth. "No one can see anything."

His hand covered mine and I waited for him to pry my fingers away, only he didn't. Instead, Xander pushed my hand against his dick, hissing at the friction.

"See what you do to me." A wicked glint flashed in his eyes, heating my blood.

With his encouragement, I dipped my hand into his jeans and boxers and fisted his silky length. "Fuuuuck," he hissed again.

"Ssh," I teased, flicking my tongue over the seam of his lips. "You're going to have to be quiet."

"Maybe I should pull you on top of me and sink deep inside your pussy instead? Then let's see who can keep quiet."

My breath hitched at his dirty words, and I smothered a chuckle. I wanted that. God, did I ever. But first, I wanted to feel him. I wanted to make him come undone.

Xander kissed me hard as I pumped him slowly, running my thumb over the bead of pre-cum.

"Fuck, don't stop," he drawled, between hot, wet kisses. "Harder."

"Like this?" I tightened my fingers as they worked him faster.

"Yeah, fuck... yeah." He panted, his hand clutching the blanket.

His eyes sparkled in the shadows, filled with hunger and raw lust. He speared his fingers into my hair, brushing his thumb over my neck as he kissed me, forcing me to swallow his groans of pleasure.

"Let me fuck you."

His words made my tummy clench.

"We can't, not here." My own breathing turned choppy as I pushed him closer to the edge.

"Then let me touch you..."

Laughter bubbled inside me. "Patience," I scolded. "Let me take care of you." I twisted my wrist slightly as I worked my hand up and down. He was close. Teeth gritted, legs tense as he kissed me through ragged breaths.

"Shit, Peyton, I'm almost... fuck, yeah..."

Xander buried his face as he came hard. He pressed a kiss to my neck, tracing his lips up my jaw. "You are... amazing."

I pulled my hand free and wiped it on the napkins we'd been handed with our drinks and popcorn.

Xander's intense gaze made my breath catch. "We need to tell them," he said, as if he'd just figured something out.

"Yeah, I know." I swallowed, the moment between us gone.

"You know, I haven't fooled around like this in a really long time." A panty-melting smirk spread over Xander's face.

"Oh yeah?"

He leaned in, brushing his nose against mine. "Yeah. Since high school."

"Well, I guess dating a younger woman has its perks." Despite the warring emotions inside me, I smiled back.

"I guess it does." Xander stole a kiss before tucking me back into his side, where I remained for the rest of the movie.

We walked the short distance back to Xander's truck, his arm around my shoulder as I ate my hot dog. It was late, time to get back to Rixon, leaving a bittersweet feeling in my chest.

Tonight had been amazing, a glimpse of how things would be once we came clean to our friends and families.

"The only thing that could make this night any better is sn—oh my God." My eyes almost bugged as snowflakes began to fall.

"Did you plan this?" I grinned up at Xander and he chuckled.

"I have many talents but controlling the weather is definitely not one of them."

A contented sigh slipped from my lips as I buried closer into his side. "I wish tonight never had to end."

"Only a few more weeks." He kissed my head.

We'd talked earlier, wandering the quiet streets of Halston and decided that although we would tell Jason and Felicity the day after tomorrow when I had no shift at the diner, that we would wait until I'd graduated to go public.

It would be hard, but at least once those closest to us knew, I could spend more time at his place.

"Are you scared about what they'll say?" I asked him as he climbed into his truck.

"Scared, no. But I suspect the fallout will be messy for a while."

My chest tightened. "I wish it didn't have to be like this."

Xander shoved the key into the ignition and the truck rumbled to life. He turned up the heater and leaned over, taking my hand. "You're worth it," he said, quietly.

"You are too, you know?" My lip curved.

Xander was worried about what the truth would do to my reputation, but it wasn't me people would judge. He was the adult, the one who should know better. People would twist that, turn it into something it wasn't.

My stomach dropped.

"Hey," he said, brushing his knuckles over my cheeks. "It'll be okay, Peyton."

"I know." So long as we were together, it would be okay.

The vibration of my cell phone pierced the tension and I dug it out of my purse. "It's Bryan," I said, scanning the screen.

"I like the kid, but I'll be glad when he isn't your cover story anymore."

"Seriously, I already told you, you don't need to be jealous of Bryan."

"He put his mouth on you. Of course I'm jealous."

"He's my friend, Xander."

"I know, but you've been with him. Do you have any idea how crazy that makes me?"

"Wait a minute, you know about that?" I blinked, confused. I'd never told him about that.

"It's pretty obvious." His lips thinned.

"Why have you never brought this up before?"

"I didn't want to come on too strong."

"And now?" My brow lifted as I fought a smile.

"Now I want to stamp my name on your body, so everyone knows who you belong to."

"Neanderthal."

"With you? Always." Xander slid his hand along the side of my neck, gently collaring me, and kissed me.

"We should get back," I said, breaking the kiss first. He let out a frustrated sigh.

"Yeah, okay."

"Thank you, for tonight. It was perfect."

He brushed his thumb over my lips, staring at me with such intensity I could hardly breathe. "Yeah, well, you're worth it."

THE NEXT MORNING, I found Poppy and her mom in the kitchen.

"How was your date with Bryan?" she asked, and Poppy snickered.

"It wasn't a date. We're just friends."

"Well, I think it's lovely that you two spend so much time together."

Her words made me flinch. "He's a good guy," I said, avoiding her searching gaze. Poppy caught my eye though, and smirked.

Since Bryan and I had been spending so much time together, I figured they all thought more was going on than either of us were willing to admit. But no one pushed me for answers.

"You have to work the long shift today?"

"Yeah," I replied, grabbing a banana from the fruit bowl. "Ten until four."

"Too bad," Poppy said. "We're going to hang out at Sofia's."

"Maybe I'll stop by after."

"I bet Bryan would like that." The corner of her mouth lifted. I balled up a napkin and threw it at her.

"Girls," her mom scolded. "I'm at the center all day, but if you need a ride, call Jase. He should be home by three. Although looking at the weather, I'm not sure how much practice they'll get in."

Rixon had woken to a blanket of fluffy white snow, but it wasn't enough to stop the town dead in its tracks.

"You know they'll spend all day in the clubhouse drinking and playing pool," Poppy said.

"Probably. But they deserve a break. Your dad works hard, sweetheart. Your Uncle Cameron too."

"I know, Mom." Her cell chimed and she snatched it off the counter. "It's Lily. She says hey."

My cell lit up a second later and I received the same message, accompanied by a photo of her and Kaiden in their fluffy white robes in front of a window looking out onto a postcard perfect wintery scene.

"Not jealous at all," Poppy grumbled.

"Your time will come, Pops." Her mom smiled. "Now if you two girls are good here, I need to head out."

"Sure, see you later, Mom."

"Wrap up warm both of you." Felicity grabbed her purse and headed out.

"Is Bryan giving you a ride to work?" Poppy asked, and I shook my head.

"Cal offered to pick me up on his way in."

"Cool. So... last night..."

"Poppy."

"What?" She smothered a grin. "You've got to know it's

driving us wild not knowing what's going on between you two."

"We're friends."

Poppy pinned me with a pointed look. "Friends who hang out, alone."

"You and Aaron hang out alone sometimes."

"It's different. He's... he's one of my best friends."

"Hmm, if you say so."

"Hey," she balked, "what's that supposed to mean?"

"Nothing, nothing at all."

"Whatever." She poked her tongue out at me. "You know, it would be okay if you like him, Peyton. You seem... different lately. Happier. Lighter. Bryan is good for you."

My stomach twisted. If only she knew the truth.

"What?" Her expression slipped. "I didn't mean—"

"It's fine. You're right. I do feel different."

My broken heart was slowly being pieced back together. The jagged holes being filled with light and love and happiness.

Only Poppy didn't know the truth.

She didn't know it wasn't Bryan bringing me back to life.

And I wondered what she'd say when she knew the truth, when they all knew the truth. Because surely seeing me this way far outweighed the events that led me to this point.

I knew people would look at me and Xander and see something wrong.

Something taboo and forbidden.

But how could something healing me from the inside out, ever be a bad thing?

CHAPTER THIRTY-TWO

Xander

THE HEAVY KNOCK at my door startled me. I wasn't expecting visitors. My brother, Jase, and Asher were at the country club. I'd declined their offer to go along, wanting to avoid them until tomorrow when I was going to officially give Jase my resignation, and then come clean about everything.

I couldn't lie to him any longer. Not when he'd trusted me and given me the job. He deserved the truth, even if it shattered our friendship.

Crossing my apartment, I checked the peephole and opened the door. "Jase, this is—"

"We need to talk," he gritted out, shouldering past me.

Dread flooded me but I didn't have time to ask what was going on. When I closed the door and turned to face him, his murderous expression said it all.

"Tell me it isn't true," he said coolly. Too fucking coolly.

I bristled. "Let's sit—"

"Sit? You think I want to fucking *sit*?" Disgust washed

over him. "I want you to look me in the eye and tell me that it's not true. I want you to tell me there's no fucking way on Earth that you've been... fuck, I can't even say it." He blanched.

I held up my hands, panic surging through me. "I can explain."

"Explain? What the fuck could you possibly say that even begins to explain how Darryn thinks he saw you and Peyton in Halston last night... *together*."

"Fuck, Huckley saw us."

My stomach dropped.

"Yeah, he saw you. Said the two of you were walking downtown looking very cozy." Anger bled from his pores. "He called me earlier out of respect."

"And to get one over on me, no doubt," I muttered.

Jase pinned me with a dark look. "*Not* the fucking issue here." He leaned back against the kitchen counter and let out a heavy sigh. "Talk to me, Xander. Tell me what the fuck is going on here."

"It wasn't supposed to happen. I tried to—"

"Are you fucking her?"

My spine went rigid. "It isn't like that."

"You're fucking sick. She's a kid—"

"She isn't and you know it," I ground out. "She didn't fall in the river that night, Jase. She tried to... fuck." I ran a hand down my face.

"And you don't think that was all the more reason not to get involved with her for Christ's sake? She's unstable, and you're... fucking hell, Xander. You should have known better."

Anger circled him like a storm. "I don't know what I'm supposed to do here. Huckley is threatening to go to the school board with this. She's a student at the school where you work—"

"She's eighteen."

"It doesn't fucking matter." He boomed, the veins in his neck pulsating. "There are laws about this type of thing. Corruption of minors is a felony... you could go to jail. Do you have any idea the shitstorm that could rain down on you?"

My fingers went to my hair, tugging the ends in frustration.

He was right.

Of course he was fucking right.

And I'd known. I'd known that this could happen and yet, I hadn't stopped myself. Because Peyton was buried under my skin, an itch that no matter how much I scratched didn't go away.

Jase stared at me like he no longer recognized me. It was a look I was used to my brother wearing, but never Jase. He'd always been the peacekeeper, the one to try and smooth things over between me and Cameron. He'd given me a shot at something real with the team, and as far as he was concerned, I'd thrown it back in his face.

I'd broken his trust.

I'd fucked things up.

"I tried to tell you I wasn't going to take the job," I said, as if it made any difference. "Right after the championship, I tried—"

"How long?" Anger coated his words, turning my blood to ice.

"A few weeks."

"I should call the police myself. It's not right. She's an innocent—"

"You think I forced her?" Bile churned in his gut. "I would never—"

"IT DOESN'T FUCKING MATTER." He roared, slamming his hand down on the counter, making the fruit bowl clatter. "You think Huckley gives a shit about that, or Principal Kiln, or Mya? All they'll see is a guy—a grown fucking man—who I trusted, taking advantage of a teenager—a fucking child—in her time of need."

"Jase, I—"

"No, Xander." He jabbed his finger at me. "You need to listen to me and listen good. Whatever you think you feel or however you've justified this to yourself, it ends. It ends now. Peyton is grieving. She's hurting and she needs help. Professional help. She doesn't need some down-and-out making things worse, confusing her and filling her head with idealistic notions about… fuck, I don't even know what this is."

I jerked back, his words physically striking me. "I'm glad to know how you really feel."

"Oh, for fuck's sake, Xander. What could you possibly offer her? She's got her whole life ahead of her. A future. A shot at something better. Once she's had the counselling and figured out her next move, Peyton can do anything she wants. You'll be nothing more than a blip on her radar."

He might as well have driven a knife right through my back. I gaped at him, trying to formulate a response. But I had nothing.

Because he was right.

I had nothing to offer Peyton. Without my job at the high school, I'd be back to dead-end jobs and living paycheck to paycheck.

She deserved more.

She deserved so much more.

But I'd let the way she made me feel blind me to that fact. I'd wanted so badly to believe we could have something together—something real. But maybe it was never supposed to be that way.

I'd given up my chance back in high school, but Peyton... she still had the world at her feet.

"You need to end it. Today. I'll handle Huckley."

"Jase, man, I can't—"

His eyes narrowed, fury simmering there. Jase was a silent storm and if I pushed any harder, he would explode.

"You can and you will. I'm not asking you. As Peyton's guardian, I'm telling you, you will fucking end it." I inhaled a sharp breath as he stormed to the door, ripping it open. "And, Xander?"

"Yeah?"

"Consider yourself officially fired." He slammed the door behind him. It reverberated through me as I sank into my worn armchair.

It wasn't supposed to go down like this.

Last night had been one of the best nights of my life.

One more day.

One more fucking day and I was going to come clean to Jase.

But part of me couldn't help but think that maybe this was karma for screwing up my life back in high school. Maybe the universe wasn't done fucking with me.

I'd thought saving Peyton that night was my shot at a second chance. That maybe she was my redemption. But maybe it was never about me.

Maybe it was about her.

Because although this would hurt her, she would get over it. She would go on to graduate, and have counselling and deal with her grief, and when she was ready, she would meet a good guy like Bryan. Someone with hopes and dreams and a shot at something more than... than this.

I glanced around my shitty apartment.

Peyton deserved better than this.

She deserved better than me.

And for as much as I didn't want to admit it, maybe, in the long run, Huckley had done us both a favor.

I SPENT the day on the couch watching ESPN, trying, and failing not to think about her.

Bryan was bringing Peyton straight over from work, although just the thought of that conversation made me want to puke. But the sooner I ripped off the Band-Aid, the better.

By the time she knocked at the door, my stomach was a tight knot.

"Hey," Peyton beamed at me, her cheeks flushed from the cold.

"Hey," I said. "Come in."

Her expression slipped. "Xander, what is it?"

"Come inside, we need to talk." I noticed Bryan backing out of the parking lot, and part of me wanted him to come and save her from this.

From me.

"Xander," Peyton slipped past me, but didn't get far before she whirled on me, "you're scaring me. Did something happen?"

"Jase knows."

"Wh-what? But... how? Bryan would never—"

"It wasn't Bryan, Peyton. Coach Huckley... he saw us last night." I let out a deep exhale. "He called Jase earlier."

"Oh God." Her hand drifted to the hollow of her throat. "But you told Jase everything, right? That you're leaving the team and I'm—"

"It doesn't matter."

Her brows knitted, confusion clouding her eyes. "What do you mean, it doesn't matter?"

"We have to end this." My calm voice was at odds with the storm raging and tearing through me.

"What... no. *No*! I know it's not ideal that he found out like this, but we were going to tell him tomorrow. I'm eighteen now and you don't work at the school anymore, and hopefully, I'm going to graduate early. It doesn't mat—"

"Yes, it does. Huckley has threatened to go to the school board." The words cracked my chest wide open.

Tears clung to Peyton's lashes as the reality of the situation came crashing down around us. "I'll tell them it was consensual. I'll tell them that I—"

"Peyton, listen to me. It doesn't matter. I'm employed by the school. You're a student. They have grounds to investigate... to press charges."

"No, I don't accept that. I need you, Xander... I-I love you. I'm in love with you."

I'm in love with you.

Her words rattled around my skull.

Love.

She loved me.

"You don't love me."

"Don't tell me how I feel," she seethed, determination glittering in her eyes as she lifted her chin with defiance. "I think I've known for a little while... and I think you feel the same. And I know it's a mess, but we'll figure it out. Together."

"No."

Peyton jerked back as if I'd slapped her. "No?" Her voice shook. "No, we won't figure it out, or no, you don't feel the same?"

Steeling myself, I inhaled a thin breath. "I care about you, Peyton, I do. But I don't... I can't love you."

"You can't love me." She repeated the words quietly, the disbelief in her voice shredding my insides. "But I felt it." It was a cracked whisper. "Every time you kissed me, every time we were together, I felt it."

She wasn't going to accept this, not unless I ripped out her heart and trampled all over it. I stared at her, silently pleading with her to understand. *Don't make me do this.*

"I'm sorry. I am. I should never have let it get this far."

"You're lying. You're trying to protect me... I get it. I do. But I choose you, Xander. I choose you and nothing anyone says or does is going to change that."

"This was a mistake." I pressed my lips together, letting the words sink in. "I'm not looking to settle down, Peyton. This was fun and all, but it was never going to last. We both know that."

Tears fell freely down her cheeks. "I see." She shuddered, her eyes shuttering on a sharp inhale.

Guilt swarmed me, threatening to topple me to my knees. Couldn't she see it wasn't only her own heart breaking?

"For what it's worth," I said, "I'm sorry it went down this way."

Peyton sniffled, drying her eyes with the back of her hand. "You know that night you pulled me from the river, I thought you were my hero. How wrong I was." Her laughter was ugly, dark and twisted, mirroring the storm raging inside me. "You're not the hero of my story, Xander. You're the villain and I will never forgive you for breaking my heart."

She moved around me to the door.

"Peyton, wait," I rushed out. "I'll give you a ride home. It's the least I can do."

She scoffed, yanking the door open. The blast of frigid air was nothing compared to the temperature in my apartment.

Her eyes seemed to look through me as she said, "I think you've already done enough."

Peyton walked out of my apartment without looking back, completely unaware that she was taking my bloody, bruised heart with her.

Two days later, I finally left my apartment. Jason had called earlier to say that he'd handled Huckley, but it came with a steep cost. I burrowed into my jacket and headed toward the familiar row of graves, crouching low to run a hand over Mom and Dad's marbled headstones.

"Hey, Mom, Dad." I let out a heavy sigh. "I messed up. Fuck, I really messed up good this time. There's a girl... and she's smart and funny, and God, she's beautiful. And she gets me. She knows what it's like to be lost. I don't deserve it,"—*I'll never deserve it*—"but I think she loves me.

"You'd love her. She doesn't take herself too seriously and she loves those cheesy holiday movies you both loved. But she deserves better..." I almost choked over the lump in my throat.

Two days and I'd heard nothing from Peyton, not that I expected to. I'd seen the utter devastation in her eyes as she'd walked away from me, the betrayal. She'd let me in; given me a rare gift, and I'd thrown it back in her face like it meant nothing.

Like she meant nothing.

Closing my eyes, I inhaled a shaky breath. When I opened them again, I heard the crunch of leaves.

"I have to go. I don't know when I'll be back, so I wanted to come and say I'm sorry. I'm sorry I didn't do better. I'm so fucking sorry I'm not the son you wanted me to be. But I'm going to try, okay? I'm going to figure out how to fix myself, and who knows, maybe there's still a happy ending out there for me."

"Xander..." Cameron said from behind me, and I stood to greet my brother. I hadn't seen him since Jase stopped by, but I knew he knew. He'd sent me a text message saying exactly what he thought of me and my *ability to continuously screw up my life.*

"I was expecting Jase," I said.

"I wanted to do this."

"If you're here to rub salt in the wound, I'm all—"

"Why?" My brows pinched, and he let out a steady breath, but his anger was palpable. "Why her?"

"Sometimes you don't choose it, it chooses you," I murmured to myself. "Have you ever thought that maybe there was a reason I was there that night? That of all the people in this town, it was me who was right there at the moment she..." I still couldn't say the words.

"What are you saying?" Cameron rubbed his jaw, staring at me with utter disbelief.

"Everyone kept going on about how I saved her that night. But maybe it was the other way around... maybe she saved me."

"Xander, I—"

"It doesn't matter now. I know what comes next."

"You know, I wish it didn't have to be this way." He looked genuinely hurt.

"Yeah, well, I wish a lot of things were different."

Cam pulled out an envelope from his jacket pocket and handed it to me.

"What is this?" I took it, peeking inside at the check with one too many zeros.

"Enough for you to start over."

"I can't take this," I said, thrusting it back at him.

"Take it. But make sure you put it to good use. You

know, I think this... time away, could be good for you. You've been lost a long time, Xander. Maybe it's finally time to find yourself."

It didn't strike me as the time to tell him I'd already found myself in the smile belonging to a blue-eyed, blonde-haired angel who should never have laid eyes on me.

"How is she?"

"Xander, I—"

"Please, just give me this."

"She'll be okay."

It was a non-answer. But in some ways, I was relieved he didn't give me the truth—I wasn't sure I could handle it.

"I know things haven't always been easy with us," he said, "but you'll always be my brother, Xander. And I'll always be here for you."

Too choked up to reply, I gave him a small nod.

"I should go, Hailee and Ashleigh are waiting for me in the car. We're heading to Bell's for something to eat."

"Tell them... tell them all I'm sorry."

It was his turn to nod.

"I'm sorry we lost our way, Xander. I'll talk to you soon." Cam turned and left. He walked away from me like there was no coming back from this.

And maybe there wasn't.

I stood there, clutching the check in my hand. I shoved it in my pocket and pulled out my smokes. But as I stared at the packet, his words rang through me. *Maybe it's time to find yourself.* I crumpled the packet in my hand and threw it in the nearby trash can.

Glancing back at my parents' headstones, a faint smile traced my lips.

It wasn't much.

A small step.

But everyone had to start somewhere.

CHAPTER THIRTY-THREE

Peyton

"HEY, CAN I COME IN?" Lily peeked around the door, her eyes brimming with sympathy.

"Sure."

She closed the door and came and sat on the edge of the bed. "We're worried about you."

"I'm fine."

Lie.

It was a big fat lie.

I wasn't fine. My heart was shattered into irreparable pieces.

Xander was gone.

He'd left Rixon and never looked back. There had been no text messages, no calls, nothing.

He'd left town—left me—and I was just supposed to get on with things, as if I could breathe without him.

"Peyton, it's been three days and you've barely left your room. This isn't healthy."

"I'm sorry if I can't pretend everything is okay..." I

clutched the pillow tighter, blinking away the tears. I'd cried incessantly after I walked away from Xander, from his poisonous, cruel words. I was surprised I still had tears left to cry.

"You know, it's for the best—"

"Don't, just don't." I gaped at her. How could she possibly say that? I loved him. I was in love with him, and people were acting like it was some silly high school crush that I would get over.

"Peyton," she shuffled closer, reaching for my arm, "I know it hurts now, but it'll get easier."

"How can you say that? I feel like I've had my heart ripped out of my chest..." And there was nothing left but an empty hole.

"My dad only wanted to protect you. If Xander stayed and the two of you... People wouldn't understand."

I heard the words she didn't say. *I don't understand.*

"You deserve so much more, Peyton."

"Oh my God," I snatched my arm away, "stop telling me what I deserve. This isn't a game, Lil. I'm not acting out because I've had it hard and want attention. Xander and I shared something. He knew... he knew what it was like for me.

"He tried to push me away. He fought the connection between us because he knew it was wrong. But sometimes, you don't choose it..." *It chooses you.* God, those words would haunt me for a lifetime.

I'd truly believed Xander was my savior.

But when it came down to it, he was nothing more than a coward. I'd been prepared to fight for us, to risk the few relationships and friendships I had, for him.

What an idiot.

"I'm sorry," Lily gave me a weak smile. "I guess I'm just finding it hard to understand... He's Xander."

"This is exactly why I didn't tell you," I murmured. She'd been hurt at first. But this was why I hadn't trusted her with my biggest secret. She didn't understand.

None of them did.

"Peyton, that isn't fair..."

"None of this is."

Her dad could barely look at me. Poppy was avoiding me. Ashleigh wanted nothing to do with me. They were all acting like we'd committed a personal attack against them, when no one had stopped to consider how hard this had been for us. For me.

The only person who had shown me even a glimpse of sympathy was Bryan, but I'd refused his numerous offers to rescue me from the Ford's house.

"Peyton," Felicity called from downstairs. "You have a visitor."

For a split second, I imagined Xander standing on the doorstep. But I knew better. He was gone, and he wasn't coming back anytime soon. Ignoring Lily's heavy stare, I climbed off the bed and pulled on a Rixon High hoodie.

Mrs. Bennet was waiting downstairs. "Peyton," she said. "I hoped we could talk."

I glanced at Felicity, and she put up her hands. "This wasn't my doing, I swear."

"Is there somewhere we can talk in private?"

"Of course," Felicity said. "You can use the living room. I'll be in the kitchen if you need me."

Reluctantly, I followed Mya and sat down on one of the chairs. "I'm assuming they told you?"

"They did." She sat opposite me. "But I didn't come to discuss Xander."

"Oh?"

"I finally heard back from the school board. If you're still serious about graduating early, they are happy to approve your request. You'll need to complete your outstanding papers, but you have enough credits and a strong enough GPA that it's possible."

"I want to do it."

"Are you sure?"

"One-hundred percent." The sooner I graduated, the sooner I could pick up more shifts at Cindy's and start saving for my own place.

"I have to ask, Peyton. This plan... it didn't have anything to do with—"

"No. I wanted this before we..." She nodded, saving me from saying the words. "I refuse to be someone else's burden."

"You know they don't feel that way."

"It's not about how they feel, it's about how I feel, and I need to know I can do this. I want to earn money, Mrs. B. I want to provide for myself."

"I understand. Once I get back into the office, I can start the paperwork. You'll also need Jase and Felicity to sign off on it since they're your legal guardians. Would you like to talk to them now about it? I can stick around if you want some moral support."

"No," I said. "This is something I need to do alone, but thank you, for everything."

"Once school is back, we'll make an appointment for you to come by my office and get the ball rolling."

"Okay." I got up and followed Mya to the door. "I'll see you soon."

"You will. And, Peyton, I know things seem bleak now but you're a fighter and I have no doubt you'll come out on top. Tomorrow is a new year, a clean state."

Like that changed anything.

Mya went and said goodbye to Felicity and left, while I

inhaled a deep breath and braced myself for the conversation I needed to have.

I FOUND Jason and Felicity in the kitchen. "Can we talk?"

"Of course, sweetheart. Let's all sit." Felicity motioned to the table. Jason could barely look at me, tension swirling in the air. I knew he was angry. At Xander, at himself... maybe even a little at me.

"A few weeks ago, I asked Mya—Mrs. Bennet—to look into my options for graduating early."

"I see," Felicity frowned.

"You know I had no plans to apply for college, not this year. Not after everything that's happened." I swallowed over the lump in my throat unable to meet either of their heavy stares. "You have both been so generous, and I am so grateful. More than you'll ever know, but I need to stand on my own two feet. It's something I have to do. And I can't afford to waste five more months in high school when I could be working, earning."

"Peyton, sweetheart, while that's admirable, it is completely unnecessary. We didn't take you in and expect you to contribute. That was never—"

"I know, I do. But it's important to me to do this. I spent my entire childhood feeling like a burden, Felicity. Feeling unworthy and never good enough... It took me a long time to get over that. But I'm not a kid anymore. I'm eighteen and I need to know I can support myself."

"I-I don't know what to say." She let out an exasperated breath, and I noted how still and silent her husband was. He was still seething over everything that had happened, but I hoped that he could put that behind us to do the right thing here and give me permission to graduate early.

"With your generosity, I already have enough for a security deposit for my own place. And Cindy has already offered me more shifts at the diner, so I'll be able to find my own place."

"Sweetheart, there's no rush. Tell her, Jase." She nudged her husband. "If this is about what happened... You don't need to leave, Peyton. We love having you here."

I finally met Jason's eyes. A storm brewed there, the air cooling around us.

"There's just one snag," I said. "I'll need your permission. Mrs. Bennet says—"

"No," he said, flatly.

"Jason!"

"No fucking way, Felicity. She's just a kid. She doesn't know what she wants."

"Peyton, honey, why don't you go find Lily, and me and Jason will discuss this."

"Yeah, okay." I got up, but not before looking at him again. "I know you're only looking out for me. But this is my life. I should get to choose how I want to live it."

I hadn't even left the kitchen before their raised voices filled the air. But I was too weary to care. Felicity would fight in my corner; she would try to get her husband to do the right thing.

Their argument grew louder, and I winced, hating that I'd come into their lives and caused all this. Digging my cell out of my pocket, I pulled up a new text message to Bryan.

Me: Can you come and get me, please?

Bryan: I'll be there as quick as I can.

I STARED out at the lake, Bryan quiet beside me.

"I've been worried," he said, finally breaking the thick silence.

"I know." I inhaled a thin breath. "I couldn't..."

"Yeah. What happened?"

"I told them I want to graduate early, and Jason was having none of it."

"He only cares." Bryan gave me a sympathetic look.

"I know that. But it's my life, Bryan. I need to take control of my future."

"Have you talked to him about everything? About Coach Chase?"

"No, we've pretty much avoided each other. I don't know what to say." When I'd first found out he sent Xander away, I'd wanted to fight. To argue and stand up for him, for us. But then I'd remember Xander's words.

I can't love you... this was a mistake.

A mistake. He'd called me a mistake. God, it had hurt. At first, I'd been so convinced that he was just trying to protect me, to avoid the potential fallout from Coach Huckley discovering the truth. But you didn't hurt someone you cared about like that.

You didn't.

"You weren't in the wrong, Myers. Coach Chase is the adult here. He should have known better."

"I knew what I was doing, Bryan." I was equally as responsible for every kiss and every touch we'd shared. I'd wanted it. I'd wanted everything from a man who was never supposed to be mine.

And I'd made the foolish mistake of thinking he felt the same.

A fresh wave of tears burned the backs of my eyes.

Bryan noticed and cussed under his breath, reaching over to pull me into his arms. "I'm so fucking sorry," he whispered.

"Yeah, me too." My hands curled into his hoodie.

"You know, I think it's a crock of shit what he said to you… I spoke to him that day. I saw the look in his eyes. He cares about you, Peyton."

"It doesn't matter."

Because it wasn't enough.

I wasn't enough.

"So you're really going to do it? You're going to graduate early?"

I peeked up at him and nodded. "If they'll give me permission, yeah."

"I'm gonna miss you, Myers." His gaze darkened.

"You won't get rid of me that easy."

He wouldn't be around forever though. He, Lily, Kaiden, and Ashleigh would go off to college and start the next phase of their lives. But I couldn't dwell on that.

I wouldn't.

"You'll get through this, you know?" He held me at arm's length. "You're so fucking strong and I know you don't want to believe it yet, but one day you'll find the right guy to sweep you off your feet."

I gave him a thin smile. I didn't want to tell him that I'd already found that. That Xander was my person. Because he didn't want to hear it, nobody did.

And maybe they were all right.

Maybe it was time to accept the truth.

Xander was gone…

And he wasn't coming back.

CHAPTER THIRTY-FOUR

Xander

SIX WEEKS LATER...

"Look what the cat dragged in," Tash said as I approached her at the bar.

"Tash, you're looking good." I planted a kiss on her cheek.

"This place looks good on you." She grinned. "The usual?"

"Actually, I'll take a soda."

"Don't tell me... you're off the smokes and the liquor?" I nodded, and she snorted. "What the hell do you do for fun around here?" Her cackle filled our section of the bar, and Jenson, the bartender, threw me a questioning look.

"Don't mind her," I said. "She's from out-of-town."

"Rixon is hardly out of... oh, whatever." Tash's eyes crinkled. "It's good to see you, Xander."

"You too."

"How have you been?"

"Good. Things are... good."

"Are you sure? Because I'm not gonna lie, I was worried when you up and left town without so much as a phone call."

"It was complicated."

"The blonde."

"How did you—"

"I saw her, with your brother, his wife, and their kid. She's a student at the high school, isn't she?"

"She was." I nodded. I'd heard from Hailee that she was due to graduate next week. There would be no fancy ceremony, but they were having a family celebration. I hadn't been invited; not that I expected to be.

"Shit, Xander. A teenager. What the fuck were you—"

"Ssh, keep your voice down."

"What the hell happened?" Her eyes bugged.

"We got caught, Jase lost his shit, and he and Cam thought it would be best if I left town for a while."

She let out a low whistle. "Shit, that's some kind of fucked up."

The permanent knot in my stomach twisted.

Tash wasn't wrong, Halston looked good on me. I was done with the cigarettes and booze. I was in therapy, and I'd recently started volunteering at a local youth center. But no matter how much I'd turned things around, I still had a gaping hole in my chest.

I doubted it would ever disappear.

Leaving Peyton was hands down the hardest thing I'd ever done. But Jase and my brother were right. I had nothing to offer her except a boat load of emotional baggage and issues she didn't need holding her back.

Our relationship had been a whirlwind, borne out of pain and grief and darkness. She'd wanted a hero, and part of me had needed to be her savior. But if time and space had taught me anything, it was that another person couldn't fix you. Only you could do that for yourself.

Fuck, I was starting to sound like my therapist.

"So here you are," Tash added.

"Here I am." I clinked my bottle against hers. "It's not so bad. I have a decent apartment,"—thanks to Cameron—"and my building has a gym so I work out a lot. It helps..."

"Helps?"

Shit.

Tasha's eyes narrowed and then widened. "Holy crap, you're still hung up on her."

"It wasn't just some fling, Tash." The defensive edge to my words surprised us both. "It was the girl I pulled from the river."

"Whoa, you don't do things by half do you?" She gave me a sympathetic smile. "Have you spoken to her since you left?"

"No." I'd written a hundred text messages and deleted every single one. What could I possibly say to fix the mess I'd made of everything? Sorry certainly didn't cut it.

Peyton had confessed she'd fallen in love with me, and I'd thrown it back in her face.

I'd called her a mistake.

Not a second went by when I didn't regret that conversation, but I knew she would never let me walk away without a fight unless I hurt her. Unless I proved to her I was everything she'd always refused to believe.

I exhaled a steady breath and ran a hand down my face.

"I get it. You fucked up. But this is you, Xan, you've never let anyone in before. She must be special if she managed to find your heart under all that stone."

"Fuck you." I chuckled.

"Seriously though, you say she's no longer at the high

school?" I nodded and she went on. "And she's eighteen?" Another nod. "So why the fuck are you still here? Unless you're... hiding."

"I'm not." The words were flat.

"So, what's the problem?"

"She deserves better," I said, quietly, refusing to meet Tash's eyes.

"Oh, spare me the bullshit. We all go through shit, Xander. Life is hard and messy, and sometimes it hurts... but we only get one shot at it." She clapped me on the back. "I get the smoking and the drinking, we could all benefit from a detox now and again, but denying yourself a shot at being happy? That doesn't make any sense to me."

Tasha's eyes drilled into the side of my face until I finally glanced over at her. "What?" I asked, unsure I wanted to know the answer. But Tasha was nothing if not honest.

"You deserve this." Her lips curved into a warm smile. "You deserve to be loved."

"Shit, Tash, I didn't peg you for the sentimental type."

"Trust me, it doesn't happen often." She smirked. "But it's you... and I've watched you drink and fuck your way out of a black hole for too long. You care about her... don't let that slip through your fingers over something as foolish as pride."

Her words reverberated inside me, but she wasn't done.

"You'll regret it, Xander. If you don't try to fix it, you'll regret it. And you already have enough of those."

I drained my soda wishing it was a beer. Tash had rattled me, forced me to look at things I didn't want to look at, not yet.

But the real question was, was I going to do anything about it?

"XANDER, OVER HERE," Lynton beckoned me over.

"Hey, buddy, what's up?"

"Julian brought his collection of trading cards in." He flipped open the binder. "Check it out. He has the Jason Ford rookie card."

"Whoa, that's pretty cool." I sat down beside him on the bench.

"Right?"

"You know, I know Jase."

"No freakin' way." He gawked up at me. "You mean, you've met him?"

"He's a friend."

"Holy crap, I mean... wow. That's..."

"Relax, kid." I ruffled his hair. Lynton was one of the regulars at the youth club for young boys dealing with an array of emotional issues. Parental loss, separation, kids in care, the center provided a safe place for them to access activities. He'd taken an instant liking to me.

"What's he like?"

"He's a good guy. I grew up with him. He's my brother's best friend."

"So cool." He grinned. "Wait until the others find out."

Julian caught my eye across the room and smiled. Lynton was a good kid, but he was a little motormouth, and I had no doubt the rest of the kids would know all about my relationship with Jase by the end of the session.

We flicked through the remainder of the binder, Lynton pointing out his favorite players and ultimate heroes. His energy was infectious, and I envied the way he wore a smile every time he walked through the doors despite his turbulent homelife.

"You two look like you're having fun," Julian loomed over us.

"Julian, Julian, guess what?" Lynton wriggled on the bench, barely able to contain himself. "XanderknowsJason-Fordhowcoolisthat?"

"Whoa, there, little guy, take a breath." The volunteer manager smiled. "I actually need to borrow Xander a second, if that would be okay?"

"Sure, I want to show Dexter and Cody the trading cards anyway. Bye, Xander."

"Bye, buddy." I lifted my hand in a wave, watching as he scooped up the binder and hurried away toward a small group of boys.

"Can we talk?" Julian asked.

"Sure." Nervous energy zipped through me as I followed him toward his office.

"Take a seat." He motioned to the couch.

"Is everything okay?"

Amusement crinkled his eyes. "Don't look so worried. This is a good talk, hopefully."

Phew. I relaxed on the couch. "What's up?"

"I know it's only been a couple of weeks since you started volunteering here, but an opportunity has arisen. I spoke to Debra and we both agreed that we'd like to give you a shot."

"I'm sorry. A shot at what?"

"How would you like to be our newest youth counselor in training?"

"Seriously?" I gawked at him. "But I don't have any formal qualifications."

"It's an internship. You would work for us while completing the necessary qualifications. The pay is questionable, and the workload is intense, but at the end of it, we'd take you on as a fully qualified member of staff."

"I-I don't know what to say."

They wanted me.

Me.

"You've made a big impression over the last month and you're already an asset to the team. That, coupled with your own life experience, makes you the perfect candidate. There's a formal application process, but me and Debra both agree it's yours, if you want it."

"Thank you, I'm... wow, I'm speechless."

"We don't need a decision today. Take the week to think about it. You'll need at least one personal recommendation, but I figured it shouldn't be a problem getting one from Coach Ford." He winked.

Julian knew about my brother, about Jase and my coaching job at the school, but he didn't know everything.

Fuck.

This was... it was a huge opportunity to finally get my life on track and make something of myself. To make a difference to kids like I'd been once. Lost and confused and afraid.

"I'll think about it, thank you." I stood and reached forward to shake his hand.

"Good." Julian pierced me with a hard look. "I think you could make a real difference here. I hope you'll make the right decision."

Stunned, I left his office and headed straight for the staff bathroom. I'd never in a million years expected this. I'd signed up to volunteer to keep myself busy and feel like I was doing something positive with my time. Something more than the endless cycle of unskilled labor I was stuck in.

But he needed a personal recommendation, and the only person able to give me one hadn't spoken to me since the day I'd left Rixon. But what was it that Tash had said to me? Don't let something as foolish as pride get in the way of what you want.

And I wanted this.

Before I could talk myself out of it, I pulled out my cell phone and opened a new text message.

Me: Hey, I know it's been a while. But I need to talk to you.

Jase: It's about time.

My lip twisted at his reply. Typical Jase.

Me: Tomorrow night, my place? Cameron has the address.

Jase: I'll be there at six.

Me: Thank you.

I didn't know what I would say to him yet. How I'd repair the damage done to our friendship. But he was willing to give me a chance...

And that's all I could ask for.

"THIS PLACE IS a damn sight better than that shithole you had in Rixon." Jase stepped into my apartment and surveyed the tidy living room.

"It's okay."

He scoffed at that. "You got any beer?"

"No, I'm... detoxing."

"Guess it's coffee then?"

I nodded, making a beeline for the coffee machine. "You came straight from work?" I asked.

"Yeah." He rubbed his jaw, perching on one of the stools at the breakfast counter. "How have you been?"

"Okay, I guess. I keep busy enough."

"Good, that's good. Hailee keeps us all updated."

"Of course she does." I gave him a wry smile.

"You never called."

"I thought it was pretty obvious from our last conversation that you didn't want to talk to me."

"Shit, Xander. I was angry. I said a lot of things—"

"It doesn't matter. It happened, and I didn't ask you to come here to rehash the past."

"You didn't?" He eyed me warily.

"No. I need a favor."

"And there it is."

His assumption made me bristle, but it was nothing I didn't deserve. I forced myself to take a deep breath. "I've been offered an internship at the youth center where I volunteer, but I need a personal recommendation."

The surprise in his expression hurt almost as much as his earlier assumption.

"I'm sorry. I just assumed you wanted money or something."

"Not this time," I said grimly.

"Xander, I—"

"Let's not, Jase. If you don't want to write it, I

understand. I fucked up. I broke your trust and put your integrity and job on the line. And there isn't a day that goes by without me regretting how things went down, but I really want this. I think I could be... good at it."

He regarded me for a second, his eyes searching my face. "You're different."

"Yeah, well, I've had a lot of time to reflect."

Time seemed to stop, every beat of silence more painful than the last.

"For what it's worth," I finally spoke, "I am sorry. It was never supposed to go down like that."

"But it did..."

"Yeah."

"Did you love her?"

"Jase, I..." The words got stuck in my throat. It's the question I'd asked myself every day since leaving Rixon.

Did I love her?

I'd told her I couldn't. That I didn't have it in me.

But there were moments, when I closed my eyes and saw Peyton's face, that my heart swelled to the point where I thought it might explode.

I wasn't incapable of loving her. I was terrified of what it would do to me when she realized I wasn't worth it. That's what it boiled down to—that I wouldn't survive loving and losing her.

"Xander?"

I blinked, shaking the thoughts out of my head. "It doesn't matter now."

Her life was in Rixon, and my life was here. And maybe it was better this way. Maybe it was the only way to protect both of our hearts from the inevitable fallout of our relationship.

His eyes narrowed. "I'll write your recommendation."

"You will?"

"What happened doesn't change the fact that you were good with the team, with the guys. You've always had so much potential. Xander. You just couldn't look past your own pain to see it. Send me the details, and I'll get it done."

"Thank you."

"Does this mean you won't be coming back to Rixon any time soon?"

"I don't think that's a good idea, do you?"

Something flashed in his expression, but I ignored it. Whatever he wanted to say, nothing good could come of it. The damage was done.

I couldn't even bring myself to ask him how she was.

"Do you want to stay for something to eat? I was going to order in."

"I can't tonight, but maybe another time."

"Yeah, sure." It came out tight as I realized the bridge between us might be too damaged to ever fully repair.

He leaped off the stool and headed for the door, texting someone.

"It was good to see you, Xander."

"Yeah, you too."

My cell pinged and I frowned, snatching it off the counter. "What's this?" I asked, as he reached the door.

"It's the details of Peyton's graduation dinner."

"I don't understand." My expression hardened, the mention of her name a burden too big to bear.

"You should come," he said quietly, as if he didn't want to say the words.

"Why?" My voice trembled.

"Because you're family... and despite everything, she'd want you there."

CHAPTER THIRTY-FIVE

Peyton

"TABLE FIVE," Cal rang the bell, and I made my way over to the service counter, loading my hands full of plates.

"Thanks," I said, winding through the tables. "Okay, I've got the cheeseburger no pickles, and the chicken salad with the sauce on the side." I placed them down. "Enjoy your meals."

"You know, you haven't stopped smiling," Cindy said.

"I'm just happy to be here."

It was my first day working a full shift at the diner. I had officially graduated and entered the world of full-time employment.

It had been a hard few weeks. I'd spent most of it heartbroken over Xander, reliving every moment we'd spent together, trying to figure out where it had gone so wrong. But when I'd finally got the green light to graduate, it felt like a weight had been lifted.

Maybe Xander and I weren't meant to be. But this,

taking control of my life the only way I knew how, was a step in the right direction.

Jason had really dug in his heels at first, refusing to even contemplate signing the permission form, but Felicity—with a little help from Lily—managed to persuade him. He had agreed with the stipulation that I didn't rush to find my own place, which was fine by me. The longer I saved up, the better choices I'd have.

Things were good.

I was good.

Sure, it still hurt to think about Xander, but I'd accepted he wasn't coming back. Moving on was going to take some time. Not that I suspected I'd ever truly move on from him. But I was determined to get there.

Somewhere in the last month, I'd realized that I hadn't survived everything I'd been through to just give up all because I got my heart broken. I was better than that.

I was more deserving than that.

Counseling has helped a lot. We'd worked through the trauma of my mom's suicide and now we were slowly unpicking all my unresolved feelings around my childhood and the neglect I suffered at her hands.

I had a long way to go, but it was a start.

A group of people filed into the diner, and I smiled. "This is a surprise," I said, greeting my friends.

"Yeah, well, we couldn't very well let you start your first day of full-time employment without coming by to wish you good luck." Lily produced a small box from behind her back. "Congratulations."

I flipped the lid and sniffed the chocolate cupcake from Sprinkles. "It smells so good. I'll eat it on my break." I'd already had my lunch break, but I'd get another fifteen minutes later.

"If you find a booth, I'll bring over your menus."

Kaiden led Lily away; and Bryan, Poppy, and Sofia followed. But Ashleigh hovered.

"Hey," she said.

"Hey."

"Listen, are we okay? I know you said we are,"—I had, numerous times—"but I can't—"

"Leigh, relax." I smiled. "We're fine. I promise."

"Okay." Her shoulders sank, relief etched in her expression. "Because you're one of my best friends, Peyton, and I hate that things have been weird between us. I know what you had with Xander—"

"Not here." I shook my head.

I couldn't fall apart, not here. Not now. Although I was in a better place, it was easier to keep him locked away in a box than talk about him.

I'd found that out the hard way, when a couple of weeks ago we'd had a girl's night at the Bennet's house and gotten drunk on Mrs. Bennet's wine collection. Lily and Ashleigh had started asking me about Xander, and before I knew it, I'd been sitting in a puddle of my tears, trembling as I tried to put into words what had happened between us.

They didn't ask again after that, and I never brought it up. But I think they realized then, the depth of what I'd felt for him.

"Okay." She nodded. "But if you ever want to talk about it... about him. I'm here."

"Thanks." I grabbed a stack of menus and walked to the booth with her.

"What's good, Myers?" Bryan smirked.

"You've eaten here enough to know what's good by now." I chuckled.

It was true. Bryan stopped by all the time to eat; sometimes just to hang out until he gave me a ride home.

Our friendship was stronger than ever, and I knew I was lucky to have him in my corner still, after everything.

"Do you want to order some drinks and I'll take your food order when you've decided?"

"Sure," Poppy said, and they all rattled off their orders.

I went to ring them through the system and Cindy helped me prepare them. "I still think you should give him a shot," she said, glancing in Bryan's direction. "He's a looker."

"It's not like that between us. He's one of my best friends."

"Friends can become more."

"Cindy!" I scolded.

"Fine, I'll stop. Hey, maybe he fancies himself a cougar?"

"Oh my God, you're so bad." Amusement played on my lips. I loaded the tray and headed back over to my friends.

"Drinks." I handed them around. "Are you ready to order?"

"Yeah." Lily smiled, ordering her and Kaiden's. Poppy went next, and then Ashleigh and Bryan.

"Great, it won't be long." They'd beaten the after-school rush. "Where are Sofia and Aaron?" I asked.

"Bennet family drama," Ashleigh grimaced.

"Ezra?"

"Who else?"

"I wonder if he'll come tomorrow," I said. The Fords had organized a small graduation celebration at a fancy restaurant in town. I hadn't wanted anything elaborate so we'd compromised on dinner.

"I wouldn't hold your breath."

"Don't worry, Myers," Bryan chimed, "I'll be there."

I grinned at him. "I wouldn't expect anything less."

Senior year hadn't gone the way I'd hoped. I'd lost my

mom, my home, I'd even lost myself along the way... But I wasn't alone. Not really. I had good friends and a family who treated me like one of their own.

It was enough.

I was enough.

And I had to believe there was a happy ending out there for me.

"THEY DID KNOW I wanted this to be low key, right?" Spying the balloons and banners, I clutched Lily's hand and we made our way through the restaurant. Her dad had booked the entire back room which was at least something. I wouldn't have to survive the night with the other patrons all gawking at me.

It wasn't everyday a student graduated early from Rixon High, and everyone had heard my story by now. But they didn't know about Xander. Jason had managed to keep that under wraps. I don't know how exactly he'd gotten Coach Huckley to stay quiet, but he had.

"They wanted to make it special."

I gave her a pointed look and Lily rolled her eyes. "Let them have this." She squeezed my hand. "They're proud of you, Peyton."

I very much doubted that, but I wasn't looking to start an argument.

Not tonight. Not when things were finally calmer between all of us.

"Here she is," Jason stood, smoothing down his fitted black shirt.

"This is... thank you." No expense had been spared with table décor and bottles of champagne sitting in ice buckets littered on the table.

We sat down just as a server appeared and handed out leather-bound menus. "I'll give you some time to decide and come back shortly. If you need anything, just call."

"Thanks, Harriet." Felicity gave her a warm smile, and I glanced at her in question. "She volunteers at the rescue center a couple hours a week."

"How does it feel then, Peyton, to be finally free of high school?" Mr. Bennet asked me, much to his wife's annoyance. She nudged his arm, offering me an apologetic smile.

"It feels... really good. I'm just excited to be earning money and to look to the future."

"Nothing wrong with that," he said, lifting his glass. "To Peyton."

"Peyton." My name rang out in the small room and I flushed.

"Way to steal my speech," Jason protested.

"You can save yours for after dinner."

"You look beautiful," Bryan whispered around a teasing grin, before giving me a super squeezy hug.

"Hands off, Hughes."

"Yeah, yeah, Myers. Get a few glasses of bubbly inside you and you won't be able to resist the Brymeister." His brows waggled, and I burst into laughter.

"Oh my God, don't ever call yourself that again." Noticing the empty chair, I said to Kaiden, "Is your mom joining us after all?"

"No, she couldn't make it. But she sent a card." He pushed the envelope across the table to me.

"She didn't need to do that."

"It's from both of us."

"Thank you."

"What looks good?" Bryan nudged my shoulder, but I

was too busy watching Jason watch the entrance to the private room like a hawk.

"Myers."

"What, sorry?" I glanced up at Bryan, and he chuckled. "You're jumpy."

"No, I'm not. I'm just... it doesn't matter." The corner of my mouth tipped as I opened my menu. "Let's see what looks good."

DINNER WAS AMAZING, but I was so stuffed, gorging myself on chicken parmigiana, that when they wheeled in the dessert trolley, I had to pass.

"Lightweight," Bryan teased, and I pinched his hand.

Jason was still acting cagey, stalking the door and checking his cell phone. I was beginning to think he'd planned another surprise. But no one mentioned anything, and I was all too happy to stay oblivious. Dinner was enough. I didn't need, or want, anything else.

Once the server had plated up everyone's desserts, Jason stood, clinking his fork against his glass.

"Speech," Mr. Bennet drawled, earning him a swift elbow to the stomach from his wife.

We all snickered at him doubled over in pain.

"You're worse than the kids," Jason said. "Now, where was I? Ah yes, Peyton." His eyes settled on me. "You came to this family at a difficult time. I didn't always know the right things to say or do, but hopefully you knew that you had a place among us. You will always have a place among us. I might not be your dad but I'm proud to be the man who gets to watch you grow into a strong, confident, independent young woman. It took me a while to accept your decision, but I realize now that it was yours to make. And I can respect that."

He lifted his glass in the air and everyone followed. Emotion pricked my eyes as I fought the tidal wave of tears building. "To Peyton."

It was the second toast to me of the night, and this time, I couldn't stop the slip of silent tears down my cheeks as everyone settled their gazes on me. It was my turn to speak.

"I just want to say a huge thank you to the Fords for taking me in and giving me somewhere safe to stay. I'll never forget what you did for me. It's true what they say, that family isn't always blood, it's the people who are there, no matter what."

"Cheers to that," Asher said, deflecting the spotlight from me.

Laughter filled the room as everyone dug into their desserts. They had all come here tonight for me. Not out of obligation, but because this group of people was family in every way that mattered.

They'd accepted me, flaws, baggage, and all.

And that was something to cherish.

"Good night," Jason said to Asher and Cameron while their wives hugged and kissed. Poppy and Sofia had already left with Aaron since they were heading to Cole's to watch a movie.

"We're going to head out too," Lily said, tucked into the crook of Kaiden's arm. "You'll be okay riding home with Mom and Dad?"

"I think I'll survive." I smiled.

"Bye." They waved and took off after everyone else, leaving me with Jason and Felicity.

"Did you enjoy your night, sweetheart?"

"I did, thank you." I glanced at Jason lingering by the door. "Is everything okay?"

"Yes, why do you ask?"

"He's been acting kind of strange."

"Trust me when I say that is nothing new." Felicity smirked, pressing her hand against my cheek. "He meant every word of it, you know? We're very proud of you, sweetheart."

"Thank you." I swallowed thickly.

"Okay?" she asked Jason as he approached.

"Yeah," he smiled, but it didn't quite reach his eyes. "Let's go." He wrapped his arm around her waist, and I trailed after them.

We spilled onto the sidewalk into a blast of cold air.

"Good thing your car is right around the corner." Felicity chuckled.

"Cold, love?" He nuzzled her neck, not caring they had an audience. "Don't worry, I'll warm you up later."

A pang of heartache went through me. Even now, after all this time—after college, a career in the NFL, Felicity's career, two daughters, and a foster daughter with more baggage than the four of them combined—they were still fiercely in love.

I wanted that.

I could recognize that now.

I'd always been too scared to let myself want it, but I did.

We rounded the side of the restaurant when a voice said, "Peyton."

My body froze, the air stuck in my lungs as if I'd forgotten how to breathe. I turned slowly. "X-Xander... I don't—"

Realization slammed into me. The empty chair. Jason

acting strange as if he was expecting somebody else to join us.

"You're late," he said to Xander from somewhere behind me.

"I got caught up with something. I'm sorry I missed it." His apologetic gaze settled on me, but I didn't know what he was apologizing for.

I didn't understand.

"You left," I blurted, my thoughts too muddled. I thought I was dealing with everything. I thought the heartache, the emptiness I felt, was slowly healing. But now he was standing there, looking at me, looking so fucking good… and I was a mess.

My carefully erected walls came crashing down around me and I didn't know what to do.

"Peyton," he said again, taking a step toward me. "You look good."

You look good.

A bitter laugh crawled up my throat. "You've got to be kidding me. I haven't seen or heard from you in almost two months and that's what you say to me?"

Guilt flashed in his eyes.

Good.

I wanted him to feel guilty. I wanted him to feel even a tenth of the heartache I'd felt every day since he uttered the words, '*I can't love you.*'

"I don't understand," I said, needing to break the thick silence. "How are you even here?" Xander glanced at Jason, and I gaped back at him. "You invited him?"

"I saw him recently. I may have mentioned your graduation dinner."

"I see."

"Peyton, sweetheart," Felicity inched closer. "Why don't we—"

"The two of you should talk," Jason said. "You're welcome to come back to the house. We'll give you some space."

They would?

I didn't understand what was happening.

Just when I finally thought I was getting somewhere, he was back.

Xander was back.

CHAPTER THIRTY-SIX

Xander

HURT SHONE IN HER EYES.

But it was nothing compared to how much it ripped me to shreds to hear the contempt in her voice.

"No," she said. "I have nothing to say to you." Peyton wrapped her arms around her waist.

"Peyton, maybe you should—"

"It's okay," I shook my head at Fee. "I won't keep you all. But take this, please." Unzipping my jacket, I retrieved the envelope from the inside pocket and handed it to her.

"What is it?" She stared at it like I'd given her a ticking time bomb.

"Just read it. Please?"

Peyton held my gaze but gave nothing away. "I'm ready to leave now." She stalked past Jase and Felicity, climbing into his car.

"It's good to see you." Fee pulled me into a hug. "I'm so mad at you for staying away this long."

"I'm sorry, for everything."

It wasn't enough, but forgiveness didn't happen overnight.

"How is she, really?" I looked over at the car, wanting nothing more than to go to her.

"She's okay," Jase said. "For much as I was against it, I think graduating early will be good for her. She worked her first full shift at the diner yesterday. We haven't seen her smile that much in a while."

"I'm going to check on her." Fee squeezed Jase's hand. "Don't be long."

He gave her a small nod, watching her leave, and then looked at me. "You came."

"I almost didn't."

"What changed your mind?"

"There's a lot I never got to say to her."

"Are you sticking around?" His brow lifted.

"Yeah, I'm staying at a motel just outside of town."

"Does Cam know you're back?"

"Not yet."

"You two need to talk."

"I know." My chest rose with the weight of the words. "Listen, I have no right to ask, but tell her to read the letter."

"Will it make me want to hunt you down and break your legs?"

"Probably, but life's too short not to go after what you want."

"And what do you want, Xander?" His cool gaze burned into me.

"I want it all."

Without explanation, I spun on my heel and took off down the sidewalk. Peyton wasn't ready to talk, but she wasn't the only one I needed to apologize to.

"XANDER?" Hailee blinked as if she couldn't quite believe it. "This is a surprise."

"Hey, is he home?"

"He is. Come in." She beckoned me inside, taking my jacket and hanging it on the rack. "Halston looks good on you."

"Thanks."

"And how are things?"

"Jase didn't tell you?" I frowned. It wasn't like them to keep things from each other.

"He said you were okay."

"I am. Life is surprisingly good." There was just one thing missing.

"Hailee, is someone—Xander." Cameron appeared, his expression grim. "So you are alive then."

"Hello, Brother."

"I'll give the two of you some space." Hailee kissed my brother's cheek and then glanced at me. "It's good to see you, Xander. Don't leave it so long next time."

I gave her a nod, watching her disappear into the living room.

"You came for her." It wasn't a question.

"I came to see her, yeah. But she isn't the only reason I'm here. Can we talk?"

"Sure, I have some beers in the refrigerator." He motioned for me to follow him.

"Actually, coffee or soda will be fine." Cameron glanced back at me and frowned, so I added, "I've been cutting down."

"Right."

I perched at the breakfast counter. "How are things?"

"Xander, you can't just turn up and expect me to shoot the shit. Not after what went down."

"I know. Fuck, I know." I dragged a hand over my face. "I don't even know where to start."

He pushed a mug of coffee toward me. "Try..."

"You know when I think back to when I was a kid, it isn't Mom I remember, or Dad, it's you. You were always there for me. No matter what. I idolized you, and when you left for college, it felt like my world imploded."

"Xander, I—"

"No, let me get this out. All I ever wanted was to make you proud. But things got all twisted up. You had Hailee and then she got pregnant, and suddenly, I wasn't the center of your world... and I know how messed up that sounds. But I couldn't deal."

I inhaled a thin breath. "Senior year, I was so fucking angry at everything. You kept pushing me about college, about the future... and I don't know, I guess I resented you. I hated that everyone looked at me and saw the football star as if that's all I was good for."

"You had it, Xander. You could have gone all the way."

"You think I don't know that? You think I don't regret that every second of every day? But deep down, I didn't want it for me, Cam, I wanted it for you, for them... and I threw it all away because I couldn't deal, because I was so messed from losing Mom and Dad... and you—"

"Xander, you never lost me." His fists clenched against his thighs. "I was always there."

"I know that now. I fucked everything up. I knew it the second I woke up in the hospital and saw the disappointment in your eyes. Things changed between us that day and rather than confess everything, I reinforced my defenses and shut you out. I shut you out because it was easier than facing the truth. I let you down. I let everybody down."

Silence ticked by. Thick and heavy with the ghosts of our past.

"When I pulled Peyton from the river, I didn't want to be the hero. It was the last thing I wanted. But when she looked at me, it was like for the first time, in a really long time, I could breathe. She made it quiet, Cam. The self-loathing, the bitterness and regrets, she made it all go away."

"Fuck..." He breathed, running a hand down the back of his neck. "You love her."

"Yeah, I think I do. And I'd planned to tell Jase, to come clean to you all because I didn't want to jeopardize what I had with her. But then Huckley saw us, and everything went to shit... and I lost her. I fucking lost the best thing ever to happen to me."

"I don't know what to say." He shook his head. "When I found out, all I kept thinking was if a guy your age even tried to come close to Ashleigh, I'd want to kill him with my bare hands. But you and her, it wasn't normal circumstances."

"No, it wasn't."

"It doesn't change the fact you went about it all the wrong way. You know that, right?"

"Yeah, I know. I'd feel the same. But honestly, I can't say I'd do any of it differently."

Because every second with Peyton had been worth it. Even when I was trying to fight it, even when I knew it was wrong, it was worth it.

"Have you told her?"

"Not to her face, no."

His eyes clouded at that. "I know I should probably pull the older, wiser big brother card here, and part of me wants to, but... you've already lost so much."

"We both have."

"Yeah, but I have Hailee and the kids. I have a life, a family." His expression fell. "I never meant to—"

"No, you're not going to do this. You're not going to swoop in and try to carry some of the burden of this. I made my choices. Me. It's time I owned them."

Cam rounded the breakfast counter and pulled me into his arms. "I'll always be here for you, Xander. Even when we lose our way, I'll always be here."

"I know, Brother," I hugged him tighter. "I know."

CHAPTER THIRTY-SEVEN

Peyton

TEARS ROLLED down my cheeks as I clutched Xander's letter, reading it for the third time.

Peyton,

Before you, I was bitter. Angry and jaded at the world. I didn't believe in love or soulmates or happy-ever-afters. Sure, I watched everyone around me fall in love and find their person, the other half of their soul, but I knew it wouldn't ever be me.

You see, I didn't want it. I didn't want to give my heart to someone, only to lose them somewhere down the line. I have always had attachment issues, a deep sense of abandonment that as I grew turned into a steel fortress around my emotions.

And then I saw you in the river that night. I didn't want to be your hero. I didn't want to be anyone's hero. But I saw the way you looked at me. Nobody had ever looked at me like that. I felt unworthy, undeserving of your attention. But the more you got all up in my face, the more I fell. And a strange thing happened. For the first time in my life, I could breathe. You didn't look at me and see Xander the constant disappointment, the down-and-out drinking his life away. You saw Xander, a hero, your savior, a guy who knew what it was like to always feel on the outside looking in.

I knew it was wrong to want you. Fuck, it was so wrong. But how could anything that felt so right ever be wrong?

If I could go back in time, I'd like to think I'd do things differently. That I'd tell you we had to wait. But the truth is, I'm not sure I would. Because although I saved you that night, what you probably don't realize is, you saved me too. You taught me how to smile, how to laugh, and love. You taught me what it means to be brave and fight for something better.

I lied to you that night when I told you I couldn't love you. I love you, Peyton. I love your flaws and imperfections, your scars and emotional baggage. I love the girl you are, and the woman you'll become. I know I hurt you. I know I don't deserve a second chance, but here I am anyway, asking for one last shot.

You asked me once not to break your heart... and I failed. But I swear, it won't happen again.

I'm staying at The Happy Days Motel, room 4B, on the edge

of town until Sunday. If you want to talk, about anything, you know where to find me.

Xander

"Peyton?" There was a soft tap at my door. "Can I come in?"

"Yeah."

Jason's head appeared around the door. "Hey," he said.

"Hey." I sniffled, drying my eyes with my sleeves. "What's up?"

"I just wanted to check in on you. It's been an eventful night."

"Why did you tell him about the dinner?"

He perched against the edge of my desk. "Because no matter what happened between the two of you, Xander is family and I thought he should be there... and I thought you might want him there."

"I didn't." I peeked up at him. "At least, I thought I didn't."

"Did you get any answers?" His gaze went to the letter in my hand.

"Some."

"I know it can't be easy talking to me about this. I was the one who sent Xander away."

"Xander is a grown man. If he didn't want to go, he didn't have to—"

"Yes, Peyton, he did. If Huckley had gone running to Principal Kiln, Xander could have been arrested. Your name would have been dragged through the mud. Hell, my name, Cam's name, our families... it would have been very messy."

"I was eighteen. I would have denied everything."

"I know, but it doesn't change the fact that he worked at the school where you were a student. Xander leaving was the right decision, the only decision. You both needed time..."

"Time?"

"You were grieving, Peyton, and Xander saved you, literally saved your life. You were vulnerable and you latched onto him, and I think deep down, a part of Xander needed to save you."

"Because of his mom and dad," I whispered.

"Yeah. Whether you want to admit it or not, your relationship was borne out of a dark place and those kinds of emotions can be intense and all-consuming. They can make people reckless."

Mashing my lips together, I dropped my gaze. He was right, it had felt like a whirlwind.

A storm that neither of us could avoid.

"Time apart would let you sort through things; let you take a step back and see things with a different perspective."

"You thought I'd get over him?"

"I had hoped you would, yes. And part of me was beginning to think that maybe you were. But I see you, Peyton. I see you day in and day out. You smile in all the right places and join in conversations and laugh, but I see the pain in your eyes. The longing."

"I—"

"It's okay, I'm not here to judge. Not this time. It's my job to protect my girls, and that extends to you. It always will. But I also respect your right to make your own decisions. You're eighteen now, you've graduated high school, and you're working full-time, and I know you're saving for your own place."

There was a protective edge to his voice usually reserved for conversations between him and his daughters.

"If you can pay your own bills and stand on your own two feet, you can choose who you love. I won't stand in the way of that, no matter how much it freaks me the hell out."

"I-I don't know what to say," I stuttered, completely overwhelmed at his words.

"You miss him. I see it every time I look at you. And do you know what I saw when I went to visit him? I saw the same vacant look in his eyes." Jason gave me a weak smile. "Sometimes love doesn't play by the rules, Peyton. Sometimes it's messy and raw and relentless. Sometimes it hurts us and sometimes it breaks us. But when you find the right kind of love, the love worth fighting for, you should never let go of that."

He moved to the door. "Think about it." His eyes went to the letter again. "Everyone deserves a second chance. If Fee hadn't given me one or two over the years, fuck knows we wouldn't be here now."

"Thank you, Jason, for everything." Tears tracked down my cheeks. "Felicity, Lily, and Poppy are lucky to have you."

He winked and said, "I guess that makes you pretty damn lucky too."

I smiled.

Yeah, I guess it did.

The next morning, I stood outside Xander's room at The Happy Days Motel, wondering if I'd made a big mistake coming here.

His letter had ripped open the fragile stitches in my heart, but it was Jason's words that had given me the courage to come here. I owed it to myself, to the part of me that knew I hadn't dreamed up every kiss and touch and stolen moment, to hear him out.

But the second I arrived outside his room, fear had gripped me in a chokehold, stopping me from knocking on the door.

"Ugh, this is ridiculous," I muttered to myself, forcing myself to take a step closer just as the door swung open.

"Peyton," Xander stared at me wide-eyed.

"I… hey."

"I was just about to head over to Jase's."

"You were?"

"Yeah. When you didn't text, I thought…" Relief washed over him. "You're here."

"I'm here."

"Do you want to come in?"

"I…" *Did I?*

Could I?

I took a deep breath and shook off the icy chill of fear. "Yeah, okay."

I followed Xander inside to a clean and tidy motel room. His small bag in the corner hinted at his short stay, but I didn't want to think about that right now. My mind didn't have enough room to process everything.

"You read my letter?"

"I did." I sat gingerly in the single chair while Xander sat on the edge of the bed, leaning toward me, the way I slightly edged toward him.

Like magnets, my mind whispered.

Except, we weren't magnets now. Because he'd pushed me away and then left, and whatever invisible tether between us had existed had been cleaved in two.

"I meant it, Peyton. Every single word."

"You hurt me, Xander. You—"

"I know, fuck, I know." He ran a hand down his face, exhaling a pained breath. "I messed up. I know that. But I think that maybe I needed to lose you to realize what I had, to realize how I truly felt about you."

"You love me?"

"I do, so fucking much. It's killed me staying away, not texting you or calling. But I needed to figure out some things. I needed to find a way to fix myself before I..." The words lodged in his throat, and I knew he'd probably never bared himself to anyone this way before.

And I got it. Neither of us were used to letting ourselves be vulnerable in front of others. But this wasn't just any person. It was Xander. And I was Peyton, the girl who had opened up to him, trusted him with my heart. I was the girl who looked in his direction and saw him. Really saw him.

"Would you have come back for me if Jason hadn't visited you?"

"Eventually, yes."

"Eventually..." I let out a bitter laugh, darting my gaze away from him.

"I can't change what happened, Peyton," he sighed. "I can only own my mistakes and move forward. But I don't want to move forward without you."

God, I wanted to believe him.

"Jason said he thinks our relationship was some kind of dependency thing because we were both hurting."

"I think he's right—"

"What?"

Xander held up his hands. "Just hear me out for a second. You were in a dark place and I think you needed a savior." His expression softened. "You needed someone to save you."

I pursed my lips. He had a point. But people bonded

over grief and pain and trauma all the time. It didn't dampen what I felt for him.

It didn't.

"What I feel... what I felt for you. It was real."

"What you... felt?" Hurt flashed in his eyes. "So, you don't..."

"Xander, that isn't fair. You left me. You just left and I didn't know if you were ever going to come back. You told me you couldn't love me. You said it was a mistake." My heart broke all over again, remembering how it had felt hearing those words. "Do you have any idea what that felt like?"

"I'm sorry."

"It's too late." Tears sprung from my eyes, rolling down my cheeks. This was too hard, sitting here with him. Listening to him try to fix what he'd broken.

"Don't say that." He dropped to his knees in front of me, sliding his hands up my thighs. "I need you, Peyton. I need you."

I leaned down, touching my head to his as my eyes fluttered closed. "I can't trust you anymore." I breathed the words, suppressing a shudder.

"You can." His hand curved around my neck, holding me as he wiped my tears away with his thumb. "I don't want to be that guy anymore. Angry, bitter... cold. You showed me another way, Peyton. You did that. I know I saved you that night, but you saved me too."

Xander's words caressed my face, and I inhaled a shuddering breath as I blinked away the tears still falling. He'd said the same thing in his letter.

"Give me another chance, please?"

Tension crackled around us as I felt my resolve slipping. He was offering me everything I wanted.

His mouth ghosted over mine, touching but not touching. "I need you," he repeated. "I need you."

"Say it." I cupped his face in my hands, staring him dead in the eye. "I need to hear you say it."

"I love you, Peyton Myers. I love your smile and sass and strength. But most of all, I love your soul. How could I not when it's the other half to mine?"

I expelled a shaky breath, my heart fluttering wildly in my chest. My arms wound around his neck, crushing him to me as our lips came together in an uncertain kiss, both of us scared the other might disappear.

"Don't ever break my heart again," I whispered.

Xander searched my eyes and he smiled at whatever he saw there. "I won't, I promise," he said, kissing me. Claiming me with his lips, branding me with his tongue, and piecing me back together with every shared breath.

"It's you and me, Peyton." He broke the kiss, nothing but love and promises for the future shining in his eyes. "You and me against the world."

EPILOGUE

Peyton

ONE MONTH LATER...

"Stop." Laughter spilled out of me as Xander tickled my waist, his legs tangled with mine, the brush of his bare skin and teasing fingers sending shivers through me.

"You know the safe word." He grinned, nuzzling my neck. His fingers painted torturous circles along my curves.

"Xander, I... have to..." They changed direction, gliding down the flat of my stomach and straight over my panties. I gasped, the sensations overwhelming.

"You were saying?" He kissed the corner of my mouth, a wicked glint in his eye.

"You are so bad."

He hooked my panties aside and pressed two fingers into me without warning. A moan got stuck in my throat, but then he was kissing me, swallowing every breath and sigh. "Hmm," he murmured, "you're always so wet for me."

"Kiss me," I whispered, curving my hand around Xander's neck and pulling him to me.

He crushed his mouth against mine, kissing me hard. Deep and bruising. His fingers curled inside me as his thumb circled my clit, sending me racing toward ecstasy.

"God, it always feels so good," I murmured between hot wet kisses.

My body was a tightly coiled spring, an intense wave building inside me as he kept working me with his fingers.

"More..."

"Greedy girl." He pressed a kiss to the corner of my mouth, lazily flicking his tongue over the seam of my lips. Licking and nipping my jaw.

Kissing Xander was my favorite thing. I loved the scrape of his stubble against my face, the taste of his tongue, the way he gripped the nape of my neck, holding me exactly where he wanted me.

"I'm close," I moaned. "Keep—"

He ripped his fingers out of me and smirked.

"Xander, what the hell?" I glared at him, and he chuckled.

"Together." His smirk grew as he moved on top of me, fitting into the cradle of my thighs.

In one smooth stroke, he filled me, and we both moaned.

Xander gazed down at me as he pulled out and sank back inside, so deep a bite of pain went through me. But it was quickly drenched in pleasure as we found our rhythm.

"Fuck, you feel good." He leaned down, capturing my mouth in a slow, dirty kiss. I lifted my hips to meet him, thrust for thrust, and he grabbed my legs, hitching them around so he could go deeper... harder... faster.

"Xander," I cried.

He lowered his head, running the flat of his tongue over my nipple and then closed his mouth over it, sucking.

My hands dug into his shoulders, pleasure sparking off around my body. "It feels..."

"Yeah, I know." Xander smiled against my neck, kissing me there. "I love you, Peyton."

No more words were spoken as he loved my body into utter bliss.

It was always intense between us, as if we both knew how lucky we were to have found each other. Our relationship didn't start conventionally, and society might have judged us—judged him—for being together, but it didn't matter.

Nothing would ever come between us again.

"I'M GOING TO MISS YOU." He pouted as we reluctantly got dressed.

"I know, but I'll only be gone for three days." Me, Lily, Ashleigh, and the guys were heading to the Pocono Mountains for spring break. Just the six of us, a pre-graduation celebration.

"I'm not sure I like the idea of you all alone in some ski resort with Hughes." His brow arched.

I went to him, sliding my arms around his waist. "You have nothing to worry about. Bryan is my friend, nothing more. Besides, we won't be alone. Ashleigh and Gav are going and they're not a couple. Really, when you think about it, Lily and Kaiden will be the odd ones out."

"I could always come—"

"We talked about this: a) you hate skiing, b) it's weird, you're their coach, and c) you'll want to steal all my time and it would defeat the purpose of me going away with my friends." I gave Xander a pointed look before stealing a kiss.

"It's only three days and you promised Cameron you'd go hiking with him."

"Yeah, I know." He wrapped his arms around me and pulled me closer. "I'll miss you."

"You know what they say—"

"Don't let your girlfriend go on spring break with another guy."

I swatted his chest. "Xander Ellis Chase!"

"Fine, fine! I hope you and your friends have a good time."

"We will. Help me with my bags?" Xander had stayed over at my place last night. I'd moved in a couple of weeks ago. Jason and Felicity had begged me to stay, but after everything, I didn't want to make things any more awkward than they already were.

Everyone who mattered had accepted our relationship to a degree, but it was going to take some time for the dust to settle. Xander had decided to stay in Halston, and I wanted to stay in Rixon given I had my job at the diner. So for now, I had my place and he had his. But it worked. We got a lot more stares in Rixon, but I knew over time, people would move onto the next scandal.

I was happy.

We were happy.

And that's all that mattered.

Xander

"Coach," Bryan approached me warily. "How's it—"

"Listen up, Hughes, and listen good," I said with a smirk. "We need to lay down some ground rules for this trip." My eyes flicked over to where Peyton, Ashleigh, and Lily were huddled together, watching Kaiden and Gav load the trunk with their bags.

"Ground rules?" Bryan balked.

"Yes. You and Peyton—"

"Whoa, Coach. You know it isn't like that. I would never—"

"Relax, kid." I smirked. "I'm just busting your balls. Watch out for her though, yeah? She's important to me." Peyton looked over and our eyes collided.

Fuck. I would never tire of the way she looked at me. Happiness radiated in her smile, and love blazed in her baby blues.

"I know, Coach. She's important to me too."

My head whipped up to Bryan and his eyes went wide. "Shit, I didn't mean—*friends*... she's important to me as a friend."

Laughter rumbled in my chest. Truth was that Bryan was a good kid. He'd kept our secret, been a good friend to Peyton, and he continued to be a friend to us both.

I was still getting used to navigating my relationship with Peyton and the fact that her friends were all still in high school, but we made it work. It wasn't much better with our families. Despite Jase and my brother giving their blessing, things were still awkward as fuck. I got it though, and so long as they didn't try to come between us again, I could live with it.

"What are you two over here talking about?" Peyton appeared, burrowing into my side. Her hand ran up my stomach, making my dick twitch. Just thinking about all the dirty things I'd done to her earlier made me hot.

"None of your business, Blondie."

She smiled up at me. I'd taken to calling her Blondie since everything. "We're almost ready."

"I'll go see if they need a hand." Bryan gave me a small nod.

"Xander..." Peyton moved in front of me and narrowed her eyes. "What did you do?"

"Me?"

"Yes, you!"

"I just reminded him that you're important to me."

Her scowl melted away. "Yeah? How important?"

Chuckling, I dipped my head and brushed my lips along her neck. "Very important."

"Hmm, I like the sound of that." Peyton's fingers twisted into my sweater as I sucked her skin.

"Xander... don't start or I'll never want to leave."

"Kind of the plan." I smiled. But she wasn't buying it, slamming her palms into my chest. Straightening, I pouted.

"What am I going to do with you?"

"I can think of a few things." My brows waggled, earning me another scowl.

"You are so bad. I should go." A beat passed, the air turning thick around us. "It's only three days, right?" she murmured, and I saw a flash of hesitation.

"Three days," I repeated.

"We can totally do three days."

"Totally."

"Okay, then. I'll call you when we get there." Peyton worried her bottom lip.

"Come here, Blondie." I hooked my arm around her waist, tugging her closer. "I love you, so fucking much."

There had been a time those words terrified me, made me want to run in the other direction. I hadn't ever believed myself worthy of love. Of someone like Peyton.

But love didn't always play by the rules, and I was so fucking grateful I'd stumbled upon her that night down by the river. I'd saved her, but she'd saved me too.

"I love you too, Xander." She gazed up at me. "More than I ever thought possible."

"Yeah?" I grinned like a fool.

"Yeah. But I really need to go, so you're going to have to..." She gave me a pointed look and then dropped her eyes to my arms still wrapped around her.

"Fine. Go. And have fun."

"I will." Walking backwards, she mouthed, "I love you."

And like the pussy-whipped guy I was now, I mouthed them right back.

Peyton

"This is the life," I said, leaning back against the hot tub edge as the warm bubbles frothed around me.

"Right?" Lily sighed. "I feel so relaxed."

Steam billowed off the water, rising up around us like a mist.

"What do you think they're doing?" Ashleigh flicked her eyes to the cabin.

Lily smiled, grabbing her cocktail off the ledge and taking a slurp. "Goofing around like guys do."

"Today was a good day," I added. We'd watched the guys make fools of themselves on the slopes and then we'd rented toboggans.

Between graduating high school, working at the diner full-time, and spending time with Xander, I didn't get to see my girlfriends all that much nowadays, so it was nice to get away with them.

"Yeah." Ashleigh let out a small breath, and tipped her head back, closing her eyes. I cast Lily a concerned look.

"Ezra," Lily mouthed.

Oh.

As far as I was aware, Ezra was more estranged from the Bennets than ever. Sofia and Aaron took it in stride, but Ashleigh had dug in her heels where he was concerned. A couple of weeks ago, Lily told me she heard them arguing, but Ashleigh wouldn't tell her what happened.

She wouldn't talk about him at all.

But maybe being away from Rixon was the perfect opportunity for her to open up.

"Hey, Leigh," I said, and she lifted her head.

"Yeah?"

"Anything you want to talk about?"

"No, why?"

"Come on, babe, this is us. And you seem... quiet."

She exhaled a long breath, hesitating. Lily looked ready to interject, but I shook my head.

Finally, Ashleigh said, "Wanting someone who doesn't want you back sucks." Tears pricked her eyes.

"Oh, babe." I reached over and squeezed her hand. "Ezra?"

"Yeah. I mean, it's stupid. We've never even... it's not like he's ever given me a sign, you know? But it's like no matter how much I try to forget about him, the more I think about him."

"Does he know how you feel?" Lily asked.

"I haven't told him, not in so many words. But I've tried to be there for him, you guys know that. But I can't keep fighting for him if he doesn't want me to."

"I don't think it's about you, Leigh. I think Ezra has his own stuff to work out."

He wasn't going to graduate. He'd failed too many classes. Mya and Asher were trying to talk him into doing the year again, but apparently, that had gone down like a lead balloon.

Ezra didn't care.

And I could see how much it was hurting Ashleigh to know he'd given up.

"Yeah, it still sucks though." She swiped a tear away.

"Aww, babe, you'll find someone. Besides, come fall you'll be at college, living your best life."

She smiled, but it didn't reach her eyes.

"I can't believe we only have a few more months together," Lily said.

A few months ago, that would have terrified me. Losing them. Being stuck in Rixon alone, without my friends. But I wasn't that girl anymore. So much had changed.

I had changed.

I had a job I enjoyed, my own place, and Xander.

Everything else was just a bonus.

My cell phone started ringing and Lily snickered. "Oh my God, he's worse than Dad."

I splashed her as I climbed out the hot tub and wrapped a towel around my waist. "I'll be in our room."

"Tell Xander we said we're confiscating your phone tomorrow," Ashleigh called after me.

"Hello," I said, answering him.

"Hey, what are you up to?"

"You know you called me four hours ago, right?" I suppressed a giggle as I slipped into mine and Ashleigh's room. "Lily and Ashleigh are talking about confiscating my cell tomorrow."

"Tell them if they do that, I won't hesitate to come up there."

"You're missing me?"

"The apartment isn't the same without you."

"Xander..."

"Move in with me," he blurted out of nowhere.

"Wh-what?"

"Move in with me. We spend every night together anyway. And I'm fed up with having half my clothes at your place and half at my place."

"But it's soon, really soon..." My heart crashed wildly against my chest.

He wanted us to *live* together.

He was right. We already spent nearly every night together, meaning one of us was always driving back and forth for work. It wasn't that far though.

"Or I can move in with you, if you'd rather stay in Rixon," he went on. "I just know, I'm sitting here in my apartment and you're not here and it sucks."

"You're serious?"

"As a heart attack. I love you, Blondie, and I plan on spending the rest of my life with you. So the way I see it, we could do the regular stages of a relationship, or we could jump straight ahead to the part where you're in my bed every night with your girly shit all over my apartment and—"

"Yes," I smiled so hard my cheeks hurt, "yes, I'll move in with you."

"Wow, I had a whole speech prepared. I even made a list."

"You did not." Laughter spilled out of me, and it was so pure, so full of love, I thought my heart might burst.

"Did too," he quipped. "So we're doing this? We're really going to live together?"

"Yeah, I think we are."

"Monday," he deadpanned.

"Monday?"

"I want you to move in on Monday, the second you get back."

"Xander, I can't move in on Monday." I had a rental agreement, I had to give notice.

"We'll see," he muttered. "Now talk to me so I can fall asleep to the sound of your voice."

"Xander, I can't do—"

"Humor me." I could imagine his pouty expression and puppy dog eyes.

Flopping back against the pillows, I let out a soft sigh. "You're a pain in my ass, you know."

"I know, but you love me."

"Yeah, I do."

It wasn't every day you got to move in with your hero. But Xander was so much more than that to me. He was my savior. My confidante. My best friend. My soul mate.

He was the man I was going to spend my life loving.

And I couldn't wait to see what the future held for us.

Ashleigh

Two months later…

"UNCLE XANDER, YOU CAME," I threw my arms around him and squeezed him tight.

"Congratulations, Leigh Leigh." He held me at arm's length, studying me. His brows knitted, his mouth thinning. "Are you drunk?"

"It's a party. Our graduation party. Of course I'm drunk." I flashed him a devious grin. "But don't tell my dad. You have to promise you won't—"

"Relax, Leigh," Peyton said, slipping under his arm and burrowing into his side. "He won't tell him. Right, babe?" She smiled up at Xander.

Jeez, it was still weird to think of them together. One day, if they got married, she'd be my aunt.

Whoa, mindfuck. My best friend and my aunt.

Peyton smothered a chuckle and I blinked at them.

"Did I say that out loud?"

"Yup. You might want to lay off the alcohol, Leigh." She gave me a pointed look.

"Shit, sorry." I hiccoughed. "I didn't mean... I mean, it'll be cool if you do get married. I'm totally up for being your niece and—"

"Leigh Leigh?" Uncle Xander said looking a little flustered, and I nodded. "Stop talking now."

"O-okay."

"We're going to find Bryan," Peyton smiled, "you'll be okay?"

"Yeah, I'm good." It wasn't a total lie. I was happy to be here, celebrating with my friends. We'd made it—we'd survived high school. Soon we'd all be chasing our dreams at college.

Well, most of us.

I searched Bryan's crowded yard hoping to see a glimpse of Ezra.

I knew he probably wouldn't come. After all, he hadn't graduated like the rest of us. But it didn't stop me from looking for him, hoping that maybe, just maybe, he would come and celebrate with the rest of us.

With me.

Ezra Jackson was my Achilles' heel. I'd spent months, years even, trying to be his friend. Trying to be his someone. But every time I thought I was getting close, he would pull away, and I would be left heartbroken all over again.

It sucked wanting someone who didn't want you back. But it sucked even more that in the rare moments where he acted like he did want me, I was too weak to deny him.

"Ashleigh," Lily and Kaiden approached me. "What are you doing?"

"Nothing." I smiled. "Peyton and Xander are here. Can you believe he came?"

"I wonder how she managed to persuade him," Lily said, and Kaiden snorted.

"You probably don't want to know." He smirked.

"Ew, gross."

"You know, one day she'll be my aunt, that's gross."

"Are you okay?" Lily frowned.

"I'm fine. Better than fine." I mustered the best smile I could. "We did it, Lil. We graduated. And now the world is our oyster."

But I wasn't really looking at her, I was looking past her. Still searching for Ezra.

Silently wishing that just this once, he would surprise me.

We partied into the late hours of the night, but Ezra never showed. Not that I really expected him to.

Bryan's house was a mess, empty cups and bottles were littered across the yard. But Kaiden and Gav had promised to help him clean up tomorrow. My head already hurt from all the liquor, but the pizza we'd eaten earlier had soaked it up enough that I no longer felt drunk.

"I'm going to take these bags out to the trash," I said to no one in particular. Gav was half-asleep on the couch, and Kaiden and Lily were too wrapped up in each other to notice me. Bryan had disappeared earlier and never resurfaced, and Peyton and Xander had left hours ago after he'd declared it too inappropriate to watch his niece and her friends get shit-faced.

His words, not mine.

I grabbed the bags and slipped out the back door, heading for the side of the house. After dumping them in the trash can, I was about to return to the house when the faint rumble of a car caught my attention. Before I knew what I was doing, I went around the front of the house, grinding to a halt when I spotted the familiar car in the shadows.

Ezra.

Even in the darkness, I could feel his eyes on me.

The first emotion I felt whenever Ezra was around was always a trickle of excitement, but usually it was quickly followed by frustration or anger.

Tonight was no different.

I stormed over to the car and ripped the door open. "What are you doing here?"

"Good to see you too, buttercup."

"Don't call me that." I seethed. "You're too late, the party's over."

"I didn't come for the party." His amber eyes bore into mine. Intense and unwavering.

"I'm not doing this, not tonight." I went to slam the door, but his voice stopped me.

"Come on, Leigh. Don't be like that." A beat passed and he released a long breath. "You know why I didn't come."

"No, I don't."

Ezra was a lone wolf, always had been. But tonight, of all nights, he could have come.

He could have come... for me.

"Take a ride with me," he said quietly.

"A ride? Now? It's almost two in the morning."

"Please?" A faint smile traced his mouth and I felt that familiar tug in my stomach. When Ezra smiled, and he didn't do it a lot, it changed his entire face.

I'd never admit it to anyone, but I lived for his smiles.

I studied him, unable to take my eyes off his face. It was a perfect canvas of strong features and full lips, and amber eyes that looked right into your soul. A silver hoop pierced his nose and a diamond stud glinted in his ear, both giving him an edge most guys in Rixon didn't have. There was dusting of hair over his upper lip and jaw, and his hair was styled into twists. Ezra Jackson stole my breath every time I looked at him.

He stared back at me with a lazy smile. One I recognized. My stomach sank.

"You're high."

"I had a smoke earlier, but I'm fine. Stop worrying."

But I did worry. I always worried where Ezra was concerned.

"Take a ride with me, come on." He pouted, dragging his plump bottom lip between his teeth, letting it slowly pop out. "Come on, buttercup, you know you want to."

Damn him.

And damn my foolish, fickle heart.

"Fine, but just for a little while." I slid into the car, sending Lily a quick text so she knew where I was.

Chilled music pumped out of the speaker as Ezra backed out of the Hughes' driveway. We didn't talk, not as the houses rolled by, silent and sleeping.

"Where are we going?" I realized he was heading out of town.

"Wanna see how fast she can go?" His eyes twinkled.

"Ezra, I don't think that's—" He floored the gas and the car shot off like a rocket. "Ezra, what the *hell*?" My hands curled around the edge of the seat.

"Relax, buttercup, it's just a little fun. Something to get the heart pumping."

"This was a bad idea; you should take me back."

He glanced at me, his jaw ticking. "You wanted me to come tonight, right? That's what all your texts were about, begging me to come."

Shame burned my cheeks. I had texted him, one too

many times. But I'd drank a lot, too much, and I hated the thought of him alone.

"You're being a dick," I said calmly, refusing to let him bait me. "I want you to take me back to Bryan's house, *now*."

"Yeah," he let out a strained breath, "whatever." Ezra slowed down to pull a U-turn in the middle of the road.

"Jesus," I hissed under my breath. But at least he'd slowed down a little.

"You're right," he said coolly, flicking his amber gaze to mine. It was darker now, almost brown with a ring of gold around the edges. "This was a mistake." He held me captive in those eyes. "I don't know why I even—"

Headlights blinded me. "Ezra, *look out*," I shrieked, bracing myself.

"Fuck!" He swerved the car, but it was too late. The truck was heading right for us.

"Oh my God," I breathed and then my world exploded in a flash of screeching metal and burning rubber. The car rolled and rolled again, glass smashing and bones cracking.

Pain radiated through every inch of my body, darkness swimming in my vision. I couldn't see... I couldn't think.

"Leigh?" someone called frantically. "Ashleigh?"

"I—I... the words barely formed on my lips, something trickling out of my mouth. Blood. God, so much blood.

"Ezra," I cried. "I'm..." God, it hurt to breathe. It hurt so much. "I'm scared."

"I'm sorry, buttercup." He sounded far away, the edges of my consciousness flickering in and out... darkness rushing in, blotting out my world. "I'm so fucking sorry."

PLAYLIST

Feel Something – Jaymes Young
Watch – Billie Eilish
Skin – Sabrina Carpenter
Perfectly Wrong – Shawn Mendes
Don't Give Up On Me – Andy Grammar
Wildest Dream – Taylor Swift
The Village – Wrabel
Train Wreck – James Arthur
Forever – Labrinth
Love in the Dark – Isak Danielson
Are You With Me – Nilu
Falling Apart – Michael Schulte
Half Light – BANNERS
Say – Ruel
Moments Passed – Dermot Kennedy
Hope is A Heartache – LEON
I Should Go – James Vincent McMorrow

AUTHOR'S NOTE

Gah! This book... this book!

I've never written an age gap romance before... I know they're not everyone's cup of tea, and I know some readers find them distasteful (especially when one of the characters is still in high school) but I always stay true to my characters and their stories. And Peyton and Xander certainly had a story to tell. I won't lie—it broke me. They pushed me and tested me and made me work for it, but I think it paid off.

Love isn't always straightforward. Sometimes it's messy and hard and sometimes, it doesn't conform to societal boundaries. And Xander and Peyton definitely had their work cut out for them... but it only makes their HEA all the sweeter.

I adore these characters, the world, and their bond between them, and I can't wait to bring you more stories from Rixon High!

As always, a huge thank you to everyone who helped bring this book to life. By now, you know who you are! And to every book blogger who took the time to read an advance copy of Tragic Lies, your reviews, messages, are everything. Never stop doing what you're doing because the book world needs you!

Until next time,

L A xo

ABOUT THE AUTHOR

Angsty. Edgy. Addictive Romance

Author of mature young adult and new adult novels, L. A. is happiest writing the kind of books she loves to read: addictive stories full of teenage angst, tension, twists and turns.

Home is a small town in the middle of England where she currently juggles being a full-time writer with being a mother/referee to two little people. In her spare time (and when she's not camped out in front of the laptop) you'll most likely find L. A. immersed in a book, escaping the chaos that is life.

L. A. loves connecting with readers.

The best places to find her are:
www.lacotton.com

Printed in Great Britain
by Amazon

41919305R00245